One for Arthur...

It was nearing daybreak when Neil Dillon awoke.

Like every other morning, he lay in bed, the realisation washing over him that he was still there, yet another day to be endured.

He looked up at the ceiling where the light bulb used to sit in its socket and tried to gather his strength to get out of bed. It was the same every morning, his reasoning's not to climb out of bed had been considered and defeated a long time before. Now, he saw it as his punishment... for weakness in a different life. He hoped, however, his punishment was near at an end.

Once out of bed, he dressed in the same clothes he had worn every day for years- a pair of black corduroy's, a checked shirt, and a black V-neck jumper. He sat on the edge of his bed and tied up the laces on his steel toe-capped boots, then stood to put on his full length, black top coat.

After dressing, he went down the stairs, sat at the kitchen table, and looked out the window at nothing in particular.

Once again, there had been a heavy frost during the night, and a film of ice had dispatched itself on the inside of the kitchen window.

Landlocked south Ulster had surely frozen during the night.

He didn't eat that morning, he rarely did anymore. Not that he didn't want to, but because there had never been any food in the house. Besides, a recluse didn't exactly fancy the idea of going to a nearby shop and making small talk with the locals. Just like the biting cold, he had gotten used to the sensation of hunger, so much that when he did eat, it almost sickened him.

He sat at the table another while and pulled on his smoking pipe. He had allowed himself that little luxury from time to time. He hadn't properly smoked it in years, as his tobacco supply had run out long before, but the stale taste that lingered long after the tobacco had been burned, offered him some form of comfort.

After a few pulls, he had to put it down. Memories began to flood back. Memories which seemed to deliberately taunt and torment, rather than comfort him. He had found that always to be the case. He had found that in life, memories could act as motivators... comforters. People could indulge in them whenever things weren't going so well, they could help inspire a person to pick themselves up and keep going. However, he knew that didn't apply to him anymore, as he saw his life as over a long time ago.

He wondered what the point of having good memories were, if no new ones were ever to be made again.

He liked to sit at the kitchen table. It gave him a sense of normality, like the feelings he used to have when he would sit at it, have a drink and plan what he would do next in his life. Plans were not to be made again though, yet he remained proud that he still actually had the table and the few chairs that sat around it, as many a cold and wet night he had to fight the urge not to chop them up and burn them as firewood. The kitchen table, the four chairs and his bed were the only surviving furniture left in the house, although all had been charred badly from the fire.

He looked through the kitchen door, into the room which used to be the living room. He would busy himself in there in a moment or so, cleaning and tidying, the same tasks he did every day, cleaning up the remains of the fire he had lit the night before.

Every night he would prepare what could only be described as an indoor camp fire. He would build it in the middle of the room and sit at it until it went out. Then, he would retire to his freezing bedroom. He knew it didn't make sense, but nothing much in his life did anymore. He had sometimes thought about making a fire in the fireplace, but always decided against it. Again, too many good memories would come flooding back, taking him back to a different time, until it would become unbearable to him.

Smoke filling up the room had never been a problem, as the house had so many drafts and openings that the smoke would always escape somewhere, although many a night he had hoped the smoke would suffocate and kill him.

It had yet to do so.

The house he lived in was quite large. His father had owned a small flax mill and Neil had converted it into a dwelling house a few years before. The house had two storeys. It had three bedrooms, a kitchen, a large living room, a larder and another large room which had been used for Christmas time and other special occasions. Attached to the house was a large outhouse, where hay and farming machinery were stored. It was the perfect dwelling for a recluse, as he fully considered himself to be, as it sat deep down a private lane just off a quiet country road, engulfed by fields he and his family had owned.

He got up off his chair and went into the living room, stooping under the doorway as he went. At six feet and four inches he was used to stooping under most doorways, especially when he wore his work boots, which would add an extra inch or two to his already considerable height. He had always been proud of his height and build. His frame was lean, packed with muscle, due mostly to the physical labour he had employed living on a farm, working from dawn to dusk every day. Some people had thought his pride in his stature bordered on arrogance, he didn't agree. However, it had been difficult not to have a slight superiority complex when the average height of a man had been around five feet and nine inches, most of whom had been humped over, due to bad posture and too much drink. He had always looked after himself physically, and couldn't understand the other men letting themselves degenerate into such poor physical forms.

His great physical presence, of which he had been so proud, had become a considerable burden to him though, as it required much maintenance. Food had become so scarce that he had lost almost all the bulky muscle on his body, so that his clothes barely fitted. It pained him greatly that his huge shoulders had all but disappeared, one of his finest attributes in the past. Luckily, because of his well-padded top coat, his profile gave the illusion of still having the large shoulders. He found he had, too, developed a slight hump, which very much depressed him. He knew there wasn't much he could do about it, as the muscles that once held him so upright and straight, had wasted away too.

He looked upon the ashes and the unburnt wood that sat in the middle of the room, deciding he would salvage the wood, put it to one side and use it again that night. He began to clear the ashes and tidy the room, the same routine he had known for as long as he could remember. Once finished, he would brace himself to go out into the cold morning to begin searching for firewood for another night's fire. He thought himself lucky in that regard, as there had always been an abundance of firewood lying around, owing to the vast number of oak trees that lined the property. He had always tried to break twigs and branches off the trees if there had been no wood on the ground, as he had been reluctant to chop any trees down. The mighty oak trees had offered privacy from the outside world. Even in the winter months, the trees bare skeletons, still, offered a great deal of solitude.

As he opened the front door that morning, the winter chill blasted him straight in the face, almost taking his breath away. He turned up his collar and walked into the icy, crisp morning to begin his work.

It didn't take long for him to get used to the biting morning air. It stimulated and refreshed him, took his mind off the other things.

As he looked around the surroundings of his home, he had always been filled with a longing. He knew exactly what he longed for…better days, happier times, but he stopped himself from thinking too much about them. It would be too much for him. Routine had to take priority, he couldn't waste another day lost in sorrow.

His home stood in a four-acre field. All around were high, majestic oak trees, that shimmied and swayed in the high summer sun, and stood deathly still in the winter months, like the skeletons of a group of hunched over giants. There had been a definite melancholy about the place.

In the distance, he heard the piercing cackle of a jackdaw, and he cursed to himself, wishing he had a rifle to blow the bastard away. The sound of the cackle sounding like a cruel, mocking laugh. That sound would continue throughout the day, along with the odd haunting scream of the fox. Those were the only noises he heard, apart from when he could make out the growl of a powerful piece of farm machinery in the distance from time to time. Those noises were rare though, as he lived a quarter of a mile from the small country road, and owned all the adjoining fields in the vicinity. Even the birds, whose sweet sounds used to provide a beautiful soundtrack to his mornings, outside his bedroom window, seemed to have deserted him. Perhaps, he thought, the birds had been spooked, afraid to enter such a cursed place as what was his.

After a time spent scouring the field for wood on the ground beneath the trees, he took the small stack back to the house, and placed it with the unburnt wood from the night before.

The cold his body had felt, replaced by hunger, so he went back outside and took a trek down to the bottom of the field to the adjoining lake, to see if he could catch something. He had caught a pike or two in the past, but didn't hold out much hope for such an act of luck to happen frequently. From the remains of meal bags that lay around the outhouse he had made a crude net. He attached the net to a brush shaft to make a very makeshift fishing rod. His family had always loved the lake, as they saw it as one of the most important components in their once successful mill business, as rival businesses did not have the luxury of a water supply so close by. However, like everything, he had begun to despise it, as he couldn't help but to notice his reflection in the water when looking for fish. His reflection only confirmed just how much he had wasted away. He tried to avoid his reflection at all costs. Also, it served as a massive disappointment to him day by day, as his efforts to find fish mostly failed, and he had to traipse back to the house empty handed and starving.

He couldn't remember how long it had been since he had last eaten. He knew it to be at least a few weeks. He often wondered how he remained alive, although, strangely, he never found the hunger too unbearable. The last time he had eaten was when a pheasant came strutting and clucking around the place one day. Although he had felt grateful for the company of another living thing, he had no choice but to catch it and break the poor creature's neck. It broke his heart to do such a callous thing, but he hadn't eaten in weeks and knew it came down to kill, or die himself, although the latter option hadn't been too unappealing an option either. The poor bird at least got a dignified send off, as he had eaten every bit of it over a few nights, having resisted the urge to eat it all in the one night.

Although it froze hard that day, and he returned to the empty house with no food to eat, it meant the best part of his day was over.

Then, when back in the house, he would sit in solitude and wait for the ensuing torment to begin in earnest. He would sit, around the indoor camp fire, the memories of that night eventually flooding back. Like a tsunami, overwhelming and cruel.

The memories of the night the bastards came and destroyed everything he had ever loved.

The night his life had been taken away from him.

The night when the lives of Máire and wee Seamie ended.

I remember the day I got the call from him, like it was only yesterday.

I had, after all been expecting it, but it in no way dampened the shock when it finally happened.

It came exactly a month after my mother died.

The day began like most days did. Waking up to another unwelcome hangover. The flat, cold, and damp, stinking of alcohol, stale cigarettes, and various other pungent aromas.

I climbed out of bed, eventually, around eleven, or shortly after, and wracked my frazzled brain to think of something I could take to ease my murderous headache. I had promised myself months before that I would stop taking another drink in the morning, as a cure. A vicious cycle had developed in the past where I had the intention of taking one drink, to take the edge off the disabling hangover, only to find myself falling into another few days of total inebriation. That then led to a few days of deep depression, when I had to get sober again because of the money running out, or having to go back to work. I resolved not to let that happen again.
I was going to turn over a new leaf. I was going to try and finally make something of my rotten life.

A big opportunity was on its way, and I was determined that there would be no way, no way on Gods earth, that I was going to blow it this time. People depended on me for once, and I sure as hell was not going to let them down.

I hoped to God I wouldn't.

I contemplated a paracetamol. My head pounded so bad, I swear I could feel my brain, shrunken and toxic, rattling around in my skull. I couldn't do anything until my headache passed, the pain almost blinding. I couldn't focus on anything else, absolutely nothing, other than how to make the pain go away. I could have gone back to bed to sleep it off, but I knew from vast experience that the pain would stop me from sleeping. The sweats would come, I would become more dehydrated and even sicker. The day would be screwed before it even had a chance to begin. I had resolved, also, a few months before that no more days were to be wasted.

Of the thirty-three years I had existed, I was sure I had spent at least twenty of those either in bed, hung-over, or getting drunk again.

Thirty-three. Where had the years gone? I was the same age as Jesus when He was crucified. It was safe to say he had perhaps packed a whole lot more into his lifetime than I had.

I took some paracetamol. I hated taking it, but I had to. Every time, without fail, after I took some I would throw up a few minutes later. As undesirable it was to throw up, it at least meant that when the problems migrated to my stomach, the headache began to dissipate... then my pain would gradually ease. I often thought it would be great to be like normal people, where I could take a paracetamol, lie in bed for a while and let the drug work its magic. Instead I had to go through the harrowing ordeal of bending over a filthy toilet (or sink, depending whether I made it on time or not) being violently sick. Maybe paracetamol worked that way on everyone?

Funny fucking drug if it did!

Ten minutes later, after a bout of intense vomiting, I lay on the bed, sweaty and exhausted. I felt pretty good though. The headache had gone, my stomach delicate and sore, but I could deal with that.

I dressed quickly to try and avoid freezing my balls off, as the gas had been turned off a few weeks before. A combination of laziness and poverty prevented me from getting it switched back on again, though I didn't like to admit that to myself. I preferred to think spring was on its way- why would I waste money on gas?

After throwing up so much, a ravenous hunger came upon me. I took it as an encouraging sign, as it had been usually much later in the day when my appetite returned. The sooner I could eat, the sooner the hangover would leave me. Of course, there was nothing in the flat, so I headed out in pursuit of a greasy breakfast.

Just after I closed the flat door, I hesitated, and weighed up the pros and cons of calling for my neighbour, Lee. I hated eating in public alone, always feeling that people were judging me, like I was some sort of nonce or weirdo.

I took the difficult decision to call for him. I hoped I wouldn't regret it, knowing that I would.

I knocked at his door.

He answered, greeting me with; "All right Tommy, you on the faacking piss again last night?"

He pronounced "fucking" like "faacking", trying, and failing embarrassingly to sound cockney and hard. I didn't like the little prick, instantly regretting knocking on his door.

The things one did for company at times.

Usually, I wouldn't let him away with that, and would reply with something cutting, something to bring him down a peg or two, setting the tone for the day ahead, but I felt too ill to bother.

"Yeah, Lee, something like that", I replied, surprising myself how hoarse I sounded. "Anyway, do you fancy going out for some breakfast or something?"

He tried to mask a little reptilian smile.

"Love to mate, but I'm a little short this week, and..."

"Don't worry about it. It's on me, I know you're good for it"

I knew he definitely wasn't good for it. His queasy little smile broadened

"Oh. Well, why didn't you faacking say so. I'll grab my coat".

I felt annoyed with myself for letting him away with it again. The problem with him, amongst many others, was that he was a tight fisted little shit. Always crying poverty. If we went to the pub, I ended up footing about ninety per-cent of the bill, as he was always "skint". Most riling of all was, his flat was decked out to the nines with all the latest technology and gadgets, it almost felt like walking into a spaceship. He had technology I didn't even know existed yet.

I had only known him for three or four months, since he had moved in next door. He was, according to himself, a big-time university graduate. Not just a normal graduate, I think he had a few degrees, each, of course, related to computers and technology in some form or another. I couldn't work out whether I liked him. He intrigued me, I had never known a character like him. Certainly, none of my friends had been anything like him.

Apparently, he came from a very well-off family, in a posh area of London, but, like a lot of posh, privileged little pricks, he had wanted to rebel against mummy and daddy, move to a rough area and mix with lowlifes like me. Well, until he got fed up, and daddy gave him a directorship in the family business.

I don't think he worked, as he always seemed to be in his flat, night and day. Of course, according to him, he worked for a huge multi-national company, and they let him work from the comfort of his own home.

May or may not have been true, I didn't give a shit either way.

One of his most annoying traits though, the one thing that bugged me more than anything else, was the way he spoke with his default posh accent when he climbed his high horse and bragged about his knowledge and expertise on computers, bragging of his qualifications. He would momentarily forget himself, and the mock cockney accent would be dropped until he had realised it.

I really hated that about him.

But...one of the only reasons I kind of half liked him, was because of his warped, twisted sense of humour. When he got going, he would spout some of the most depraved, fucked up stuff I had ever heard- most of it including his mother, grandmother and sometimes his family pets. All of it lies, no doubt, but it amused me greatly. Also, he had been the most sexually successful man I had ever known, even though I never once witnessed him with a woman.

For a five foot five, pot-bellied little weirdo, he certainly had a way with the ladies... imaginary or not.

No, I really don't think I liked him.

We took the stairs down to the ground floor, as the elevator was still broken. It was always broken. We didn't even bother to check if it worked, because of the stench of stale piss in it.

It had been a damp, rain sodden, grey, depressing fuck of a day when we got out of the flats onto the street.

The usual North London climate.

We walked for about ten minutes down the road, getting rained upon, until we arrived at Greasy Greg's. It wasn't officially named Greasy Greg's. The faded, dated sign read "The Rainbow Café", but it was known by all as Greasy Greg's, because of Greasy Greg himself, the proprietor.

"Well boys. What are ye havin'?", Greg cheerily asked from behind the counter, as we walked in.

Greg had always been happy to see customers walk into the café as the place was almost always empty.

The name, Greasy Greg's, had maybe not been the most powerful marketing tool he could have hoped for.

"Two full Irish's, please Gregory", I answered.

The custom would have been to order two full English breakfasts, as we were in her majesty's territory, but Greg was a fellow Irishman.

Gregory O'Donnell was his full name. Hailing from County Mayo in the west of Ireland, he was a short, stout man, probably around sixty-five years old. He always wore a white shirt while working in the café, and the time of day could always be told according to how dirty it was, due to the build-up of grease and dirt which would accumulate on it as the day progressed. He had been chef, maître d', and dishwasher, all rolled into one. His shirt on that occasion was quite clean, possibly due to how early in the day it was, and from the lack of trade.

"Take a seat, boys", Greg instructed us, "I'll get one of the boys to come out and take your orders".

"One of the boys, Greg?", I asked, "I didn't know you were taking on new staff?"

"I wasn't, Tommy", he answered, "The two boys are grandnephews of mine. They've come over from Mayo for some work experience, for school".

"They've come over from Ireland to get work experience in a London greasy spoon?", Lee whispered to me under his breath, "And they say kids these days lack ambition".

"Shut the fuck up, Lee" I hissed under my breath.

I supposed he had a point though.

We took our seats beside the window and Greg's nephews came out with the cutlery and a pot of tea. The two of them were dressed in black trousers and jumpers. Both had jet black hair and ivory white skin... strange looking lads. Many dubious looking stains adorned their black trousers. Lee must have noticed them too at the same time, whispering "Stay clear of the mayonnaise, Tommy".

My stomach did a somersault.

They very unprofessionally plonked the pot of tea down, and, after fingering every piece of cutlery, clattered it all on to the table.

The breakfast, when it arrived, had been edible at best, as always, but I could feel my hangover dissipate by the minute. I started to feel a lot better, and Lee began to irritate me less, his tales of sexual conquest becoming more amusing. All of it complete bullshit, but it took my mind off everything, for a while.

When we finished, I squared Greg up for the breakfasts and made the usual inane small talk about the weather, his lack of business, and sport. I even tipped the two lads on their wanky handed service, regretting it immediately as we left, as I spotted the two of them sniggering and pointing towards Lee and myself. God knows what they had done to our food, the little shits.

We headed back to the flats. The rain fell harder and we arrived back looking like, and in my case, feeling like a pair of drowned rats. The feel-good glow the fried breakfast had given me, becoming a distant memory. Lee spun some bullshit about having to go back to work on a top-secret project for a world-renowned client. Glad to be rid of him, I sloped back to my freezing, damp flat.

I sat for a while, a million thoughts racing through my mind, until I finally fell asleep.

Yet another day wasted.

There was nothing much I could really do, until I got that call. It was a waiting game.

How long? I didn't know. I had to be patient, I had to be ready. It had been a month. Patience had never been a strong point, but I had no other option.

Just that evening, the shrill ring of the telephone awakened me. Still half asleep, and momentarily caught in a dreamlike trance, I lifted the phone.

"Hello, son" spoke the Irishman.

Then a moment's silence, before he spoke again.

"God... it's been a while."

A long pause.

"Do you... do you know who this is?"

It took me a while to answer.

I knew who it was, all right. I had, after all, waited long enough.

"Now it begins", I almost said aloud.

CHAPTER 3

Growing up in North London as a Paddy had been tough. Life as a Paddy getting older got much tougher.

I had always been supremely proud of my Irish heritage. I bragged about it to my friends in school, and to anyone else who would listen. It didn't matter if I didn't speak with an Irish accent, I was Irish... to the core. I had a proud heritage. My people were great artists, poets, writers and fighters, there would be no one in Ireland herself, who felt prouder to be Irish than me. I told all my classmates tales about how the great warriors of Ireland would rebel, overthrow, and defeat their English tormentors to reclaim what was rightfully theirs. Those stories had been great to tell in primary school, however, as the years progressed and I moved to secondary school, more of the boys would take greater offence, resulting in a lot of black eyes and split lips. But, I never stopped telling those tales, regardless of what happened. So, I would get beaten up a lot in the earlier days, but those beatings hardened me, making me more resistant to the next beating, until, eventually, I became the beater, not the beaten. Those delicate early years had taught me a lot, but never enough to diminish my pride in my native country.

Indeed, I would become even more patriotic as the years progressed.

But, as with most things in my life, there always lurked something in the shadows of my mind. Always something that would torment my subconscious, until eventually my mind would become polluted and toxic. The main issue- I wasn't totally allowed to bask in the self-indulgent idealism I believed in.

Why?

Because of one person. That person was none other than my lunatic, alcoholic mother.

She planted the seeds of doubt in my mind about my heritage. She had always told me from as long as I could remember, to never label myself as Irish. She was Irish herself, but she had always warned me to keep my heritage a secret. The reason... because if someone from the IRA got wind of the fact I existed, I would be killed.

Nice bedtime stories for a child to hear.

Why would such a horrible thing happen? It was why my mother had to leave her homeland for London in the first place.

She had fallen for a British soldier, apparently, back home, during the troubles, and I had been the product of their love affair. I felt she always resented me for that very reason. She had to leave her family, her home, and friends to rear and protect me. To me, as a staunch Irish nationalist, being the son of a British soldier felt the equivalent of a Baptist preacher finding out he was the son of Satan himself! Of course, I tried not to believe a word of it. She was so drunk most of the time that she could barely string two words together. But, what disturbed me most of all, was how her face would distort into a vile sneer when she would recall the story of her and my 'Brit' father. No matter how much I didn't want to believe what she said, that pain had obviously turned to bitterness with time. There *was* something behind her story, and that is why I couldn't be certain I wasn't the bastard child of a British soldier after all. My surname, Smyth, taken from my father, certainly didn't confirm any hint of Irish heritage. If I had been Murphy, O'Neill, or McGuiness, I would have an argument, but Smyth, well, that name could have been from anywhere... possibly even from a British soldier.

So, through my childhood years, she would always put a heavy dampener on my romantic ideology of having an Irish pedigree. She would tell me to keep a low profile, keep my mouth shut, as I was the product of British rule in Ireland. If the wrong person were to find out that information, I would be hunted down and shot. She told me I could have a decent life living in London. I had an English accent, an English father and could pass myself with no problems. If I started broadcasting my nationality, I would have many problems in life, as I would be regarded as no more than a mongrel, unwanted by both sides

Did she have a point?

Possibly.

I could never admit it though. I *had* to believe she lied, otherwise, if I believed her story, I don't think I could have lived with myself. It felt that bad to me, like I had been infected with a horrible virus.

But, why would I believe her?

She had probably been so drunk at the time of conception, she wouldn't remember who my father was anyway. I knew I had been born in Ireland, she had let that slip a few times, so if I was born in Ireland and at least one of my parents was Irish, that was good enough for me.

Or so I tried to tell myself.

Regardless, I defied her orders and broadcast my nationality to anyone who listened. I would never, ever tell another living person what my horrible little secret was. And, I suppose to be fair to her, she didn't either. It became our own poisonous little secret that would fester, and eventually rot away any bond we had with each other, in the years that followed.

Life growing up with my mother had been no picnic either, and that was only when I *was* living with her.

I would spend a lot of my childhood in and out of children's homes, at times when my mother was deemed unfit to look after me.

Back in those days, anyone with poor mental health had been viewed very differently than in more modern times. Society wasn't as understanding. It would be years later that she would be correctly diagnosed as a manic depressive. Manic depressives in the modern age would be afforded greater compassion and help with their illness, illness being the operative word. However, back in the seventies and eighties, a sufferer would simply have been judged by society as odd, strange or the much-bandied slang term 'mental'.

So, growing up Irish in London, when the troubles were at their peak, with an insane, drunken mother, whilst being thrown in and out of children's homes, all added up to a pretty traumatic childhood.

I never would have referred to myself as an optimist, probably more a glass half empty type, but as hard as it is to believe, I didn't think my childhood and adolescent years were that bad. Perhaps, to the casual listener of my tale, a person who deemed themselves as having a normal upbringing...two parents, a sibling or two and a family pet, they would probably think my childhood was hellish. But, as I had never encountered normality, I thought my life was normal.

I couldn't miss what I never knew.

Again, the optimist in me viewed my childhood as advantageous in a way, as I grew up quick, tough, and streetwise- vital components for living in London as an adult. I knew people in their late twenties and thirties who, in my eyes, never properly grew up, quite possibly the result of over protective and overzealous parenting. I would always view such people as being bigger fuck-ups than I was. People who received all the privileges of a stable home life, good education, and a loving family.

Those people had no-one to blame only themselves.

I am, probably, being a little harsh on my mother. To be fair, when she was sober and had her faculties about her, she could be kind and loving, a completely unrecognisable person to that of when she was drinking or having a particularly down day. When things got really bad with her drinking or depression, the social services would soon be alerted by the neighbours and I would be chucked into the children's home for a few months, until she recovered.

As bad as it sounded, I didn't really mind going, from time to time. The first few times were rough as I would get teased and beaten up quite a bit, but as the years passed and I became bigger, stronger, and more streetwise, I would eventually become the top-dog. When that happened, *I* didn't beat up any of the kids.

Always hating bullies, I vowed never to become one.

One of the other reasons I didn't get into any fights after a while was because I didn't have to. My reputation preceded and protected me in various ways, as the boys would talk and tell stories about me when I wasn't there. The stories were mostly bullshit, and with each fresh telling of the tales, they would grow increasingly exaggerated, until my reputation took on an almost mythical status to the new kids who had yet to meet me.

Most of the stories originated from one actual true occurrence.

I had received a bad beating from an older kid, a vicious, horrible bully called David Thompson. He had taunted me about my mother, and I went for him. Being much bigger he punched me to the ground, then, kneeled on my chest and pummelled me until he got tired. When I eventually left to go back to live with my mother for a while, I hardened from a few fights and scrapes at school. Coupled with a good growth spurt where I shot up about three inches in the intervening six to eight months, I returned to the home and kicked seven bells of shite out of him! I had gotten lucky though, as I connected sweetly with my first punch to his jaw, weakening him from the start.

Let's just say, I wouldn't have fancied a re-match.

But, the damage had been done. A bully hates it when someone stands up to them, everyone else loves it. And so, that story had defined me for the rest of my time there.

I, had been one of the luckier kids, as my mother, to her credit, never gave up on me, always trying, and mostly succeeding to get me back home, visiting me at every opportunity. I would always have other visitors too. Mrs Kingston, our neighbour, would come, bringing sweets, comics, and her infectious laughter. Later, a very special family, who would eventually see me as almost one of their own, would come visit too. I had people who cared. As a child, it mattered…a lot! Some of those poor kids didn't have anyone to visit them. Children of alcoholics, druggies, and fuck-ups, they had never asked to be born, but paid the price for their parent's selfishness and stupidity. It would make me feel guilty when my visitors arrived, with their gifts and laughter, only to see some of the other kids shuffled off to their rooms, as the carers didn't want them to be in the way.

It wasn't fair, but what could I do?

So, instead of fighting with them, I took on a Big Brother role, sharing my sweets and comics, when the visitors had gone home.

Because I had seen a slice of life from the other side of the fence, I could never really, truly, hate my mother, no matter what she did, or said. I was all she had. Her, all I had. She had many problems, and could be cruel and spiteful at times, but I always appreciated her visiting and not giving up on me. The problem, though, was when she would win me back, her problems would return, and back into the home I would go.

As she would resume heavy drinking after I came home, it only reinforced my theory that I was indeed the problem. To her, I must have been a reminder of why she had to leave her homeland… because of the mistake she had made with the British soldier. Then, her stories about how much of a mistake I had been and her constant nagging for me to shut up about the Irish stuff would start once again, and we were soon back to square one. I would hate her, and she would hate me. It was a poisonous, vicious circle that would continue for many years.

Despite all the unrest I faced in my home life, I was always glad it didn't cause any disruptions with school.

In the children's home, a lot of the kids were having to move to different schools, as the home remained a long way from where they came from. Thankfully, that problem didn't relate to me, as the children's home was only about two miles from my mother's flat, and the school was situated equidistant between the two.

I attended St Anthony's Catholic School for boys, and absolutely loved it. Not in a bookish, nerdy sort of way- I fucking hated schoolwork... but the ritual of routine and discipline appealed to me. School acted like a sanctuary, an alternative to the real world. I could meet and play with my friends, have fun, and feel normal for those few hours. I always kept my private life a secret, and because school was never disrupted because of the turbulence at home, I could do so entirely. None of the other kids in my class would have known what a children's home was, as everyone I knew seemed to come from a single or double parent family.

Maybe they didn't, maybe they hid something like I did... who knew? Regardless, I wanted to keep everything to myself. I was ashamed of my life, ashamed to say I was ashamed of my mother.

Anyway, kids could be very cruel, and if word got out I was in and out of children's homes, it could have led to trouble.

Another reason for my optimism was largely due to what I heard about some of the other kid's single mothers. Most of the stories were told by boys about other kid's mothers, but worst of all were the boys who told stories about their own. Stories about strange men joining them at the breakfast table, men with smug, satisfied grins. Although those kids were young and innocent, they weren't stupid. They knew the reason for those men's smugness. Some of the men would hang around and eventually turn violent towards their mothers, and even to the kid's themselves. Those stories would cause upset and anger in those boys. Sadly, a lot of them would let that anger build up, affecting them later in life. Some would end up in prison, but even worse, some would end up becoming those men they so despised.

To my mother's huge credit, she never took a man home. Never did I even see her with another man. I had to respect her for that...begrudgingly. As I said, I was an optimist. Things could have been worse. That was one of the ways I would learn that no matter how bad one thinks their troubles are, there are always other poor fuckers out there, somewhere, whose problems are a thousand times worse. It taught me that no-one in life had a trouble-free existence- a depressing fucking lesson!

One day, when I turned up for school on the first day of term in primary seven, my life got a lot better.

Sitting at the back of the class was a new boy. He was around the same size as me. Scrawny, brown spiky hair, and a menacing scowl on his face which interpreted in any language as "Don't even fucking think about it". Of course, regarding myself as one of the tough kids in class, I didn't want to back away. I swaggered up to him and spoke:

"I'm Tommy Smyth... and who are you?"

His scowl lifted momentarily, making way for an impish little smile.

"Fuck you Tommy Smyth. It's none of your business who I am. Now piss off, before I kick the shit out of you!"

I nearly shit. Not with fear, but with surprise and intrigue. Because, from that little brown-haired boy, came the exact same sound my mother made. Same accent, same charming directness of speech. He was Irish, and I couldn't get enough of it. Forgiving his aggressive stance toward me, he was immediately promoted to my new best friend, whether he liked it or not.

In the years that followed, Brian McManus and his family would share with me a friendship and bond I had never experienced before... or would do again.

CHAPTER 4

Brian McManus' family hailed from Co. Down, in the north of Ireland. His father, Dan, was a builder, who had been forced to leave Ireland, as work had been so scarce he could no longer support his wife and three children. It had been the early 1980s and times were particularly bad in all sectors of industry... particularly in construction...especially in Ireland.

At that time, there had been a lot of Irish families living in and around London, most with the same predicament as the McManus'. In England, during that era, suspicions were always raised about the Irish living abroad, as the actions of the IRA had been particularly rife. Almost all Irish people had to deal with the paranoia of the English at one time or another, which could simmer over, turning nasty and violent at times. Brian and I would experience a lot of that later in our lives.

At that time, when we were still in primary school, we revelled in the notoriety, bragging, quite innocently, that our fathers were famous IRA soldiers. Deadly men, feared both in England and Ireland. We made it clear, again, quite naively, in a "my dad is bigger than your dad" type way that anyone who dared mess around with us, would be dealt with by our fathers in the deadliest possible manner. As I've mentioned earlier, we could get away with saying such things in primary school, however when the time came to attend secondary school, the response of the other boys would be a lot more abrasive.

Brian and I immediately became best friends, after our first contentious encounter. Like most boys, we had to iron out our differences, by having a few fights. Some, he won, some I won. We were very similar, we fought similarly, and eventually we found we had a very similar sense of humour.

After a few weeks of fighting and conflict (I had initially been reluctant to fight with him, but his Irish temperament and the chip on his shoulder compelled him to go up against one of the tough kids in the class- I didn't back down either) for those first few weeks, it seemed that we had tested each other to the limit. We both seemed happy with each other's results, so both parties merited the other with best friend status.

Brian and his family would eventually play a huge part in my life, growing up, and beyond. They lived close to us, in a small two storey house in a rundown housing estate, where the only attraction had been a large, grassy area in the middle of the development. I loved to visit his house after school and at the weekends, as the sense of normality and warmth demonstrated by his family was a tonic to the disruption I was used to.

After school, we would rush to his house, drop our schoolbags off, and then go out to the large grassy area and play football for an hour or so with all the other kids from the estate. Brian, myself and about ten other boys would split into two teams, and the match would begin. Jumpers and coats would create makeshift goal posts, and the matches would be epic encounters, usually ending up with a score line of around ten-nine each day, largely due to the poor standard of goal-keeping on show. I loved those matches, they offered pure and utter escapism. Every time I had possession of the ball, I was Ossie Ardiles, the great Argentinian footballer, who played for my favourite team, Tottenham Hotspur. Brian would become Kenny Dalglish- his favourite player from his favourite team, Liverpool, much to the disdain of his father, a Manchester United fanatic. Usually, the matches would end when some of the mothers would come out calling the kids in for dinner, until the teams became so decimated in numbers, the game would be called as over. Those calls from the mothers would be dreaded, a sorry sight to see the boys traipsing reluctantly into their houses, red faced and mud stained, retiring for dinner.

After a few months of knowing Brian, I got invited to dinner by his parents. I gladly accepted, however, in the earlier days before they knew my true situation, I sometimes made excuses, lying that my mother was preparing a roast beef dinner, trying to allude to some form of normality. I would relish and look forward to those dinners. Theirs was a world completely alien to mine. I couldn't comprehend how a family of five people could be so happy and content with each other and their lives. When I would enter their home, hot and sweaty after playing football, a warm glow could be felt coming from the kitchen. Not warmth from the oven, but one of actual human kindness and love. This was in complete contrast to my own home life, where I would climb the cold, smelly stairs of the concrete jungle where we lived, finding my mother lying in bed with the curtains drawn, no dinner on the table. The other extreme was where she would screech at the top of her lungs, asking where I had been, reeking of booze, the smell of burnt meat emanating from our grease ridden tiny kitchen, the sound of Country and Western music blaring from the stereo.

Life in the McManus household was the life I could only dream of.

Brian's mother, Kathleen, was a slim, blonde haired woman. Perhaps, mid-thirties, though she looked much younger. She had a kind, pretty face and had a lovely infectious laugh that was both heart-warming and comforting.

Francis, was the baby of the house, who sat mostly in his high chair and giggled and gurgled at almost everything he saw. He was less than a year old, and unlike most babies I had ever seen, very rarely cried.

Brian's older sister, Maura, was three years older than both of us, and had been my first crush. She was a lot taller than me and looked a lot like her mother, only she had the cutest dimples and the most beautiful, dazzling white teeth I had ever seen. I rarely spoke to her, as I was too shy, finding myself blushing like a smitten schoolgirl anytime I was near her. I think I was in love with her, though I would never let Brian know, as I feared he would fall out with me and that would be the end of the McManus family visits. I would never tell her either, as she had a stern look about her, and a razor-sharp tongue that put the fear of God into me.

Brian's dad was the main attraction of the house, in my eyes. Growing up, he would become my hero. I had always wished that one day my mother would tell me all the stories of my parentage were untrue, and in actual fact Dan McManus was my dad. That certainly would have made me the happiest boy in the world.

Dan was in his late thirties, perhaps early forties, although like, Kathleen, could have passed for much younger. He had a fine head of hair on him, jet black, so black it almost appeared blue under a certain light. It was styled like many of the pop stars of the day, much in the style of Shakin' Stevens. He had, what can only be described as a toothy demeanour and reminded me a lot of Brian Ferry from Roxy Music. He was tall and slim, even from a male's point of view, one could tell he was very handsome. Unlike most handsome men, he did not seem to realise it himself, and instead of having an arrogant swagger, he was of a very humble disposition. He carried himself with a slight hump, like many of the men, especially most of the Irish... a symptom of the back-breaking nature of their construction jobs.

His greatest attribute, though, was his sense of humour. He was an extremely funny man, the funniest person I had ever, or would ever meet in my life. Brian and I would be infected with his humour as we grew up. It was impossible to be immune, so deliciously contagious it was. The way in which he not only viewed the world, from the darkest recesses of his twisted mind, but also the way he described and interpreted what he had seen, could only be described as genius... or madness!

They made up the McManus family. They played an instrumental part in my development into a barely functioning adult. I believed, and always would do, that without them I wouldn't have seen adulthood at all. I loved them all, like normal people love their families. I loved them as much, if not more than my own mother.

They were certainly easier to love.

In turn, they made me feel like a member of their own little family.

Times had always been good when I was with them.

I just wished I could have been with them a lot more often.

CHAPTER 5

Neil sat at the kitchen table. He sat on a different chair each day, as the chairs, like everything else in the house, creaked and groaned, making him fear the chairs would break into pieces under his weight. He tried desperately to cling on to some sense of normality, the intact table and four chairs surrounding it, helped him a little to do so...he didn't know why. He longed to take a pull on his pipe, but, as he had indulged in that little luxury earlier that morning, he decided to hold out until later that evening to do so.

The shadows began to loom larger in the kitchen by the passing minutes. He knew that half an hour later, it would be dark once again. It must have been November, he thought, possibly December... early December. He felt annoyed that he could not determine what month of the year, or even what season it was. He felt embarrassed, as a once proud farmer, he couldn't even determine the season of the year. Not spring or summer, possibly autumn, but the intensity of the cold made him lean toward winter.

"What difference does it make" he said to himself, under his breath.

A farmer always had to be at least one step ahead of the weather. The weather could have a positive or negative effect depending on the circumstances. A sunny week with no rain would be perfect weather to make and harvest hay, the same climate for a few weeks could mean drought, a complete opposite and adverse effect.

It didn't matter to him anymore. He had lost interest in the weather years before. What was the use in monitoring the weather when a man had nothing to look after or harvest anymore?

As to what time of the day it was, he hadn't a clue either. The sun rose and fell at different times throughout the year. He would awaken at sunrise and retire to his internal campfire at night time, the time in-between irrelevant.

There was only one thing in the world that scared him anymore. It didn't only scare him, it absolutely terrified him- the risk of ensuing insanity. He sensed it was inevitable, but when or how it would arrive, he couldn't determine. He knew a man couldn't continue with the existence he endured without utter madness taking an eventual hold. The routine he persisted with, a mere distraction method for his mind to keep functioning, without being overwhelmed by an irresistible sense of insanity.

It confused and intrigued him why, even though he had lost everything and seen his life as over years before, he retained a primeval survival instinct. He didn't understand it. However, he knew the will waned every single day he awoke, until it eventually hung by a thread. Something deep inside still wafted the flames of life within him, although he wished the same spirit would wither and die, so that he could do the same himself.

The air around him suddenly became almost unbearably cold, in direct correlation with the diminishing sunlight. He wouldn't allow himself to go to the living room and light the wood he had collected that day, until total darkness had descended. Through chattering teeth, he counted, almost chanting to himself, until he reached five hundred. Then he would consider lighting the fire, only to stop himself by setting a challenge to count to five hundred once more. Then he would do it again, and again after that, until the cold became all-consuming and he could no longer remember what number he had counted to. Those little endurance challenges he would set himself throughout the day. They alleviated the boredom and passed the time. He hoped it would hone discipline too. He didn't know if it did or not.

Then, when the darkness had truly fallen, he would kindle the fire. The dancing orange and blue flames would visually excite him. The crackling, popping rhythms sounding to him like the most beautiful song, until an intense, bone dry heat would arrive at the end, the searing heat, stinging his skin, the most delicious, painful sensation he would encounter all day. Those feelings gave at least a few of his senses some form of daily exercise.

His life was ruled with the aim of mastering total discipline and self-control.

He knew it needed to be.

He knew his unwavering self-control was the key to keep madness at bay. At times, he knew madness was imminent, when he would sit at the fire or at the table, roaring uncontrollably until his throat would burn and no further sound would come. At other times, when out walking the fields during the day, he would roar, horrible inaudible noises that would horrify even himself, if he sensed another living thing in the vicinity. He knew those acts of impulsiveness were the first tell-tale signs of madness. Although he tried with every ounce of his being to stifle those occurrences, he couldn't. It was the desperation and helplessness, the realisation that no matter how much he roared into the ether, it was never going to change what had happened...he was never going to be able to recoup what he had lost.

He knew if self-discipline could be maintained, it was the key to gaining revenge on the bastards who ruined his life. He had always been a patient, unimpulsive (unless riled to breaking point, by a select few) man, who had taken measured steps in everything he had done in his life. The issue of revenge would remain, as with everything else, well thought out, well planned, and as the old saying went...best served cold. Those thoughts mildly comforted him. He believed he could depend on himself to come up with something, although, disappointingly, he had yet to think of anything.

It would be easy to track down the bastards who were responsible and take their lives in an equally horrendous and brutal fashion, but he knew it would only appease him for a short while. He had to try and think of something that would hurt those people much more than that. Death was too easy. He could perhaps kill their families, he had thought of that, but knew that made him no better than them. Their families were to remain unharmed. It had nothing to do with them, and he wasn't going to start killing innocent people.

He hoped to God he wasn't buoyed by delusion or false hope in the aim of thinking of a revengeful master plan.

The light from the dying sun finally extinguished. He could see his breath again in the pale blueness of the evening and he knew it was finally time to light the fire.

He walked to the living room, and after a few minutes of trying, the little bundle of sticks finally began to smoke. He sat for a while, when the flames finally appeared, and basked in its wicked heat. The shadows shortening and lengthening around the room, the fire moving from left to right, up and down, due to the draughts in the walls, yet still it burned, never giving up.

"My only friend" thought Neil, "So resilient and alike myself in many ways" He smiled bitterly into the fire, saying aloud, very quietly to himself;

"My only friend. My only friend, the one who killed my family...some friend"

He gazed into the fire, watching the beautiful element wreak its deadly magic, and began to picture the man who had caused it, destroying everything that night. He could feel a fire rising from within himself, but using all the self-restraint he had honed during the day, he managed to douse it before it took complete control. Not roaring like he desperately wanted to, he restrained his anger to a fine hiss, as he spoke the name through gritted teeth:

"Dessie McNamee"

He shook his head, took a pull on his unlit pipe, and spat into the fire.

CHAPTER 6

Dessie McNamee could only be described as a weed. That was the best description for him. In the garden that was humanity, some people were beautiful and fragrant, like the rose. Some people were ugly, though wholesome, like the potato, but Dessie McNamee...was a weed.

He thrived on the misfortune of others, growing in stature from the decomposing hopes and dreams of his fellow man. He would associate himself with good and beautiful people, then eventually strangle them with his poisonous aura until everything associated with them began to resemble him. He was like a bacterium that could sour a cream with its presence. He was toxic.

Neil had known Dessie McNamee all his life. He never liked him, and he knew the feeling was certainly mutual. McNamee had worked for Neil's father in the mill. Neil's father had employed many of the local community back then. He owned a flax mill business and there was always plenty of work going. He also ran a cattle farm and grew potatoes in some of his fields that required harvesting at a certain time of the year. He was a successful businessman and well respected in the area. He had been an outgoing, friendly, and likeable man, who liked a drink (a little too much, most of the time, which in turn led to his demise).

Neil had been different to his father. While his father had been outgoing and popular with the locals, Neil had always been withdrawn and mostly unpopular. Many of the locals viewed him as arrogant, as he rarely conversed or socialised with them. He was the only son of a successful man, who one day would inherit it all, without ever really doing much to deserve it.

That's what they thought.

The truth was, Neil disliked most of them and had no interest in joining into, what he deemed, pathetic conversations, most of which revolved around who was going to inherit what land, who was courting who, or who were making fools of themselves at the local pub every night.

After the workers went home at the end of their shifts, Neil would continue working. There had always been cattle to feed and look after. Outhouses had to be cleaned out daily and the mill had to be readied for the next day, when the workers returned in the morning.

Those were the things the locals did not see. Neil had been regarded as aloof and a bit lazy, but the locals had only seen what they wanted to see.

His education, like many of the children of the day, ended at thirteen. Where most rich men would send their children to grammar school to obtain an education, Neil's father sent only his daughter. Kathy went to school and became a doctor.

Dessie McNamee worked as a handyman around Neil's fathers place. He would fix any broken machinery in the mill and was also an accomplished builder and farmer. An odd-job man would have been a good description for him. To his credit, he was good at what he did, and he was a hard worker. Neil's father liked him.

Neil began to work around the place properly, full time, from around the age of thirteen. McNamee was ten years older, but around the same height as Neil at the time. He was about five feet seven, stocky in build and seemed to be all trunk. He had abnormally short arms and legs. Although still only in his early-twenties, he had already begun balding. He had a small, pug nose and sandy red hair, which matched his sandy red face.

Neil had originally disliked him, as he thought of him as a "smart arse". He had always something smart to say for himself, and would always deliver one of his put-downs with his customary smirk.

Neil had to work closely with McNamee, as his father wanted him to pick up the skills to successfully run the business himself in years to come. He hated working with him. At quitting time, Neil's father would usually appear, mostly drunk or well on his way.

"Well Dessie. How'd the boy get on today?" he would ask.

"Do you really want to know?" McNamee would laugh, in reply.

"Do ye reckon we can make a handy man out of him?"

"Handy man fuck. Sure, ye have to use your hands to be a handy man. I'm surprised he can even wipe his own hole, he's that unhandy of a prick" McNamee would reply.

Both McNamee and Neil's father would laugh.

"I should have sent *him* to school and let Kathy take care of the place, eh?" Neil's father asked.

"Ye should have sent him to the priesthood instead. Isn't the idiot in every family sent to the priesthood?"

They both laughed heartily at that remark.

"Good man Dessie, off ye go. I'll see you in the pub tonight"

Neil would stand silently and rage. He had done everything McNamee had asked him to do. Sometimes McNamee would even praise him, when they were alone, for his work. However, when Neil's father would appear on the scene, he would suddenly change and begin to ridicule him, much to everyone's amusement.

Neil despised him for that.

It was little known that Neil's father, although charming and friendly to the outside world was indeed a horrible, nasty drunk whilst at home. He would dredge up all the criticisms McNamee told him earlier that day, using them to ridicule and torment Neil that night, whilst sometimes, if fit, brandishing a heavy beating upon him.

"Why the fuck couldn't God have given me a decent heir to this place?" his drunken rant would normally begin, "Instead, he gives me you. A stupid, good for nothing, wee bastard. You walk around like you're God almighty. Who do you think you are? When I was your age, I had nothing, not a pot to piss in. I didn't have a big daddy looking after me. I had nothing. I worked my fingers to the bone, and built this place from nothing. And what reward do I get for all that? I get you- gobshite. Oh, why wasn't Kathy born a boy? She'll make me proud yet, she'll be a Doctor, but you..."

The rant would continue until he got tired and went to bed.

Neil's mother had died from T.B when he was very young, so the main womanly duties were performed in the house by Neil's aunt, Maggie. She was Neil's father's sister. Her husband had also died from T.B years before too, so she had sold up and moved in with Neil and his father. Much like Thomas, Maggie appeared both charming and friendly to the locals, only really to be just as nasty as him in the domestic environment. When his father would come home at night from the pub, drunk, to ridicule Neil, she would encourage him further, stoking the fire as it were. She would sit at the fire, knitting, and smiling as his father began the onslaught, chirping in with her own criticisms from time to time, encouraging his father to continue.

It was a sign of the times that a man would bequeath most of his land and property to the sons in the family. The sons carried the family name forward and the land would be kept in the family name. The daughters would marry and take another man's name, and most fathers, if possible would have preferred to leave it to the sons to carry the legacy on. Neil's father had every intention of doing so too, but he seemed to detest the idea that Neil was the only option.

"Don't you go getting notions above your station about this place when I'm gone, sonny Jim. If it were up to me. I'd gladly leave it to Kathy. But she has no time for it- she's going to be a Doctor, going to make something of herself- unlike you. But don't worry, there's ways of getting around these things, you might find yourself getting a nasty surprise when I'm gone"

Neil would indeed find out what that surprise was later in his life. Because McNamee was a close drinking friend of his fathers, Neil would always be deeply suspicious in later years that it was *him* who had put the idea of the will into his head.

Yet another reason he hated him.

There were many, too many reasons why he so despised the man, but one of the major reasons being the deterioration of his relationship with his sister.

Unlike their father, Kathy was a friendly, outgoing, and likeable person. Not only to the outside world, but also to Neil.

She was five years older and had always looked out for him. She had mostly been away from home at various boarding schools but always came home for the holidays and would help with the work around home. Neil found himself fascinated by tales of her friends, their lives in big cities, and everything else she was doing in her life. When she won her place to study medicine in a Dublin university, no-one had been prouder of her than Neil. He never once resented or felt any jealousy towards her for receiving so many opportunities. He had never liked school and only ever found himself interested in farming anyway. He idolised her and found himself living his life through her in many ways. She would always write when she was away, updating him about her various experiences and adventures. Neil relished and looked forward to those letters arriving in the post.

He looked forward to the day when he would drive down and spend a day with her, and her friends in Dublin. They had agreed the date to be his seventeenth birthday.

Kathy, being the apple in her father's eye had sweet talked him into giving Neil a day off to visit on his birthday. Their father begrudgingly agreed and Neil began to count the days.

It never happened.

It had been about two months before his seventeenth birthday. Kathy was at home on holidays. It had been a Sunday. All the Dillon family had been to mass that morning. When the mass ended, Neil's father got talking to some of the local men outside the chapel, and yet again, found himself persuaded into going for a drink in the pub next door. It was the local custom after all. The men would usually stand outside the chapel when the sermon was in progress, smoking and talking amongst themselves. The priest, without fail, every Sunday, would stop the sermon and bark at the men to come in and sit down amongst the congregation. The men simply ignored him, never coming in, much to the annoyance and disgust of the priest and the women in the mass. The tut-tutting from the women would eventually die down until the priest continued with the rest of his sermon. Every week the same routine, until it became as much a part of the mass as communion. Neil's father, however, being a respected businessman in the community would not be seen partaking in such a rebellious manner, and would instead sit in his Sunday best, at one of the top rows in the chapel.

When the mass ended he would converse with the men who had been standing outside and inevitably the talk would turn to going for a drink. Just one drink, they always promised. He would always turn to Maggie, shrug his shoulders and say; "Sure it would be rude of me not go for one. You all head home and start the dinner, I'll be home in an hour".

Like the priest chastising the men outside the chapel, it was a weekly ritual. He wouldn't ever arrive home an hour later, always arriving home late that night, roaring drunk.

That Sunday, Neil, Maggie, and Kathy had been standing outside the chapel waiting on Thomas, waiting for the inevitable shrug of the shoulders. As usual, McNamee was in his company, laughing at all his jokes and back slapping him at every opportunity. Neil's father had been in the company of about five other men at the time, when suddenly McNamee broke away from the group and approached Neil and the women. Neil braced himself for some smart arsed comment directed towards him for the benefit of the women's amusement, when uncharacteristically McNamee nodded at him.

"Good morning Neil" he said.

Neil stood, baffled by his manners, still awaiting the put-down, but instead he turned towards the women, smiling;

"Mrs Clarke. Kathy. Good morning ladies. How are you both?"

Both smiled back at him.

"Oh Dessie" said Maggie "We're grand. What are you up to today?"

She looked over at Kathy who was blushing and nervously playing with her hair.

"Not much, Mrs Clarke. I might head in for a drink with Mr Dillon and then head home for my mother's Sunday dinner- nothing much exciting"

"Good boy. You tell your mother I was asking about her now" said Maggie.

"I will surely. I'll see you all later. Good luck" he replied.

He walked back over to the group of men, and from time to time glanced back at Neil and the women, smiling.

"He's a lovely boy, that Dessie" said Maggie. "Such a hard worker too. Your father really thinks a lot of him"

Neil knew better than to respond. A clip around the ear would bring great laughter from the men, especially from McNamee.

On their way home from mass that morning, Neil walked with Kathy as Maggie walked alongside their neighbour, Mrs Dunne. Neil half whispered to Kathy:

"That McNamee's a right hateful wee bastard, isn't he?"

Kathy smiled to herself.

"Ach, he's not that bad Neil. Sure, daddy thinks the world of him"

"What?" replied Neil, in disgust "Do you not listen to the stories I tell you about him. He's a weed".

Kathy smiled and continued along the road. Neil shook his head in disbelief and tried to change the subject.

Later that evening, after dinner, Neil went out to watch over the cattle in the fields. He particularly enjoyed that certain chore as he found himself refreshed after a good rest and a hearty Sunday dinner. Mostly he enjoyed it as it gave him the opportunity to be free from Maggie's nagging. He would normally steal a few of her cigarettes and walk around the fields smoking them. The solitude, tranquillity, and beauty of the evening countryside, invigorated and recharged his batteries for the week that lay ahead.

It began to get dark when Neil decided it was time to head back for home. The light had faded to near darkness as he reached the road. When he had walked further up the road nearing the turnoff to his lane, he thought he heard stifled laughter.

"Who would be around here at this time of the evening" he thought to himself, as the roads would always be deserted after dark until after closing time at the pub, when the odd drunk could be found staggering home, or sometimes even lying in a ditch sleeping, during the summer months.

As he got closer to the sound, he could just about make out the shape of two bicycles. Straining his eyes further, he realised one of the bicycles belonged to Kathy.

"Kathy" he shouted. "Is that you? Where are you?"

A moment later, after a little tittering and giggling:

"Uh, Neil, is that you?"

"Yes, it's me. Where are you? What are you doing out here?"

He heard rustling and whispering. He leapt over the gate towards where the noises were coming from. He then made out the shape of Kathy, getting to her feet, adjusting, and fixing herself. There was a man, there also, lying on the grass, attempting to get to his feet too.

As his eyes adjusted further to the darkness, he realised, to his horror and disgust, that the man was no other than Dessie McNamee.

"What the fuck are you doing with him, Kathy?" he asked, his voice beginning to rise in anger.

"Neil", Kathy replied, nervously, "Watch your language, especially today- a Sunday of all days"

"What is he doing here, Kathy?", asked Neil, hissing the words out.

"Oh...Dessie just wanted to take me out for a bike ride, that's all"

McNamee stood behind Kathy, a sly smile spreading across his lips. Neil pointed his finger towards him, and snapped:

"You go anywhere near my sister again and I'll fuckin' kill ye. Now... get the fuck down that road, or God help me, I'll kick you down it"

Just then, Kathy grabbed him by the collar and shook him.

"Calm down Neil. This has nothing to do with you. Dessie is just a good friend of mine; we were only having a chat"

"He's a fuckin weed. How many times have I told you about him? And what do you do? You betray me and go and do this. Now, let go of me you fuckin' hoor"

Kathy reeled back in shock, reflexively putting her hand over her mouth in horror, staring wide eyed and in disbelief at him.

"Don't you speak to your sister like that, ye pup", shouted McNamee. It was too much for Neil and before he knew it he had launched himself, fists and boots flailing towards him, knocking Kathy over in the process.

He landed a good few punches on the top of McNamee's head, but being considerably older and a few stone heavier, McNamee eventually overpowered him, throwing him to the ground, before he sat with his two knees on his shoulders, his elbow wedged into his throat.

"Who's the big man now, eh?", McNamee breathlessly spat out, spittle landing on Neil's face; "It's about time someone put some manners into you, ye brat. Walkin' around all day like your something, lookin' down your nose at the people. So… what are ye gonna do now, eh?"

McNamee was relishing his moment, Neil knew that. He couldn't breathe. The situation was hellish to him- he couldn't possibly think of anything worse. Full of an intense rage, he couldn't do anything, he was trapped and humiliated at the hands of his sworn enemy. He thought he was going to die. Then, McNamee would marry his sister and live happily ever after, inheriting his family property in the process. Those were the thoughts rushing through his mind, when finally, just as he thought he was about to lose consciousness, McNamee said; "Say sorry to your sister… say sorry and I'll let you go"

"Sorry", Neil gurgled, with the last of the breath that was in his lungs.

McNamee took his elbow out of Neil's throat. He gasped in a huge lungful of precious air, the night sky turning from black to pink to blue through to red before turning black again.

He looked towards Kathy, who was crying. "Neil… please don't be like this. You don't understand…you're too young"

Neil stood, bent over, sucking in air, trying desperately to regain his composure. Rage burned through his bloodstream. He knew he would rather die than let McNamee get the better of him at that moment. Kathy continued crying and blubbing when he spotted a small rock nestled in the grass directly below where he stood. He glanced up at McNamee who was hovering above him, still on guard, and obviously enjoying every second of Neil's humiliation. He quickly dropped his hand, picked up the rock and in one fluid motion, sprang up, ramming the rock into the side of McNamee's head. McNamee stood still for a moment, in a daze, looking at Neil with no expression, before falling sideways, like a felled tree.

"You bastard", Neil shouted, before kicking him hard, twice in the ribs, until Kathy ran at him, pushing him over. He got to his feet quickly and looked down at Kathy who was on her knees tending to McNamee.

"You've killed him, ye mad wee bastard", she cried; "No wonder both daddy and Maggie hate you…you're not right in the head"

Neil looked down upon her, sneering, and replied; "Good. I hope the cunt *is* dead. Fuck him and fuck you too. I won't forget about this Kathy".

He then began to walk towards home.

McNamee didn't die that night. He came to after twenty minutes. He couldn't attend work for a few weeks after, as he had sustained many broken ribs.

Neil, in turn received many beatings from his father during those weeks, for the cowardly act of hitting a man with a weapon during a disagreement. He was then labelled a coward by all in the country and McNamee received much sympathy.

Neil never spoke to his sister again, after that night. Their relationship was killed, like everything else by association with McNamee. He later heard she married an American doctor in Dublin a few years later, immigrated to America and was rarely heard of again.

Life went on as normal for him, only then people had a proper reason to hate and ridicule him.

About three months later, after much barracking and baiting, Neil finally agreed to fight McNamee. That day, after work, in the field beside his father's mill, beside his own home, a skinny seventeen-year-old slip of a boy, took an almighty beating from a twenty-seven-year-old grown man, much to the delight of everyone who had witnessed it, including his own father.

Justice had been dished out and everyone went to the pub, happy. His father announced that there were no cowards in the Dillon family and his son had learned that lesson the hard way. Everyone drank to that. It was Neil's turn to miss work for a week because of his injuries.

He vowed to get his revenge on McNamee one day.

However, that episode was only a part of the reason he despised McNamee so much. The other reason would come later in life when both were very different men.

CHAPTER 7

After I put the telephone down, I found my head spinning. It had all happened so quickly.

I sat on the bed and stared out the window. The window eventually steamed up with my breath as the room was so cold, although I was too wrapped up in my thoughts, I hadn't noticed. For about an hour, I didn't feel anything. I just sat, from time to time wiping the window clear so I could look out upon North London, its piss coloured streetlights twinkling and dimming against the vast black sky.

All my life I had felt like an outsider, an unwanted alien in a foreign country- an alien no-one gave a shit about. It was probably the reason I had drank so much. Drink had always given me confidence whilst also seemingly switching off the part of my brain which made me worry, feel bad and suffer anxiety. When the alcohol invaded and took hold, I gladly and timidly surrendered. The next day, of course, the hangover would arrive. Again, I sort of welcomed it- no matter how bad the fucker felt, it served as a distraction. Anyone who has ever suffered from a horrible hangover knows the feeling. It consumes a person- one cannot feel or think of anything else, other than the immediate pain the hangover is bringing. Well, that is what I liked about it. It gave me something to deal with, other than reality...a painful distraction. Most of the time the only way to make a hangover disappear was to get drunk again.

That was fine with me.

Did I consider myself to be an alcoholic? I didn't know. Who truly ever admits to such a stigma? When they do, they are usually fucked anyway, and it's too late. A drinking problem, certainly, but most people I knew had a drinking problem.

One thing was for certain, I considered my mother to be an alcoholic.

However, the revelations she made to me in her final few weeks made me love her for who she was, helping me understand all the more why she had behaved like she had.

Why hadn't she disclosed those truths to me years before?

I supposed she had her reasons.

Life was going to change. The man on the phone had confirmed everything my mother had told me.

He talked, and I listened, listening intently to every single word he uttered. He had spoken like my mother had in her final weeks. He spoke with anger, but his tone was laced with empathy and sorrow. I barely spoke, but I felt I had told him my life story. He knew without asking, just how I felt. No one had really understood how I felt before...that man did.

I felt like my life was just about to finally begin.

I felt excitement, but also fear. I felt relieved, but also that the weight of the world weighed heavy upon my shoulders. I had never felt such happiness, but my heart was also broken into pieces.

When the man finally stopped talking, a silence fell between us. It was a comfortable silence. He knew I was busy digesting everything he had told me. I sat doing exactly that. Although my mother had told me the exact same tales in her final weeks, they didn't seem completely real or true until the man confirmed them.

I finally broke the silence between us, asking him what to do next. He spoke for a further few minutes detailing his plans. He had been busy arranging plans, and all I had to do was follow them.

Things were finally going to happen.

I was jolted back to life by a huge shiver that bolted directly down my spine. Only then did I realise how cold it had been in the flat. I reached around to scratch an itch on my back, and realised I had been drenched in sweat. An icy cold, clammy sweat.

I got up off the bed, put on some extra clothes, went to the fridge, and opened a beer. I knew I would finally have to break the rotten habit of excessive drinking, but on that occasion, it had surely been the ideal time to have one.

I downed the beer in about three or four gulps, went to the toilet, took a piss, came back, and opened another. I lay on the bed once more and thought it all over again. I thought about all the good and bad times I had seen. I thought about my mother, the McManus' and Andrea. I knew I could finally make things work between us. I knew, potentially, that I could give her the kind of life she deserved.

I thought about all those things and drank the rest of the beer that had been in the fridge. I put on my coat and headed to the off-licence, enjoying the walk, realising it had actually been warmer in the outside evening air than it had been in my flat.

I came back, lay on the bed, drank the beers, and let my thoughts take hold once more. The chance I had been waiting for my whole life was finally arriving. I was determined to make a difference. I was going to pay people back in extreme ways- good and bad, in equal measure to how good and bad they had treated my mother and I in our lives.

I drank the rest of the beers and fell asleep on top of the bed sheets. I knew I wouldn't be hung-over the next day.

I had a purpose. I didn't have time for hangovers anymore.

CHAPTER 8

As I grew up, life had moved forward very fast. I had to grow up quickly. Childhood was a dangerous time, and I knew the quicker I grew out of it, the safer and better I would be for it.

I got into fights, became interested in girls, and moved to secondary school, all whilst still being dumped in and out the children's home.

The one positive outcome was how my relationship with the McManus family grew and prospered. I was delighted that Brian and I moved to the same secondary school together. It was there, however, where we would learn most of life's bad habits.

We began smoking at thirteen, drinking at fourteen, and fucking at fifteen...well, Brian did anyway. I would claim to have been a late developer in that field.

There had been some good and happy times as well. As I stated previously, contrary to common perception, being tossed in and out of the children's home was not all bad. I supposed I had grown up with it as a constant in my life, and didn't know any other way, but it certainly had some good points. When life with my mother became almost unbearable, when she was going through a turbulent spell of her own, the home would offer me a sanctuary for a while. I could go for a few weeks or months and renew old friendships.

What I found tough was seeing some kids dumped into the home, who up to that point had lived completely normal and happy lives. *I* had been used to it, so became hardened at a young age to it, but it was sad to see kids come in for the first time. They all came from a variety of backgrounds, for a variety of different reasons. Some would arrive because of a death of one or sometimes two parents and because there was no-one left to look after them. Some arrived because of marriage problems between their parents, newly found lone parents unable to cope mentally or financially with the pressures of bringing up a child. There were many reasons, though none good.

The home I attended had about fifteen to twenty kids in residency, all from different cultures, ethnicities, and class divides. I was the only Irish kid, as Irish parents back then would stick together through thick and thin. It was almost unheard of for Irish couples to separate or divorce, the Catholic Church putting the fear of God into them.

It saddened me to see little children arriving into the home who knew of no other home life than days at the beach, happy family birthdays and Christmas morning presents, mummy, and daddy omnipresent in all. I thought it must have been a horrible shock for them. Those were the kids I tried to protect most. Some of the older, more hardened kids would laugh and sneer when they heard the new children's stories, probably through jealousy that these kids had experienced some form of happiness and stability in their lives at some point. I never saw it that way. I supposed I had always imagined what it would be like for the McManus kids to enter the home, if something horrible happened in their lives. Because I had witnessed first-hand what their happy family unit felt like, I could probably empathise more because of that.

I had mentioned before how I had carved a tough guy reputation. A reputation I was terrified to lose and utterly determined to keep, in equal measure. To recap, I got a bad beating from the resident bully, David Thompson. Then, I returned after a good growth spurt and a bit of hardening up on the outside, to finally beat him the second time, although I still felt I had gotten lucky and wouldn't have fancied my chances again if there had been a round three.

David Thompson was about two years older than I was. He had a big, thick head, big sticky out ears and big rubbery lips. He was Neanderthal-like in every way. His story had been sad though, both his parents had been smack heads and he had been resident in the home from about six years old. The home would be visited from time to time by prospective foster parents and Thompson would be the main kid the carers would try to flog to them- mainly because of the length of time he had been resident, but more likely because *they* were fed up dealing with him. Unfortunately for him, and the rest of us, he never got chosen by anyone.

As much as anyone tried to empathise with him, he made it very difficult, as he was a nasty bully. They say there is no such thing as a bad child, and that is probably mostly true, but there wasn't much good to be seen in Thompson.

One of his favourite things was to find out the background of the new kids arriving in the home, then use that information to ridicule and torment them during their first few weeks and months. He had done it to me when I had first arrived, taunting me about my "loony, pissed-up whore of a mother". I cracked and went for him, receiving a bad hiding in the process.

He really enjoyed inflicting pain too. I will never forget the look on his face, the horrible, gleeful smile he wore when he was on top of me, taunting and tormenting me more with his vile words than his punches. I made sure not to cry that day. I wanted nothing more than to curl up in a ball and cry like a small child, to let the pain and anguish flood out.

I didn't though.

Blood streamed from my nose and lips, but not a tear was shed. I was proud of myself that day, even with the beating I received. It pissed him off too. He got a kick out of humiliating other children. I wasn't going to let him humiliate me.

It was a different story when the tables were turned. The day I gained my revenge he cried and roared like a pig, running to the carers, telling tales, and blubbing like a pathetic creature. I had felt like a fucking He-Man that day, receiving a cult-like status amongst the other kids from then onwards. He remained a bully afterwards though. He just stayed well clear of me. I heard from other kids about what he had been up to when I wasn't around.

Worst of it all was, the carers didn't really give a shit. It was impossible for them not to notice what he was up to. I got the impression that most of them were cruising along, not wanting to rock the boat too much. As long as they received their pay cheque at the end of the month, it was easy to bury the head in the sand and plod along as if everything was good in the world. The other kids were too frightened to tell on him, in-case he found out- then they would receive a worse beating later if he did.

I knew after our second fight he was afraid of me.

Strangely though, Thompson offered me a way out of the home for good...and into the home of the McManus'.

I remember the day it happened vividly. It had been during the summer holidays between second and third year in school, so I must have been about thirteen or so. It had been a Thursday, and that was visitor's day. The morning had been brilliant as the McManus' had come to see me.

I had made an extra effort that morning in getting ready as I knew Maura would be with them. I had brushed my teeth, twice, and tried sweet-talking one of the other boys to let me use some of his hair gel, to make my hair nice and spiky. Of course, that didn't work, so I struck a deal with him that I would give him a bar of chocolate later that day in return. Mrs McManus always brought me a bar of chocolate, so I would give it to the other kid that night.

The kids had learned at an early age how to strike a deal in that place.

All five of the McManus family arrived that morning, including Francis who was changing from a gurgling baby into a little tearaway toddler. Maura, of course looked beautiful, wearing a figure hugging flowery dress with her blonde hair tied back in a ponytail. The whole duration of the visit she barely even glanced at me, instead sitting, chewing gum, looking bored and reading a magazine. But I was pleased she was there, nonetheless. Maura's surly attitude didn't matter too much anyway, Brian and his dad, Dan, were on brilliant form, cracking jokes and telling stories about what they had been getting up to in the past few weeks. Brian's mother, Kathleen, would sit and rock little Francis on her knee, looking around at the other kids in the room commenting on the "poor little things" the whole time. I think it upset her a little by being there, witnessing it all, but to me it meant the world they had visited.

Kathleen told me she had been to visit my mother. I tried not to let it show, but I was shocked and disappointed that she had. The last thing I wanted was for those lovely people, living their carefree, happy lives to be interacting with her. I was embarrassed. Those people lived their lives in sunshine, my mother was a dark raincloud, threatening to burst at any moment.

"Your mother sends her apologies she couldn't make it today, Tommy" Kathleen said. "She's not…feeling very well. But she said not to worry, she'll be better in a few days and she'll be in to see you then".

I couldn't help but feel annoyed. They were *my* people, my escape from the dourness of our lives. I didn't want my mother getting involved. The worst part was that they seemed to really like her. It wasn't a lie either, to spare my feelings, they were honest people.

In my childish immaturity, it enraged me a little, in a "these are my friends, go find your own" type of way.

Brian and Dan must have sensed the bad vibes I was sending out, so in their usual way began messing around once more.

"Do me a favour, Tommy", Dan said, his face awash with devilment; "Pull my finger for me", and we all knew how that ended.

Too soon the visit ended and I was left with my usual bar of chocolate from Mrs McManus (which I reluctantly gave to my hair gel friend) and my "Dandy" comic and "Match" magazine, my mother sent with them (God love her!).

"Don't you worry Tommy", Kathleen said as she put her jacket on; "Your mother is getting a lot better and she promises she'll have you home in no time".

She gave me the warmest hug I ever received. Dan grabbed me in a headlock and ruffled my nicely spiked hair, much to my annoyance, Brian punched me on the arm, little Francis giggled and waved and Maura put her magazine down, mumbled something inaudible and sloped off without even looking at me.

I barely had time to pine for them before I was visited by my second visitor. It was our neighbour from the flats, Mrs Kingston.
Mrs Kingston, like the McManus' was a good person. A genuinely good-hearted soul. Probably in her sixties, it was hard to tell as her silky smooth, black skin could have belonged to a woman half her age. Not a single wrinkle on her face. The only sign of any advanced age being her white hair and her slowness of movement- and the fact she had grown up grandchildren. She was a large woman who had emigrated from Jamaica to London many years before. She was a deeply religious woman, who attended church every day, and much like the McManus family lived her life with

unbridled happiness and joy. A very positive and enjoyable person to be around.

Even though she was an older lady, I could relate directly with her as she had a fantastic sense of humour. I told her jokes and funny little stories and she would always find herself bent over, slapping her large thighs, and bellowing out laughter like a madwoman. She just didn't give a shit, and that was one of the reasons I liked her so much.

As I have mentioned before, it was hard to hate my mother. Probably the main reason was because so many good people, like the McManus' and Mrs Kingston genuinely held her in high esteem. They must have seen something in her that I didn't. Mrs Kingston gave me updates and told me she was keeping a close eye on her, reinforcing what the McManus' told me about her good progress.

Mrs Kingston always visited.

My mother and I had always thought of her as family. I had known her since I could first remember. My mother and I had lived in the same block of flats since she moved over from Ireland, and Mrs Kingston had lived there from before that. When I was younger and my mother began drinking heavily, going through one of her dark periods, Mrs Kingston would step in and take me to live in her flat, sometimes for as long as a week. She had always looked after me, helping my mother out, until her own health eventually began to fail. It was only when she began to be visited by nurses several days a week that it was time for me to go into care.

She could hardly convince the nurses the small white boy constantly in her flat was her grandson.

It happened when I was about six or seven, and it broke her heart- she constantly reminded me. But, what could she have done? She required as much outside help as my mother, and it wasn't fair on her to be looking after me.

The first time I was returned to my mother from the care home, the social workers visited some of the other neighbours and asked them to keep an eye on our situation. So, anytime the neighbours got wind of my mother's bad behaviour, straight back into the home I went.

I always got the feeling Mrs Kingston felt guilty that I was in care, I didn't know why. My mother and I certainly never blamed her, it wouldn't even have crossed our minds, but she had been old school, and believed in a sense of community- an all for one, one for all mentality. I think she felt she had let us down because of her ill health, like it was some sort of weakness or flaw in her character. She couldn't have been more wrong.

I loved her like a grandmother, and even my mother had loved her as if she had been her own mother.

She was immensely proud of her own family, even her youngest grandson, who was currently doing a stretch in jail. She seen the good in everyone and I always thought I had reminded her of him, as she would always mention him and myself in the same breath, sometimes even calling me by his name. I didn't mind. I fully expected to be in prison later in life anyway.

Sometimes she would be accompanied by one of her three sons, who were all tall and built like brick shit houses. Big scary looking fuckers, would have been a good description for them. But, as with most things in life, appearances could be deceptive, as the three of them were every bit as kind and warm-hearted as their mother, when I got to know them.

On that particular day, she arrived on her own. She had had to take a bus over. She had looked very tired and was sweating quite a bit, constantly wiping her brow. She took her seat and appeared very out of breath.

"Sorry child", she said to one of the staff; "You wouldn't go and get me a nice cool glass of water?".

She was brought the water and drank it down in two gulps. She finally focused her eyes solely on mine and said, smiling; "Now, how's my little Thomas, you been a good boy?", in her thick Jamaican accent.

"No, Mrs K. I've been a big bad boy", I replied. She let out a howl of laughter, and continued to wipe her brow.

The conversation between us flowed on in that manner, both of us laughing and joking, until she looked around and suddenly became consumed with a pained expression.

"Now, isn't dat sad" she said "Dat little boy over there, young Alan. He's Mrs Fuller's boy. Oh…poor child, it just breaks my heart"

I looked over at the boy in question, sitting in the next room watching television. He was a little black boy. I had noticed him a week or so earlier, but hadn't really paid much attention to him, as he was very quiet.

Mrs Kingston filled me in on the story. She had known his mother, Gloria Fuller. She knew both her and her husband from church. Mrs Fuller had been a teacher and her husband a bus driver. They had been good people, who had a happy family unit together, with their little son. They always attended church on a Sunday and were a very likeable family. However, tragedy struck as Mrs Fuller was diagnosed with cancer and had died soon after. Her husband had fallen to pieces and began to drink heavily after her death. Eventually he was deemed unable to look after his son by Social Services, and little Alan was sent to the care home.

Mrs Kingston continued to gaze towards the little boy. "Dat poor, poor boy. Now, you keep an eye out for him Thomas, look after him for me", she asked.

I promised her I would.

When our visit ended, Mrs Kingston hugged me and told me not to worry, at the same time wiping her eyes trying to conceal her tears. As a child, it had made me sad as I didn't want to inflict any sadness upon her as she was such a happy person. She asked a passing member of staff if she could have a word with little Alan, and explained she knew both him and his family. She wasn't allowed to, so she hugged me once more and waddled out the door, clutching her little handbag, wiping her brow as she went.

That evening I went over to speak to Alan. He was only a small kid, about eight or nine years old. It had been difficult to make conversation as he was very guarded and withdrawn. I asked him if he liked football.

He did.

I asked him who he supported.

He gave a one-word reply-Arsenal.

I told him he mustn't know much about football if he supported that lot. He smiled and asked me who I followed.

I told him Tottenham.

He laughed.

He opened up a little and began to tell me how Arsenal were the top team in London, if not England, whilst also ridiculing Tottenham. If anyone else had said those things, they would have risked a fat lip or black eye, but I took it in good jest and let him have his little victory. I went to my room and brought back a few of my football annuals to give to him.

"Here, take these", I said; "Read up and expand your knowledge. Who knows, maybe you'll start to support a good team when you learn a little more."

He smiled and went off to a corner, thumbing through the pages with great relish.

It had always made me feel good, doing things like that. Sometimes, however, I wished I had someone to look after me like that. But, as I was growing older and bigger, I was to be the protector, not the protected.

The day had passed by lazily, like any other summers day. There wasn't much to do, but it had been nice. We were all called for supper at about six that night. Supper had always been around that time of day, the younger kids going to bed immediately after, the older kids, like myself, allowed the privilege of sitting up and watching television until around nine-thirty.

That particular night we were given tea, toast and a banana. I had noticed before that Alan had a strange habit of breaking off strips of toast before dunking them into his tea, sucking the tea from the toast, before finally swallowing the sodden bread. He had performed the very same ritual on that night. I had noticed, but didn't think anything of it, as I knew it to be his little habit.

The table had been quiet, apart from the obvious slurping of tea and chomping of toast, until David Thompson bellowed;

"Ewww, you're putting me off my tea, you little black fucker. Stop eating like that or I'll punch your fucking head in"

The room grew even quieter.

"Leave me alone, meathead", Alan replied.

The whole room, including myself, began laughing. Not a joyous laugh, but one derived from sheer nervousness.

Thompson even laughed. Unlike the rest of the room, his was completely sinister.

"Meathead, eh? You disgusting little bastard", he shouted back.

Then, he kicked his chair out from underneath his feet, and lunged, grabbing Alan by the throat. He slapped him in the face two or three times before throwing him to the floor.

I froze for a second.

To be honest, I didn't want another ruckus with Thompson. He had been looking even bigger and stronger recently and I didn't know if I could take him on and beat him again. A thousand thoughts rushed through my brain in that split second, the main one being, if I went for him and he beat me, my carefully constructed reputation would be in tatters.

I swallowed my fear and let instinct kick in. Before Thompson could really start kicking Alan on the ground, I shouted; "Leave him alone, Thompson. Why don't you pick on someone your own size?"

The room suddenly went deathly quiet. I could feel all eyes upon me.

"Well, if it's not Blacky's boyfriend", he said, a large, sinister smile appearing on his face; "I've been waiting to get another crack at you for a good while now. You got lucky the last time, you little faggot".

He was squinting at me, menacingly.

I could feel my heart in my mouth. My throat was as coarse as sandpaper. It had all happened so quickly. I didn't know if I was ready. The scariest thing being, he certainly was. I had an almost irresistible urge to run away, but the words came out, almost on their own; "You gonna run crying like a bitch, just like last time, *you* little faggot?"

That had done it. He charged at me, grabbing me by the waist, ramming me up against the wall. My head slammed hard against it, and when I looked up, all I could see was a fist coming towards my face. It struck me hard and the room began to spin. I could hear a buzzing sound in my ears and thought that was it- I was going down. I knew if I did, he would pummel me into the ground. I thought I was finished until my eyes regained some form of focus again and I could see the fist making its way toward my face again. Just at the last second, I ducked and heard the crack of it on the wall behind me. I heard him yelp in pain, then knew I would have my chance. On the way up, I uppercut him below the jaw. His head snapped back and he retreated about ten steps back in shock. He got his bearings very quickly, jumping high into the air, swinging his leg towards me, like a karate kick. He was trying to kick my head off, the vicious bastard. Unluckily for him, I could see his kicks coming a mile off, so I timed my punches every time he landed. I caught him a few cracks to the jaw and could see he was weakening. He persisted with the karate kick strategy until he eventually ran out of energy.

Then I knew I had him beat.

I began to enjoy the fight then. He finally stood, pathetically trying to swing his fists. I punched him twice, one landing on his ear, and the other square on his nose. He put his hands up to protect himself. I leaned in and tripped him up. When he was on the ground I couldn't resist finishing the bastard off, kicking him in the guts, before he cried for me to stop.

He deserved more.

I turned to see the reaction of the watching kids, to be suddenly grabbed by one of the carers, and marched into the staffroom. I didn't remember much after that, not realising my nose was bleeding very badly and I had a large gash at the back of my head.

Social Services were called that night.

An hour later, Mrs Henry, our social worker, came to see me. She told me the carers were basically fed up with me. They thought I was too violent and they couldn't put up with it anymore. I had been warned after I had last beat him, and this time was to be the final straw.

I felt let down and hurt by her words. As usual, the adults who were supposed to have been protecting us, overseeing our welfare, had only seen what they had wanted to see. They hadn't looked at the bigger picture to see where the problem originated from, and had simply used me as a scapegoat.

I was terrified they would place me in another care home, further away. If that were to be the case, I would have to move schools and I wouldn't be able to see Brian and the McManus' again.

I sat in the room alone, listening only to the loud ticking of the clock on the wall and felt like crying, when the social worker was out on a phone call.

The woman came back into the room; "Ok Thomas. I have been making a few phone calls", she said; "First things first, we are going to have to bring you to hospital and get that nasty looking gash on your head looked at. Secondly, I may have found you a temporary foster home for you to stay in...until your mum gets better"

My heart was racing. I began to realise the severity of the situation.

"No, Mrs Henry, please don't do this.", I began to plead. "Let me stay here. I can change. It wasn't my fault, ask any of the other kids. David Thompson is a bully. I was only sticking up for little Alan, *please* don't..."

"That's enough, Thomas. I know…I know", she said. The look in her eyes told me she believed me.

Tears stood in my eyes, but I wouldn't let them fall. She could probably see that, speaking then with a softer voice.

"Thomas. We have been speaking to your mum about a few issues recently, after some interest was expressed in you"

"No…please don't" I begged.

Strangely, she smiled.

"Thomas, these people are friends of you and your mum. The McManus family have kindly offered to foster you on a temporary basis, pending their performance, and your mum's state of health"

I nearly pinched myself. I hoped the gash on my head wasn't so bad that I was beginning to lose consciousness and daydream.

"The McManus'?", I asked, in disbelief.

"Yes", she replied, her smile growing wider; "See Thomas, it's not all that bad now, is it?", she said. "They have faced strict background and compatibility testing recently, and with the consent of your mother, they have been deemed suitable. On a trial basis, of course"

It felt like all my wishes had been granted at once.

"They want to foster me. And my mother…my mother has agreed to this?", I asked, to be completely sure.

"Yes", she confirmed; "Listen, we all know you're a good boy. I have known you a long time now, and I know you're not a bad lad. You have been through a lot, but you must learn to respect the rules a little better. I know from speaking to the other children what really happened, and I understand that you thought you were doing the right thing. But it wasn't. We all feel that if you are in a more stable family environment, you will improve as a person. You just need a little guidance, and we feel that the McManus family can offer this to you."

She smiled at me again; "Happy, Thomas?"

"It's like Spurs have just won the double", I replied.

She laughed and began to pack up her briefcase.

"Right. Let's get you to the hospital first. Your clothes and things will be picked up and brought to the McManus' for you".

"Just one thing, Mrs Henry", I said; "My football annuals. Tell whoever is packing my things to give them to Alan."

"I will", she replied.

As we walked out of the building, past the room where all the boys were, I glanced in to look at them, one last time.

Some of them waved at me.

I waved back.

I spotted Alan.

He didn't look over.

He sat in the corner, reading the annual I had given him earlier.

I felt sad, yet had never felt happier. I couldn't believe what the McManus family were going to do for me.

I would make them proud. I would repay them for their belief in me...one day.

I promised myself that as I left the care home and got into the car.

Life continued as usual for Neil in the years following the McNamee incident.

His father gave him more responsibility around the farm, so he didn't have to be around the mill as much as he used to.

A major bonus was that he didn't have to work closely with McNamee anymore. That was the only good thing that came from the fight they had. His father had been embarrassed by what had happened, and twinned with the negative reports he received from McNamee about Neil's work, he deemed it best to separate the two. He thought it best to try and pass some farming skills onto Neil, instead of pursuing the lost cause of making a handy man out of him.

He relished the new role. He took more control of the farm, McNamee then effectively running the mill for his father, as his health began to steadily deteriorate.

Neil became more involved in the buying and selling of cows, and would develop a specialist eye for those animals. Over those few years he had learned many skills, essential for running and maintaining a successful farm. Haggling with suppliers and negotiating with buyers of his produce became vital aspects of his work. He had originally struggled with those skills in the earlier days as he had been almost crippled with shyness, but eventually he would overcome it to become a successful negotiator. He realised the wide margin of profit, or large savings that could be made by simply querying the first asking or bidding price. A large part of farming, he realised was knowing the value of everything one would produce or buy. He witnessed a lot of farmers at markets and trade events who accepted the first offer and paid the first asking price. Men who had been in the business twenty or thirty years longer than he had, making those elementary mistakes. It always amused and baffled him. He wondered how such men could continue to run a business when they were essentially being ripped off, day in-day out.

Neil, however was no-one's fool and soon learned the value of everything.

He particularly thrived on the livestock part of the farming trade. He had a good eye for cattle. At the beginning of each year, he would attend the Marts in the local neighbouring towns of Dunbay, north of the border, and Ballymoy, which lay in the south, to buy calves and cows. He would graze the cattle on the land throughout the spring and summer and would sell them to either the mart or the slaughter house in the autumn. He always kept a few selected breeding cows over the winter and would sometimes breed them with a good quality bull, producing pedigree calves the following year. If the calves were male, he would squeeze them, producing good bullocks which he would rear and sell the following autumn. If the calves were female, he would breed the best ones to a bull again and the cycle would continue.

His father owned a lot of acres, so Neil would sacrifice a few of them to grow the grass, harvest it into hay in the summer, using it to feed the cattle during the winter.

He became a perfectionist, and became almost entirely obsessed about anything he put his mind to. Most farmers he knew seemed to be very careless and disorganised. Where most of them were losing a lot of cattle to various diseases, Neil rarely had any losses. He grew very particular about getting the cattle dosed by the vet and believed more in preventative maintenance than last ditch medication. A lot of the farmers either couldn't afford a call-out from the vet or didn't believe it to be of any use. Neil believed his cautious and methodical approach was the reason for his success.

Keeping the animals in the best of health wasn't the only measure he had taken. Growing up, he had become disillusioned with his father's farm as he had always found himself running around, night after night, looking for cattle that had broken out of the fields. When he took the reins, he knew that to prevent such occurrences happening so often, he would have to extensively fence the land that held the cattle.

The fencing in the fields had become patchy, at best. Where segments of fencing had broken, little bushes had been put up in place, in a vain attempt to patch it up. It had never worked, and the cattle always continued to escape. To avoid future occurrences, he invested the time to remove the old fencing, putting up new posts and fencing in its place. It was an investment he knew would pay off in the long term. In the future, he experienced very few breakouts, whereas the other farmers would continue to lose cattle, because of their poorly fenced fields. Most men would lose a few cattle throughout the year, Neil would never lose any from then onwards.

It was because of those stringent methods, Neil knew gave him the advantage over the other farmers. A cow was a large investment. A lot of time was put into looking after it and a lot of money put into its upkeep…feeding, dosing and transportation to name but a few. To lose a cow to illness, breakout, theft, or natural causes was a large setback for any farmer, so Neil, through preventative maintenance, built his farm on that philosophy and would stick to it rigidly to make his business a success.

His father could see he knew what he was doing. He could see from the money going into his bank account that Neil was making more than what he had over the years. He would never mention it to him, instead telling him he needed to concentrate on the arable aspect of the farm, as "the cattle could look after themselves".

His father's attitude frustrated Neil to no end. As Neil's success in the cattle farming sector flourished he began to look at other aspects of his father's business.

Firstly, he couldn't understand his father's reluctance to let go of the mill. Most mills in the area had shut-down ten to fifteen years before, as demand had declined drastically. Buyers were looking elsewhere, to countries who could supply the product at a fraction of the price. He knew it must have been making his father a huge loss, month after month to keep the mill running.

He did, however, know why his father did such stupid things…pride. It was a status symbol to be a mill owner. His father surely had a huge ego, and because the workforce in the mill was quite large, Neil knew his father would never let himself lose face by shutting the business down. A lot of people were dependant on the mill for a living, Neil understood that, but he couldn't understand why his father would sacrifice not losing face with the people of the country, over losing money hand over fist.

His father was not moving with the times. He was happy to delude himself that he was a successful mill owner who had the respect of the community, whereas the truth was quite the opposite. People knew the mill was failing, his father confirming public belief by selling two large fields to a neighbouring farmer. Neil found it difficult to stand by, watching his father sell off large chunks of land for the sake of keeping his pride in-tact, keeping people, who didn't care an ounce about him in employment.

Secondly, it frustrated him that his family had to endure living in such squalid conditions, when across the lane stood a building that was being used daily to drain the family's money.

He always believed it could have been converted into a fantastic dwelling house. The house they occupied had been a very old, damp, two up-two-down shack that shook to its foundations anytime a door was closed or a light wind blew outside. The walls had been crumbling with boast, and rats could sometimes be seen scuttling over the dining table when he came downstairs for breakfast in the morning. It annoyed him (as he had to move downstairs to sleep in the room that used to be the sitting room, since Maggie moved in) that a lot of the people who worked in the mill owned houses twice the size of theirs. A lot of the mill workers had owned farms of their own and probably would have been able to get by without the mill anyway. It didn't make sense to Neil why his father seemed content to live in squalor, whilst trying to lord it over the rest of the people, simply because he was the mill owner.

Thirdly, Neil couldn't understand his father's reluctance to let go of the potato farming. He seemed to have cared more about that aspect of the farm than he did about livestock. Neil had always hated the potato farming because of the memories of the back-breaking work he had endured during his childhood. As he grew older and took more control of the farm, he grew to hate it even more because of the financial aspect. He couldn't work out why his father cared so deeply about it. The amount of labour and time spent, didn't equate to profit or satisfaction, the way livestock did. From the tilling, seeding, and growing, to the harvesting, there were too many variables that could conspire against the farmer yielding a good crop. A bad blight, too much or too little rain or many other factors could be detrimental to the farmer's profit margin.

Neil sometimes doubted himself, because of those negative thought processes, doubting his own sense of humanity and romanticism. He knew those were the exact reasons his father continued with the potatoes. His father seen himself as a proud Irishman, continuing to grow his own spuds and play his part in growing the Irish economy.

Neil didn't buy into it.

Farming was a business- he knew there was no point in doing something half hearted, just for the sake of being seen doing it. His father had his fingers in too many pies.

Neil was different though.

He seen the virtues in sticking to what he was good at, concentrating all his energies on those things. He knew rewards would surely be reaped if he stuck to that philosophy. He knew the rearing and nurturing of livestock was his skill, knowing that was where he could develop and grow the farm into something big.

He knew; however, he would only be able to do that on a small-scale basis when his father was still the boss.

He spent those years, from the ages of seventeen to twenty-one, honing his farming skills, yet still growing the potatoes and helping in the failing mill business, until the day came when his father's health failed him one last time.

It happened on a grey, drizzly day in the middle of February, in Neil's twenty-first year. He had just returned from the mart in Dunbay and was in good form having purchased four great looking calves for a very decent price. It was those small victories he relished. Sometimes it would make him very angry when he would spot a heifer or bullock with great potential, only to enter a bidding war with a rival farmer. He would never pay over the odds for the animal and would become greatly annoyed if the rival farmer would outbid him for what Neil termed "silly money". He viewed it as a loss to both of them- the rival would never recover much of a profit from what he initially paid and Neil would lose out on a big profit and a good animal. Neil knew his father would try and outbid a rival, even if it meant making a huge loss in the long term.

Pride cost a lot of money.

Luckily though, it would be a rare enough occurrence and Neil would normally get his animals for the correct amount, and would always make a good profit on them too.

When he arrived home that evening, he noticed the mill was not in operation. That occurrence was not totally odd as his father, sometimes, after a bottle of whiskey that morning, and in good spirits would decide to let everyone go home early on a Friday. However, on that occasion it had seemed like all work had stopped suddenly. Usually when the workers had been allowed to finish early, the mill would be tidy, ready for work the next day. On that day, the place was left untidy, an air of chaos lingering, like something unexpected had happened.

Neil walked over to the house and shouted up the stairs. There had been no answer. He walked upstairs to his father's room, where he had resided often in the recent past - no sign of him. That was the moment it dawned on him that his father was either dead or at death's door.

His father had been unwell for a long time- around three years or so. The doctor had been called out on a few occasions when he had been throwing up large volumes of blood and falling unconscious. The doctor had told him he was to stop drinking immediately- as it was literally killing him. His father had many stomach ulcers, brought on by excessive whiskey drinking that had burst a few times before. He lost a lot of blood on each occasion- each episode weakening and ageing him considerably. After each of those traumatic experiences, he vowed to never drink again, only to recover slightly.

Eventually, though, the whiskey bottle would make another unwelcome appearance.

Those previous six months to that fateful day, his health had grown progressively worse. He had turned from his usual Irish ivory colour to a sickly shade of yellow. His eyes grew hollow and black around the rims and he would remain in bed for days at a time. When his father turned from the sickly yellow to a greenish hue, Neil knew then his days were numbered.

There had been nothing he could have done to halt his father's decline. Maggie, on the other hand, he knew, could have. She had been the one who had been sent to the pub to buy the bottles of whiskey to bring back to his bed. Neil had tried, and failed, to talk any sense into him- in fact he was barely allowed to even speak to him. If he ever uttered any word of advice or raised any concerns when he witnessed his father shakily drink, he would have been met with the stern reply of; "Shut up, boy. A drop of whiskey never did any man a button of harm. Anyway, before you start talkin' shite to me, you remember I built this place up on me own- no help from anybody. We'll see what you'll do on your own. Fuck all, that's what. Now leave me alone. If there was ever a man who deserved a drop of whiskey it's me, after doing all I've done and having to raise a boy like you".

It would continue in such a manner, as it had done for years. Neil would give up and say nothing in reply. He had known years before that his father hated him.

He never knew the reason.

Sadly, he had started to hate his father in return.

Maggie had been different, though. Neil's father liked and respected her- she could have imparted some helpful advice.

She never did.

Even in his father's most weakened state, when he had asked her to get a bottle for him, she would descend the stairs, put her coat on and get ready to go.

"You're not goin' to get him another bottle, are you?", Neil would ask.

Buttoning up her coat and smiling, she would reply; "Ach, sure if a man can't take a drop, what kind of man is he"

"A fucking drop", Neil would say sarcastically under his breath. He wouldn't have minded if his father took a "drop", but a bottle or two a day for a man who was barely fit to get out of his bed was somewhat excessive.

He had rowed with Maggie about her going off to bring him back whiskey in the past, all to no avail.

She didn't seem to care.

His father didn't seem to care either.

Eventually Neil thought to himself; "Then, why should I?"

So, on that grey, drizzly day in the middle of February, Maggie arrived home.

She walked in through the front door, Neil anxiously greeted her.

She unbuttoned her coat, shook the rain from it, turned to Neil with the same smile he had grown accustomed to and said, very calmly;

"Your father passed away earlier today. The doctor was called out, but it was too late. The doctor made arrangements to take him away, and I went with him. We'll have to arrange the funeral. But first, I'll have to have a cup of tea...I'm choked".

And that was that. That was how Neil found out his father died.

He had strangely found a knot in his stomach...but he didn't cry.

He never shed a tear over his father, neither did Maggie.

He wondered if anybody did.

To him, that was the saddest part of all.

CHAPTER 10

The days between the realisation of his father's death and the funeral went by in a blur for Neil.

The coffin they bought for him was the most expensive in the funeral parlour- just what he would have wanted. Maggie arranged almost everything, and the Dillon pride gene obviously ran in her blood too, as she also wanted the best of everything for the funeral.

She spent a fortune on flowers for the graveside. She made a large donation to the local choir to sing at the service and it astonished Neil to see the large wad of notes she put in the envelope for Father Flanagan, the parish priest who performed the ceremony.

To her credit though, Maggie had done a fantastic job, leaving no stone unturned and Neil had felt grateful for her being there.

He couldn't help but to feel embarrassed and angered about the whole wake/funeral ordeal.

As he had always known, his father took a great deal of pride in his appearance and the way in which he was perceived to the people of the country.

That pride, though, had all been a front, as he lived in squalor in what was nothing more than a shack.

So, the great Thomas Dillon eventually ended his time on the planet lying dead in the finest coffin money could buy, in a damp, decaying house that was collapsing around him.

Neil had viewed the coffin in contempt. To him it looked grotesque in its indulgent splendour. He knew it probably cost more than the house itself. Neil knew that when he died, he would rather be buried in a cardboard box, leaving his family to live in comfort rather than squalor. He knew, however, his father had a different outlook.

Maggie took the role of chief mourner. People offered their condolences to her first, then to Neil...mostly as an afterthought.

She had been in her element. She had played the misty eyed loving sister to perfection. Neil couldn't help but to resent her though, thinking that if she only tried to talk some sense into her brother, he might still be around.

He knew he had to get through those few days as best he could, simply out of respect for his father.

He knew it would be hard.

There would be people he could barely stand, congregating in his home, laughing behind his back at the tiny decrepit house at which they inhabited. Pride most surely took a fall, but it seemed unfair to Neil that he was the one who would be falling hardest, paying the price for his father's.

Neil's tolerance for bluffer's and bullshitter's was minimal and he knew he would have to face torrents of them in those few days. Fake sympathy and insincere gestures would be rife. He knew he would have to hold his tongue and get through it, knowing he would probably never have to deal with most of those people ever again.

Word filtered through that Kathy would not be attending the funeral. Neil at first felt relieved he would not have to face her, but later found himself feeling angry and resentful because of her absence.

She had, after all, been the apple in their father's eye- the golden child. Blood was thicker than water, basic respect didn't cost anything. Neil, although being the black sheep of the family, knew he wouldn't miss his father's funeral for the world- regardless of what went before.

The public reason Kathy couldn't attend was because she was eight months pregnant, so she hadn't been allowed to fly from America to Ireland. The story was broadcast by Maggie, to many; "Ach, poor Kathy. She must be heartbroken. God love her" sentiments from the mourners.

The real story, which Maggie told Neil, making him swear he wouldn't tell anyone else, was that Kathy's new husband, the Jewish American doctor, was a controlling manipulator who had been consumed with a manic jealousy. He had forbidden Kathy to travel home as he believed that if she went to Ireland, she would never come back. He had apparently threatened to divorce her whilst holding their young son in custody and had threatened extradition too. He supposedly had a family full of high powered lawyers and judges who would back him to the hilt. "A nasty piece of work" Maggie had uttered throughout the telling of the tale.

She had a great taste in men, thought Neil. First McNamee and then this piece of Yankee shit, he almost said aloud.

Again, he bit his tongue.

He couldn't help but to feel bad for her, though. He knew he could never forgive her for her betrayal towards him, but as her brother, it pained him that another man was ruining her life. It pained him to think she must have been in an awful situation. She, unlike him, had deeply loved and respected their father and he knew it must have been killing her that she couldn't attend the funeral. He tried to blank those feelings out, almost muttering under his breath to himself; "She has no-one to blame only herself. She's a well-educated, intelligent woman who should have known better", but he couldn't shake the dull ache he found in his stomach every time he thought of her.

The two days his father had been waked had been very long, hard days for Neil, to say the least. He behaved so well, though, even Maggie couldn't fault him.

He spoke to everyone who visited, listened to all their clichéd statements about his "great" father whilst at the same time throwing subtle insults his way.

"Sure, you have a hard act to follow son- you'll never be half the man your father was", they would say, smiling into his face.

He held his own though. He made tea, poured whiskies, and opened all the bottles of stout Maggie asked of him, whilst all the time keeping his opinions to himself. He had been busy and enjoyed being so. Once the last of the mourners had left at around eleven each night, he would busy himself clearing away all the stout and whiskey bottles, brushing the floors and washing up any of the cups and dishes that had been used. He let Maggie go to bed as she had been worn out from all the organising and meeting and greeting of the day. He didn't mind the hard work. It kept his mind active, but more importantly kept him distracted from the knowledge that his dead father lay a few feet away, in the corner of the room.

On the second night, the night before the funeral, just before putting out the light and retiring to bed, he walked over to the coffin and looked down upon his father. He realised that it was probably the only time in his life he had shared a quiet moment alone with him. A rush of sadness bolted through him and he wondered why his father had seemed to hate him so much in life.

He would never understand why…it was far too late to start asking anyway.

He shook his head, said a prayer for him, bent and kissed his forehead, before putting out the light and climbing the stairs to his father's old bed.

He barely slept that night. Before long he heard Maggie up and about too. Maggie always had her annoying habits of "accidently" banging doors and clanging pots, all whilst she sang at the top of her lungs like a rabid banshee.

Neil knew it would then be impossible to get back to sleep and wondered if he had slept at all. Maggie continued to bang, clatter and sing, irrespective of the dead man in the corner of the room.

"Aul cunt", Neil grunted as he got out of bed and began to dress, dressing quickly, the heavy frost during the night making the room almost unbearably cold.

Maggie had been preparing breakfast when Neil arrived downstairs. She had always been a terrible cook and she served him a bowl of lukewarm, grey coloured porridge.

Neil sat at one end of the table and ate, Maggie sat at the other drinking tea and smoking a cigarette. Like every other morning, they sat in silence.

Maggie, after a few minutes finally spoke; "The undertaker will be here soon. The funeral is at eleven, so we will be leaving for the chapel at ten thirty"

"All right", Neil answered, concentrating on getting his porridge down. He knew he would certainly need all his strength that day.

"I've been trying to think who your father would have wanted to carry his coffin", Maggie continued, smoke jetting from her nose; "So, I have arranged for you, your uncles Gabriel and Bernard and young McNamee to do so".

Neil almost choked on a mass of undercooked porridge. Coughing and trying to recover his breath, he gasped; "Are you away in the fuckin' head woman? Dessie McNamee? No way is he havin' anything to do with this funeral."

Maggie slammed her cup down onto the table, tea splashing up from it and onto her cigarette, almost extinguishing it; "What type of foul mouthed talk is that to be at? And your father lyin' dead not a few yards away from where we sit".

She glared at him intensely; "You'll do what you're told, sonny. I'm the one who is paying for this funeral and you'll do well to remember that. Young McNamee was like a son to your father...", Maggie's voice tailed off at that, she didn't need to elaborate for Neil to know what she meant.

She pulled on her cigarette and stood, fixing herself, as was her manner. Neil remained seated, enraged but silent. He couldn't argue with her. He knew it was true. As much as he despised McNamee, he knew his father held him in high regard and would have wanted him involved.

He eventually stood and went to the front door, before turning to see Maggie, as usual after one of her outbursts standing with her back to him.

"Fair enough, Maggie. My father thought the world of that weed, and I see you do too. God knows why, but that's the way it is. But, just so you know, after today there are going to be some changes made around here. You may not like them, but they are going to happen...and that's that"

Just as he turned to walk out the door, Maggie cackled with laughter.

"Just who do you think you're talking to?", she almost spat; "So you think you're the big man now your father's not around, do you? Well we'll see about that. Don't go thinking you rule the roost just yet sonny. You may have a little surprise coming your way soon...ya boy ye"

A cold shiver ran down Neil's spine. The venom in her voice and the scowl on her old wrinkled face conveyed a genuine hatred towards him. He thought the unthinkable at that second. The unthinkable being his father had done something completely stupid and hateful, such as signing the place over to McNamee, cutting him out of the will.

Surely not, he thought, but the reaction of Maggie surely got him thinking of worse case scenarios.

He looked her straight in the eye, trying to detect a bluff somewhere on her features. She returned his gaze, never flinching, until he shook his head, turned toward the door, and walked out, hoping and praying to God his worst fears would not be realised.

The mourners arrived in their droves and Maggie magically morphed from the wicked old witch to the sweet heartbroken old dear in a matter of minutes.

The only positive of the day for Neil was seeing his two uncles, Bernard, and Gabriel. They had both worked in England for years and had arrived late the night before the funeral. They were his late mother's brothers'. He had always liked and respected both men and had always noticed a difference between the two of them and a lot of the other men from the country.

They had travelled to a foreign country, setting up a successful building business between them, on their own. He always liked their easy-going nature and the way they didn't take themselves too seriously, unlike most men from the country. Neil enjoyed his few minutes catching up with them as it had been refreshing to hear a different point of view from most of the people he dealt with daily.

He laughed at both men's witty putdowns and sarcastic comments about a lot of the men in attendance that morning. Both men had grown up and knew most of the people there, so knew them as well as Neil did. It seemed to Neil though that because they had lived in England for years they could take a step back and view such people almost with an outsider point of view. They had stood and laughed with Neil about the small village prejudices and mentalities of some of the people in attendance that morning. Neil couldn't help but to admire their views on life.

He enjoyed their company so much, he had begun not noticing what was going on around him, only then to be interrupted by a shriek from Maggie.

"Ach, good man Dessie" she shrieked "Good to see you son"

McNamee hugged and consoled her in the smarmy, smug way only he had, the scene appearing to Neil like that of an incestuous couple.

McNamee walked up to Neil, arm in arm with Maggie. He offered a handshake. Neil accepted, realising how watery and insincere it felt. He had judged a man on his handshake whilst dealing with men in the buying and selling of livestock, and wouldn't have judged McNamee too highly based on his.

"Sorry for your troubles, young Dillon", he solemnly said, looking Neil straight in the eye.

"Thanks", replied Neil, scanning his eyes for a certain glint- not finding one.

It unsettled him.

He knew that to hate someone so much, one would always need to continue to find reasons to justify the hatred, otherwise the hater would start to feel hateful himself. But, he reassured himself in the knowledge that a man such as McNamee wouldn't be as careless to insult or annoy a mourning son in front of all present. To do so it would broadcast to everyone just how much of a weed he was.

He was too smart for that.

Neil stuck rigidly to his resolve to behave himself, trying to ignore the fact that his sworn enemy was not only standing in his house, but would also be carrying his father's coffin. The time was coming to close the coffin lid and he knew it would all be over very soon.

The undertaker asked who was to carry the coffin. Neil and his uncles stepped forward. Maggie then very publicly asked McNamee if he would do so too, as Thomas Dillon had thought so highly of him, and would be honoured to have such a fine young man carry him to his final resting place. McNamee visibly grew in stature and choked out some words about how it would be an honour.

Neil wanted to clap sarcastically at their misty-eyed performance.

Neither the time nor the place he realised.

Neil had reached his full six feet and four inches by that stage of his life. Gabriel stood around six-one and Bernard about five-nine, so the undertaker instructed Neil and Gabriel to carry at the back and McNamee and Bernard to take the front.

On the initial lift, as Neil had been head and shoulders above the two at the front, he let out a small grunt as he took the majority of the weight- the two smaller men at the front yet to feel any until it fell on their shoulders. McNamee let out a belt of laughter.

"Bejaysus young Dillon- you do the gruntin' and we'll do the liftin'. Have ye any strength in them big shoulders at all, ye long hoor ye?"

At that, most of the people in the house tried in vain to conceal their laughter, including his two uncles, much to Neil's embarrassment and disappointment. McNamee turned his head slyly and winked at him.

"You cunt. Still the same weed you always were", Neil desperately tried not to utter, instead biting hard upon his tongue.

He got through the funeral and the rest of the day and went home afterwards. He almost patted himself on the back for his behaviour...at least no one could have faulted him.

His father's enormous shadow had passed by. He knew he could begin to live. He could finally be his own man.

His future was finally bright.

So he thought.

CHAPTER 11

They were the happiest days of my life.

I remember shopping for uniforms that year before returning to third year in school. It was late August- a time of year I usually hated, doing a task I hated even more. That year I looked forward to returning to school.

The thought of getting up and having breakfast with those lovely people, going to school, seeing my friends, then home to play football in the park before being called in for a home cooked dinner, homework, then bed seemed like heaven to me at that time. It was the normality, the routine that kids needed, I craved.

It had been a time of optimism. I vowed to make that year's school football team. With so much practice, good food and quality sleep I knew that goal could be easily achieved. Also, for the first time ever, I was determined to do well in school. I knew I wasn't stupid, I knew that if I applied myself and worked hard, I could turn those 'D' and 'E' grades into 'A's and 'B's... well maybe 'B's and 'C's. I wouldn't be skiving off anymore and the back chatting to teachers would end too. I wouldn't bring trouble to those people. I was going to work hard and make them proud of me.

It had been a lovely day, that Saturday in late August. We arrived home that evening and played football until dark. I scored six goals.

"Fuck it", I thought. That year I wouldn't only make the school team...I would captain it!

The start of September saw us return to school. The contrast between living with the McManus' and my mother couldn't have been any greater.

I woke up on the first morning of school, went to the bathroom and washed myself in the sink with hot water and sweet-smelling soaps. My mother's flat barely ever had any hot water and we would have been lucky to have a bar of even the most basic soap in the house.

I pulled on my crisp, well ironed shirt. The soft, well-fitting school jumper, jet black trousers with a crease running down the side of each leg and shoes so black and shiny that you could see your reflection in them. I had been used to putting on a uniform that had been worn the year before. A jumper with holes in it, a shirt stained and smelly with sweat marks, trousers so short they barely reached halfway up my shins and shoes that had to have the front glued together to stop them flapping around- soles so riddled with holes that the skin on my feet began turning to leather itself.

I went downstairs that morning, welcomed by a delicious waft of cooked bacon, toast, and tea. Conversation flowed, laughter hung in the air. Little Francis toddled around, giggling, and smiling. Maura had acknowledged me, even though it had been a surly little grunt, but it was an acknowledgement. Dan hadn't been there as he started very early on the building sites. He had been my idol before I moved in, but when I witnessed at first hand his work ethic, all done with a smile and a joke, I admired him even more.

He inspired me to become a better person.

Mrs McManus had fussed over me, making sure I wouldn't leave the house before I was almost bursting at the sides with breakfast. The radio had been on in the background, Brian and Maura fighting over which station they wanted to listen to until a good song would come on and both would be happy to leave it.

Mornings with my mother would usually be either one of two scenarios.

The first scenario, I would wake up to find her lying on the sofa, fast asleep with one of her Country and Western records blaring at full volume, the room stinking of gin and the big fluorescent light glowing, the curtains closed. Scenario two would see her fully sober, rushing around the kitchen trying to prepare breakfast, like the fucking Tasmanian devil. She would give me motivational talks about trying to do well in school and staying out of trouble whilst telling me her plans about getting a job and going on holidays somewhere nice in the summer. If I opened my mouth to say anything she would immediately fly off the handle and accuse me of being just like everyone else, putting her down etc. She would then tell me to cook my own breakfast, before storming back to bed muttering to herself about her own son even putting the boot in, leaving me to butter my burnt toast and trying hopelessly to rescue a pot of eggs that had turned to near concrete.

Never once had she sat with me, being civil whilst I ate, the outcome always remained the same. I didn't know which scenario was worse. At least when she lay unconscious on the sofa I didn't have to deal with the confrontation.

School that first day, whilst living with the McManus' had been great. Brian and I walked there and back, and the craic had been good. I was focused on my studies, I had a bellyful of good food and there was no shit rushing around my head about how angry and pissed off I was. I was contented and could fully concentrate, whereas when living with my mother I would have been full of rage about what had happened that morning, dreading going home that evening. Sometimes I would have felt so angry that I would have gotten into a fight with another kid at school or would have told a teacher to go and fuck themselves. Either reaction would have led to a letter home or a suspension, leading to a complete breakdown on my mother's behalf, resulting in me being thrown back into the children's home for another stint.

It was a vicious fucking circle which I couldn't break.

It had always led me to believe that *I* was the actual problem. I was the reason my mother was having all her breakdowns. Deep down though I knew I wasn't such a bad kid and she was the one with the problems. There was nothing anyone could have done to improve the situation, but I knew my behaviour had not helped things, so the guilt had always lingered.

That night, after a productive day at school, we played football for a little while, under the warm, early autumn sun. Mrs McManus, who was a stickler for homework and discipline called us in after half an hour or so. Brian, disgruntled, told her we didn't have any homework as it was only the first day back and begged her to let us back out to play some more. She was adamant though that the first week back was one of the most important times of the school year. Homework or not, there were books to be backed, timetables to be studied and normal routine had to be administered to once again. No more staying up late like what had happened during the summer holidays.

We were disappointed not to get back out to finish our game, but after a delicious homemade meal we began to enjoy backing the books with old wallpaper and organising our things for the next day.

Dan arrived home around eight that evening and after eating his warmed-up dinner, proceeded to joke around with Brian and myself, as was his custom. So, we laughed, cracked jokes, wrestled, and took the piss out of each other whilst backing our books until Mrs McManus gave us the dreaded fifteen-minute warning that bedtime was coming up. We complained, half-heartedly, mostly for the sake of it but didn't really mind as it had been a long, tiring day.

As soon as my head touched the pillow, I fell asleep, dreaming happy dreams.

That day had been a million miles away from what it would have been like arriving home from school if I had have been living with my mother.

Again, like breakfast time, I would have encountered one of two scenarios. Scenario one would see me arrive home to find the flat in complete darkness, curtains closed while she slept in bed. No dinner would have been made so I would have made myself a sandwich of whatever was available-crisps, bananas, tomatoes…I even made a cornflake sandwich once. My mother would get up, heavily hung over and rant and rave about a letter she received from the school about me, then tell me to wise up or I was going to fuck my life up and end up just like her. She would either slope off back to bed or sit at the kitchen table and cry, before eventually returning to bed. Scenario two would see me return home, the large fluorescent light glowing, Country and Western music blaring and a smell of burning coming from the kitchen, my mother sloping around, glass in hand. When she saw me, she would scowl and tell me to stay away from the Irish brat, God forbidding his family of terrorists find out about my Brit father. Or, she would smile warmly, hugging, and kissing, me telling me how good of a boy I was. That warmth from her would always turn once again to coldness as the drinks flowed. The volume of her voice would rise considerably over the evening in direct proportion to how many "wee drinks" she consumed, until her shouts began to turn to screeches. At that point, I would either go to bed or go out and try to find something to do, which was difficult living in a concrete jungle, all to escape her madness. Homework would have been forgotten about and the next day I would have gotten into more trouble at school for not doing it. Another letter would be sent home, and it all started again...the vicious fucking circle.

The contrast between the two different home lives was incomparable. Mundane, every day stuff like getting ready for school or coming home to do homework was a real privilege at the McManus'.

Life living it with those people was good...too good.

As with everything in my life, if things were going my way, if I was happy, I would begin to get an uncomfortable, uneasy feeling that things were going to go wrong again... as they usually did.

September and October came and went, autumn turning to winter and I had never known months to fly by so quickly.

The first day back at school that I had enjoyed so much, had not turned out to be the stereotypical "turning over a new leaf" phenomenon that lasted usually two to three days. I continued to enjoy school and schoolwork for a few months. Mrs McManus helped me stay organised and I always produced my homework on time. I learned new things and because of good wholesome morning breakfasts, my concentration span improved tenfold. I made the school football team and began to play well, better than ever before. Brian and I had carved out a great on-field partnership. He played directly behind me, I played up-front, the two of us scoring and assisting many goals between us. I didn't make captain, however, that honour being bestowed upon the coach's very mediocre son...to no one's surprise. I didn't really mind though. It was hard to complain about anything when life was so good.

I didn't get into any more fights. No more letters were sent home.

Teachers had actually complimented me, (much to my great embarrassment) as they handed back assignments and tests I had completed with a few 'B' grades scrawled in red ink at the top right-hand corner of the page. I became more popular with my classmates and received more attention from the girls, probably because I didn't stink anymore and was much more groomed and better presented than I had ever been.

I was having the time of my life. I couldn't understand it when Brian would complain about how boring his life was and how he would wish for something exciting to happen. To me his life was better than any excitement I could have wished for.

That feeling, however, the one I always got when I knew things were going too well, began to intensify, until I could almost hear alarm bells go off in my head.

I wasn't one bit surprised then when my gut feeling had been confirmed...but it didn't dampen the disappointment.

On a Wednesday evening in early November when returning from school we found Mrs McManus sitting having a cup of tea with a middle aged, sandy haired woman wearing a cheap suit. She might as well have been wearing a uniform with "Social Worker" on a band around her arm like one worn by the captain of a football team, or perhaps more fittingly like a Swastika armband on a Nazi!

"Aah, Thomas. Just the man", she said, reinforcing my suspicions that she was a social worker there to deliver bad news. They rarely brought good news.

"You'll be pleased to hear your mum has made a good recovery from her illness. She's like a new woman now...and guess what, she wants to bring you back home to live with her again"

She sat smiling at me. "I bet that's made your day, eh?"
I felt like I had been punched in the guts. I felt like vomiting.

Then the anger kicked in.

Why had the bitch been so happy to let me rot away in some shithole institutional kid's prison for six to eight months at a time, but then suddenly, when I'm happy and content with the McManus', she recovers in double quick time to spoil the best time of my life?

I couldn't help it. Even though I was not technically a child anymore, more a teenager, I acted like a petulant child in my response.

"No...I want to stay here. I don't want to go home. I'm doing well in school and I'm stayin' out of trouble...I'm being good"

Then I looked at Mrs McManus, trying hard not to cry or sound too whiney.

"Tell her Mrs McManus...tell her...please"

At that my voice croaked with emotion and my eyes filled up with tears, blurring my vision of the room momentarily. Mrs McManus looked at me, pity writ large across her features; "Sorry Tommy, I really am. If it were up to us we'd keep you forever, but she's your mum. She wants you back, and as a mum myself I can only imagine how bad she must be feeling about all this"

I could tell from looking at her she meant every word. She couldn't lie. Unlike the social workers, she spoke what was in her heart.

I wasn't going to argue with her. It was a difficult position for her to be in, I knew that and didn't want to make things harder than they were. I wiped my eyes, embarrassed, hoping no one noticed the tears standing in my eyes or the croak that had been in my voice. What could I do? As usual I had to do to what the social workers told me.

"Okay" I said; "I'll go pack my stuff then"

"Oh" said the social worker; "Mrs McManus has kindly done it already for you. If you don't mind, maybe we should get going. Your mother will be expecting us."

Sure enough, my bags were sitting there on the dining room table, all ready to go.

Mrs McManus stood up and came over to give me a hug. We embraced warmly, I didn't want to let go, until she eventually pulled away and gave me a kiss on the cheek.

"You be a good boy for your mum, now.", she said; "You need to look after each other. You're all the poor woman has, God love her. But, don't forget, we are always here for you son, no matter what happens"

She walked me to the door. Brian stood idly by watching everything unfold, in silence. The social worker took my bags. "Righto young man", she said; "Let's get you back to your mum then. She's dying to see you".

"I bet she is", I almost said aloud.

Just as I walked out the door, I turned to Brian who stood awkwardly by.

"See you at school tomorrow then", I said, in a vain attempt to break the awkward silence.

"See you then" he replied quietly, looking down at the ground.

And there ended the best two months of my life. In hindsight, the saddest thing of all was, they ended up being the happiest times of my entire life after that point too.

We drove in silence to the concrete jungle we called home. When we arrived, the social worker knocked on the door of my mother's flat. She answered almost immediately, which made me think she had been eagerly waiting, perhaps watching out the window for us.

She looked different. Younger looking, fresher. She had a new hairstyle and wore a nice yellow dress which looked odd on her, as I was used to seeing her in dark colours. She embraced me warmly.

"Ach my wee Thomas. I'm sorry son. That's it… never again", she said to me.

Unfortunately, I had heard those promises many times throughout the years, knowing they were as likely to be true as Ireland winning the next World Cup. All the other times I had come home, I had been glad to do so, as it meant escaping the children's home…for a while, but not this time. She had ruined any hopes I had for the future. I was going places at the McManus', I had passions and purpose. I knew life would be endured once again, instead of enjoyed.

I could feel myself getting angry again- useless, futile anger.

Anger and passion are two closely related emotions. The major difference between the two being passion drives a person to desperately want to achieve something, anger makes the same person want to desperately destroy something.

I knew at that moment some poor kid was in for it the next day at school!

And so, it came to be. Like all the other times it panned out the same.

For the first few days she had been a changed woman, all hugs, and kisses, hopes and dreams. Then, gradually that would all change to scowls and put-downs, self-pity, and tears. Then the drinking began once more. Slowly at first until it was ramped up eventually to the excesses of before. The bright hair and clothes slowly darkened once more.

Tragedy struck a few weeks later.

Mrs Kingston died.

My mother had been close friends with her for years. When she heard the news that morning she just said; "Ach. How sad" and went back to bed. She never mentioned her again.

I had been very upset. She had been like a grandmother to me, but my mother's reaction upset me too. I couldn't understand how she could have been so nonchalant about it all after their many years of friendship. However, I didn't try to understand her, for fear if I tried to, I might see her twisted logic and end up thinking and behaving like her too.

Mrs Kingston's death had greater implications for us too.

All the neighbours who had kept an eye out for my mother's tell-tale signs of madness had eventually moved on, leaving Mrs Kingston the last person to keep in close contact with us. When she passed away there was no one left to keep the social workers informed of my mother's behaviour. The social workers had never exactly been pro-active in keeping tabs, so I knew then there would be no more long-term stays at the McManus' whilst my mother sorted herself out.

I knew then I was on my own with her. I knew I would just have to slog it out.

I had been fourteen by then.

I just had to endure four more years…and endure I just about did.

CHAPTER 12

A week passed since the funeral.

A weight had been lifted from Neil's shoulders. He was the new boss and he had major plans he wanted to implement.

The mill and the dwelling house had been very quiet, something he and Maggie were not used to. It seemed to unsettle Maggie, but to Neil the silence had been golden.

Of course, as it would have been his father's wish, all the workers had a week off to let the family grieve.

A week off on full pay no less.

Neil had felt angered when a few of the men had approached him shortly after the burial, caps in hand muttering; "Sorry for your loss, young Dillon... but we were just wondering about maybe getting a few shillings up front for next week's work. Sure, ye know how it is, we all have men knocking at the door to be paid for bits and bobs".

Neil knew how it was all right. Men to pay? Publicans to pay more like.

"I know, I know", he replied, as calmly as he could; "I have nothin' on me at the minute, but call to the house later and I'll have it for you then".

The men had sloped off, without a word in reply. They weren't due to be paid for their week off until the following Friday, yet had the cheek to ask for payment in advance at such a delicate time.

Neil didn't react or snap in a temper. He knew it would be the last payment they would be getting from him.

On the Thursday of the week after the funeral, Neil arrived home after feeding the cattle to find Maggie packing her bags. He stood at the doorway in silence, watching and hoping she was packing her bags for good.

"Now your father's gone, there is no need for me to remain here anymore" she said, not stopping to look at him while she spoke. "I have taken lease of a small house in Dunbay. It has everything I need and I will find it more convenient living in town rather than out here in the country".

Dunbay was the nearest town to them, about five miles away, where the farmers would go to trade livestock and other produce.

"I have a man from Dunbay coming out to pick me up in an hour or so, so I will be gone by then", she continued in her matter of fact tone, still not looking up at him when she spoke.

"All right" he replied, not knowing what else to say.

"You may or may not know, but your father's will is to be read in Mr Blayney's office next week, so make arrangements to be there", she said, cramming the last of her things into one of her bags.

"Righto", Neil replied before going out to do some work in the mill.

He heard the car come and go and worked on, regardless of Maggie leaving, for another few hours. When he finished, he returned to an eerily quiet house. Part of him felt sad. It was after all the end of an era but he mostly felt happy. The house had been full of unhappy memories. Days and nights had been spent in misery as his aunt and father belittled and put him down at every opportunity. The only laughter there had ever been from cruel jokes between the pair at his expense.

He began to feel happy and optimistic. He knew the rest of his life could begin that day. He planned to make changes, starting almost immediately and he vowed to make a success of his life.

As he walked into the quiet house, he turned, looked at the mill and shuddered. A shiver ran down his spine like someone had put a melting ice-cube down the back of his shirt.

He entered the house, made himself some tea and a sandwich and went to bed a contented man.

Monday morning came quickly. He didn't eat any breakfast that morning. He tried to eat, but the food just wouldn't go down. Nerves had gotten the better of him.

He tried to tell himself he was doing the right thing. He knew it was, but the thought of *doing* it made him sick to his stomach. No matter how he tried, he couldn't remove the image of his father being present as he made the announcement.

He could almost feel his father's fury, even from beyond the grave.

He always vowed that whenever he was given the chance, he would do it.

The time had arrived. *His* time. He knew he had to step up.

The workers had arrived in dribs and drabs that drizzly, dark-grey morning. When they all finally arrived, Neil made his entrance. He contemplated standing on a step to address the workers, only realising he hadn't needed to, as he stood head and shoulders above them all anyway.

He glanced at many of the faces. A lot looked tired and drawn as many had spent all weekend working on theirs or their father's farms. Other faces bloated and sweaty, the result of a long weekend spent in the local public house. Others were like that of McNamee, smirking and cruel, wondering what the jumped-up brat was going to lecture them on now.

He knew his words would be carefully listened to, then mocked, laughed at, and twisted out of context later in the public house.

He felt bad for what he was about to do as some of the people were decent, honest, and hardworking. He had reassured himself many times that his decision was not one to spite the McNamee's of the world (although it was incredibly sweet to do so), but a smart business move that should have been taken years before. The fact that his father died in a rundown hovel of a house with people laughing behind his back, after he had kept them in work for many years at great personal expense was enough to validate Neil's reasoning's.

"Listen everyone", Neil spoke addressing all the workers, glad his voice sounded clear and strong with no audible hint of nerves; "I don't think it will come as much of a surprise to anyone here, but this industry is not what it once was. Small businesses like ours can't compete anymore with the larger ones that are springing up around the larger towns and cities. We've even lost a few good employees to those other businesses, as we couldn't compete with the wages they are offering and the opportunities available."

He paused to take a breath and a quick lick of his dry lips, before continuing; "I hope you all realise this decision has not been taken lightly, but the truth is, this place has been losing money hand over fist for a long time now and I just can't justify keeping the place running anymore. If I don't do something now, the bank will step in and act *for* me. It's as simple as that- that's how bad it is."

He took another deep breath "So, I am sorry to say that from today onwards, the mill is closed for further business".

As he expected, an audible rumble of discontent occurred immediately. The men swore and some of the women began to cry.

He resumed quickly before the situation became out of control.

"I appreciate all the work you have done over the years in keeping the mill running. In acknowledgement of all your hard work, I have contacted several other mill owners my father and I have dealt with in the past and gave them a list of all your names and the jobs each of you do. Most of these mills are looking for workers, so you all have a good chance of getting another job if you approach these companies and mention you worked here. If you need a reference, just let me know-anytime"

Neil had been true to his word and had contacted other mill owners, listing names and job descriptions of each of his workers. He had even included McNamee, in the interest of fairness as he had been a good, solid worker and a skilled handyman.

His conscience was clear. He believed he had done the right thing. He could concentrate all his energies on farming, his true love. The dead weight of the mill could finally be let go.

"I'm sorry everyone. I haven't made this decision without a lot of thought and many sleepless nights. I wish you all the best of luck in the future, and that is all I really have to say"

Neil turned to walk back to the house. As he turned, amid all the swearing and crying, he could see McNamee whisper into the ear of a man named Henry McKeever.

Henry McKeever was a man in his late forties, who had worked in the mill for as long as Neil could remember. He had been quietly spoken, perhaps a little light in the brain department, but a pleasant enough fellow. He drank with both McNamee and Neil's father and had been a good, steady worker.

"Young Dillon", Henry spoke, above the murmur just as Neil had turned to walk away.

Neil turned to face him.

"Yes, Henry"

At that point, most of the murmurs grew quiet.

Henry, visibly nervous, obviously not used to public speaking, his voice trembling, never looking up at Neil, only at the ground, asked; "Have you spoken to your aunt about all this?"

The crowd began to laugh. Above all he could hear McNamee's hysterical, cruel cackle.

Henry, buoyed by the laughter, continued; "I mean, we all know who pulls the strings around here and has the final say...and it sure as fuck isn't you"

At that, the crowd erupted. Henry received pats on the back from many of the men, McNamee shouting; "Young Henry ye boy ya. You tell him, hahaha".

Neil scanned the area, seeing many sneering faces, the ones that had been filled with anger and rage a minute before, now full of gleeful scorn. He tried to contain his own rage, squeezing his hands together tightly, trying to retain control.

"Firstly Henry, that's disgraceful language to be using in front of women. You should be ashamed of yourself. Secondly, my family's business is absolutely none of yours. You can spout all the rubbish you want, but my decision is final, and that's the end of it. Now if you don't mind, I would like you to leave now".

"Aye, is that so? Well, what about Kathy?", shouted another man, Paddy Gray.

Paddy Gray had been another of McNamee's cohorts. A younger man, probably in his late twenties. He lived just down the road from Neil and much like Henry, Neil never had an issue with him before.

His outburst had taken Neil by surprise.

"Kathy... my sister Kathy? What about her?", he asked

"What about her? Exactly...what about her?", he shouted back.

Neil laughed nervously.

"Have you forgotten to take your tablets this morning Paddy?", he asked, finally earning himself a small chuckle from the crowd.

His response seemed to enrage Gray further, his face reddening and his body beginning to shake back and forth.

"What about *her* share of the family inheritance, eh? Sure, the poor lassie is afraid to come back into the country over the head of you...ye fuckin' bully"

Neil's head began to swirl. A mixed feeling of confusion and rage flooded his senses.

"What the hell are you talkin' about Paddy? Maybe you should go home and sober up before coming around here and talkin' rubbish."

He knew at that moment he shouldn't have. He wanted to remain calm, rise above all the bitterness and scorn, but he couldn't resist it.

"By the way, Paddy, I very much doubt you came up with that idea yourself. Did your boyfriend there, McNamee, help you with it perhaps?"

At that, Gray made a dash for Neil.

"Ye bastard Dillon. I'll fuckin' kill ye"

McNamee and Henry McKeever restrained him just as he made off.
Neil laughed. "Let him come boys...I'm shakin' in my boots"

Gray letting out a frustrated roar, like a wounded animal, broke off from both men's grip and set off on his way home, slamming the door on his way out.

Neil laughed, defiantly this time. It had been difficult for him to get angry with Paddy Gray. He had been in more of a state of shock than anything else. He never had a problem with either Gray or Henry McKeever, yet there were the two of them trying to ridicule him so viciously in front of everyone in the building.

He knew where all the bitterness had stemmed from though. Both those men were the puppets, the puppet master slyly standing back laughing and pulling the strings.

He let it wash over him, the words of fools didn't worry him.

He was, much to his annoyance, shaken a little about the rumours Gray had brought up. One thing he had never been was a bully. Kathy had been educated at his father's expense. She should have been reaping the benefits of her high-flying profession, yet she had made such a fundamental error of judgement in marrying such a bastard. He couldn't help but feel angry that he was the one to take the blame- the great Kathy wouldn't have a bad word said against her.

"So, has anyone else anything they want to get off their chests before we all go our separate ways then?", he asked the people who remained in the building.

No-one spoke, much to his disappointment as he had been inwardly gearing up for a row.

"Fair enough", he continued; "Again, let me apologise for this news. I wish you all the best, but if you don't mind, I would like to be left in peace now"

The crowd finally dispersed, the disgruntled mutterings gradually fading out as the last of the crowd left the building for the final time.

Neil returned to his house and sat at the kitchen table. His blood boiled and he half wished he had reacted violently, teaching both men who spoke against him a lesson. The other half of him was satisfied of his dignified response though. To have raised his fists would have played into McNamee's hands. He and his cronies would sit in the bar and talk of the brute who lived by the old mill, castigating, and ridiculing him to anyone who would listen. Those men, he thought, had been the ones to make fools of themselves...not him.

McNamee's dirty tricks had not worked that time.

As he stood to boil the kettle for tea, he heard a knock at the door.

"Come in...the door's opened"

A young woman, Annie Rafferty walked in. Annie, probably in her mid to late twenties, had been a good friend of Kathy's.

"Ach, hello Annie. What can I do for you?", Neil cheerily asked.

She had always been nice to him in the past and offered a welcome tonic to the bitterness he had faced earlier.

Annie Rafferty was a small slip of a girl, no more than five feet tall and weighing no more than about six stone. She had a tom-boyish prettiness about her, short brown hair styled in a bob and freckles that made her look even younger than she was. She had worked in the mill on and off for around five years or so, spending most of her time looking after her bed-ridden father who seemed to have been dying for most of his life. Her mother had died years before and she had been the only girl in a family of three boys. Neil always felt she had a "notion" in him, as she always smiled and flicked her hair in a clumsily seductive way anytime he had been in her company. The attraction, if it was indeed there, had only been one way, as Neil had liked his women to have a little more meat on their bones as what Annie had.

Despite her diminutive appearance, she had been a feisty little woman with a tongue on her to prove it.

"Those bastards...oh those bastards", she rasped, pointing out the door at something that had long gone.

Neil couldn't help but laugh.

"Annie...that's shocking language from a little lady like yourself", he said, jokingly.

"My language, shite, Neil. That's not right what they said out there. It's not fair. Thon wee bastard Gray, and that auld prick McKeever...bad luck to the pair of them"

Neil laughed again. She was incorrigible.

She considered his eyes and asked how he was. She had been the first person to ask him that question, sincerely, since his father had died. He couldn't help but to feel touched.

He walked over to the small stove in the corner, checking the water that had been boiling for his tea.

"I'm all right Annie, thanks.", he half lied; "I'm makin' a drop of tay here if you want some?"

Annie nodded in approval, reached into her coat pocket, and pulled out a packet of cigarettes. She gave one to Neil and he struck a match lighting both his and hers. Inhaling deeply and speaking through a cloud of exhaled smoke, she continued; "You know we don't believe any of that bullshit about you and Kathy...don't you?"

Neil took a pull of his cigarette and gave a dismissive wave whilst stirring the teabags in the pot.

"Kathy thought the world of you. I know you had your differences, but sure what brother and sister don't?"

Neil nodded and poured two mugs of tea.

"Do you still keep in contact, Annie?"

"We used to. She used to write. I loved all the stories she had. The parties, the big nights out in America. It was better than any film to me, so glamorous. Then, it changed... her stories. Her words that had been so full of happiness and excitement, became more downbeat as the months and years passed. I could detect a sadness in her writing. I knew it was because of that bastard she married. The nights out stopped, she became more withdrawn and she would speak of missing home and began asking about *my* life, instead of elaborating on her own. It seemed that her dream was slowly unfolding into a nightmare."

Neil took a sip of his tea, then asked; "Is that all you are going on. What about this prick she married. Has she actually *said* anything about him?"

Annie nodded.

"Yes. He is the cause of it all. Eventually she began telling me stories about him. He controls her completely. Ever since she had the baby she had to quit her job... for good. I mean, for God's sake, it's not as if they couldn't afford a nanny."

Neil nodded in agreement.

"You know more than anyone how hard Kathy worked to become a doctor. Now she can't do that anymore. Sure, for God's sake, didn't she tell Maggie she couldn't attend your father's funeral because the bastard wouldn't let her go, threatening to extradite her, and keep the baby for good in America. Fuck that Neil. I don't know what kind of prick she's got herself involved with, but he's not good."

Neil nodded sombrely again.

"I haven't heard from her in a few months now. She's probably forbidden to even write now. The poor girl, I feel so sad for her"

Neil sat in silence. He didn't know what to say. He felt bad for his sister, he didn't want her to be living in misery, no matter how things had been left between them.

He shrugged his shoulders and said; "Sure what can we do about it, Annie. We can't be going over to America, kidnapping babies or whatever...sure we'd never get out of the country ourselves. Kathy's a smart woman, she'll work things out"

He hoped he was right about his last sentence, but deep inside he wasn't so sure.

Annie smiled sweetly at him.

"She thinks the world of you, you know. She asked about you all the time. She feels bad about what happened, but, you know Neil...she still feels a bit angry about what you did too"

Neil nearly choked on his tea, spluttering; "What *I* did, Annie? What *I* did? Does she feel bad about that gypsy McNamee beating the livin' shite out of me in front of my own father and everyone in the country over what happened that night? Does she fuck! Why? Because she was away at her fancy school with her fancy friends, and I had to stick around here, living amongst these people"

His voice had been steadily rising and his blood had begun to boil. To calm down he finished his cigarette and walked to the basin, rinsing his mug.

Annie sat in silence, sipping her tea, visibly embarrassed.

He turned to look at her when he had finished rinsing the mug.

She gave him a knowing smile. He stretched and yawned loudly.

"Sorry for swearing Annie. Anyway, it's been a tiring morning, I'm beat. I'm goin' to hit the sack for a while"

"All right" Annie replied as she got up to leave.

Neil yawned again. "Right. I'm away up".

It was his turn to give a knowing smile, before adding "Are you comin'?"

Annie, never averting her gaze from his, took the last pull on her cigarette, stubbed it out in the ashtray and replied; "All right".

A week passed since the mill had closed. Neil had busied himself around the farm, there had always been plenty to do...and he thrived on it.

A big job he had taken on during the week was digging out ditches, as the drainage system his father had employed, or the lack of such system, had seemed almost medieval to him. Drains had run from one shuck to the next and in turn the water would overflow and almost always return to where it had come from. A few days of digging had made a big difference, the peace of mind he would receive over the coming months and years, worth every shovel of shite he had dug. He knew it was the small sacrifices that would pay out the big dividends. The days sacrificed performing menial chores such as digging ditches, putting up new fencing and herding up cattle to dose, meant that he could have what most farmers could only wish for- peace of mind when they went to bed at night.

To spend his entire days working on the farm, in peace and quiet without annoyance from either mill or workers was bliss to him.

Time flew too quickly for him, as the following Monday morning came around much too fast for his liking.

On that day, he dressed in his Sunday best. The last time he wore it, to his father's funeral. He hadn't been to mass since.

He drove his father's old Volkswagen into town. The morning damp, cold and grey as usual.

Mr Blayney's office was a small hovel of a place that sat above a small supermarket in the middle of Dunbay town. Neil had only ever been a handful of times before, usually on the days he and his father had gone to the mart. He had never been interested in what the two men had spoken of, always being bored rigid.

On that morning, however, Neil could not have been interested in anything more in the world.

When he arrived, Maggie and Mr Blayney were sitting at his small desk, laughing, and making the usual small talk. Both ceased laughing when he entered the room, taking on the stern look of grown up adults talking business.

Clearing his throat and standing to shake Neil's hand, Mr Blayney said; "Young Mr Dillon, it's been a long time. You're looking well"

If only Neil could have returned the compliment, he thought.

Mr Blayney had been quite a tall man, perhaps around six feet, but his bulk had made him appear very squat and rotund in appearance. He wore a navy suit and tie, his shirt straining at the buttons, pale white flesh peeking out between each button hole. His head was bald and his face looked like an over ripe tomato.

Neil, not being a man for niceties, or indeed falseness, did not return the compliment.

"Thank you, Mr Blayney. Yes, it's been a while"

He took a seat beside Maggie.

"Good morning Maggie", he said quietly as he shuffled uncomfortably in his chair.

Maggie nodded in acknowledgement before addressing Mr Blayney; "If you don't mind, Mr Blayney, maybe we should start. I have a few messages to run in town today and I really need to get cracking-lots to do".

"Yes, yes, of course Mrs McGuigan" Mr Blayney replied, flustering, and rifling through a mass of papers on his desk.

Neil almost felt sorry for him. Maggie had a manner about her that could make anyone feel like an idiot. It was her way, but, in fairness it didn't take much to make Mr Blayney look like a bumbling fool.

"Right", he announced, putting on his glasses and reading the papers in front of him; "We have here the last will and testament of Thomas Patrick Dillon. You two are the only beneficiaries, so I will begin"

Neil could feel his pulse quickening. A sudden queasy anxiety attacked his stomach. He hadn't felt like breakfast that morning and he worried what he might bring up if he threw up in that very instant.

"I can read out the will in its entirety, or I can quickly give you the brief-this may be a lot quicker and easier to understand"

"The brief", Neil almost shouted, surprising even himself with his eagerness; "If that is all right by you, Maggie?", he continued, reigning himself back in.

Maggie looked directly ahead at Mr Blayney, her expression one of absolute calm, a faint knowing smile on her lips; "Go ahead. The brief is fine Mr Blayney"

"Righto" Mr Blayney started; "Basically, to break this down to its fundamental core, Mrs McGuigan is to take full control of the late Mr Dillon's property and assets. Mr Dillon's savings and monetary amounts are also to be guarded by Mrs McGuigan, and it is in her that Mr Dillon trusts his finances will be distributed in a sensible fashion"

Neil felt himself sinking into the ground. He thought his heart had stopped beating. The room began to spin and he had to subtlety hold onto the desk in front of him to stop himself from falling off his chair. A thousand thoughts rushed through his mind all at once. His inheritance had been severed. He always knew his father had disliked, perhaps hated him, but he had never imagined his hatred was so intense that he would do something so drastic to spite him.

"However," continued Mr Blayney; "Young Mr Dillon is permitted to reside on the late Mr Dillon's property and in conjunction with Mrs McGuigan, run the businesses as deemed best. Mrs McGuigan must approve any changes Mr Dillon requires to implement, if she deems it in the family's best interest. The deeds of the land and any bank accounts will remain in Mrs McGuigan's control until her death."

Mr Blayney paused, before continuing; "If you have children, Mr Dillon, Mrs McGuigan will relinquish any power she has when the first of your children reaches eighteen years of age. The late Mr Dillon has willed it that his grandchildren will be given the family estate. If, for instance, you fail to have any children, Mrs McGuigan retains the right to will the estate to whoever she wishes...family members or not"

Neil suddenly felt like a man who had been drowning, only to have been thrown a lifeline. He actually took a breath like a man who had taken his first after being submerged in water so long he was on the verge of death.

He reached into his pocket to take his cigarettes out, his hands shaking noticeably, struck a match, and lit one before inhaling the soothing smoke deep inside his lungs. He let it sit and disperse into every air sac before jetting it out of his nostrils slowly, trying to let the calmness wash over him before he spoke.

"That's it then?"

"That's the gist of it anyway", Mr Blayney replied.

Maggie sat staring straight ahead as she had done. The knowing smile finally revealed to him.

"Hmm. I don't know whether to be relieved or angry, to be honest", Neil added.

Maggie let out a small laugh, laced with bitterness. "Sure, what would you be angry about?", she asked.

Neil took another drag. He knew not to speak in haste around her, knowing she would be waiting with a readymade reply that would cut him to the bone, making him look like a fool to whoever was witnessing the exchange.

Choosing to ignore what Maggie had said to him, and addressing only Mr Blayney, he said; "So, to get this straight. I can still run the farm and live in the home place. But, Maggie has the final say on things and I need her blessings to make any changes. The place remains in her name, until my children come of age. But...I never own the place outright...am I right?"

Mr Blayney stole a glance across at Maggie, then back to Neil.

"Yes. That is right, Mr Dillon. It was your father's wishes"

Neil took another drag, then tapped the ashes lightly into the ashtray.

"My father didn't trust me with the place, which was plain to be seen. But, what he didn't know is that I love that place of ours, and would have never sold a blade of grass anyway. It makes no difference to me what way he has willed it. I will farm it and do my best to make it a success, then my children will be guaranteed their inheritance. The place will remain in the Dillon name, in our family's blood, so what's not to be happy about. I'm very pleased about this. My father was perhaps seeing the bigger picture after all, God rest him"

Neil gathered that Mr Blayney may have thought there would be conflict or trouble with the results of the will, as his relieved reaction of sitting back in his chair, raising his arms above his head and exhaling deeply, visibly showed.

"Righto", he said; "Everyone happy then. It makes my job seem almost worthwhile to see satisfied customers. Mrs McGuigan, are you happy for me to keep the deeds and things in the office?"

"I am", she replied.

"That's great" said Mr Blayney, clapping his hands together; "Anyone any further questions before we head our separate ways?"

"No" both replied.

Neil rose first from his seat.

"Maggie. Can I offer you a lift?", he asked just before he was about to leave.

"Yes. You can drop me off at the Post Office on your way home, I suppose. It will save me from the rain".

As she went to get up from her seat, Neil offered her his arm. She took it.

"Aul cunt", he thought; "She really does think she is Queen Bee now"

They thanked Mr Blayney, who in turn gave them a very hearty, if not clammy handshake.

After leaving the office, they both got into Neil's father's Volkswagen and headed towards the Post Office at the top of the town. When they arrived, Neil turned to her and asked in a small, nervous voice which surprised him; "So, what do you want to do about all this then?"

Not turning to look at him and in her usual matter of fact tone, she answered; "I would like it if you visited me once a fortnight. You visit the mart in town quite frequently, so you won't have to go out of your way very much by coming to see me on your way home. You can let me know how things are going and if you need help financially or otherwise, then I will see what I can do. I heard you shut down the mill. Now, you didn't know about this arrangement we have, when you did, so I am not going to harp on about that decision. I know you didn't know what way the will was going to go, but I did, as your father had spoken to me a lot about it before he passed away. I could have prevented you from shutting down the mill, but didn't. In fairness, I think you have a good knack for farming and perhaps the mill wasn't doing as well as it did years ago. But, the point I am making is...from now on, any big decisions like that are to be run past me first. No matter what you may think, I'm not an unreasonable person, and I want to see the place do well. You look after me, and I will see you right. Be honest, don't go behind my back in case you don't think I will approve of something- I will find out. We will operate as partners, every decision a mutual one. Your father has trusted my judgement and experience; I would like it if you would honour his trust"

Neil nodded his head in agreement.

"I do Maggie"

"As for the money, your father left", she continued; "I am a woman of a certain age. I have few needs and I have enough savings of my own to let me live within my means... in case you are worrying I will spend all your inheritance"

Neil laughed an embarrassed laugh.

"No, not at all"

"I am going to keep my little leased house in town. It is handy for me and I am sure you don't want me living out there with you, not if you are to marry in the future and make a family home for yourself. I think you will find it fair and reasonable I put an amount aside for Kathy. You will make a living from the land, and you have a home to live in, so it's only fair Kathy receives her share. It's what your father wanted."

She sneaked a look at Neil to monitor his reaction, to see if he showed any displeasure at the mention of Kathy and her share of the inheritance.

He hadn't.

"So, those are my plans. Come and see me every other week, keep me informed of what is happening and we will both be happy. Cross me and risk my wrath. Are we straight?"

Neil sat at the steering wheel, looking straight ahead also.

"We're straight"

"Good day to you then" Maggie replied; "I'll see you Friday week"

She opened the car door and left.

That damp, cold and grey day, Neil drove home looking out at men tending their animals on their own land. He couldn't figure out whether he had lost or gained a farm of land that day. That morning when he had woken, he had felt like a land owner, but on the drive home he knew he wasn't, and never would be.

But, he couldn't help but feel happy.

If anything, he knew he wouldn't grow old with the pride that had so afflicted his father. Unlike his father, he wouldn't own anything, but his children would. His children were guaranteed an inheritance. There was nothing anyone, not even himself, could do to stop that.

He smiled, sat back, and began to enjoy the drive home.

The Dillon's were guaranteed to remain in his beloved little part of the world for at least another generation.

He couldn't have wished for anything more.

CHAPTER 13

I realised growing up that people cope.

People cope with all sorts of shit life throws at them. People lose their jobs and wonder how they are ever going to manage, cope. People receive bad news from their doctor and think their lives are going to end slowly and painfully, cope. Some people lose loved ones and think that the dark, painful throb in their hearts that seems to worsen with every day that passes, cope. Life is shit, but as people must deal with certain horrors in their lives, the next series of horrors come along quickly, making the previous set look not so bad after all.

That is how I seen life. Today's problems always seem so huge, but tomorrow or next week they look small compared to the present. I think I should have tried to learn something from this realisation, but trying to think in that manner when dealing with that day's worries, well... I was too busy worrying.

Typical.

The point I am making is that I survived my childhood...barely. I was seventeen years old. A young man in the eyes of the world, though I felt like a grizzled veteran of life.

My mother remained the same, only worse. At least when we were both younger she looked good to the casual observer. At least she could have covered up how ghastly she was behind closed doors with her youthful and fresh looks. No matter how much drink she consumed she always looked fresh. It was the good Irish breeding she would say. As a woman in her early forties she could have passed for a woman in her late twenties. Now, she was forty-seven and instead of looking like a woman of thirty-seven, or even forty-seven she would have been lucky if the man on the street passed her for sixty-seven.

The babyish cheeks had been hollowed by vodka. The smooth and radiant complexion ravaged and pockmarked by gin. Her thin and athletic body left bloated by wine. But, worst of all, her fine little porcelain teeth had been decayed and eroded by cigarettes and neglect. Her hair, always having been mahogany brown, unaided like most other women by hair dyes, was now a lank, greasy mass of grey. She had literally turned from a fresh-faced girl to a dried up old crone in what seemed like a matter of months.

I could see it was hurting her. It seemed strange that a woman who had obviously given up on life years before, could be so hurt over the loss of her looks. Maybe it was different for women than men? I suppose it was, but I could see it was killing her inside every time she glanced at herself in the mirror. I couldn't help but feel sad too. I thought my mother was indestructible, and in turn I was too by association. But, in seeing the ravages of time and alcohol, I knew that not to be the case anymore.

I think it was killing me, as much as her to see her degrade in such a manner.

School for me was over. Like most of my friends I left with no qualifications. I wouldn't have known how to use them even if I had them anyway. Jobs were scarce, or so we were continually told. I spent most of my time hanging around with Brian and the other young guys from the area, wasting our days shoplifting, smoking, hanging around public parks and trying to get off with girls. Usually the days would end with me going home on my own as only Brian would be successful in his attempts with the girls…the Irish accent, always a winner. In a vain attempt to win favour with the girls I would tell them I was Irish too. They didn't believe me, didn't care- I didn't have the accent, I never stood a chance. But even through my petty jealousy of him, I still liked to see him score.

Sure, didn't it give the rest of us hope?

Life changed in a big way in my seventeenth year. My mother nagged me constantly. Not in a normal motherly way but more an insane drunken rant to get my ass out and start earning money, as she wasn't getting anything from the government for me anymore and I would have to support the both of us, as I was now a fully-grown man.

As usual, the McManus' came to the rescue.

Brian had mentioned a few times before that his father was giving him an apprenticeship as a bricklayer, working with him on the sites. I congratulated him and told him how lucky he was, as most of us didn't stand a chance of getting a job. He told me to ask Dan that night if he had any other work going.

So, I did.

To my great surprise he *had* a lot of work on and he told me he and his partner would give me a trial run. They couldn't guarantee work every day however, but they would try and give me as many days as they could. I was over the moon at the news. Now I could spend my days in the company of Brian and Dan and get paid too. It couldn't have worked out any better for me. I was to start the following Monday.

Even my mother seemed pleased that night when I told her.

The work was tough, but I couldn't have been happier. I worked as a labourer. Brian was on-site with me most of the time, except when he had to go to the tech for his training. Dan encouraged me to do the same, but it didn't interest me. If I were to do it I wouldn't have gotten paid for the days I wasn't on-site. Dan told me it would be worth it overall, as bricklaying was a good solid trade to have and I could earn even more money in the future, rather than labouring. Being in the first flush of the arrogance of youth however, I obviously knew best and politely declined the advice. I had never earned money before and I had a plan to earn enough money so I could move out and get a place of my own.

What a job! Where before I was hanging around street corners trying to kill the days as best I could, mostly by petty criminal activities, now I was on a building site with my best friends. I was exercising my muscles, getting plenty of fresh air and earning good money too. Of course, there were days, especially when I had been badly hung over, when it was hard to get out of bed and get motivated to go to work in a freezing, damp building site, but when I would arrive and meet the boys, it would get a lot easier.

Dan and his partner, Sean Carragher from County Cavan, had met in Australia years before. They both sub-contracted work from big contractors in London and headed up a team of around eight to ten men, depending on how much work was available.

Most were Irish and all were great characters.

There was Fergus Fox from County Monaghan. Fergus was a man in his sixties and never really said too much, but anything he said, the phrase would always end with; "Dogs cock, dog's balls", to punctuate the sentence. For instance, if you asked him what he did the previous night, he would perhaps reply; "Went to the pub for a few pints, then went home to bed... dogs cock, dog's balls".

A man of very few words, but every sentence had the; "Dogs cock, dog's balls", punctuation.

No-one knew why. No-one ever asked why either.

Then there was Larry Dolan from County Carlow. A strange one Larry was. I could never understand a word he said, because of his thick accent and the way in which he laughed all the time, even mid-sentence when he spoke. Any time he ever spoke to me I would usually just nod and agree with whatever he said; "Yea Larry, that's right. Oh, I know, a-ha, a-ha, absolutely", even though I hadn't a clue what he was saying. There was one day however when I sat next to him on a plank whilst having lunch. I don't know why, but I could understand him a lot better on that day, maybe he was less giddy, but he was certainly a lot more audible.

He told me he had lived in Greece for a few years previously. He spoke of the food, the weather and inevitably the women. My ears pricked up at that.

"Greek women, eh Larry? What were they like?"

"Well" he replied - "Greek women are a strange breed. They are really beautiful; I mean the most beautiful girls on earth when they are young. Lovely. Jet black hair, olive skin, pert little tits, tight little arses, mmm, just beautiful. But...once they hit a certain age, they turn into complete barrels of shite. It's the same for every Greek woman I've ever known. Beautiful...then with age, all goes to shite"

"Fuck me Larry" I said- "Sure isn't that the case with most women. I wouldn't say it was purely a Greek thing", I laughed. I couldn't see his logic.

"No, no, no son. You don't understand. You see, what you're saying applies to women as they hit middle age or even old age- usually after they go through the change of life or whatever they call it. Greek women turn to shite a lot younger. I'm talkin' about girls of eighteen or nineteen turning to shit, not women in their fifties or sixties. A Greek girl of around the age of fourteen or fifteen is hard to beat... hard to beat I tell you son"

I looked at him, studying his face, waiting for him to laugh, to say something to indicate he was only joking in some particular way, but he simply got up, brushed the breadcrumbs from his trousers and said; "Righto boys. I'm away for a shite. Be back in five minutes".

All I could do was laugh to myself. What else was there to do? There was no point in saying anything to him, I don't think he'd have understood anyway.

It came as no surprise that neither he nor Fergus were married men.

Blondie was another colleague. Colleague was a very generous term for him. Like me, he was also a labourer, but being a major arse licker, he worked his way into the position of an unofficial foreman. When Dan and Sean weren't around, Blondie was the boss, although no-one ever took any real heed of what he said. His major problem was that he was a complete Mummy's boy. A local boy, he was a neighbour of Sean Carragher's. His mother having tired of having him lying around the house all day asked Sean if he had any work going. That was how he got his "start". He was an only child and like most "only" children (and I categorise myself here too) was a bit odd. His father had left his mother years before and she had obviously spoiled and doted upon him.

I never in all my time knew a man who was as well fed as Blondie. At lunch time every day, all the men would open the lunch boxes their wives, girlfriends or themselves had prepared, to find the usual limp sandwich accompanied usually by a packet of crisps and a few stale biscuits.

Not Blondie though.

The first day I worked with him, I couldn't help but wonder what he had in the rucksack he carried. I thought he must have had a change of clothes to put on after the day's work to visit his girlfriend or something. I couldn't help but feel shocked though, when at lunchtime, he opened the bag to produce the largest lunchbox I had ever seen, accompanied by a flask of tea, two packets of crisps and a full packet of chocolate digestives. He proceeded to open the massive lunchbox which consisted of two bread rolls, two bananas and two large tin foiled objects. In astonishment, I watched as he unwrapped the tin foiled objects, to find a huge turkey thigh in each. He reached into his rucksack again, hoking out a bottle of salt, then after he shook the salt over the thighs, tore into them with all the zest of King Henry VIII in his heyday.

Sensing my amazement in witnessing this exhibition of gluttony for the first time, Dan quipped; "Bejaysus Blondie, you must leave some serious coil of shite behind you".

Dan's comment brought a bout of laughter from the rest of the men, and in the background Fergus Fox could be heard commenting; "Coil of shite, ha-ha. That's a good one all right, aaah, dog's cock, dog's balls".

Blondie wasn't fazed, he ate away, too busy enjoying his lunch to participate in the craic around the site. His whole lunch, of course, had been prepared by his mother that very morning.

Blondie, for all the energy he consumed, never converted much of it into his work. He was the best bluffer I had ever seen. His bluffing could have been deemed a skilled trade itself, so impressive it was. Hugely annoying to observe every day, but I had to hand it to him- he had a certain knack.

Every day the work would begin with the unloading of the van. Blondie drove the van to the site every day and it was the responsibility of the man working with him (usually me) to unload it for the day ahead. Nothing too taxing in the summer months, but in the depths of winter, a different matter. Unloading wet, freezing tools and bags from the van, usually getting soaked to the skin in the process, wasn't the most pleasurable experience to start the day off with. Blondie, of course, every morning would have an excuse.

"Tommy, mate, Dan wants me to go and have a word with Larry on the other site. I should be back in half an hour or so. You wouldn't mind...would you?", he would say, pointing towards the van. The same scene would play out every morning. He would return, dry and clean where I would be covered in all sorts of shit and soaked through. But, the most annoying thing was, sometimes a ring of shiny grease could be seen around his mouth.

The fat fucker had not only been skiving off work, but he had been stuffing his face in the process, fuelling himself for a day of dossing.

Once the van was unloaded and we were set up, we would work on the plan for the day ahead. Some days we would be attending a brickie, other days it could be anything from tidying up the site to carting iron girders from one site to another. It varied from day to day and site to site. My favourite job was attending a brickie, especially if it was Dan or Seamus. The craic would be great all day and the work would be very straightforward. Keep the bricks and mortar coming and everyone was happy.

My most detested job, however, was tidying up the site. This would involve filling the skips with broken bricks and slates that lay around it.

I hated it.

It was hard work, sure, but it was the monotony of it that got me, not to mention that many of the sites had no toilets, so all the men were pissing anywhere they could find. We then had to pick up pissy bricks and the rest, then had to eat our sandwiches at lunchtime. Most sites had limited water and the water that was available for making up the mortar was probably piss contaminated too. Gloves could have been worn, only they wouldn't have lasted long with the abrasive materials being handled, not to mention the mickey taking that had to be endured from the men on the sites for wearing them.

If I ever mentioned my annoyance to Dan, he would say; "Good for your immune system Tommy. I haven't had a cold since I was fifteen years old"

He had a point. The work certainly toughened a man up, all I had to do was look around at the hard bastards I worked alongside for proof.

As I said, Blondie was a bluffer extraordinaire. If we were given instructions to unload a shipment of blocks or any other materials, myself and the rest of the men would get stuck in. Blondie would walk about, looking around him. It was highly aggravating for the rest of us, but as he was the boss in Dan and Seamus' absence, there wasn't much we could do about it. After a while we would run out of steam; "Fuck it" one of us would say (usually me); "We'll have a fag and a rest for a couple of minutes".

We would light up, some would lean against a shovel, and some would sit down. Blondie would disappear, coming into view only to mope around in his usual manner.

"That Blondie wouldn't work on batteries, the fat cunt" someone would usually quip. We would all laugh. As soon as we knew it, mid fag, and in the middle of a good laugh, Dan and Seamus would arrive out of nowhere. They never said anything to us about it, but we could tell they weren't happy. After all, they were under pressure to get the work done by a certain deadline and there they were, to their knowledge paying a squad of dossers. They had a way of not saying anything yet exuding a certain body language and expression that made us feel guilty. We all needed our jobs and those men treated us well. It wasn't a pleasant experience getting caught out like that, especially for me as I was so close to Dan. We would stub our fags out and turn to get back to the job immediately, only to find Blondie, red-faced, sweating heavily and working like a man possessed.

It was unbelievable.

Every time, every single time we were caught taking a break, Blondie could be seen working like a maniac.

No wonder Dan and Seamus had made him boss.

No one knew how he did it. He had an almost sixth sense to detect when the bosses were about to arrive, it was uncanny. We even tried keeping an eye on him when we were having a sneaky break, so we too could detect when the bosses were arriving, but it never worked.

He was too elusive.

For such a fat fucker, he moved like a ballerina when he needed to.

That was Blondie. He was some boy.

Another of the men I worked with was Michael McKeown from South Armagh. He was another of Dan's friends from home. Even though his name was Michael, he was known as Mickel… like Nickel, with an M. He was middle aged, perhaps late forties, early fifties…it was hard to tell. As lean as a whippet and as hard as nails, I never seen him eat a crumb. He smoked like a train and drank like a maniac at every opportunity. He had a way of talking through his nose, sounding like someone who is inhaling a cigarette and talking at the same time.

I liked him a lot. An abrasive character, but very likeable. He reminded me of Robert De Niro. He had that same cocky looking smile, the famous De Niro expression, the tongue sticking out slightly and the eyebrows raised. He certainly wasn't everyone's cup of tea, he spoke exactly what was on his mind, no matter what company he was in.

Mickel was an unusual case, as he still lived at home in Ireland, coming over to England to work for a month to six weeks every year. He lived with his brother back home, both never marrying, which didn't surprise anyone, as it would have taken a brave woman to put up with him. The two brothers owned a farm, the other brother obviously taking more of a hands-on approach than Mickel. When he came over to England, he would always stay with Larry Dolan. Every morning when the two arrived to work, I could almost find myself getting drunk on their fumes.

I always looked forward to Mickel's arrival throughout the year. Not just because of the pints we would share after work, but because of the craic he brought with him to the site. As I said, he never ate a thing, so at break times when we would be having our sandwiches and tea, Mickel would smoke a few cigarettes and the stories would flow. I couldn't get enough of them. All the men I worked with were Irish, apart from Blondie, but their stories from home grew stale over time. It was almost as if they became anglicised themselves the longer they stayed. Mickel, on the other hand was current. He might have arrived that very morning and he would be full of fresh stories. To me, someone who had never even been to Ireland, but felt Irish to the core, it was like receiving letters from home every time he would settle into one of his hilarious monologues.

One day he arrived on site unexpectedly after about six months of absence. No-one seen him coming, as he now walked with a heavy limp. He looked to have aged about ten years and appeared even leaner than normal, his face haggard, a nasty looking six-inch scar running down the back of his head.

"Good man Mickel" said Larry; "What the fuck happened you?"

Smiling, Mickel replied; "Ach, I had a run in with that cunt of a bull of ours"

Everyone laughed and he told the story in full.

He had been feeding the cattle one morning, of course after he and his brother had sat up all night drinking after the pub. Usually the Friesian bull they kept would graze on its own when the cattle meal was put in the trough, only coming up to feed when Mickel or his brother were safely out of the field. On that occasion, however, Mickel hadn't noticed the bull huddled in amongst the herd of cows. The next thing he knew was he was face to face with the bull at the trough. Unlike most normal people, who would automatically drop the bucket and run to the safety of the gate, Mickel stared straight into its eyes, shouting; "Get away to fuck, ye big ugly cunt, before you get my boot up your hole".

Not totally amused at Mickel's confrontational manner, the bull reacted angrily, butting him with its head, almost knocking him backwards. Mickel, relieved at still being on his feet and unfazed, propelled himself forward, lunging at the bull, punching it three or four times between the eyes.

He then found himself waking up in hospital with a big assed nurse leaning over in front of him. He went to say something to her (probably about her big ass) only to realise his jaws had been wired together.

The bull had butted him against the trough, and when he fell to the ground, gored him until it got tired. Mickel didn't remember any of the ordeal (or so he told us). He ended up with five broken ribs, a broken jaw, a shattered pelvis, a large gash to the back of the head from where he fell backwards and three broken fingers from punching the bull. He was in hospital for a few weeks afterwards. He said the doctors told him if he hadn't had so much alcohol in his system keeping him supple and warm, he would have been a dead man. That was one of the reasons no one ever dared to mess with Mickel.

If he could get into a fight with a bull and come out the other side, what could he not do to any man?

That question was answered one day when we were all sitting around having a tea break. Mickel was in full flow with one of his stories when he suddenly became distracted by something in the distance. The look that only he possessed, the half wily smile, half squint, colouring his features, which meant devilment was brewing inside.

"Aah, sweet holy Jaysus" he said; "Would yis look at the big sow headed over this way".

Theatrically he blessed himself, took a last drag of his cigarette and stubbed it out under his boot, a wicked little smile on his lips.

"I have never in all my time seen such a barrel of shite. A fat animal like thon should be put down. Oh, sweet Mary, mother of God, such a pig's ass I never did see"

At that point, everyone looked around to see a large tattooed woman bounding towards us carrying a flask and a bag. Everyone laughed heartily at the poor woman's expense until a gruff cockney voice could be heard above the laughter.

"Wot you facking say Mick? That's ma facking missus that is"

My heart sank and I felt a sudden queasiness when I saw who it was.

It was Skipper. Skipper was a foreman with one of the other contractors on the site. He was a big, mean tattooed fucker who lifted weights in his spare time and was built like a brick shit house.

Mickel didn't even look over at Skipper, as he replied.

"And what do ye want me to do? I'll tell ye what you should do though, try to distract her from the ring feeder for a bit...that might be a start".

He spat on the ground, then looking over at Skipper, added; "And maybe you should keep away from it too, ye stupid lookin' cunt"

At that point Skipper roared in anger and went to rush towards Mickel, only for his mates to hold him back.

"He's not worth it Skip. He's not worth gettin' the sack over", they said.

"I know where you drink, Mick", Skipper roared; "I'll facking see you tonight"

Mickel laughed and walked away, bowing his head at Skipper's poor bemused wife on his way.

Later, Dan said to him; "Ye fucker, Mickel...you knew exactly who that woman was, didn't ye?"

Again, the wily smile appeared.

"I've never seen that poor woman before in all of my life".

Dan laughed; "You're some cunt Mickel".

That night, everyone who had been on the site that day, and all their mates, went to the pub. It was an Irish bar, "O'Reilly's", we went to every night and there had always been a good crowd in-mostly Irish. On that night the place was heaving, English, Irish, Scots, Welsh, Europeans, men of every background came to see what Skipper was going to do with Mickel. Mickel, of course was at the bar with us, holding court as usual, not a care in the world. As ever, he was sinking bottles of stout and shots of whiskey at an astonishing rate. Dan was standing beside him; "Mickel, for God's sake do you not think you should take it easier on that stuff...tonight of all nights?"

"Tonight, of all night's? What? Sure, what's so special about tonight, Dan? I have a serious thirst on me and I intend to drink until I kill it"

With that he ordered us all another round. It was at that moment I retired to the toilet. I hadn't shat properly in about three days or so before that, too much beer and not enough roughage obviously my problem. I fought my way to the toilets and as usual when I finally got there I had to squat over the piss soaked rim whilst trying to keep the door closed with one hand in a vain attempt to cover my modesty. After not having shat in over three days and after the initial pain of squeezing out a large stinging turd, I relaxed and began to enjoy my intestinal extraction. It was at that moment, mid shit that I heard the roar from the bar and I knew I was missing the fight. I tried to hurry it up, but it just kept coming. All I could do was wait until it all emptied out. I wanted to be out there to help Mickel, if Skippers mates got involved, but I wasn't prepared to do that with a trouser full of shite. I enjoyed a good scrap as much as the next man, but there were more important things in life, like not having a squelchy arse when I was walking around.

The commotion in the bar quickly died down and I knew the fight had been taken outside. Once finished my mammoth shit, I quickly wiped with the complimentary newspaper someone had left in the toilet and rushed out to the bar. As I guessed, it was empty, apart from old Mrs O'Reilly who was tidying up tables and lifting empty glasses. I burst out through the front door to be met with a chorus of heckles and jeers. Men began returning to the bar, most of whom wore a disappointed expression.

"Some fight that was. Talk about an anti-climax...and him supposed to be a hard cunt too", a man said to another on his way past.

My heart sank. Poor old Mickel. I knew the reputation he had as a hard man, but surely the goring he had taken from the bull had taken its toll. I hoped he hadn't been hurt too badly. Skipper was a dangerous man, Mickel had been brave (or stupid) to go up against him. My heart sank even further when I saw a crowd of concerned looking faces huddled around Mickel on the ground.

"He's not responding...somebody call an ambulance", one man shouted.

My blood boiled. That big bastard Skipper, a big pumped up bully, half killing little haggard Mickel. It just wasn't right. I began to look for Skipper, not caring what he would do to me, my temper surely roused. I walked up to one of the men at the back of the huddle.

"Where is the big fucker?", I shouted at him; "Where the fuck did he go?"

The man looked at me angrily, and shouted back; "Who...who the fuck are you talking about?"

"Skipper...the cunt" I hissed back. I reckoned this guy was one of Skipper's hangers on. I'd start with him first. Blood boiling and rage tunnelling my vision towards the man, I went to grab him by the throat, before someone spoke from behind me.

"Tommy, you're here?"

I looked around. It was Dan.

"Where'd you go? You missed it all"

I was confused. Why was he not with Mickel?

"What the fuck, Dan? Did you not help him out?"

At that, he began to laugh.

"You really did miss it all, didn't ye? Come on. Let's go inside and see the champ"

I looked around again, only to see Skipper eventually being helped up. He held a blood-stained rag to his mouth and wore a startled look on his face.

I laughed, mostly from relief. Dan filled me in on the way back to the bar. He told me that, just after I left to go to the toilet, Skipper came at Mickel from behind, putting him in a headlock dragging him out into the street. He threw Mickel onto the kerb and kicked him twice in the ribs. Mickel stumbled to his feet and Skipper threw a few punches which landed clumsily on Mickels shoulders and arms. All the while, Mickel was ducking and measuring Skipper up. Then, out of nowhere he threw a precise uppercut right under Skippers chin. Skipper's eyes rolled in his head and he fell back in a heap. At that, Mickel stood back, saw Skipper wasn't going to get back up and retreated to the bar to finish his drink.

We got back into the pub. It was considerably less packed than it had been. The ghouls hadn't seen the bloodbath they so wished and expected to see.

Mickel stood at the bar and ordered another round. He wore his usual wry smile, the one like Robert De Niro.

Dan put his arm around him.

"You're some cunt, Mickel McKeown...you are *some* cunt"

CHAPTER 14

The years passed by fruitfully for Neil. The mill had long since ceased. Over the years, between happily farming the land, he converted the mill into a dwelling house for himself to live in, bit by bit. He took great satisfaction in all his work, but converting the mill was his greatest achievement. Finally, he had a dwelling that mirrored his success in business. He no longer had to endure living in the run-down shack his father had lived and died in, no longer being the laughing stock of the country.

He continued to honour his father's will and give Maggie her due respect, mostly begrudgingly, but he did it as best he could. She had turned out to be not as hard to deal with as he had originally feared. He would go into town to visit her once a fortnight, usually on mart day. She would always be ready and waiting for him, coat, and handbag already on. As soon as Neil got to the front door she would be on her way out. He would drive her to the shops for her groceries and that was when the business would be discussed. He would tell her his plans and she would sit staring straight ahead nodding in approval at what he requested. Very rarely did she ever disagree with any of his plans or ideas, and if she did, Neil found that a little bit of gentle persuasion usually did the trick to get her to approve what he asked for.

In all fairness, she was a good partner.

Maggie would go into the shops and do her shopping whilst Neil would sit smoking in the car. When she came out, he would take her bags, put them into the boot and drive her back home. Once there he would get out, carry the bags up to her doorstep and leave them for her to take in. He never entered her house. She never invited him and he never asked. Before he left to go back to the car he would recap what his plans were to make certain there was no misunderstanding.

"You all right with that Maggie?", he would ask and she would usually nod and enter the house.

The rest of the week would be spent farming the livestock and maintaining the land. The bane of his life for years had been the ripping out of hedges and amalgamating lots of little fields into larger ones, tedious work that seemed to never end but had been immensely satisfying when eventually completed. It had annoyed him over the years that his father's land had been made up of tiny fields separated by hedges running along their borders. It never made sense to him as he knew the hedges and ditches were taking up unnecessary space, so he ripped them all out, making four or five little fields into one "super" field. The large field would have a proper drainage system installed, using more modern pipes under the soil. Once finished the large fields were ploughed and reseeded, to produce beautiful large areas of dark green grass, the likes of which had never been seen before in the entire country. The fields made him immensely proud, but they had come with much sacrifice- it would eventually take him years to realise his vision. Many days he worked from dawn until complete darkness drew over the land, until he could see no more. Most days all he ate were a few slices of bread and jam. He didn't mind- he was so engrossed in his work that he mostly had to force himself to stop and eat out of pure necessity. He wouldn't realise how hungry he had become until he got back to the house that night. By then he would be too tired to eat anyway.

He lived a lonely existence, but he couldn't have been happier. It was all he had ever wanted to do. His sister had always wanted to go to school, take exams and eventually become a doctor. Neil had never been interested in any of that- farming was his passion. He was happy to dig ditches, plough land, run after cattle, buy, and sell livestock, repair, and operate heavy machinery and muck out cattle sheds- he couldn't think of anything that could be better.

Neil had an eye for land as good as what he had for cattle. A sign of the times seen many of the men from the area emigrating as they had fallen on hard times-some sold up and never returned. Neil took full advantage of that situation. He would visit Maggie and put forward his plans to buy more land and she would eventually be talked into signing the cheques to make sure it happened. At times when she was harder to convince, he would take her out to see the prospective land, and she would always agree they would be good investments. He would show her the work he had been doing to his father's fields, and although she would never say much, he could tell she was impressed by what he had done.

When he had finished buying up all the best ground in the area, he owned over one hundred and fifty acres of Ireland's finest land, growing it from the hundred acres he inherited. He couldn't help but to feel proud of himself. He had proved his father, and Maggie, wrong. Unlike a lot of the other young men who had inherited their father's farms, he had grown and improved his, whereas they would sell and waste theirs. Even the great Dessie McNamee, whom both his father and Maggie had thought so highly of, sold much of his father's small farm to fund his lifestyle, and pay for his emigration across the water to England. According to sources, McNamee had taken to living in England like a duck to water, apparently being made a partner in a large quarry after only working in it as a general handyman for just over a year. "Driving around England in Rolls Royce's", his admirers' would say, obviously exaggerating.

The legend of the great McNamee lived on, looming large over the country.

Neil didn't care though; his absence was one less thing to worry about. When McNamee put his few acres up for sale, Neil hadn't bothered enquiring. Firstly, because it sat on top of rocks and would be of no use to him, secondly, because he didn't want to give McNamee the pleasure of refusing to sell to him.

Neil was feeling happiness for the first time in his life. Life was good, the only piece he felt was missing was the lack of a wife and possibly a child or two.

He had entered his mid-thirties and most of the men he knew of his age were settled down with a family of their own. He felt he hadn't had time to look for a woman up to that point of his life, the building of the farm had been all consuming, almost obsessional. But, he knew that if he didn't start a family at some stage, all his work would be in vain. His fathers will was clear- he had the farm his day, then it was to be inherited by his children. If he didn't pro-create, the will was left in Maggie's hands and God only knew to whom she would bequeath it to.

He knew he would have to see the bigger picture, he would have to find himself a woman. He would have liked to have started a family regardless, but the terms of the will made him more eager to do so. He didn't want to settle for second best in the act of finding a wife. He had many dalliances with girls over the years, finding a girlfriend had never been particularly hard for him, but he wanted the best. He had never been in love and he didn't want to father a child to a woman he didn't love.

Luckily for him, that part of his life came right in his thirty fifth year. Not only that year did he meet the woman who would later become his wife, but also a man who would turn out to be his only true friend.

It all began on the day he visited Maggie to discuss his plans. When he had finished his business, he decided to call into the butchers on the way home. He would buy a pound of beef sausages and a pound or two of stewing beef. He made a great stew and a large pot would keep him fed for at least three days, the sausages accompanied with a few slices of bread would sustain him through the rest of the week.

It had been a while since he had visited that butchers, but the first thing he noticed when he walked in was he didn't get his usual jovial greeting from big Dermot Meegan.

Big Dermot had been the butcher in town for many years- a man mountain, dwarfing even Neil himself. His health hadn't been good for years and he had recently complained that the work was getting a bit much for him. He had talked, for as long as Neil had known him, about retiring, and selling up. Neil didn't believe he would as his heart and soul appeared to be firmly rooted in the business, a man certainly well suited to a sociable trade where he could be in contact with the public every day. However, he realised he may have been wrong when a young man walked through the multicoloured tasselled curtains and appeared behind the counter. Clapping his hands together and rubbing them quickly he smiled, asking; "Well young fellah, what can I get for you today?"

Neil did a double take. There was something about the man's manner and his features that stoked up something in his memory. He knew he recognised the man from somewhere, but he couldn't think from where. His mind busily delved into its archives at the same time he ordered the meat. The man, smiling at him as he lifted out the sausages, putting them into a plastic bag whist twirling it, then spoke; "I hope thon aunt of yours isn't making life too hard for you, Neil?"

He then put the bag through a little device that put a red tag on it, sealing it, before continuing; "You don't remember me, do you?", whilst laughing heartily.

Neil took a long, hard look at him. The man was tall and thin, not as tall as Neil, but few were. He had sandy coloured hair, a little wavy in parts and a fine, prominent jaw. His features were very fine in general, not unlike feminine, but he had a steely look about him, very deep blue eyes. Neil could tell the man hadn't done much physical labour in his life, he wasn't a farmer, but he didn't look like a butcher either.

Laughing to himself the man continued; "Well I certainly remember you. Ye have the same big square head on ye as when you were a gasun."
It was then Neil's turn to laugh. He took another look at him before blurting out, even before he could think of what he was saying; "Jesus, you're not Kelly…eh, Pete…Pete Kelly, are you?"

The man smiled and nodded.

"Indeed I am. Long-time no see, eh Neil?"

"Jesus, it is all right", replied Neil; "Must be over twenty years. Fuck, if I haven't changed, then you surely have"

Neil remembered him from school. He had been a year younger, a very small, thin child. People had always thought there was something wrong with him. He had been a very sheltered child. Whilst the rest of the boys from around the country were out gathering potatoes or helping on their parent's farms, Pete would have been housebound with his mother. Neil immediately felt a sense of shame as he remembered he and a few of his classmates used to call him names and laugh at him. He remembered when his mother eventually took ill and died, when Pete was only about sixteen or so. He remembered his own father's reluctance to attend the funeral.

"Never trust a Kelly" he would say; "There are Kelly's scattered around the four corners of God's earth and not one of them can be trusted. They'd bloody well live in your ear and rent the other one out, if they could".

Some people judged others on their religion, the colour of their skin or their nationality, but Neil's father judged a man on his name, and his mind was never for changing.

Shortly after Pete's mother died, he immigrated to England and had lived there ever since. Neil had dealt with his father only a few years before, when he bought a few acres of land from him. He had disappointed himself when he had done so, as the land was rocky, buying with his heart and not his brain.

Frank Kelly had approached Neil to see if he was interested in buying some land off him. He hadn't really any interest in it, but he bought it anyway as he could see Frank was short of a pound or two. He also paid over and above what he thought it was worth to help him out. Although his father never had much time for Frank, Neil thought of him as a decent and honourable man, so he didn't want to stick the boot in when he could see the man was struggling, so much that he had to approach him cap in hand asking him to buy his land.

Neil, having an eye for a bargain also had an Achilles heel when it came to sentimentality.

Pete had greatly changed. It seemed to Neil that being cut from his mother's apron strings had finally made a man of him. He had grown up and whilst still very thin had a wiriness about him that seemed to radiate an inner strength. He also seemed to have acquired a charm in the intervening years. As a child, he had been terribly shy and introverted, though now he had a great likeability twinned with an affable nature.

"I tell you what, Neil. How about I store these sausages for you and we'll go for a few bottles? I'm about to close up anyway"

Neil nodded in agreement and the two men headed towards the pub a few doors up from the butcher's shop. The two drank until they could barely stand anymore. The conversation had begun with the two telling what they had been doing for the last twenty odd years.

Pete told Neil of the life he led in Bristol.

He had tried to get into the construction industry only to realise he just wasn't cut out for it. He then found himself stumbling into the butchery trade when he had shared a flat with a young butcher. The young butcher had managed to get Pete an apprenticeship with a friend and Pete took to it like a duck to water. He had been a butcher ever since and had made a living out of it. He told Neil of his incapacitating childhood illness, a disease of the kidneys the doctors predicted would eventually lead to his early death, but which he later went on to beat against all the odds. Neil couldn't help but to feel bad hearing about his childhood illness. It had made him feel like a bully thinking back about all the things he had said to him in their childhood, about his appearance and mannerisms. He hadn't been the only boy, of course, to chide him about it, but it didn't make him feel any better because of it. He felt he had been as much of a bully to Pete as McNamee had been to him. He spent the night sombrely apologising, Pete waving his apologies away.

"Sure, how were you supposed to know. For all you knew I was some sort of fairy, some sort of sissy boy- how would you have known any different. I probably would have done the same myself- boys will be boys after all"

Pete's understanding struck a chord with Neil. He didn't think that he himself would be a big enough man to sit and have a drink with Pete if the boot was on the other foot. He admired him for it. Pete went on to tell how his father had gotten in touch to plead with him to come back to Ireland. His father had told him that Big Dermot Meegan was selling his butchers shop and he would help him buy it, everyone knowing the shop was a goldmine, and it was too big an opportunity for Pete to miss. That was how he had ended up back home. Once home he rented a small house in Dunbay, a few doors up from where Maggie lived. He told Neil of how he had spoken to Maggie on several occasions, either meeting her in town or when she came into the shop. He spoke of his happiness at being home, the only downside being the lack of female attention he was getting. As the drink flowed and both men loosened up in each other's company he told Neil of his many escapades with the ladies of Bristol. Neil couldn't contain his amusement or excitement, the two men whooping and roaring with laughter at the stories he told.

"No...I'll never get those experiences with Irish girls", he said; "The Catholic Church has too big of a hold on their knickers"

The two men drank and talked until closing time and then went back to Pete's house for more. Neil, in a moment of drunken sincerity told Pete what his father had said about never trusting a Kelly. The two men roared with laughter.

"I heard Hitler, after dealing with the Jews and the homosexuals was going to come after the Kelly's next", Pete joked.

"What do you mean?", said Neil; "Sure Hitler *was* a fuckin' Kelly!"

"Listen", he continued after the laughter had died down; "My father talked a lot of shite. He always told me to head north for women and south for cattle. Now, I always found the opposite to be true and I would consider myself a far better cattle dealer than he ever was"

Pete's ears pricked up.

"Head south for women, huh?"

Neil smiled.

"Come with me to Ballymoy some night. I'll show you some fine women"

And with that, the two men's friendship was borne.

Most Saturday nights the two would meet for drinks in Ballymoy. They would talk about the weekend they had experienced at the start of the week, and plan the next one at the tail end of the same week. They would do this in the evenings after Pete had finished his work in the butchers, later coming out to help Neil on the farm. Neil had been impressed with his work ethic. As he thought, his slight frame *had* been deceiving, as he was as strong as a bull underneath it all. He could carry a bale of hay under each arm from one length of a field to the other, striding at a pace Neil could barely keep up with, whilst smoking a cigarette out of the corner of his mouth, talking non-stop and laughing heartily, all at the same time. There eventually came a time where Neil wondered what he would do without him, the standard and efficiency of Pete's work was so high. Not a penny he would accept from Neil either, Neil always offering and arguing with him to take something, even trying to stuff money in his pockets before he left.

"Get away out of that", Pete would say; "Sure, don't I come out for a bit of craic-what else would I be doing with myself of an evening, apart from pullin' the balls of myself?"

Even when the two would go into own for a drink, Pete would always go round for round with Neil, never allowing him to buy an extra one as a payment for his work. It felt refreshing for Neil. Most men from the country would sit and let someone buy drink for them all night if they could get away with it. To think his father had always said the Kelly's would "live in your ear if they could".

Well, he should have known how that felt, Neil thought. After all, he had let half the country live rent free in his, for most of his life.

A few months went by and the two men frequented many watering holes in the pursuit of craic and women, and they received their fair share of both. Pete ended up doing a semi steady line with a girl, Sarah Jones. She was a nice girl, a tad on the heavy side for Neil's liking, but a nice jovial and easy-going girl all the same. Both she and Pete made a good couple. Pete would spout wise-cracks all night and she would sit and laugh at them. If the craic was good and the vodka was flowing, she was happy.

Neil, however, had still never found that one girl who made his heart flutter. He had plenty of dalliances, but they never lasted too long, most borne from loneliness or horniness, and when one or other of the feelings had gone, the women were usually gone with them. Of course, he wanted to meet a special girl, but he doubted he ever would. Time was ticking by too quickly for him.

Everything changed on that front, though, on the night Sarah announced she was bringing her best friend for a drink with them the following Saturday night, as she had recently split up with her boyfriend and needed cheering up.

"Well, that's all I need", Neil complained; "Some night this is going to be. You two away courting in the corner and me, left to mop the tears of some quare one. I can hardly wait!"

Sarah assured him it wouldn't be like that as her friend would put a brave face on and was great craic regardless. She also teased that he would be exactly her type and her, his.

"I doubt that, Sarah. If she's the same age as you, she'll be a bit too young for me. What are you-twenty-three, twenty-four? I'm afraid I'm no cradle snatcher...like your man here", he said, pointing at Pete.

Pete laughed.

"If their old enough to bleed their old enough to butcher"

Sarah giggled and slapped Pete on the arm playfully.

"For fuck sakes, yis'll get me locked up, the pair of ye", Neil replied, totally defeated.

That Saturday night, Neil met with Pete in the bar as usual. After three or four drinks, the craic really began to flow. Neil wished the women wouldn't show up, so he and Pete could simply get drunk and talk bullshit for the rest of the night. He knew when the woman arrived (not Sarah as she was used to it) they would have to tone down their vicious humour for fear of offending her.

"Pete, never mind Sarah and your one tonight" he said; "Let's do a runner to another pub where they can't find us. This craic is too good to water down, and sure don't these women love it when you treat them mean? So, let's go"

Pete sipped his drink and looking beyond Neil, a broad smile breaking out on his face, replied; "Too late my friend. They're already here"

"For fuck sake" Neil replied.

Finishing the rest of his drink and wiping his mouth with his sleeve, he turned around...and his heart fluttered.

CHAPTER 15

It couldn't last forever

I knew it wouldn't.

The news was dominated by stories of strikes, long dole queues and general doom and gloom in the country. The country's economy was in the pits and there I was, working in a job I enjoyed with a bunch of friends and great characters as colleagues. Men arrived home from work with various aches and pains from their day's labour. I, however, came home with an ache in my side from laughing all day.

Life had been good. I was twenty-one and I had finally afforded to move out of my mother's place a few years back. My little flat was nothing special. I still lived in a high-rise block of flats, only about a mile or so away from where I was brought up, but it was my little sanctuary. I had peace, something I never had before. When I came home from work, I would lie on top of my bed, put the TV on and usually dose off for a bit. It was a simple existence, but I loved it.

I visited my mother a few times a week to make sure she was all right and I made sure she wanted for nothing. I gave her money every week and sometimes brought her shopping around too. The money I gave her was supposed to go towards her shopping bills, but I could see the only shopping she was doing was at the local off-licence.

Some days when I visited after work, she wasn't even out of bed. Other days she would sit silently and smoke, then there were days when she would be as drunk as hell and give it to me with both barrels. The same shit I listened to for years; "Keep away from those Irish gypsies you're running around with. If they ever find out who you are, they'd cut your throat. The son of a British soldier! Oh, if they ever found out". Then the other broken record piece; "Why didn't you stay in school and get yourself a proper job, instead of being a patsy to those bunch of bastards?

Those visits would usually end with me roaring back that I never stood a chance, with her as a mother. The same old scenes played out repeatedly. A cocktail of shame, anger and sadness would wash over me, almost always pointing towards a bender, and I'm sure she did the same too. It truly was a depressing situation.

Apart from my obligatory visits to my mother, life had been good. Dan paid well and I was putting some money away. I was even contemplating finally doing a day release scheme and pursuing a trade. I was gradually given more responsibility on the sites as I grew more experienced and I surprised even myself by being something of a natural at joinery work. Joinery was the trade I was willing to pursue. Some of the joiners I had encountered could almost have been described as artists. It was amazing what some of those men could do with a few pieces of wood, a bag of nails, a saw, and a hammer. Brian had already qualified as a brickie. Like his father, he was very good at what he did too. He was moving forward with his life, taking on different jobs and earning a lot more money than me. It didn't bother me though; I was happy for him. Money had never been a motivator for me. If I had enough to pay the bills, look after my mother and some left for a few nights on the piss, I was happy. I never worried about not having enough money. If I was young, able, and willing to work, I knew I would always get by.

As I said, things had been good. But, I knew things were about to change for the worse when some of the men began getting laid off. Despite all of Blondie's bluffing and blagging, he was the first to get the chop, much to everyone's surprise. Blondie had been the boss in Dan and Sean's absence, so to see him go had been a big shock.

It all happened so quickly too.

Blondie didn't show up one morning and Dan and Seamus arrived on-site at around eleven. They assembled us all for a group meeting and told us Blondie had been let go. They tried to reassure us by saying they had been working overtime to win more contracts, but the work was really beginning to dry up. We all knew this, however. Times were tough and construction was usually one of the first sectors of commerce to get hit. As the weeks and months went by, more men were being let go. Fergus and Larry went back to Ireland and even Mickel's visits became less frequent, eventually stopping altogether.

From the initial squad of around ten men, we had been reduced to about four. Brian, after garnering a good reputation, quit working for his father and gained work as a free agent. Through his training and Dan's acquaintance's he found a steady supply of work, mostly private- extensions to domestic buildings and so forth.

I could see very clearly that Dan didn't want to let me down, even though I knew I was becoming a dead weight to him. I had been kept on the payroll even though some days all I had done was brush a floor that had been brushed one hundred times already. Dan would put on a brave face and tell me; "Don't worry young fella, this is only a flash in the pan. Once I get more work in, I'll get the aul squad back together. Mark my words".

His body language told a different story though, not to mention his physicality. He had lost weight, was pale, and dark shadows circled his eyes. His shoulders drooped and his usual easy smile began to look forced. I knew I was a problem for him that should have been fixed quickly and easily. Those last few weeks I had felt sick receiving my pay cheques, I felt like I had stolen from his family. Even Seamus' frustrations began to get the better of him as he lashed out a few bollocking's over the smallest of things in those last few weeks. I knew it would break Dan's heart to let me go. He was too proud.

So, to protect his pride I did what I thought was the decent thing to do-look for another job.

The trouble with only being qualified to work as a labourer and having no recognised skills was, everyone wanted the same job. A strong back and a weak mind were the only criterion...a lot of men possessed those essentials.

I wouldn't have particularly wanted to work for another squad of builders anyway.

I wasn't having much luck with my job hunting until I came across a vacancy one night, completely unexpectedly. I had been trying to get a date with the new barmaid in my local for a few weeks with absolutely no success. After all my crap chat-up lines and jokes had failed to impress her, I resorted to spending some serious money. I promised her I would take her into the city for a night out-comedy show, dinner, drinks, the whole works. Like with most girls, it worked, though unfortunately the evenings never usually ended the way I wanted them to. I knew I would starve for the rest of the week and would have to avoid my landlord for a while- but I hoped it would be worth it. Sometimes spending a very expensive evening with an attractive girl was worth all the shit coming down the line.

That night, as we sat in the back of a cab on the way home, in the middle of a very one-sided passionate kiss, I was interrupted by a large guffaw of laughter by the cab driver.

"Fuck. I've seen it all now", he said; "A caretaker's assistant, eh? Since when did they get so fuckin' uppity?"

We had been driving past a secondary school when the cabbie seen the sign on the school gates. Not wanting to show any interest in such a petty job in front of the bored barmaid, I kept my curiosity to myself and simply laughed along with the cabbie.

As predicted, when we arrived outside her house, she gave me the usual line; "Listen Tommy I've had a lovely night...and you're a lovely bloke. But, my dad's back home from working up north this week, and he'd kill us both if I brought you in."

Then, the little smile, quick kiss on the lips and; "Maybe next week, eh?", finisher. To be fair, I wasn't too disappointed on this occasion, as I wanted to get back to get the details of the job on the school gates.

"No problem Lauren", I shrugged; "I'll call you sometime"

The strange thing was, *she* called me the night after, obviously impressed with my not-give-a-fuck attitude.

Women?

Once she left, I leaned forward to the cabbie; "Right, let's get that uppity caretaker cunt's number then, mate".

He laughed, obviously thinking I was taking the number down to ring the next day as a prank call.

The next week after making the call, I had a new job.

My new boss was called Herbert. He was a little old man, like a little goblin. He wasn't a stereotypical caretaker; working class and perpetually skint.

Herbert had class.

Always dressing with a neck-tie, his shirts always new and pristinely ironed, always wearing a variety of coloured trousers-red, green, blue, yellow, but very rarely black or grey. He wore his trousers high above his waist so his socks were always plainly visible. Like his trousers they too were the colours of the rainbow. He would arrive to work looking like a nineteenth century nobleman, velvet, or tweed jackets in a variety of colours, accompanied usually by a gentleman's top hat. When at work, he would always slip into his grey caretaker's coat, an unusual look for him, but no more unusual than his choice of career.

Herbert had interviewed me on his own, which I thought a little unusual. For most governmental jobs, a member of HR or a bigwig of some sort would be on the panel- specially to weed out and expose any possible nonces. The interview itself was also strange. On arrival, I was told to take a seat by the secretary until I was met by this strange, eccentric looking little old man. I straightened myself up and shook him firmly by the hand, thinking he was the principal and wanting to make a good first impression. Then, I was led into his little fusty smelling, extremely untidy office which had the usual caretaker items- mop buckets, floor polishers etc. I looked at him again, my brain confused as to who or what he was. In the corner of his office sat a desk on which stood a very old looking television on top of a very modern looking video player. The penny dropped that he was indeed the caretaker when he sat down on his tattered armchair and instructed me to sit beside him on a classroom plastic chair. He looked at my application form and asked his opening question;

"So, dear Thomas, do you enjoy western films?"

Thrown a little by his bizarre line of questioning, I answered;

"Western films? What, like cowboy films?"

"Yes, yes, cowboy films. Do you enjoy them?" he asked again, a little irritated.

"Yes, umm-hmm, I do indeed.", I lied, trying to impress him. His face lit up and I knew I was onto a winner; "I love them, can't get enough of them. Clint Eastwood is a big hero of mine".

Surprisingly, he looked a little disappointed by my reply.

"Hmm, Eastwood. A little over-rated in my book I'm afraid, but the masses do seem to disagree. How do you feel about Wayne…Cooper…Hudson and the rest?"

Trying to redeem some lost ground I replied; "Yes, good fellow's the lot of them. I'm a particularly big John Wayne fan. Big, big fan."

Taking a sip out of his cup, he smiled and asked what my favourite film was. This interview was tougher than any formal one I had ever had, at least I could have bullshitted a little in them. But, this fucker was sitting in anticipation for an answer that would really assist him in judging me. My mind began to race. I couldn't even think of any Western film. If one came on TV I would normally turn it off rather than watch it. Then, whilst racking my brain, a flashback suddenly came to me.

I remembered a Christmas Eve whilst living with my mother. I played on the floor and she was watching a western- it was her favourite one. I could see some of the scenes play out in my mind's eye. What was it?

"Oh, let me see now. God, that's a good question. So many good ones, how to pick a favourite", I waffled on, playing for time trying desperately to pull the name of the film from the archives of my mind.

Bingo-it surfaced.

"Hmm, if I were pushed I would have to say, "The Searchers""

His face broke into a broad smile and he stood up, going to one of the cupboards.

"Aah, good choice young man. Ford is a particular favourite of mine. A classic by all means"

He foraged into his cupboard, taking out a few videotapes. He handed one to me.

On it the cover read; "The man who shot Liberty Valance"

"Another favourite of mine" he said, looking up at me as if for approval. I smiled and nodded, quickly scanning for information on the cover.

"Another Ford masterpiece. A genius in the truest sense of the word"

He gave me an even broader smile this time. He put the videotape back in the cupboard and shook my hand.

"Congratulations young man, you have the job. When can you start?"

God bless John Ford... whoever he was!

I started on the following Monday. The pay wasn't half as much as I got on the sites but the work was a hell of a lot easier. The money didn't bother me. Like I said, I had never been greedy for money. If the rent got paid, and I could afford a loaf of bread to sustain my hunger and most importantly a fridge well stocked with beer, I was happy. A lack of ambition, some would say, especially my mother, but it kept *me* happy.

The school was a Catholic maintained grammar school for boys. Of course, the brotherhood and priesthood had a large role to play in its running. The principal was Brother O'Brien, an incredibly clean looking man. His skin looked as if he had washed himself with a wire brush every morning (he probably did) as it looked red raw first thing in the morning, regenerating into a smooth, flawless complexion late afternoon. His grey hair was precisely brushed into a side shade and whatever hair product he used seemed to make it gleam almost preternaturally in any light setting. I always thought of him as quite pleasant, and of course he was Irish too, which influenced my judgement.

The vice-principal on the other hand was a less savoury character.

Miss Dixon or "No Dix" as she was less than affectionately known by the pupils, was the dominant force in the school. A bull in a china shop type character. Small, built like an Olympic weightlifter and with the temperament of a steroidal maniac to match. A highly unpleasant character to say the least, and she fucking hated me from the moment her beady little eyes were laid upon me.

Her nickname, "No Dix", was largely due to her spinster lifestyle. She had a little hard-core clique of ass lickers who boosted her ego daily. All, unsurprisingly had fast-tracked from being ordinary young teachers to heads of departments and so on. It must have been clear to the rest of the teachers that to get ahead they would have to lick her behind and try to gain access to the clique too.

Thankfully, most seemed to have more self-respect than that, and remained in their lowly positions.

The gang of three consisted of Mrs Williams, Miss Campbell, and Mr Baker.

Mrs Williams taught history and seemed to be Dixon's favourite pet. She was the blandest person I ever knew. The type who would blank you if you met her in the corridor. Dan would describe such a person, as having an expression like a cow gazing at you over a hedge. She seemed to be next in line as vice-principal when Dixon moved up to the top job, and no-one seemed to work out how she climbed so high. She didn't seem to ever take responsibility for anything. If there was a problem, she would refer it to Dixon, if Dixon wasn't there, it went to Brother O'Brien- she passed the buck at all times.

Another of the trio was Miss Campbell. A spinster in her early forties, the opposite of Mrs Williams, she had a sickly-sweet manner about her, "Too sweet to be wholesome" Mrs McManus would say. She couldn't be nicer to a person's face, but when their back was turned she would let rip. I overheard her criticisms about fellow female teacher's lack of personal hygiene, canteen staff member's lack of intelligence and the unattractiveness of some student's parents. However, I had also witnessed her complimenting their said attributes directly to their faces, all delivered without a hint of sarcasm. What was her chosen subject? Religious Education.

Head of department...of course.

The third of the trio, Mr Baker was in my opinion the most sickening of all. A young man, probably late twenties, early thirties. He taught Science and was both head of department and Year head too. Any female member of staff that moved, he tried it on with. Unfortunately for him though, any female who had a low enough self-esteem to have anything to do with him in the first place, usually dumped him within weeks. Then, without fail he would display all the hysterics of a full-blown drama queen in the company of Dixons gang. He would try and act the Jack-the-lad around the school, but it was plain to be seen he was just a shithead, a mummy's boy in the truest sense of the word, and in school his mummy certainly was Dixon.

She ate out of the palm of his hand, and he knew it. All he had to do, to maintain his position in Dixon's inner circle was flirt, throw in the odd compliment, laugh at her bitchy comments and he was a made man. He never liked me from the start either. So insecure he was, he probably seen me as a rival young buck, threatening his pissing ground.

A complete asshole!

Dixon, an utter ego-maniac thrived on her brood. Throughout the day, every day, they would be seen walking down the corridor in a line. Dixon always at the front, bounding into her office they would go, no doubt to slander some poor soul.

As I observed this daily, it made me even more confused about how Herbert remained in employment for so long. They obviously didn't like him. He irritated them, which was plain to be seen. When spotting them bounding down the corridor in their troupe, he would always bow theatrically in front of them and exclaim loudly; "Her Majesty, and her loyal subjects", much to the amusement of staff and pupils standing by. Mrs Williams would wear the same bland expression she always wore, obviously aware of his sarcasm, Miss Campbell would smile and reply with a; "Hello Herbert", and Baker would glare at him in a failed attempt at intimidation. No one could intimidate Herbert, though. Dixon, bullish and brash as she was would strangely give him an uneasy smile and remain walking.

Herbert remained in employment, employment being a very loose term for what he did. The only person I had encountered who did as little work as Herbert, had been Blondie.

Blondie had been a bluffer extraordinaire though, Herbert didn't even attempt to masquerade his idleness.

Apart from Western films, the only other interest he seemed to pursue was that of photography. He had a collection of some very expensive cameras, some very old-antique like, and some very modern.

Some of the photo's he took were actually very good. My favourite was of a robin redbreast perched atop a railing, eating a crumb of bread. The railing had a covering of snow, the red brick building in the background together with a deep blue winter sky backdrop, prevalent even in soft focus. The contrasts of the different colours were quite beautiful. The robin cut a forlorn figure as the focus piece, offering the photo a distinct sense of melancholy. There was no doubting anyone who captured such an image had a sensitive soul.

It was just hard to believe it belonged to Herbert.

To be fair, a lot of his other photos had been crap. The usual photos of buildings, nature and of course some naked women, had been mostly bland and stereotypical. But, amongst them were some gems.

Herbert had been a great colleague, except for the actual working part of our relationship. Any little bit of work that was required to be done around the school, I had to do. Never anything too taxing- setting up seating arrangements for assemblies, painting classrooms and hallways, unblocking toilets and general maintenance. No job satisfaction was to be gained like what I had working on the sites, but I kept my head down, listened to Herbert's orders and got on with it.

Herbert throughout the day would always sip orange juice from his little mug he kept in the office. I never thought anything of it- he liked orange juice, he liked to keep hydrated. One day though, as we sat watching a western film in his office, he reached around to his desk, opened the top drawer, and took out a bottle of vodka, poured a good shot into his mug then topped it up with orange juice. Possibly remembering I was in his company he looked over at me and asked if I would like a little dash too.

I declined. I had enough issues with alcohol at home without having to deal with it at work too.

That was how Herbert and I put in our days at work. I would have my jobs finished by lunchtime, then we would spend the rest of the afternoon in his dingy little office watching westerns, Herbert eventually getting more shit-faced as the day progressed. No one bothered us and Herbert would have a nap for an hour or so after lunch, before putting another western on to see us through to the end of the day. I began to enjoy the films, the more of them I watched.

I could never understand how or why Herbert got into the caretaking trade. He certainly wasn't the usual type. From his dress, his manners, and his accent it was obvious he came from a very privileged background. I just couldn't figure why he would lower himself to such an occupation. Not to mention that he was well into his seventies too. Why did he even need to work, when he could be drawing his pension?

Herbert was old school, not one for initiating conversations, especially about his private life. So, one day after a few months of getting to know him, after he awoke from his nap, I summoned up the courage to ask. To my surprise, he gave a very frank answer that explained everything.

He told me, that as a young man he had been a reckless playboy. He gambled, drank, womanised, and generally brought shame on his family. He came from a long line of Earls and was the heir-in-chief to a very large estate. However, seeing that he had a wild streak in him, his father put a clause in his will that Herbert would have to hold down a steady job to avail of his legacy. His father died a few years after, but his brothers and his brother's children still kept an eye on him and made sure he stayed within the straight and narrow. When I asked him why they thought it was necessary for him to work into his seventies he told me, with a devilish look in his eye;

"Oh, I was only required to remain in employment until retirement age. My family may be a lot of things, but they are not of such cruel intent as to flog an old man to death. No, you must understand Thomas, I rather like it here. I have been here for a long time and I am content and happy in these surroundings. As an old man, I can reflect and see my father was correct in his reasoning...routine suits me. It lends a certain discipline to one and I quite thrive upon it."

Taking a sip from his mug, he continued;

"And, I may add that there is a certain level of satisfaction that comes to a person when one's presence may cause great frustration and annoyance to others"

My ears must have physically pricked up at his last sentence.

"Who does it annoy Herb? No Dix, is it No Dix? I can tell the bitch doesn't like you. *What* have you done, you old git?"

The devilish little grin he had worn suddenly slipped and he almost shouted;

"Herbert...Thomas, its Herbert. What is this Herb you refer to me as? A man's name is his legacy. I have the decency to address you as Thomas, not this common Tommy as you seem to be known. So, from here onwards, please refer to me as Herbert. Now, what will we put on next? Scalp hunters or Jeremiah Johnson?"

That had been Herbert's way of changing the subject. Old git!

He must have been the only school caretaker in England who wanted to go to work when he didn't have to...certainly the only caretaker who called a plush little apartment in the middle of Kensington, home.

A great character and a great working relationship we were to form.

As new relationships were formed with old people, old relationships were beginning to strain with the middle aged.

Feeling flushed recently as I had been staying in quite a bit due to the disbandment of the old building site crew, I decided to pay my mother a visit.

It was a delightfully warm and bright Friday evening. I felt good. I had money burning a hole in my pocket. My bills were paid and I had a good dose of vodka coursing through my veins, courtesy of Herbert and a lazy Friday afternoon. I had torn into a six-pack of beer when I had gone home to get ready for the evening, so was in fine fettle. I planned to sort my mother out with some cash, remain civil for as long as I could, then head across town to a new pub that Brian had raved about, to meet him and his new mate from college.

As I lived quite close to my mother, I walked to her flat that evening. The sun had slowly dipped into the pale blue sky; a lonely fluffy white cloud was slowly emigrating to find some company. There was a fresh, warm breeze wafting around, just enough to take the heat from the atmosphere. Young couples walked aimlessly around hand in hand. Kids played ball games and rode on their bikes. Old men sat contentedly outside pubs, smoking, and sipping beer. It was a good evening to be alive, the world seemed to be in good spirits.

Hopping up the stairs, taking them in threes in my mother's apartment block, I naively almost thought that the contagious sense of wellbeing may have spread to her. Once I reached her flat and after knocking increasingly harder on the door, I let myself in.

She was sitting on the sofa when I entered the room. All the curtains were pulled and the artificial light filtered through the smoky haze, more a dense smog in the room. Glen Campbell's dulcet tones wafted along the gloomy thickness of smoke, interspersed with despair.

"How ya keepin', ma?", I cheerily asked as I sat down opposite her. She stared at me, like someone looks at the first person to aid them after receiving a heavy blow. It really broke my heart to see her like that. She had lost even more weight, weight she didn't have the luxury to lose. Grey, limp hair hung around her eyes. Her eyes themselves were sunken and black, the whites yellowish. Her hands also were stained yellow from smoking, her blouse discoloured too from the same weed. Her face was blotched and her teeth seemed to be drawn back from the gums, turning to black too.

Despite everything that had happened through the years, I still loved her. She was all I had. I didn't have any other family, not even a distant cousin. We were both all each other had. When she would finally go, I would be alone. I wished I could tell her how I felt. I wished I could take her in my arms, carry her to the bathroom to wash her hair and brush her teeth. I wished I could take her to a hairdresser, a dentist, a beauty salon. But I knew none of those things would work. I knew the only place to take her would be to the doctors, to properly fix her. I wanted to talk to her and tell her how I felt. I wanted her to tell me, how she felt. I wanted us to hold each other and cry until all the pain washed away. But...we weren't like that. We were too Irish. We were too proud. She continued to look at me, as if in a concussed state, saying nothing until I broke the ice.

"Ma, for fuck sake- are you not going to talk to me?"

She suddenly seemed to jolt into life. Half sneering and half laughing she shook her head and took a drink from her glass.

"Here ma, that'll keep you going for a while", I said, chucking her an envelope containing half my wages. Looking at the envelope and lighting a cigarette, taking a deep draw, she stared straight through me once again. She exhaled through her nostrils and shaking her head, began to laugh again.

"So, to what do I owe the pleasure of your company?"

"Ah well, I haven't been around in a bit. Here, why don't you let me open these curtains for you, maybe open a window too? It's a beautiful evening outside."

I got up to open the curtains and a window.

"Leave them alone. I don't want them open."

I sat back down again. I felt anxious. I knew from the atmosphere and the look in her eye, trouble was brewing.

"Yeah…so I've been doing OK in work so I thought I'd sort you out with a few quid", I said, in a futile attempt to lighten the mood.

She broke into the bitter little laugh again.

"He's doing all right in work and he thought he would sort me out with a few quid. Indeed"

She looked me straight in the eye. I didn't like it. I averted my gaze and tried to change the subject.

"Been out and about recently?"

She didn't answer, instead sitting staring at me, still smoking and drinking. I knew she was having one of her episodes, so I decided to make my excuses.

"Well", I said, standing up and looking at my watch; "I'm gonna have to go. I'm meeting Brian and one of his mates from college. You get yourself some good food with that money, ma. Try to go easy on that vodka too, it's not good for you, you know that", I walked towards the door, thinking inwardly that I got away very easily.

"One of his mates from college, eh? How come you never went to college?"

A cold shiver ran down my spine, her words had been laced with ice. I turned as defiantly as I could, and replied; "I don't know ma. Never found a course I was really interested in"

"Oh, is that right? Ach, isn't that a shame", her words couldn't have been more sarcastic; "Well, that's all right then- all right for you anyway. I'm the one who has to sit and listen to that bitch mother of his gloat about her fantastic son, when she comes around"

Taken aback by her harsh assessment of such a kindly person such as Mrs McManus, I replied; "Come on now. Why do you call her such a thing? You've got the woman completely wrong"

"Wrong…wrong? You don't have to listen to her. Brian this, Brian that. And you…what have you done with your life, eh? What can I brag about? Nothing- that's what. Hanging around with those Irish gypsies on building sites and bars. You're a fuckin' skivvy, a patsy…a joke! Look at the little Brit trying to be Irish. The English look down their noses and belittle the Irish and here are these shower of bastards doin' the same to you. I rear a laughin' stock of a son…God give me strength"

Her voice, as always had went from relatively calm, to a banshee like scream. I tried desperately to remain calm. I shook my head.

"You don't know those people the way I do. They are good people, the best. They look out for me, they look after me"

"Don't make me laugh", she hissed; "Look after you, do they? Let me tell you this, boyo. If any of those lowlifes found out who you are, you'd be found lying in a pool of your own blood down some back alley. Who'd be left in the shite then, eh? Me, that's who. I don't have the money to bury you, you'd be left to rot, thrown to the fuckin' dogs of the street"

She stopped talking, to have a smoke and a sip of her drink, before continuing.

"We came to England when you were just a child, and the English have never done us a button of harm. Over here no one gives a damn who or what you are. You get your head down, keep it down and get on with it. If you do that, you will do well- I have always told you that since you were no age. But, what do you do… the fuckin' opposite. You go and get involved with those gypsies who want to know everything about you. Who you are, where you came from, why you're here. What do you tell them, that's what I'd like to know, because it's certainly not the truth, I don't think you are *that* stupid?"

My blood was boiling. The room seemed to shrink and my rage focused entirely on her, as she now dominated everything I saw and raged against. She sat puffing on her cigarette like a poisonous old dragon.

"Don't you dare talk about those people like that- don't you *dare*", I almost shouted back at her, trying to keep a lid on my temper.

"I don't understand why you speak of them the way you do. They're good people, they've been good to us in the past", I continued.

I knew she wasn't listening to me though, as she sat talking to herself in a semi-psychotic mocking rant; "My Brian's doing this, doing that, living in a lovely flat, helps us out, blah blah fucking blah! Bitch! Who does she think she is? And what do I have to brag about? My boy's working for a homosexual geriatric. Holy good God. Why didn't you make something of yourself? You went to a good school, had all the opportunities and you wasted every single one. You could have been a teacher, a doctor, engineer-anything. Then you come around here throwing me a couple of measly quid, telling me you're doing all right. Ha! To think I left my home and family to raise something like you..."

She tailed off her rant, exhausted. I went to walk out the door, in silence. I should have walked out the door, drunk my frustrations away, but unfortunately, I didn't. I turned and looked at her, straight in the eye and a strange sense of calm washed over me.

"I could have been anything I wanted, huh? That's a good 'un. Going to school every day after sleeping maybe two to three hours the night before because I was worried you would burn the flat down in your pissed-up stupor. Listening to you scream and cry, rushing into my bedroom telling me I was no good. Sitting in class every day, worrying about what mood you would be in when I got home. Boys and even some of the teachers teasing me about the state and smell of my uniform because you were too off your face to buy washing powder, or any new school clothes. Walkin' around with my plastic schoolbag and my shoes flapping about like a pair of fuckin' flippers. Walkin' around shitting myself that some Irish bogeyman was goin' to hunt me down and torture me because I was the son of a British army man. Hmm- opportunities, opportunities. And then, when I turned sixteen, didn't I have to go and get a job to support the both of us? You certainly weren't goin' to. And don't get me started on..."

I was cut off mid rant. She was sitting, fag hanging out of the corner of her mouth, theatrically playing an invisible violin.

"Aww, poor wee Tommy. Do you want mummy to give you a hug? Maybe you want mummy to get her titty out and give you a suck- is that it? Ha ha ha, little orphan Tommy".

She finished her drink and got up to refill her glass.

Now, my temper was in full flow. Still surprisingly calm, I spoke through gritted teeth.

"Oh, mummy dear. I'll tell you what you can do, shall I?"

She turned to me, sarcastically smiling.

"Yea- go on. Tell me what I can do"

"You can go and fuck yourself. You stinking aul pathetic bitch. The fuckin cut of you"

I regretted saying it immediately. I will never forget the look she gave me. Until I die, that look will stay with me. A mixture of rage, shock, and worst of all hurt, etched on her face. As horrible and nasty as she could be, she occasionally let the mask slip and I could see just how vulnerable, fragile, and scared she really was.

I wanted to apologise immediately, to beg for forgiveness and tell her I didn't mean what I said.

But... I couldn't.

I felt like crying.

I wanted to slap her until she cried.

I wanted to hug her.

She continued to stare at me...that look. Then, she turned and filled her glass from the bottle. The glug-glug sound from the bottle, the only sound rising above the blanket of silence that enshrouded us.

I opened the door and left.

Halfway down the stairs I stopped and punched the wall until my fists were drenched in blood.

CHAPTER 16

Everything seemed to be coming together nicely for Neil.

He had found the woman who held his attention in a crowded place.

Her name was Máire. She was twenty-six, ten years younger than him. When she looked into his eyes, he felt the rest of the world fade away. When he spoke, she gazed at him as if in wonder. There was a childlike innocence about her. When he told a joke, or relayed a funny story, she held her stomach, much like a jolly fat person would. Sometimes when he spoke to her, she would play with her hair, not in a flirtatious way like most women would.

It was different...innocent and non-self-conscious.

Her hair was a deep brown that hung over her shoulders. Her face had a youthful freshness about it. Some would describe her cheeks as slightly chubby, Neil would say full and youthful. He knew from her features that by the time she hit sixty years, she would look no more than forty. Her skin, like her hair also had a glow to it. Some would say beauty is skin deep, but Neil knew the glow from her originated from her core...her soul. There was a goodness about her, a kindness that radiated through her skin. Her body was perfect. She was tall, about five six or so, but looked taller than she was. She had an athletic figure. Slim, but there were curves were there were supposed to be. Neil used to judge women like he judged cattle, trying to figure out which ones would produce a strong healthy child, but he suddenly thought of such behaviour now to be crude. She was slowly changing all his previous pre-conceptions and biases about life in general, changing them for the better. Her teeth had been one of the first features he noticed about her. Very small and uniform in size, splendidly white. He told her when he first met her that night.

"God...look at your teeth", he blurted out, his nerves getting the better of him. She had been taken aback slightly, self-consciously raising her hand to her mouth, replying; "Why, what's wrong with them?"

"No, nothing's wrong with them. They're very nice...very small". He began to blush.

She laughed and showed him one of the teeth that was still a baby tooth. It almost fitted in with the rest of her teeth, they were so small, validating his point entirely. She laughed at him all the time he rambled on about the size of her teeth, trying to dig himself out of a hole. Her beauty made him nervous and almost queasy at the same time. He wished for her to like him half as much as he liked her. A different feeling that was for him. Most women he didn't want to like him- didn't want them to get too attached to him. She was like no other woman though. Still nervously rambling on about her teeth he continued;

"You know you can tell how old a cow is by its teeth. Sure, why don't you open up and I'll see if it works on you"

She laughed heartily, again holding her stomach like a jolly Santa Clause.

"Ho ho, you are funny Neil. That is like something my brother would come off with", she said.

Neil realised that night he knew her brother, Fintan Smith. He was about four or five years younger than Neil, from outside Ballymoy. Neil had dealt with him in the past and had been impressed by his fairness and knowledge of cattle. He was a quiet fellow, but a very nice one too. Neil liked the fact that he knew and liked her brother. It made a big difference, he knew she was from good stock.

They arranged another few dates after that first night, each date being very relaxed and enjoyable, as Pete and Sarah would be there too. They made up a happy foursome. Pete and Sarah became more serious too. Pete told Neil after dropping him home one night he was thinking of proposing. Neil was glad. As much as he enjoyed his wild nights out with him, he didn't want Pete to dump Sarah and expect him to do the same with Máire. He was content now with Máire and wanted Pete and Sarah to be contented too.

A few weeks later Pete and Sarah broke up. Pete had been very quiet all week and Neil didn't want to ask him what was wrong, but he sensed something was up. He knew something was very wrong when Pete cancelled a night out in town that weekend. He claimed he wasn't feeling well and Neil didn't probe any further, taking his word for it. He however got the full story from Máire that night when he met her.

"Well, I'm glad the bastard didn't have the cheek to show up tonight", she said after Neil told her Pete wouldn't be coming out. Shocked at Máire's outburst, he asked; "Pete? Why, what's happened? What has he done?"

"He hasn't told you? The bastard. He only went and cheated on poor Sarah"

Taken aback by her response, Neil ordered at the bar, quickly trying to gather his thoughts and replied; "He cheated on Sarah? Who with?"

Máire then told him the story. The Saturday night before, after Pete took Sarah home, she invited him in. They both began to drink her father's whiskey they found in the cupboard. After a lot of whiskey Sarah rushed outside to get sick. Pete stayed in the house and continued drinking. It was then that Sarah's eighteen-year-old sister arrived home from a local dance. She had been sober, but later claimed that Pete told her it was his whiskey and more or less forced her to have some. He gave her a few large measures and seeing that she was becoming quite drunk, put his arm around her. He sweet talked her and eventually began kissing her. Just as he was getting into his stride, the girl's father, confused and sleepy, entered the room. Noticing the expensive bottle of whiskey that had been barely touched, now near empty, he went mad.

"Me fuckin' bottle. Ya wee fucker. Who the fuck do ye think ye are drinkin' me fuckin' whiskey?", he roared and began to run around the room after Pete, who was laughing because the man's Long Johns had come open at the front and his todger and balls were half hanging out, flapping around as he ran. Pete escaped from the house, jumped into his car, and drove home. The girl, frightened that her father would find out she had drunk his whiskey too, told all the next morning. Of course, Sarah had missed the whole episode as she had fallen asleep under a bush outside where she had been throwing up.

"Poor Sarah. I tell you Neil, if I see that bastard Kelly again, oh, God help him".

Neil had sat and listened to the whole story. He was saddened as he hoped the two of them would settle down with each other, but he couldn't stop himself from bursting into laughter.

"Oh Jesus, that Pete one. I'm not saying what he did was right, but was Sarah's daddy really running after him with his boyo flapping about?"

"It's not funny Neil", Máire defiantly replied, but her features were beginning to brighten and moments later the two of them were bent over laughing.

"It's not funny Neil, we shouldn't be laughing. But I'll tell you this much Neil Dillon, if you ever did that to me, you wouldn't *have* a boyo to flap around, as I'd cut it off the first chance I got"

The two then laughed even harder at that. He knew it was at that moment he made the decision to buy a ring the next day. Two weeks after that night, after leaving her home, he gave her the ring. She accepted and it had been the happiest moment of their lives.

Six months later they got married. It was a small wedding. Neil didn't have much of a family and certainly hadn't many friends. Máire seemed to be the same too but most of the congregation came from her side, and she complained her mother was the one doing all the inviting, not her. Pete performed the best man duties and Sarah was Máire's bridesmaid. Funny enough Pete and Sarah had made up, rekindling their relationship. Máire was even begrudgingly happy for them, knowing they made a good couple regardless of what had happened.

Máire moved in immediately after the wedding and Neil noticed a huge difference in the house in those first few weeks. She brought with her all sorts of little knick-knacks, little things that made a house feel like a home. Before she moved in, anyone could tell a lone male lived in the house. Now the walls that had once been bare, had mirrors and pictures hanging. The dusty, dirty floors now had rugs placed upon them, rugs that Neil secretly walked over bare footed at night as he loved the feel of them under his feet. Gone was the pungent smell of cow manure from his wellies, replaced with the sweet smell of fresh flowers and perfume. His favourite change was the delicious evening meals he was served at night, instead of the usual stale sandwich and lukewarm tea. Now he ate until he was full, before returning to his cosily furnished living room, to pull on his pipe and enjoy conversation and laughter with Máire for the rest of the night. They would talk until they were tired, then retire to bed where they would lie, holding each other, listening to the rain tap-tap off the roof. They were happy, Neil had never been happier. Every morning he woke, he would jump to his work, working all day on the farm, looking forward to his nights with Máire. He wanted for nothing, he felt his whole world was complete.

Relations with Maggie were even improving. He could see she liked Máire, even Maggie couldn't dislike her. The farm was thriving, Maggie even admitted one day that he had been right to close the mill and concentrate on the farm. He hadn't expected such a concession from her. She also seemed to be fond of Pete. It greatly pleased Neil to see that. He began to think she wasn't such a bad judge of character at all. Pete, only living a few doors from her had been good to her. He would deliver her meat from his shop and would never charge full price.

"He's a nice fella that Pete Kelly. Mind you, your father hated the sight of his, but I'm not one to judge a man on his father's past actions, as you know", Maggie said one day. Neil had a little laugh to himself at that statement. Sometimes Pete would give Maggie a lift out to Neil's as she liked to get out to see how things were going around the place. Máire would cook dinner and the four would sit and talk about what was happening around the country.

They were good times.

Although he had had his differences with Maggie over the years, he could see she was getting old and it saddened him, against his will. She seemed to be mellowing with age and she was his flesh and blood after all. He had to look after her, he had to see she was all right, Máire would have made him do it anyway, even if he hadn't wanted to.

He and Máire worked hard. He loved her work ethic. The two would get up at about half five every morning, breakfast was prepared and Neil would tend to the livestock. Máire would perform the housework and then help on the farm. Neil had always been organised with paperwork and keeping his taxes up to date, but Máire took it to a whole different level. She had performed all the paperwork for her brother and father, and still did when required, and her organisational skills were second to none. Her work had been so meticulous it had flagged up how bad Neil's record keeping and filing methods had been. She had tutted in disdain when Neil had shown her the little shoebox he had kept his receipts and different property certificates in. Within an hour she had filed everything in a filing cabinet she had brought with her. Everything had a place, Neil would no longer have to rifle around in the box to find some important piece of documentation when he required it.

She was a great gardener too. At the back of the house lay a small patch of grass, mostly weeds that Neil would occasionally take a scythe to, cutting them down so they wouldn't grow out of control. This had annoyed Máire. She made it her mission to convert the small plot into a beautiful little garden. Her father had come around and built a little wooden fence around it and Máire quickly got to work digging and reseeding. She had soon converted a weedy, lifeless eyesore into a vibrant and beautiful garden, complete with all sorts of beautifully coloured flowers, fruits, and vegetables which she would pick when ripe. They would be delicious when she incorporated them into her salads and desserts.

Neil, as a proud farmer had felt embarrassed when he only learned from Máire the virtues of compost in the growing of fruit and vegetables, grass, and plants. He had retired to his chair after another one of Máire's delicious cooked meals, as she cleared the dinner plates. Puffing hard on his pipe, trying to get it properly lit, he watched as Máire emptied potato skins and cabbage leaves into a large black bin, just out the back of the house. He walked out and stood beside her as she was scraping the last of the scraps into the bin.

"Máire, what are you doin' woman? This isn't the rubbish bin. I don't even know where it came from- did you get a new one?"

He looked inside and almost recoiled from the smell. The fumes of rotting food were sickening. Trying not to cough too much he said; "Jesus, Máire. I think this bin needs emptying. It shouldn't smell like that."

"My God, Neil" she replied; "Are you telling me you've never made your own compost before?"

"Compost? Sure, that's horse shite and straw is it not? What good is it if you're not growing mushrooms?"

Máire sighed. "There are different types of compost. If you let fruit and vegetables decompose it will produce the finest plant food you could ever imagine"

Neil laughed. "Worm food more like. Sure, you'll have the place coming down with rats and maggots in no time"

He could see she was trying to control her temper at that point. She would always pull a funny kind of expression and would remain quiet for a few moments before replying. He supposed she was counting to ten to calm herself down. He knew she had a feisty little side to her and it amused him greatly to wind her up sometimes and watch her go through these little motions of hers.

Suddenly, smiling sweetly and busying herself once more with the remains of the dinner, she responded; "Whatever you think Dillon. You keep the livestock alive and I'll keep my plants alive. I'll show you the results over time. I don't think you have the intelligence to understand"

Neil laughed and headed back to his armchair, thinking he had married a mad woman. That very spring, however, Máire indeed did prove him wrong. The little garden out the back bloomed with all the vivid colours of the rainbow. Never had Neil seen such an intensely coloured garden. Roses came up a deep, dark red. Daffodils were almost a luminous shade of yellow and the snowdrops looked like the flowers of heaven. She had re-seeded the weedy plot in the autumn and the grass that shot up resembled an emerald carpet- he had never seen grass like it.

"My God, Máire. What kind of fertiliser did you use on this garden? I've never seen growth like it in all my life."

Máire, then realising Neil had forgotten all about their little argument over the compost months earlier, gleefully took the opportunity to remind him.

"Well, well, well. Now, do you not remember giving off to me a few months back about throwing all the dinner leftovers into that bin outside? You said I'd have all the rats in the country about the place."

Suddenly remembering, he replied; "Aye, I do. Aul bits of leftover food and that. You said you'd turn it into compost?"

"Well, that's just what I did. I told you it was the best plant food known to man and you laughed at me", Máire replied, very satisfied with herself. "Come here to I show you it"

Neil walked over and opened the lid. Máire took a small trowel full of it out of the bin, and scattered it around the base of the rose bush.

"You see, I have been applying small amounts of the stuff to my plants all along and I also sprinkle some over the grass from time to time. No manure, no fertiliser, just this, homemade compost. The best plant food on earth."

Neil, taken aback by Máire's revelations, said; "You're damn right. I've never seen such growth. This garden is a wonder. And you tell me this stuff is simply made from rotting fruit and vegetables?"

Máire smiled triumphantly. "Yes, decomposing fruit and veg, that's it"

Neil stood back, taking in the grandeur of their garden. "Hmm, from rotting food, a beautiful garden is created", he said, feeling quite poetic.

The two stood, hand in hand in the beautiful morning garden. The sun was rising, its light reflecting off little crystalline drops of sleepy dew on the bushes. The birds sang sweetly and the slumbering cows in the back meadow lazily mooed and lapped water from the ditches.

Máire gave a satisfied little sigh and staring into the beautiful spring landscape, said; "Ah, from decay can come great beauty"

Gazing upon what she had created, Neil agreed whole heartedly.

Little moments like that occurred regularly throughout the years between the two. They constantly surprised, amazed and at sometimes annoyed each other. Their arguments never lasted long, Máire being the feisty one and Neil always having to make the first move to make up. But, their lives together had been mostly blissfully happy. They socialised very rarely, mostly only with Pete and Sarah, Maggie and Máire's parents. They both worked hard and enjoyed the fruits of their labour together.

Neil, encouraged and inspired constantly by his wife, became even more of a ground breaker in the farming trade. He built the first five link silo the country had seen. A monumental building, it took him two and a half years to erect, with the help of Pete and Máire's brother and father, building it mostly themselves. The year after the silo was built, he harvested silage -the first in the country to do so. Breaking the mould of making hay as a winter food for his cattle, he produced silage, a modern foodstuff requiring more modern machinery and farming methods. People had come from far and wide to witness this process in action. Neil barely noticed as he was totally immersed in his work, it all being new to him and quite stressful in its complexity. Máire noticed the flocks of people coming to witness all the new machinery he was employing and could barely contain her pride. Her brother and father, both seasoned and experienced farmers, also, commended Neil on his industry. The year after that he spread slurry on the fields. Again, people hadn't witnessed a large slurry tank out in the fields spraying sludge all over the grass. He had always been interested in farm machinery and new innovative techniques. He had relished those few years as farming technology was beginning to boom. The manual tasks were becoming automated. He had suffered through the years, like most other farmers, painstakingly carrying out manual chores that were too time consuming. He had always thought there had to be more efficient methods available. From the magazines and manuals, he subscribed to and received on a quarterly basis, he was learning that the farming machinery manufacturers were beginning to avail of technologies available to the automobile, manufacturing, and construction industries. To him, he wasn't a ground breaker in his field. He had simply researched through his magazines about what was happening in England, Europe and even America.

The other farmers in the country mostly annoyed and frustrated him. He could hear their sarcastic comments when at the mart and farmer's yards. "Ach, look at the big Yankee walkin' about, him and his big ideas", they would mock; "Thon boy doesn't want anything to do with us aul bollixes", he heard when passing by some men on the road; "All this machinery so he doesn't have to get his hands dirty".

He had heard all those snide, mocking whisperings when he was younger, now he was hearing them all again. Typical Irish hillbillies, too afraid to move with the times, who would rather do things the hard way, unnecessarily, rather than use their brains, Neil thought. The same men would sit in pubs at night, covered in shite, exhausted and feeling sorry for themselves rather than try a more efficient approach. Neil would get the work completed quickly, wash and change into a suit if he was heading out for the evening.

"Ah would you look at the big dandy walkin' about in his suit, boys", he could hear them utter under their breaths as he entered the pub and ordered his drinks. He didn't care though. He would enjoy the craic and his evening with Pete or Máire or whoever else was with him. He would always have the last laugh on those who attempted to mock him though, as he watched on as they slumped over the bar and various tables snoring like pigs when he was leaving.

"These fuckin' people annoy me Pete. Sitting up laughing at what I'm trying to do. I work harder than any of them, I just try to engage my brain to make a make a job go a bit smoother. If that means buying a bit of equipment to do so, then so be it. Look at the fuckin' cut of them Pete, fuckin' degenerates the lot of them"

Pete laughed. "Don't talk to me Neil, don't I know these men are numbskulls. They embrace the Irish stereotype of gallant failures. Too stuck in their ways and too ignorant to embrace any change, even if it is for the better and might make their miserable lives a bit more bearable."

Taking a draw on his cigarette, his eyes narrowing into little slits, he looked at Neil sincerely and said; "You, Dillon, are an innovator. A leader. You are ahead of your time, boy"

Neil laughed; "And you, Mr Kelly, are full of mad dog's shite"

"No. I'm serious. You have to be admired. You do your own thing, don't give a fuck about what people think about you. Look at what you've done to that place of yours. You could have sat back like the other assholes in this country with your father's land. Farmed a few acres, made a bit of a living and been happy with your lot. But no, you do things on a bigger scale. You've bought up more ground and grew and grew. You're bigger than your father ever was. Even Maggie talks about you fondly some nights when I drop her home."

Neil laughed; "Aye I'm sure she fuckin' does"

Pete drew on his cigarette and exhaled through his nostrils.

"You underestimate her. She'll never tell it to your face, but you can tell she's proud of what you've done to the place. She's not a bad aul sort you know"

Again, Neil laughed; "Aye, she's all heart. Let's not talk about the aul bag if you don't mind. I don't like thinking about her at night in case I get nightmares"

"Aye, fair enough" conceded Pete.

They parted ways and went home. Driving home, Neil began to think about what Pete told him about Maggie, about her speaking well of him. He laughed aloud though when thinking about it further as he had learned to take what Pete said with a pinch of salt. He couldn't help to wonder though if she did indeed speak highly of him. It certainly would be a first he knew, also very unlikely, but deep down he hoped it was true. He arrived home and as usual recounted the whole episode of his night to Máire, who laughed and felt angered in equal measure to himself about the night's events.

They had been together for just over three blissfully happy years. His house had become a home and his business had thrived ten-fold since. However, every time he looked into her eyes he couldn't help but feel a dark blend of anxiety and sadness washing over him.

He had always done right by her. He had money to burn, their lives were happy and comfortable, but he could see how badly she yearned for a child. He did too, more than anything. Most people who married followed suit with a baby within the first year or two, but it hadn't happened for them. It pained him. She would soon turn thirty and he, himself would soon turn forty. Most women in the country of Máire's age already had three or four children, most had even stopped having them by that age. He could see she feared it not happening for them. He knew they would both gladly give up all they had and all they had built, to be blessed with a baby. They knew they had so much to offer a child too. He wouldn't repeat the mistakes of his own father and he knew Máire would make a great mother. They never spoke about their desire to have a child openly, perhaps both thinking that if they brought it up, it would only raise an issue that perhaps wasn't even there. Even so, Neil knew that if they couldn't produce a child, they would still be happy growing old together anyway.

But, still he knew the lack of a child created a huge void in their lives.

Six months later, he dropped Máire into Dunbay. He was heading to the mart, and Máire wanted to go shopping. He kissed her goodbye and they went their separate ways. A few hours later, he collected her from Maggie's house. She seemed different to him that day, seemed to have more of a warm glow about her than usual. In the car on the way home, he spoke excitedly as per usual of his purchases, telling her how great the new livestock would prove to be. She seemed distant, not as attentive, and excited about his news as normally.

"Hi...are you ignoring me? Why are you not hanging on my words like you usually do?", Neil joked.

As if being awoken from a dream, she suddenly sat bolt upright in her seat. Smiling sweetly at him she said; "I got a new purchase today in town too"

"What did you get? Anything nice?", Neil asked.

She beamed at him and tapped her stomach.

"Oh, I see", Neil laughed; "Treat yourself to a wee cup of tea and slice of cake in town, did you? You should have said and I could have joined you"

"No. I haven't eaten all day. I've...been to the doctors"

Neil glanced quickly at her, then set his eyes back on the road.

"The doc...", it was then the penny dropped. He looked at her. Tears were standing in her eyes, but she beamed from ear to ear. He pulled the car over.

"You're not...", he pointed to her abdomen; "Are you?"

She nodded. A little teardrop fell onto her cheek.

At that moment, they embraced, Neil punching the steering wheel of the car in delight.

In that embrace, the two of them felt the rest of the world melt away into insignificance.

Now, they felt complete.

CHAPTER 17

Neil sat at the defeated fire. It saddened him that something that only an hour before had burned yellow and red in magnificent, powerful ribbons of heat, had now been reduced to a small mass of greyish cold matter. Such was life he thought.

He poked at the ashes with a length of metal he kept for such purposes. No change occurred in the ashes, no flames arose in defiance. He didn't expect them to, but he thought it would be wasteful not to at least try. He hated that moment. Every night it happened. His fire, that he worked so hard to put together would burn out and die, leaving the room which was impossible to heat, with its various drafts and cracks, to grow even colder until it was unbearable to endure anymore, forcing him to go to bed.

He hated his bed and bedroom. He hated to go to bed alone, to put his arms out, only to be met by a cold, damp mattress instead of the warm, sweet smelling body of his sleeping wife. He couldn't bear to walk past Seamie's bedroom, with his little bed in the corner of the room. The emptiness of the room echoed the emptiness of his own soul. The door remained closed. If he couldn't see inside, he could imagine Seamie was inside, dreaming his beautiful dreams, lying flat on his back with his little arms outstretched above his head as he always had.

He rose from his chair, stretched himself as if he were going to retire to a warm bed for a night's sleep and headed not up the stairs, but outside into the cold night instead. The wind seemed to blow straight from the Arctic Circle itself, though he didn't flinch. He was as cold as ice already, the thought of what he intended to do, chilling his soul to the core.

He headed directly to the out-house directly opposite his dwelling. He opened the door, the interior bathed in darkness. It didn't matter to him how dark it was. He could walk to where he was going unaided by light or even memory, he had walked it so often. When he arrived at the spot, he could almost feel the groove marks of his boots from previous visits. He felt around for a little until he took hold of what he was looking for. His eyes were beginning to adjust to the darkness of the building. He could suddenly see everything as if daylight had suddenly appeared through the cracks and crevices of the building.

He took up his position, balancing himself on the edge of the cattle trough. He swung the rope out to make it taught, straightening out any kinks which had manifested on it since the last time. He placed the noose around his neck, then placing one hand above his head and the other around the noose, he pulled both ends until he was on the verge of choking. He waited for a minute or so, still balancing on the trough, hoping this time he would succeed. He felt no fear or horror about what he was to attempt, afraid only that he would once again fail. Always being spiritual, fully believing, and faithful in the existence of God and Heaven, he knew he would soon be reunited with Seamie and Máire. Because of his belief, he allowed himself one little luxury, one little memory about them before he jumped.

He thought of the day Pete had driven him home after taking a dozen or so cattle to the slaughter house. He had always been sentimental and felt deeply guilty about selling the cows he had reared from calves for their meat. He almost felt like he had betrayed them. It had been a beautiful summers evening, the type of evening that made a man think God had indeed made the *earth* as his heaven. Still hot, yet with a fresh smelling summer breeze that blew lazily through heavily leaved trees. The senses overloaded, the type of evening when youth is universal and death, decay, and illness all seemed impossible.

He walked down the lane that evening towards home, not sober, but not exactly drunk either. His melancholy about betraying his beloved cows for money, slowly being eased by the beauty of the evening. Then, in the immediate horizon, two figures came into his view. One was tiny, the other larger. The little figure began moving quickly towards him, unsteady at first, but then suddenly finding its feet and gathering speed. The larger figure followed in its trail. Then he could hear them as they grew closer, both giggling, Seamie shouting "Daddy, daddy". Neil ran towards them, gathering Seamie into his arms, laughing too and slightly out of breath. He kissed Máire and she said; "We've missed you today Daddy"

"And I've missed you both too", Neil replied.

"Hope your hungry big man. I've been cooking and baking all day, and wee Seamie's been helping me too"

The three of them continued down the lane towards the house, laughing and joking together in the warm evening sun. They knew there couldn't have been a happier family on the face of the earth.

As Neil stood on the brink of the trough, balancing himself, as if on a knife edge, he allowed himself a smile at that last blissful memory. That summers evening to him had been the closest to heaven he thought possible in his mortal life.

He knew the one little step forward would bring him back to that moment.

He would be with them again.

He hoped it would work this time.

He decided to count to three.

One…two…he jumped. Numbness followed. Darkness.

He had done it. Finally, it had worked.

He waited a few seconds wondering if he would see the "white light" people talked about in near-death experiences.

He waited another few seconds. Then…the horror visualised in front of him. As he opened his eyes, after a few seconds, his eyes adapting to the darkness, he began to see the familiar surroundings around him. The two windows on either side of the door, the wheel barrow in the corner. He found himself lying on the ground. He lay there for a few moments, fumbling around to locate where the rope was. His eyes were fully adapted to the dark now and he could see as well as he could in the daylight. He looked up at the various broken rafters from his previous unsuccessful attempts. The rafter upon which he had tied his rope around had remained unbroken on this occasion. He fingered the rope to see if it was still in place. Then he found it. The rope had snapped in two, just above the noose. He couldn't believe it. He sat on the ground aghast.

"How many fuckin' times?" he roared. "How many fuckin', fuckin', fuckin' times?"

He sat with his head between his hands, totally defeated. He wondered just what type of cursed existence he had, it seemed even death had turned his back on him.

He couldn't help at that moment think of the day he and Pete ploughed the field at the bottom of the road. Could that simple, ignorant mistake possibly have caused all the tragedies that be-felled him. It must have, he thought. Why else had so much misfortune visited him?

As he sat there thinking about it, a sudden gust of wind blew through the outhouse. Out of nowhere appeared a tatty newspaper. Even through the darkness he could almost see the brownness of it from age. He remained where he was, not moving. The paper fell directly in front of him. He could make out the large headline at the top of the front page of the local paper;

"The Dunbay Times"

As he read the headline it seemed as if a lightning bolt ran down the base of his spine.

"TWO DEAD IN LISNADERRY BLAZE TRAGEDY"

He slumped further to the ground. He couldn't read any more. He wretched unproductively, he hadn't eaten in days after all, perhaps even weeks.

He lay on the cold outhouse concrete floor and sobbed uncontrollably, his body rocking back and forth.

He cried the cry of a child.

Unapologetic, futile and with the full gusto of despair.

CHAPTER 18

I should have gone straight home that night. I should have stopped by the off-licence on the way, bought a bottle of vodka and drank it until I fell unconscious. I was too angry to be in the company of others. No good could possibly have come from it. But, like the fool I was, I decided to go and meet Brian anyway.

He had been raving about a new bar that opened in the city. It was supposed to have been frequented by actors and pop stars, London's cool crowd. The cool crowd that Brian was desperately attempting to be part of recently.

He had grown his hair long and began wearing a lot of leather. He started hanging out with new people who had long hair and dressed in a lot of leather too. He even began ending his sentences with the word "man" a lot, much to my annoyance and Dan's great amusement. "Thon hairy wee gobshite", he would laugh; "What is he tryin' to be- a fuckin' hippy or something?".

I didn't know what he was turning into, but I didn't like what he was beginning to partake in.

I arrived at the bar earlier than Brian and his friends. I ordered a double vodka and received little change from a twenty. It made me even angrier. Fuck him and his pretentious asshole friends I thought. I would rather have been in a boozer with sawdust and blood on the ground with all the building site crew. I finished quickly and ordered another double, wondering how long I could last with those prices. I realised if I bought one round for Brian and his friends, my week's wages would be almost gone.

I received my drink and turned around to see Brian and three others swagger into the bar.

"Tommy, my man. What's happenin'?", Brian greeted me clasping my hand in a vertical handshake. His behaviour embarrassed me a little. One of his ears had been recently pierced and he wore a pair of skin tight black jeans and a large pair of Dr Martens. One of his friends, Rick, had a large ring go right through his nose. It looked to be infected though, as under closer inspection a crusty yellow mass of tissue surrounded the hole. There was another man with them, a very small man with lank greasy hair and a little weasly looking moustache. His name... Pisscoat. I was about to ask why he was called that, until I caught a whiff of him and no longer felt the need to enquire. The fourth member of the group was a Scottish girl named Karen. She too wore a heavy looking leather jacket and had many piercings on her face. I was trying to figure out if she was the girlfriend of someone, doubting very much she would be with Brian. He had always been a ladies' man and she was certainly not his type. She was around five feet tall and probably the same in width. She waddled when she walked and sure didn't make up for her shortcomings in appearance with personality.

If Brian thought those were the cool kids, I hoped he didn't label me as such.

They all headed to the bar and bought halves of beer each, much to my relief- as I said, one round and the week's wages were as good as gone. We sat in the corner of the bar around a little round table. Pisscoat sat rolling a joint whilst taking very small sips from his beer. The conversation was bland. They talked about obscure bands and weird films. Pisscoat passed the joint around. Everyone in the bar was smoking. It was one of those places were no-one batted an eyelid at such activities.

Brian took a pull on it. "Ah man, that's some good shit", he said, wearing a stupid look on his face. "Take a pull on that Tommy".

"Nah, I'm OK thanks. Been on the piss most of the day and I feel weird when I mix them", I replied.

It was the truth... to a certain extent. I liked to feel either stoned or drunk and when I smoked and drank at the same time, I felt neither or. It felt like some sort of strange equilibrium state. The main reason I didn't want to partake in the smoking though was because of the company I was in. I liked to smoke in the presence of friends, people I trusted and could have a laugh with. I neither trusted or could have a laugh with these people.

Pisscoat seemed OK. He was a jovial little creature. He talked nothing but bollocks, but seemed harmless- if not a little on the thick side. The girl, Karen, had no spleen. I knew she had no spleen within two minutes of meeting her. She spoke with a broad Scottish accent and laughed like a hyena if Brian or Rick said anything remotely funny. If I, or Pisscoat said anything amusing, she would merely look at us, stone-faced with a readymade sarcastic reply.

I was quiet at first. I was trying to assess these characters. They fascinated me to a certain extent. I couldn't figure out why Brian was associating with them. We always shared the same circle of friends, always liked the same type of people. These people certainly weren't my type and I couldn't see how they were his either.

Everyone bought another drink for themselves and I got another double vodka. They smoked more joints, then Brian and Rick went to the toilet together and came back at the same time. It was obvious they were coked up. The two babbled on relentlessly, jumping from one tedious subject to another in no logical sequence. Rick seemed to be the focal point of the group and when he went to the toilet the conversation dimmed. At that point I leant over and whispered to Brian; "What the fuck? You're on coke now. When did you start that shite?"

"Relax man. It's only a bit of nose powder, we're all doing it in college. Feel free to try some if you want, it's really good gear"

"Nah, you're all right. You must be earning some dough to be able to afford that shite?"

"Ha-ha. Work hard and play hard. That's my motto man"

I didn't like it. This wasn't the Brian I knew and grew up with. He was acting completely differently. I worried about him. These people seemed dangerous...cold. I knew he was only doing it for a different experience, but he was like me, he had an addictive personality. Cocaine did not exactly lend itself well to an addictive personality.

"Well, just be careful" I said; "Don't be buying it for all these assholes".

At that point, Rick walked back to where he had been sitting. I'd forgotten how drunk I was up to that point and had forgotten to whisper the last sentence into Brian's ear. Rick sat down and stared at me. Brian nervously laughed. "OK, fuckin' daddy". They all laughed, except Rick and me, of course.

I hadn't liked the look of him from the off. He was a big fucker. He had a huge head, almost horse like. Big and muscular, all his fingers decked in rings and a heavy looking pair of Dr Martens on his feet. He looked like he could cause a lot of damage.

"Who are the assholes?", he asked, looking straight into my eyes.

"Ah, just these dickheads we work with on the site, Rick. Typical fuckin' Paddy's, tight as a duck's ass. You know the type.", Brian lied on my behalf, trying desperately to avoid any violence between us.

They all laughed. Rick looked a little disappointed nothing was going to kick off. I remained quiet, took a sip of my drink, and felt a little disappointed too. Much to my relief, Brian stood up, put on his coat and said; "Hey fuck this place. I wanna get fucked up and the only thing getting fucked is my wallet with the prices these cunts are charging. Let's go somewhere else"

No one objected. We all downed our drinks and got up, grabbing our coats to join him.

"I'm gonna kill that wee cunt Rob" said Brian. "The place to be in London, eh? Classy women...easy classy women to be exact, and great music. He didn't mention the prices, did he? Little prick"

We headed to another bar about half a mile down the road. Brian and I had been there before. It was a lot more down market but a whole lot less expensive. It had a good atmosphere, the previous bar having the atmospheric nature of the moon.

When we arrived, the place was hiving. We managed to get another little corner of the bar to sit in. They automatically went to order their own drinks, a round system not even considered...unsociable pricks. I didn't mind though as I was on the doubles and didn't feel like downsizing to singles for the sake of others buying rounds. I knew people who would insist on ordering doubles whilst in a round and I always thought of such an act as incredibly disrespectful and greedy. I sure was greedy for it, but would never expect anyone to pay for my greed.

I picked up the pace even further, the reduction in prices encouraging me to do so. Brian noticed and said; "Man, fuckin' relax. How much have you put away so far?"

"Not fuckin' enough"

They went back to their bland conversations and I couldn't be bothered with them anymore. My mind turned again to the encounter with my mother and the vodka seemed to fan the flames that burned within me. I didn't care. I wanted to erupt, needed to erupt. Sometimes I couldn't bear the thought that she was inside me. I was part of her. She, her flesh, and blood were like a cancer or virus that existed within me. No matter what I did, she was there. At least some cancers could be cut or burned out. She had ruined my life, but I knew I shared a lot of her characteristics and it killed me that I did. I thought on many an occasion that my father must have been almost saintly as I knew deep down I wasn't all bad. Surely that must have come from him, his goodness balancing up my personality so I wasn't a complete monster.

Brit or no brit he must have been all right.

I could feel my mother's genetics being expressed in me, as I was now in the mood for a row. Some people, when they felt that way would say they felt the devil in them. Not me. I could feel my mother there instead and I hated myself for it.

My thoughts were interrupted when Karen shouted across the table to me; "Are those bastards at it again?"

She was referring to the three others who had disappeared once more to the toilets.

I wasn't in the mood to talk, especially not to her.

"Yea. Think so".

She laughed. "What are they like?"

I looked over at her. She was now smiling at me, playing with her hair a little.

Oh, shit! I knew it. I knew she would eventually find the attraction. I had never been a Casanova, far from it-Brian perhaps could claim a stake to that title. However, if I walked into a room with ninety-nine beautiful, intelligent, heart achingly desirable women and one total weirdo with weight, hygiene, and personality defects it would be guaranteed the ninety-nine would be attracted to Brian and the one bomb scare to me.

I looked over at her. She had even begun to bat her eyelids at me in what she probably thought was a seductive and playful little gesture. She couldn't have been more wrong. Her lashes were caked in mascara, appearing as one clump instead of many pretty little individuals. The whites of her eyes had an unhealthy yellowish hue. I felt queasy just looking at her.

"So, do you snort a bit yourself?" she asked

"No", I answered; "You?"

The flirtatious smile disappeared and her expression changed instantly to anger, brows furrowed and nostrils flaring, she shouted; "I've goat nay fuckin' spleen", the volume loud enough to alert other drinkers nearby to stop chatting and look over at us.

I laughed. "Really? You've no spleen? I never knew"

Her expression changed again to a flirtatious one.

"Oh, I'm sorry. I should have told you"

She sure was a rare case.

"I was being sarcastic. You've only told me you've no spleen about twenty-five times since I met you. And, so what? What the fuck is the big deal about having no spleen anyway? It's not as if you don't have a liver.", I snapped back. Immediately her expression turned to one of anger again.

"Ya fuckin' cunt", she shouted "How would you like to have nay spleen, eh? Ye huv nay fuckin' idea"

I leant over the table towards her. "Listen. I'd cut my own spleen out right now with a rusty kitchen knife and give it to you, if it meant that you would finally shut the fuck up about it"

She looked horrified. She didn't reply. She shook her head and inevitably began to cry. I got up and went to the bar to get another vodka.

When I got back to the table the three had arrived back, Karen obviously still sobbing and milking the sympathy vote. Pisscoat and Rick were sitting hugging her, trying to console her. Brian, obviously coked off his tits, sat fidgeting with his fingers, sniffing relentlessly. He looked at me and said; "What'd you say to Karen, man? She's really upset"

"I just asked her what a spleen was and told her she could have mine if she wanted"

"Ya lyin' bastid! No ye didn't. Ya dinnae understand. It's a fuckin' disability, and you talk to me the way you did? Ya piece of fuckin' scum". She was screaming now. The situation was turning ugly. People were quiet around us. I would have been embarrassed on any other occasion, a hysterical bitch screaming at me in public, but I didn't care. I was too pissed and numb to care. Again, I felt the anger rise within me. I was just about to give the bitch both barrels when Brian reached over, touched me on the knee and silently pleaded with me not to start on her. I took a deep breath. I had never been a charmer with women, but I knew I could get around this one. As I said, the attraction was there.

I put my hands up. "Ok, Ok. I was out of order. I'm sorry love. I've had a hard day and I lashed out. Unfortunately, you were in the wrong place at the wrong time. Don't take it personally, I'm just an insensitive dickhead. Sorry" I lied through my teeth. I had meant every word of what I had said when insulting her, but I didn't want to ruin Brian's night.

It worked. She was drying her tears now and a smile surfaced on her face. "You're a right bastard, aren't ya?", she playfully asked. "OK. I accept your apology. You're probably too stupid to know what a spleen is anyway"

"Yea. I thought it was somewhere up your asshole", I lied.

"Up your fuckin' asshole! Ha-ha, oh my God", she laughed.

And that was that, all was forgiven. I just had to sit there for the rest of the night and pretend to be nice to her unless she would kick off again.

Annoying as she was, she wasn't exactly the main irritant at the time. Rick had begun staring at me very menacingly. He didn't like me, obviously, and I sure didn't like him either.

The drink kept flowing. I became even more drunk. I became so drunk that I glanced in Karen's direction at one stage and doubted my previous assessment on her hideousness. My semi-conscious screamed at me though to stay well clear. To wake next morning, angry and sick beside such a being would probably be enough to push me over the edge.

If Brian had been desperately avoiding an argument or violence occurring, then I don't know what he had been thinking when he brought up the subject of Anglo-Irish politics.

"I mean. I don't know what the fuck they're playing at. Don't they realise they're making it so hard for their own people living in Britain and around the world. Going around blowing shit up, killing and maiming innocent people...fuckin' animals man"

He had upped the tempo with the coke taking, they all had. Not only were they disappearing to the toilet every ten minutes but they were now brazenly snorting it from a key where we sat. He was talking at one hundred miles an hour when I butted in, against all my better judgement; "They're not just blowing shit up for the sake of it. They must do it, to make a statement"

Rick leaned forward to me. I had given him his opening.

"And what statement would that be?", he asked.

"The statement is clear. Get the fuck out of our country or we will continue our war. We have taken your shit for over eight hundred years and now it must fuckin' stop", I replied.

"Who has to get out of the country. The soldiers?", he asked.

"Yea. Soldiers...Brits. Out to fuck"

"And how do you get them out? Kill them?"

"It's a war. Casualties are inevitable", I nonchalantly replied.

His immediate laugh was laced with bitterness. He shook his head in disdain and said; "Do you know my uncle was blown up by an IRA bomb in Belfast. How'd you feel about that?"

"He shouldn't have been there in the first place. What do you want me to say? Simple as."

I looked around at the others. Karen was once again glaring at me. Pisscoat was fidgeting and Brian was sitting with his head in his hands. Rick laughed and leaned forward in his seat towards me once more.

"Well. It appears your mother doesn't share your extreme views, does she?"

My head began to swim. I was thrown completely. "What? What are you talking about?"

"Well…", he started, before taking a large sip from his beer and looking around at the others, smirking; "She was fond of a bit of Brit cock, was she not?"

My blood boiled. "What? Who the fuck told you that…", before the penny dropped. I looked at Brian. He remained sitting with his head in his hands. He stole a glance at me through his fingers.

"You bastard. Who the fuck told *you* about that?", I shouted at him.

"Your ma, Tommy. She told mine years ago. I'm sorry for telling these ones. It slipped out. I didn't mean any harm"

I couldn't believe it. The evil old bitch. She had always threatened to tell people, but I never believed she would go through with it. My mind raced. Brian, Dan…all the building site crew must have known. Oh, God. What must they have thought of me? They had either felt pity or were laughing behind my back. I didn't know what was worse. I snapped back to the present as Rick was now standing over me.

"So, dickhead. Do you want to come outside and see how much mouthing off you can do out there then?", he said, very calmly which was disturbing given the explosive circumstances.

I had never backed down from a fight before and certainly wasn't going to start now. I was ready for the cunt. I gulped down what was left in my glass, and smiled, through gritted teeth. "Certainly"

I got up from my seat. Brian was pleading with the both of us not to go out. I looked at him, straight in the eye.

"Fuck you", I said; "Fuck you for the back-stabbing cunt you are".

He merely sat looking at the ground in shame. He didn't reply.

"Come on then prick, or Rick or whatever the fuck they call you", I said, heading towards the door.

"Rip his fucking head aff Rick", I heard Karen screaming from behind us.

As I approached the exit, I frantically wracked my brain thinking of what way I would approach the fight. Go for a one punch wonder or grapple with him until I got him to the ground. He was a big fucker so I knew I would have to go for the former option to stand a chance.

Just as I went to push the door open, I felt a sudden blow to the top of my head. I struggled to remain conscious, the room and the people in it swirled around me. I could hear screams from women, then noticed the shocked and horrified faces looking at me. I felt a warm stream running down the side of my head. I put my hands up and found them covered in blood. My legs buckled from under me. When I hit the floor, I looked up to see Rick standing above me, broken bottle in his right hand.

The cowardly bastard had bottled me from behind!

The next thing I remember was him kicking me twice in the guts. I saw Karen jumping up and down with glee behind him. Brian stood behind her, a look of horror and shame plastered all over his face.

The last thing I remembered was a boot straight to my face.

To my surprise, it didn't come from Rick.

The culprit...Pisscoat!

Then the lights went out.

CHAPTER 19

Nine months passed by and the baby was born. They named him Seamus, after Máire's late grandfather. Both parents couldn't believe what they had created. To them, he was a little bundle of perfection. An absolute bruiser of a child too, obviously taking after Neil. Nine pounds and eight ounces he weighed, with a full head of brown hair. Maggie even fell in love with the child. Neil had never seen her so affectionate and caring around another human-he never believed she was capable of it, but... she had surprised him.

Neil, Maggie, and Pete had gone to the hospital on the night the baby was born, to see him for the first time. They told Neil to go in first and spend a few minutes alone with Máire and the child, the first minutes of being a family together.

When he walked into the room, Máire was sitting on the edge of the bed cradling the sleeping baby. He had never seen her look so tired, she looked almost grey in colour from her exertions. When he first laid eyes on little Seamus, he had to use every ounce of restraint not to burst into tears. Máire smiled sweetly at him, he had never seen her so happy.

"Well... say hello to your new boy, Daddy"

Neil leant down beside them and took the baby's tiny hand in his own.

"Hello Seamus", was all he could say, so lost for words he was.

The baby didn't stir. Máire laughed. "Are you not going to take him?"

"Aye, all right", he replied, unsure what to do next.

"Here...hold him like this, cradle like him so", Máire instructed him.

Awkwardly, Neil took him into his arms. He had never handled anything so delicately before.

"Well done", Máire said, smiling. "Well, what do you think of him?"

"Ach Jesus, he's perfect."

"He sure is", Máire replied.

The door knocked, and Maggie and Pete walked in. No sooner had Neil taken Seamus into his arms he had to let him go. Maggie almost ripped the baby from his arms in her eagerness to hold him.

"Hello little man. What do we call you then?", asking the parents in her round about manner.

"Seamus", answered Máire. "We're still thinking about a middle name, but we have plenty of time for that"

"Seamus?", Maggie responded, not taking her eyes off the baby "That's...interesting". They could tell by her reaction she didn't like the name. They didn't care. Seamus was their child, not hers and they liked the name.

"He's lovely Máire. Well done", said Pete.

Neil was beside himself with joy but felt bad when he looked at Máire, seeing how drained she was. Bloodstains were visible on her nightgown and she groaned in pain whenever she moved. He knew from calving hundreds of cows in his time that childbirth was a brutal business.

"Oh", cried Maggie "Someone's done a poo-poo", lifting the baby's bottom to her nose. Like most women of her age, even though she never had any children of her own, she turned out to be a dab hand at changing nappies. Máire had offered to change him and Neil noticed her relief when Maggie insisted. He knew she would probably be as clumsy as him at that early stage.

Maggie was a natural, though. Neil always thought she should have entered the medical profession. There was no warmth in her personality, she was almost clinical, cold. He thought she would have made a great matron.

Neil almost did a double take at the baby when Maggie was in the middle of changing him. Unluckily for him, Pete was on hand to give a running commentary.

"Holy good God. Would ye look at the size of the tool on him. You tell the men in your family they have my respect, Máire. I've seen the big man's boyo and this child doesn't get *that* from his side of the house."

Máire laughed.

"That's terrible talk to be at Peter", Maggie scolded, but it was obvious to all she was trying to subdue a smile forming on her lips.

"Aul cunt", Neil said under his breath. He knew she would like Pete's statement, as it was both derogatory to him and laced with filth. He knew deep down she was a frustrated, repressed old crone who loved a bit of smut. He threw a dirty look at Pete, Pete shrugging his shoulders in innocence and both men began to laugh.

"He sure is a fine lookin' baby", Neil said, and all agreed.

They left about an hour later to let Máire and the baby get some sleep. The birth had been a difficult one and the hospital wanted to keep them in for a night as a precautionary measure. "Nothing to worry about", Máire told Neil. "They just want to build me up as I haven't eaten and barely slept in three days and I'm a wee bit unsteady on my feet. I'm fine. You go and have a few drinks with Pete. Not too much, mind you, as I need you to come and collect us in the morning"

Again, Pete and Maggie went out first to give the new family a few moments on their own. They were finally a family. Both had never been happier. After much kissing and many failed farewells, Neil eventually left, driving Maggie home before heading south to Ballymoy. There, he met with Pete and Máire's father and brother in their local pub.

They drank the night away. He lost count of the number of times Pete told the men about young Seamus and how well-endowed he was, much to their amusement. Soon the whole bar heard the story too, everyone laughing and congratulating the party on their new delivery. Of course, after a few drinks, Neil saw the funny side and eventually joined in, playing along to how under-endowed he was himself. The stories became more exaggerated and all in the pub remained in high spirits for the rest of the night.

It had been the best day of Neil's life.

Later that night, as the stories dried up and the laughter eventually dimmed, Máire's father and brother left the pub, leaving Pete and Neil alone together at the bar. As was his usual manner, Pete would change from his jovial self to one of a more serious nature.

"Listen, I was thinking to myself just today…", he said, until Neil interrupted with; "Did it hurt?"

"No…no, shut up you. I'm tryin' to be serious here. I was just thinking today that things are going to change for you and Máire…in a good way, a very good way"

"Jesus, you don't need to tell me, I know that more than anyone"

"I know…I know you do, but I was thinking financially. I mean, children cost a lot of money and let's face it you don't have too much floating about right now"

Neil straightened in his chair, a large frown descending upon his features; "What the fuck do you know about my finances, ye bollocks?".

He tried to keep his response upbeat and jovial, but he couldn't help being slightly riled by Pete's statement.

Pete took his response in the spirit it was meant. Laughing he replied; "No, no, I don't know anything about your finances, but I just thought you mustn't have too much cash at your disposal with the amount of ground you've been buying up recently. I mean, you must own half the country by now…the greedy cunt that you are"

Both men laughed at that.

"I'm just sayin', you're bound to have all your money tied up in land and machinery and whatever. I just thought now you are building a family, you'll need a few quid in the bank that you can actually spend"

Neil sipped at his drink.

"You're right…you're spot on. I never thought of that. I suppose I could sell a few cattle from time to time to gather up a few quid-couldn't I?", Neil replied.

"Well…I suppose you could, but you could end up living a very hand to mouth existence doing that. You're not the type of man to do that. Most assholes around the country live that way, not you though. You're too fuckin'…smart"

Neil smiled. He liked that compliment.

"Well, what would you suggest then?", Neil asked. This time it was Pete's turn to straighten up in his chair.

"Sell some of that land of yours. I mean, what do you need all that land for anyway?"

Pete's suggestion surprised Neil.

"Well...land is land. They can make everything these days, but they're not makin' any more land, are they?"

Pete nodded. "I agree"

"A man's property is his legacy when he dies. All I possess will go to that wee man born today, when I go. That's the way I see things"

"Oh, I agree with you one hundred percent", Pete replied.

Neil laughed and added; "Not to mention, who would I sell to anyway? Who's got money to buy land around this country, and sure the fuckers would put an insulting bid in if they could, to annoy me"

Pete straightened up further in his seat. Hc coughed, to clear his throat.

"Well come to mention it, *I* was actually thinkin' about buyin' a bit"

"Good man. Good for you", Neil replied, "Where were you thinkin' of buyin?'"

"Well, I've been thinkin' about it for a while. I could get a loan against the butchers, a good-sized loan too. I was going to talk to you about it, but never got a chance"

"Talk away. What's on your mind?"

"Well, my father done a lot for me in the past. I mean, it's no secret he funded the buying of the butchers and got me set up with a place to live and all. As much as I enjoyed England, its fuckin' good to get home and he played a big part in that"

Neil raised his glass. "To Frank Kelly. A decent man". The two men clinked their glasses together and drank.

"He done a damn lot for me and I would like to pay something back. I'd like to make him proud of me"

"Good man. And I'm sure you will", Neil remarked.

"So...I was thinking, and I think it's a damn good idea that's goin' to help everybody-you included..."

Neil laughed; "Sure what's any of this got to do with me?"

"You see, I was thinking about buyin' my father's land back that you bought from him. I would give you a fair price. You would be helping me out and I would be helping you-it would be money in the bank for you and the family"

Neil sat for a few moments. He was trying to process what Pete had just said, before answering. Pete waited silently and patiently for a reply.

"No. I'm not goin' to sell to you. The reason I won't, with no disrespect to your father's land, is because it's too rocky. If you can get money from the bank and are planning to buy land, do so, I highly recommend it. But *that* land, it's not up to a hell of a lot"

Pete took a sip from his drink, before replying; "You're missing the point Neil. It's not about the quality of the land, it's about pride. I would be proud to buy my father's land back. He would be proud of me for doin' so"

Neil's expression suddenly changed to one of anger. "Don't fuckin' talk to me about family pride. Look at my father. Pride ruined him. There's a good reason it's one of the seven fuckin' deadly sins. Fuck pride. Use your brain. Be your own man. You take that money and buy yourself better quality land, more land than what you started with, too. I paid way too much…"

He stopped himself at that point, realising what he was about to say.

"What? What do you mean you paid too much? Are you sayin' you were doin' my father a favour? Fuck that. We didn't need any charity!"

Neil waved his hand to dismiss the idea. "Don't listen to what I'm sayin' Pete. I'm drunk. It's been a long day"

"I'll pay you more than what you paid for it", Pete pleaded, his voice tinged with a hint of desperation.

Neil could see how serious he was about it.

"Pete, it's rocks. What can you grow up there? What can you feed? Take my advice, swallow your pride, and buy something better, get value for your money. I'm not goin' to let you fall into the same trap as my father did. Buy something better than what you started off with. Let it go. Be your own man and make your mark on this world. I'm telling you this as a friend"

Pete's face had turned a shade of red. "Fair enough Neil. My father and I aren't stupid though. We know the ground is not for farming, it's as barren as fuck"

Neil shook his head in confusion. "Well, what do you want it for?"

"You see, my father always reckoned the stone was of a certain quality that a great quarry could be made of it. To be honest, I always had that in mind from when I was a child- turn it into a quarry and make a living from it"

Again, Neil waved his hand as if to dismiss the idea. "Fuck sake Pete. Do you know all you'd have to do to get permission to open a quarry, not to mention the start-up capital? Then there's getting contracts in place and all the rest that goes with it. I very much doubt it could be done, at least not without spending a fortune on it. As I said, forget about it, go do your own thing"

"But this *is* what I want to do. Why don't you just sell me the fuckin' thing and be done with it. If it blows up in my face, so be it-it would be my own fault"

Neil looked at him. He could see how passionate he was about it.

"No. I'm not a seller. I don't sell land, that's it", he replied, shaking his head.

Pete stood up and drained his drink. "So, it's like that, is it?", he asked.

"Ah, come on Pete. Don't take it that way", Neil pleaded. Pete put his coat on.

"Fair enough. I can't argue with you. I'm too drunk. Maybe you're right. You're a smart bastard, I'm goin' to be smart too and take your advice", Pete replied, before smiling and adding; "Ye fucker ye".

Neil got up and put on his coat too, any trace of animosity dissolved in both men's laughter.

Neil drove them home and Pete slept on the sofa. Pete never enquired about buying back the land again.

The next day, a hungover Neil drove to the hospital to bring Máire and Seamus home. A beautiful summers day, all was good with the world and the Dillon's.

Seamus proved to be the perfect baby. He slept when he was supposed to, he ate all that was put in front of him and he smiled from morning until bedtime. Of course, Máire did most of the rearing, Neil continuing to run the farm. All of them were happy and the future seemed limitless. Maggie played a bigger part in family life too. She helped Máire on many occasions and visited more than she ever did before Seamus was born. She gradually grew fonder of Pete as time went by. Neil thought maybe she wasn't such a bad judge of character after all. He hadn't expected her to like Pete, as a character such as McNamee seemed to be her cup of tea. The two men couldn't have been more different. Neil thanked God on many occasions that McNamee was still over in England. "And long may the fucker stay over there", he prayed.

The softness Maggie showed to Pete, Seamus and to a lesser extent Máire, had still to reach Neil. The years had mellowed him towards her, but the feeling certainly hadn't been mutual. He could see she was getting very old and he respected her age and authority as much as he could.

One day, after they had eaten dinner, Máire busying herself with the dishes and Pete gone to the toilet, Neil found himself alone with her. She was cuddling Seamus and most likely trying to rile Neil, whispered into his ear; "So, little man, we finally have an heir to the Dillon estate. Thank God. Your old aunt was burdened with it for too long. It's all yours now, son"

At that, it only just dawned on Neil what Maggie had said. A broad smile adorning his lips, he said to Maggie; "You know, Maggie, that's the first time that had occurred to me. I had forgotten all about it until now"

Maggie looked up at him, an expression of disbelief on her face.

"Fair play to ye, wee man. The place stays in our name. Thank God for that". He raised his cup in a toast and Máire smiled, raising a sud filled cup from the sink. "To Seamie", said Neil and Máire repeated the sentiment.

Pete walked in at that point. "What's happenin'?", he asked. Neil briefly explained and Pete waved his hand not wanting to intrude on personal business, saying; "Oh, that thing with the will, right, yes…to Seamie", and they all raised their cups once more.

Neil slept easy that night. He realised the will his father made had been for the best after all. He was going to pass the farm onto Seamie in his own will anyway, so it didn't make any difference in the end. He couldn't help but to feel relieved though. He had many a sleepless night thinking about what would have happened if any tragedy befell him before he had a child born. God knows who Maggie might have signed it over to, he often wondered. Everything would be good for them from that moment on, he knew. Never one for sitting on his laurels, he would work even harder to secure a good future for his new family.

He did exactly that for the next year. Life couldn't have been better for them all.

But…things began to change for the worse, in the autumn of the following year.

On a balmy evening in the middle of September, after a long day ploughing in the field, Neil had paused for a moment to wipe his brow and had been relieved to see the long, rangy figure of Pete walking through the field towards him. For most of the day, after the relatively easy job of ploughing, Neil had been stooped over picking rocks and stones from the ground whilst also pulling the roots from hedges and bushes along the way. Neil always liked to merge many smaller fields into larger ones, as he had always been annoyed at the wastage of grass when harvesting smaller fields.

The two men made small talk for a few minutes, but sensing the urgency in Neil to get the work finished before dark, Pete asked what he wanted him to help with. Neil asked him to go into the little three-cornered field and pull out some of the hedges. Pete took his directions and went about his work.

The two men worked solidly for a few hours, past dusk and well into darkness. For the last hour of the evening Neil could hear the chainsaw being worked solidly. "Lazy hoor", Neil laughed to himself as he had meant for Pete to pull the roots out, not to cut the bushes down with the chainsaw. He carried on working regardless, as he trusted Pete's competency and judgement in the job at hand.

Just when the light had dimmed so much making it nigh impossible to see what he was doing anymore, Neil decided to call it a night. He downed tools and walked towards the little three-cornered field where Pete worked. The chainsaw growled away relentlessly in the background and Neil laughed to himself knowing that if he didn't call time, Pete would happily work away until the sun rose again.

He climbed over the little rusted gate and entered the field, only to witness in horror through the murky nightlight what Pete was doing. Before he could register what was happening, he found himself sprinting toward Pete. He grabbed him by the shoulder, Pete turning around in shock, almost cutting his head off in the process. Neil was shouting at the top of his lungs; "Switch it off. Switch the fuckin' thing off".

Pete done as he was instructed. Neil was hopping up and down like a child who had just cut his finger by accident. Pete almost laughed, but restrained himself as he could see Neil was obviously upset.

"What the fuck are ye at?", Neil shouted; "Fuckin' hell, what have ye done?". He was still jumping up and down. Pete thought that he was on the verge of tears.

"What…what?", Pete asked.

"What do ye mean, what? Do you know what you've done? Jesus Christ Pete, come on. For fuck sake"

"I don't understand what you're gettin' cross about. You told me to take out these bushes and that's what I did. Jesus", Pete protested.

"Yes, but not this one. NOT FUCKIN' *THIS* ONE!", Neil roared back. Foam began to appear at the corners of his mouth, he was now pacing back and forth frantically, fists clenched.

Pete stood silent for a minute or so. Neil continued marching around, gesticulating wildly before running out of steam and sitting down beside the fallen bush. He cradled a length of the bush in his arms. Much to Pete's amazement, he began to talk to it. "I'm sorry. I'm sorry. It was an accident. We didn't mean it. Sorry, please don't retaliate, honestly…we didn't mean it"

He then began to sob.

Pete was in complete shock. He walked over to Neil and put his hand on his shoulder.

"I'm sorry. I don't know what I've done, but…Jesus I'm sorry. You should have told me to leave it alone if it mattered that much to you. It's only an aul bush"

Neil shifted his shoulder away from him. "It's only an aul bush, is it? Ye haven't a fuckin' clue, have ye?"

He stood up, still cradling the length of sawed off bush. "Do you know the name of this bush?", he asked.

Pete studied it. "I dunno…I really haven't a clue. What is it then-you tell me"

Neil considered his eyes, unbelieving of what he was hearing. "You *really* don't know?"

"No", Pete replied again, almost laughing.

"Didn't your fuckin' people ever tell you about this? I mean, Jesus, my father warned me about it since I was just about able to speak. I thought it would be common knowledge around this country."

He walked a few steps away from Pete, pondering what he was saying. He turned and looked at him again, straight in the eye, seeking for some clue of deception. Pete didn't flinch. Muttering almost to himself, he conceded; "Oh, you really don't know"

"No. I fuckin' don't know. Now tell me what is so special about this thing", Pete shouted.

Neil, still cradling the bush in his arms said; "This...this is a Gentle bush"

"Never heard of it", said Pete.

Still as if in a world of his own, lost in his own thoughts, Neil continued; "The Gentle bush. My father told me many years ago, never to harm it. If you're ploughing, leave at least a fifteen-foot radius around it. Look at the grass surrounding it. See the difference? That ground has probably never been ploughed before. The Gentle bush is a sacred thing. Under no circumstances should it ever be tampered with...ever."

Then, laughing to himself and looking straight at Pete, he added; "And certainly, never is it to be fuckin' sawed down. Never...ever". He laughed to himself again before adding; "You're a lucky man to still have your two arms in-tact. I've heard stories about men taking a hatchet to a Gentle bush only to lose a finger, arm or even their lives. You're a lucky man...for now anyway"

It was Pete's turn to laugh. "God almighty. Such bullshit. Am I dreaming or what? I didn't know this bush existed five minutes ago, and now I'm hearing it's some sort of magical plant that chops peoples arms off or even kills them. Holy shit. And just where does this bush get these powers from?", he asked.

"FROM THE FUCKIN' FAIRIES", Neil roared back in response.

At that, Pete fell to the ground in hysterics. "Oh, sweet Jesus. To think I've always praised your intelligence to anyone who would listen...then you go and say one of the stupidest things I've ever heard"

Neil stood in silence. He didn't respond for some time, before saying; "You might laugh at me Pete Kelly and think I'm some sort of eejit, and you might be right- I hope you're right. But...I'll tell you this, what just happened is a very bad thing, an awful thing. Nothing good will come of this, there are too many stories for them to be untrue. I hope, God I hope, all the stories are old wives' tales, but there is something about this bush, something...otherworldly. I hope to God nothing bad happens to you or me because of this.". He paused, Pete this time sat silent on the grass, before continuing; "Gather up your bits and pieces and we'll finish up. There's nothing more we can do tonight. And by the way, for God's sake, don't tell anyone what happened here, and please, please don't mock me or this bush to another living soul. Please be to God nothing comes of this because of your ignorance on the subject"

Pete stood, stony faced and replied; "Fair enough."

With that, the two men gathered up their tools and went home, never mentioning what happened again.

In later years, Neil would always look back upon that evening, wondering if that incident was the very reason for his family's demise.

CHAPTER 20

It felt like the worst hangover imaginable. A hangover compared to what I felt would have been a pleasurable experience, a walk in the park. My head felt like someone was trying to Kango hammer into my brain. I lay there almost paralysed with pain, wondering why the hell my head hurt so bad. Then I looked up and realised I wasn't in my own bed, or anyone else's bed…more disappointingly. Then I saw the woman in the room and it dawned on me I was in hospital. A large, middle aged woman with a bee-hive style haircut sat across the room from me. When I remembered what happened the night before, the pain seemed to surge to new levels. I raised my hand to my head to feel what was there.

"Ah-ah", the nurse scolded.

Just then a very young-looking doctor entered the room.

"Ah, Mr Smyth", he said; "Good to see you're awake".

Before I could ask anything, he continued; "You had a fairly nasty bump to the head, to say the least. Now, we have stitched you up as best we could and we think you'll be fine. You shouldn't suffer any lasting effects. However, you have lost quite a lot of blood, so we would like to keep you in for a little, just to monitor how you are doing before we let you go home. So, relax and enjoy your stay with us". With that, he exited the room without saying anything else.

I looked over at the nurse.

"Quite the conversationalist, wasn't he?", I said.

She sat where she was, wearing a vacant expression, silent. I didn't mind though. I wasn't in the mood for small talk.

"What shape is my head in? Why can't I touch it?", I asked.

Remaining silent, she came over to me, holding a small mirror. I took it from her and looked in the reflection. I looked like a ghost. I was deathly white. My eyes were rimmed with deep, dark circles. More upsetting was the numerous faint red lines that had streamed down my face.

"Could you not have wiped my face?", I asked her.

"Finished?", she asked, reaching out for the mirror, the vacant expression never leaving her face.

"No", I answered. I took another look. The wound looked horrific, like a huge bloody slug had been planted on top of my head. I thought about the scar it would leave and didn't feel too bad about it then. If I was ever stuck for small talk, I thought.

I handed her back the mirror. I lay back in the bed, trying to remember exactly what happened. When it all came flooding back, I grew angry. I didn't know who I was angrier with-the bastard who did it, or Brian for his betrayal. I found a jug of water on the bedside table, drank it all in one go and fell asleep.

When I woke up, Dan and Kathleen were sitting at my bedside.

"Thought you were never goin' to wake up...ya lazy hoor", said Dan.

Kathleen nudged him in the ribs and scolded him, much in vain.

When she looked at me I could see she was on the verge of tears, the soft-hearted soul she was.

"Oh Tommy. What did they do to you?", she asked.

Tears stood in her eyes and she raised a tissue to stop them from falling.

"Ach Kathleen, its worse looking than it really is", I answered. "It couldn't make me any uglier looking. Sure, wont it add some character to my bland head too?".

They both laughed.

Dan cleared his throat. "Listen, Tommy. I don't know what happened, but what I don't understand and can't accept is why our boy didn't stand in for you. He fuckin' stood there and watched it happen and done fuck all about it. That's not right. He's only known those fuck-heads two minutes, you're his aul mate and he should have been there for you".

Kathleen patted him gently on the arm to calm him down.

"Don't get yourself annoyed about this Dan", I said to him, "Shit happens". I was lying to him. I felt the same way as he did.

"Look, Tommy", said Kathleen; "Brian is very upset by what happened. He came home last night as white as a ghost and told us what happened"

"I went fuckin' ape shit by the way", Dan interrupted.

"And that didn't help things, and it's not helping things now", Kathleen butted in. "You see, Tommy, he's very upset. He has fallen in with a bad crowd and he's confused. We will get him sorted out though. He's been acting very strangely recently and we're worried about him..."

"Never mind him", Dan butted in; "It's not about him today- we'll deal with the little prick later"

There was a slight pause. "Listen" I started, "I'm not a completely innocent victim here. I have to admit I said a few nasty things about your man's uncle who got killed in the troubles"

Dan raised his hand to stop me; "Brian told us about that Tommy. We know you can say things you don't mean in bad temper, we all can. But, that is not the issue here. It was a cowardly act what that bastard did to you. In my book, you never hit a man from behind, especially not with a fuckin' bottle. He could have killed you. Brian should have clocked the cunt"

"Ok, Ok, let's not start on that again", Kathleen stopped him.

"All right, Kathleen, Ok. Anyhow...we think we know why you got so annoyed in the first place". He began to shift uncomfortably in his seat. It wasn't like him. This was the great Dan McManus, Mr Smooth himself. He wasn't supposed to get flustered like this.

"It was the taunts about your father, wasn't it?"

I panicked, feeling nauseous about the subject of my Brit father being brought up in front of these people.

"You know that's all bullshit, Dan, don't you? That's the rantings of my lunatic mother", now my turn to shift uncomfortably in my bed.

Again, he raised his hand. "Tommy, Tommy relax. Nobody else knows about this. None of the boys on the site, no-one. I promise you"

"But, you know it's not true-don't you?"

"I don't care if it's true or not. We like you for who you are. Who cares what someone's parents did in the past. Its irrelevant Tommy, don't worry yourself about something like that"

"Dan, it's not true. There is no way in hell my father was a Brit. I'd rather die than having someone like that as my father. You know that, don't you?"

"Tommy, calm down. You can't help who your parents are. If you say it's not true, ok, I believe you. The point is though, we couldn't care less about any of that. You're you, you're Tommy and we love you for it. It wouldn't matter to us if your ma was Maggie Thatcher. So, take that chip off your shoulder and forget about all that shit. No one cares, and anyone who does, aren't fit to call themselves your friends. But, please believe me when I tell you that no-one else knows, and won't ever hear anything from us. And that is why we are so annoyed at Brian. He had no right to tell anyone your personal business, especially not dickheads he has only known for two minutes. He has let us down. But...no matter, that is for another time, you just get yourself better and stop fuckin' worrying."

We sat in silence for twenty seconds or so. The air was thick, almost moist with emotion. I broke the silence. "Thanks folks". I had never meant anything more in my life.

Eventually the talk grew lighter hearted. "Did I tell you that eejit Mickel McKeown is back in the country?", Dan asked.

I let out a belt of laughter. "You're joking? How come?"

Dan looked over at Kathleen and a little smile formed on his lips. "He's back stayin' with Larry for a while. You see, Sean and I might be getting a few of the boys back on the job. We've contracted a few jobs recently and done them well. Word must have spread and now the phone's been ringin'. We've had to bring a few boys back as the demand has been more than we can cope with. We reckon if it stays this good, we might be getting the aul crew back together again"

"Fair play, Dan. I'm delighted for you", I said.

Kathleen smiled at him, giving him a nudge.

"Oh aye. By the way, if things get better I was thinkin' you could maybe come back too. All the boys would love to have you back and I'm sure it would be better craic, and maybe better money than what you're doin' at the minute?"

I nearly jumped out of the bed, but restrained myself.

"Dan, this isn't your way to make me feel better, is it? I told you before, I don't want to be a burden on you and wouldn't feel comfortable knowing I was some sort of charity…". Dan stopped me there.

"Will ye fuck up, ye wee cunt"

Kathleen slapped him on the arm; "Dan, that's terrible"

I laughed, as I knew what way to take him, and asked; "Are you sure? When will I know?"

"Listen, I was goin' to phone you last week before all this. Just give me a few days to see what's happenin' and I'll get back to you. But, the likelihood is, I'll be callin' ye. Ok…bollocky balls?"

We both laughed, so did Kathleen despite her protestations.

I was discharged the next day. I rang Herbert and told him what had happened, and bought myself a few days off. I went home, via the off-licence where I stocked up for a few good days drinking. That was my idea of convalescence.

The whole episode hadn't been all bad though. Whilst in the hospital I got talking to a pretty, blonde cleaner called Andrea. I told her how much I admired her sweeping skills, as I was an assistant caretaker and had an eye for such skills. She laughed.

"Assistant caretaker?", she asked and I told her about Herbert and the rest of the people I worked with at the school. She enjoyed the stories about Herbert, Dan, and the rest, and said she would love to meet such great characters. It was then I cheekily asked her to come out with me and perhaps I could introduce her to them. It must have been the bump on my head that led me to ask that question, as I had never asked a girl out when sober. It must also have been the bump on the head that stirred some form of sympathy from her, as she said, much to my surprise; "Ok, here's my number. Give me a call during the week and we can arrange something".

I couldn't believe my luck.

A few days later Dan rang and confirmed what he had told me in the hospital. I was to start as soon as I could. Again, I couldn't believe my luck. I was going to be back on the sites again with all the old crew. Perhaps I could even gather up enough money to show Andrea a few good nights out on the town?

The day after Dan rang, I went back to work in the school. Herbert was sitting in his office, feet up, sipping vodka and orange. It was only a quarter past nine in the morning.

"Ah, Thomas. My dear boy. Oh, what a nasty gash you have on your head. Do tell me what happened."

I told him the entire story, much to his amusement.

He said he told Dixon I got mugged coming home from work, but he didn't think she believed him. Apparently, she was on the warpath and I would need to be careful. I told him I didn't give a shit as I was quitting anyway. He said he was pleased as he didn't think a young man like myself had many prospects in the caretaking industry. He said she would make it difficult for me, make me see out a whole months' notice. I hadn't even thought of that. I couldn't bear to miss out working on the sites for a month to stay in the school. He told me I would have to, as she could cancel my pay if I broke the contract without seeing out my notice. I couldn't do without that months' pay.

Just as I contemplated my options, a wry little smile broke over Herbert's face.

"You have mentioned in the past, Thomas, you feel I have a certain hold over Ms Dixon, that she appears to regard me with a certain mixture of hatred and fear. This may well be true. Would you like to know why this may be?"

"Yes...yes, of course. Why, what has happened to make her like that around you?", I replied, barely able to control my excitement.

He asked me to reach for a set of keys that hung above my head, on a little hook. I grabbed them and handed them to him. He opened the chest of drawers below the T.V and took out a little metal box. He used one of the keys to open it. Inside the box were many photographs and bits of paper, receipts, bills etc. He found an envelope and opened it, a devilish smile breaking across his lips as he took a photograph out. He handed it to me. My initial reaction was one of shock, followed by revulsion. Then I fell into hysterics. Herbert was laughing too.

The picture was one like I'd never seen before, not in real life anyway. The expressions of the two people in the photograph was the funniest thing I had ever seen. The look of sheer surprise, and horror in being caught did not befit the situation they were in.

"How'd you...I mean, what the hell?", I asked, totally confused and shocked.

He merely smiled, took a sip of his drink, sat back, and told the story.

It had happened years before, when Dixon had only been a young teacher. Herbert, back then, actually had to perform some form of physical labour to keep his job and satisfy his family. He had been out the back of the building, burning boxes and rubbish in the furnace, when he noticed a fox in an adjoining field. He dashed back to his office to fetch his camera, spending an hour, or so hiding in the bushes taking snaps, trying to get that perfect photo. Not realising the time, he finished loading the furnace and went back to the school to finish the last few jobs on his list. The building was empty, as it was well past six, an hour past his usual finishing time. He went about his rounds, locking up and checking the rooms. As he walked down the long corridor, directly opposite the Principals office, he could hear the shrill sound of a woman's voice, sounding extremely angry. Even back then, he knew it was Dixon, undoubtedly making some poor kids life a misery.

He walked past the office, trying to sneak a peek at what was going on.

He stopped in horror. He had to perform a double take, through the cracks of the Venetian blinds in Brother O'Brien's window door. Once he realised what an opportunity the scene playing out in front of him could potentially mean for him, he quickly rummaged in his bag and removed his camera. Then, taking a deep breath, he burst through the door, camera at the ready.

"Say cheese, you disgusting deviants"

And there, the scene was immortalised on film.

Brother O'Brien was on all fours on the floor. He had the feared leather strap between his teeth and was naked, apart from a pair of white Y-fronts that was pulled down at the back. Dixon stood over him, dressed in a leather one piece, and a pair of leather boots that must have had at least an eight-inch heel on them. She towered over Herbert, the huge heels making her seem like a giant. Her black hair was slicked back and she held a whip in her right hand. The one thing Herbert noticed more than anything was how red Brother O'Brien's ass was...she must really have been giving him the whip.

Neither of them said a word, they just looked at him in sheer horror. Herbert didn't speak either. He took another picture for good measure and walked out of the office.

From that day, onwards, neither Dixon nor Brother O'Brien gave him any trouble again. His job became one of sheer leisure from then on.

Herbert and I then drew up a plan which would enable me to leave on that very day, whilst still receiving my pay without giving the full notice.

We sat for a good hour, talking, and laughing, Herbert drinking away steadily. After that, he got up, shook my hand, and wished me the best. I would certainly miss him. A mad, eccentric old bastard...but what a great character.

I walked to Dixon's office, knocked the door, and entered. The usual suspects sat around her desk. Miss Campbell greeting me with her sickly-sweet smile, Mr Baker shifting nervously in his seat puffing his chest out in a pathetic attempt at intimidation and Mrs Williams, staring straight ahead, the blandness of her expression nauseating.

Dixon remained sat at her desk, much like a sitting bull. I could see how this could be an intimidating atmosphere for a visiting staff member.

"Yes?", asked Dixon, glaring.

I pulled up a chair, taking a cigarette out of the packet. Lighter at the ready, I put the fag in my mouth.

"You don't mind, do you?", I asked her.

"Well, actually I do", she replied, sneering.

"Good", I replied, lighting my cigarette at the same time.

An audible gasp could be heard in the room.

"What do you want?", Dixon hissed.

"Just came in for a chat"

She leaned forward, looking me straight in the eye.

"Why did you not attend work on Monday and Tuesday. I heard you had some trouble?"

"Yea- I did", I answered.

"I'd like to know what happened"

"Some dickhead bottled me in a bar"

She looked disgusted.

"I was told you had been mugged. This changes things now. Do you think it is befitting of a member of this school to be out bar-room brawling at the weekend? What if the pupils or any of the board of governors found out about this? I would have to dismiss you immediately. In-fact, owing to your behaviour in this office I may well do so, with instant effect."

She paused, largely for effect. I didn't let her continue; "You don't have to, Miss Dixon. I have come to hand in my notice. I got my old job back and start tomorrow"

At that moment, as I expected, a smile broke out across her lips.

"Oh, so you're starting a new job tomorrow, are you?", she asked, her words riddled with sarcasm.

"Yea"

"Well, I regret to inform you that you must give the school, your employer, one months' notice, otherwise you will not receive any pay and we may instigate legal action against you."

"Nah, that's not gonna happen", I replied, taking a large drag on my cigarette, trying in vain to blow smoke rings.

She looked at me in astonishment.

"Tommy", intervened Miss Campbell; "I don't think you quite understand what Miss Dixon is saying", she said, very patronisingly.

"Shut it bitch", I interrupted.

The office was stunned into silence. Miss Campbell sat with her mouth open, aghast.

"Excuse me?", she asked.

"You heard"

"Just leave it, Lucinda", a very nervous and rattled looking Mr Baker said.

Inevitably, her true, nasty colours rose to the surface.

"No, Wayne- I won't leave it. You, sunshine, are disgusting. You and that old pervert sitting in that stinking office watching television and drinking alcohol during working hours. You both walk around thinking you are something. You are *caretakers.* Oh my God, I don't think any other school in the whole country would tolerate such lowlifes." Stopping to look over at Dixon, she continued; "I don't know how you put up with the two of them, Florence?"

I pulled on my cigarette. "You finished?", I asked.

"I haven't even started", she smiled.

"Well don't. I don't have time to listen to it, ya mad bitch. Listen, I am leaving now and I want my pay cheque before I leave"

"He's absolutely nuts", an exasperated Miss Campbell interrupted.

"Bitch, shut it. You three fuckers should be ashamed of yourselves. Don't you realise how stupid you all look following her around all day? Climb out of her ass and be your own people...please"

Mr Baker stood up in front of me. "Tommy, I think it's maybe time for you to leave", he said, his voice croaking slightly from nerves or fear, possibly both.

"You gonna make me?"

He sat back down again.

I looked over at Mrs Williams. "You gonna say anything?", I asked.

She stared straight ahead, refusing to look at me. She shook her head and laughed. "You're in so much trouble right now, sonny"

"That bland statement matches your face", I said. She didn't react, just sat looking at Dixon, blandly.

"Now", I continued, addressing Dixon; "Could you arrange for my cheque to come?"

All the while, she had sat quietly, her face crimson with rage. She looked so angry, I thought I could see steam coming from her ears.

"What planet are you living on? Where did you come from?", she scolded.

"Don't worry. I will go back to my home planet when I get my cheque"

She leaned forward once more. "You have as much chance getting that cheque as I do walking on the moon. You are sacked. Get out of my office and never come back. You have five seconds to leave before I call the police"

I smiled at her and started counting; "Five, four, three..."

She smiled back at me, and lifted the phone. She began to dial.

"Old Herbert is some bloke, isn't he?", I said; "Did anyone know he is a very talented photographer? Yep, very talented. You know...he has been showing me his portfolio, and I must say, he has a particularly interesting one of you Miss Dixon. It really captures your true essence, what you are really all about", I said, locking eyes with her.

She put the phone down, leaning back in her chair. She paused for a few moments, still holding my gaze.

"Hmm, I don't know. I don't know if we should get the police involved?", she said, asking the group.

"What?", an exasperated Miss Campbell asked.

"It's ok. Leave this with me. I've dealt with Tommy's type before. Let me speak with Tommy one on one. I think he's playing up a little because he has an audience...isn't that right, Tommy?", she asked, nodding at me in encouragement.

"Yea, Miss Dixon. I suppose you're right", I replied, merely playing the game.

"Please", she asked the group; "A couple of minutes?"

They all got up. Mr Baker almost bolted toward the door, Mrs Williams walked blandly past me and Miss Campbell walked past muttering; "Asshole", under her breath at me.

I winked at her. "Bye bitch", I smiled.

Dixon sat at her desk, still resolute.

"What's this talk of the photograph?", she asked, as if I were one of her naughty students.

"Oh, I think you know what I was talking about"

She fidgeted nervously. "What do you want?"

"All I want is to leave here today, so I can start my new job tomorrow"

She smiled at me; "OK-go"

"Not without my pay"

"Not possible"

"I have *photos*"

"That's blackmail"

"I don't know what that means"

"Yes, you do"

"I don't. Now go get my cheque and not another word will be said of this filthy matter"

"That old bastard Herbert. He's been blackmailing me for years, and now you... it's not fair"

"I'm the only other person in the world who knows about it. He hasn't told anyone else. Now, if you get my cheque, I will leave and you will never hear from me again. This isn't blackmail, I want what's owed to me. I don't want to work here for another month. So, please give me what I want"

"Ok, ok", she said; "I will get it for you now. Give me twenty minutes"

She went out and twenty minutes later came back with my cheque.

"There", she said, handing it to me, glaring.

"Ok. You'll be glad to know I'm leaving now. But, there are several factors at play on me leaving on good terms. First, if you cancel this cheque when I leave, so I can't cash it, or there are any repercussions suffered by Herb, then, as Mr Schwarzenegger once said, "I'll be back". I've got a copy of that photo (I hadn't) and if any shit happens, I've a mate who works in a printer's and I will get that photo blown up fifty by fifty feet and put it on the side of the school building"

"You disgust me", she responded.

"No...*you* disgust *me*", I replied; "And by the way, I'm not a blackmailer. If I was, I would be asking for a cut of your salary every month. I just want what is owed to me. And for Herbert, read the same. We really should report you to the authorities. Having twisted, perverted deviants like yourselves running a school is quite sickening and shouldn't be tolerated"

I folded my cheque in two and headed towards the door.

I looked back and blew her a kiss.

The next day I started back on the sites.

CHAPTER 21

As superstitious and respectful of the Gentle bush curse as he was, Neil didn't suffer any bad luck in the immediate aftermath of the night Pete cut it down.

The farm was thriving, Seamie was coming on in leaps and bounds and the three of them were content and happy. The months passed by so happily that Neil almost forgot all about the event. Pete remained a big part of their lives, always helping out whenever he could and Maggie, although growing old and losing a lot of her mobility, remained within the family ranks. She loosened the stranglehold on the farm and the property, Neil knew he had earned her trust. She knew he was no fool.

His life was a simple one, the kind of life he had always wanted. He worked on the farm each day from dawn until well past dusk, but the moments he most cherished were when he was called in for lunch and dinner. A good hearty meal in the company of the two people he loved more than anything in the world. Bedtime for Seamie always meant another break in his work, cuddling, and kissing his son before Máire would take him up the stairs to his cot. His nights were usually spent in the local pub with Pete, or watching television with Máire, before he would go to bed and get up to do it all again. They were happy times for all.

About a year after the Gentle bush was felled, Neil began to feel his luck was changing after all. The farm had been thriving and he and Máire were even talking about having a second child.

All that changed the evening a large black Mercedes made its way down his driveway.

It had been a long day. Neil was about to down tools for the evening when he heard the car approach. He looked up to see who it was, making out two figures sitting in the front two seats. He had to squint to see if he recognised them as the light was dimming quickly. The window rolled down and he heard the unmistakable voice. He instantly felt nauseous.

"Young Dillon, long time no see". It was McNamee. A million thoughts raced through his mind- the first; "When did this bastard come home?".

McNamee had been living in England for years. Neil had heard all sorts of stories, mostly about how well he had been doing, but he tried not to dwell on them too much. Restraining himself and trying to be civil, he approached the car.

He nodded his head to him; "Dessie".

He bowed to look who was in the passenger seat. It was none other than McNamee's personal puppet, Paddy Gray. He remembered the last time he had encountered Gray, the day he closed the mill and Gray had shouted the odds at him in front of the whole country. Neil didn't forget moments like that.

"Paddy", Neil acknowledged, nodding his head at him. Gray half smiled, "Neil".

Neil could see life in England had agreed with them, both having put on at least a few stone each. Both wore expensive looking suits, unlike the rags they used to wear, and their hands and wrists were adorned in jewellery.

"Yis are back then?", Neil asked, hoping desperately it was a flying visit.

"Oh yea. Back and badder than ever", McNamee replied, Gray sniggering in the background.

"I see you've done well for yourselves anyway", Neil said, tapping the roof of the car with his fingers. "I'm sure this cost you a pretty penny. Nice yoke."

"Ach, this aul thing. You should has seen us over there, driving around in Rolls Royce's and all sorts, weren't we Paddy?", McNamee replied.

"You were on your shite", Neil said, half laughing.

"Oh, we were. I'll show you the photos some night"

"Nah, you're all right".

There was a brief silence, unusual for McNamee Neil thought, as he seemed to love the sound of his own voice.

"So, what do I owe the pleasure?", Neil asked.

"Ach, you know. We're back in the country and we thought we'd visit all our aul friends", McNamee smiled.

"Well fuck, don't let me hold you back from visiting them", said Neil, about to walk back to his house.

McNamee and Gray both laughed.

"Jesus, you were always a funny cunt, Dillon", said Gray.

"And you were always a funny lookin' cunt, Gray", Neil replied, laughing.

Gray stopped laughing.

"Now, now boys", McNamee interjected, laughing loudly. "I hear you're married, good man yourself. And a wee boy too, fair play to ye"

Neil felt uneasy with McNamee being so civil towards him.

"Aye. Yourselves?"

"No, no. Too busy makin' money. Isn't that right, Paddy?"

"Too fuckin' right", Gray replied; "Make the money first and you have the choice of the hoors"

Neil laughed loudly at that statement. "Sure, I heard the two of yis were riding each other over there"

Gray reacted immediately. "What kind of fuckin' talk is that to be at. I've a good mind to get out of this car and..."

"And what, Paddy? Anytime you think you're fit. You've gotten very tough since you've gone away. Fuckin' clown!"

"Now, now boys", McNamee laughed; "We're not young fellas anymore. Our fighting days are well behind us"

"Aye, if I remember, Dessie, you like batin' up young boys, don't ye?"

McNamee stopped laughing.

"Look, Dillon. We're back in the country and we thought we'd call round and see some of the boys. I suppose that's the problem with these wee country areas, too much bad blood flowing, people remember too many things"

Neil begrudgingly had to agree with him. He, after all, had been saying the same thing for years.

"I hear you've befriended young Kelly. He's home and all too?", McNamee continued.

Neil nodded. "Aye. Pete's all right"

"Aye. I hear he's all better now. He was sickly for a long time, wasn't he?"

Neil nodded.

"Listen, you probably heard, but me and Paddy were runnin' a big quarry over in England", McNamee continued.

"No, didn't hear that" Neil lied.

"Well, we were...and damn good at it too"

Neil shrugged his shoulders in indifference.

"So, we plan to get back into the business, now we are back in the country", McNamee continued, looking up at Neil from under his eyebrows.

"And what's this got to do with me?", asked Neil.

"Well, we heard you bought land off Frank Kelly a few years back"

"I did"

"How much did you give for it?", asked Gray.

"Never you mind", Neil replied.

"We'll double the price", McNamee interrupted.

"Why?"

"Why do you think? We want to make a quarry out of it", said McNamee.

Neil laughed. "Listen, you have no hope. You'd never get permission from the council, the locals living next to it would complain and those wee roads are too narrow for lorries up and down it all day long"

"Sell it to us and we can worry about all that", said McNamee.

"As much as I'd love to sell you a field of rocks and see you bollocks it up, I'm not selling. Pete himself asked and I wouldn't sell to him, so I certainly won't go above his head and sell it to you"

"That's fair enough, and I understand", replied McNamee; "But, he wasn't going to pay treble what you paid for it"

"I thought you said double?"

"I want it. I thought I'd up the bid"

Again, Neil laughed. He took his cigarettes out of his pockets and offered one to both men, against his will. Both declined, to his relief. He lit his cigarette and pondered the bid.

"Now, after all the fuss you are makin' about this land, what's to stop *me* from stealing your idea?"

It was McNamee and Gray's turn to laugh.

"Contacts, Dillon. Contacts. As you've said yourself, how could anyone get permission. The locals would be up in arms, the roads are too small for large machinery up and down it every day. But if you know the right people and promise to create some jobs to boost the local economy, then things suddenly change. I could employ local people in their own backyard- just like your own father did, God rest his soul"

Again, Neil laughed. "Jesus, I can't make up my mind about who you've turned out to be, Al Capone or Saint Dessie of Lisnaderry?"

McNamee opened the palms of his hands out in front of him. "I just want to make a few quid and try to help the area a bit. What's wrong with that?"

Neil didn't buy it. "Good luck with your plans, but it won't happen on my land", he said, and went to walk back off into his house.

"I'll pay quadruple what you paid for it, Neil", McNamee shouted after him, his voice tinged with desperation.

Neil stopped in his tracks and stood there, a thousand thoughts racing through his mind. He hated McNamee with a passion, but business was business. He had always resolved to be unlike his father, never to let pride or personal feelings get in the way of business. He could take the money, McNamee could get his quarry, local people would get employment and Neil could use the money to re-invest in better, more productive land.

He turned around. "Let me sleep on it. I'll talk to you about it another time".

"Good man", said McNamee; "We'll be in the pub most nights, so you know where to find us"

Neil didn't reply. He had a lot of thinking to do.

That night he talked to Máire. He told her the history between him and McNamee, the offer on the table, what they could do with the money and about Pete asking to buy it back, and how he turned him down. Máire told him to think about it and talk to Pete. He listened to her advice.

The next evening, Pete came out to help move cattle from one field to another. They were walking down the lane behind the cattle, sticks in hand, when Neil said; "Pete, did you know thon wee cunt McNamee is back in the country?"

"Fuck. God help us"

"I know, hateful wee prick. Anyhow, him and that shitehawk Paddy Gray visited me last night"

"Right?"

"Aye, I know. I was wondering what the fuck too. Listen, I'm goin' to get straight to the point here. They want to buy that land I bought from your father"

"What the fuck?"

"I know. Turns out they have the same idea as you…about the quarry"

"Right. And you told them where to go?"

"Of course, but…here's the thing. The fuckers reckon they can get permission to set-up and operate the quarry. They say they can employ local people and bring a lot of business to the area."

"Same thing I planned to do, was it not?"

"Yes, it is. But these cunts seem to have serious financial clout. McNamee has friends in high places and money to make things happen. You or I couldn't get that thing up and running- we don't know the right people"

"And what are you goin' to do? You can't sell it to him, surely not after I asked first"

"I think you're missing the point here Pete. We can't make a quarry out of it, he can"

"Ach, for fuck sake Neil. Don't patronise me. How much is he offering?

"Right, here's the thing"

Pete laughed bitterly. "Oh, I fuckin' see now. You won't sell to me because I was offering too little. Friendship doesn't mean much to you."

"Pete, shut the fuck up and listen", Neil shouted; "He's offering a lot of money. He's offering fuckin' four times what I paid your father"

Pete remained quiet. The two men walked in silence for a few hundred yards.

"Pete, as much as I don't want to sell it to him, this is what I plan to do…"

Pete petulantly threw his arms in the air. "You're goin' to fuckin' sell it to him, aren't ye?", a blaze of anger and disbelief in his eyes.

"Pete, seriously, fuckin' shut it"

Pete looked at him, fury in his eyes; "Go on then. Tell me what you're goin' to do about this. I *really* want to hear what your plan is", his words dripping with sarcasm.

"This field here", Neil instructed, the two men directing the cattle through the open gate. When all the cattle had entered the field, Neil closed the gate and leaned up against it.

"Pete, I don't want to sell it to the little prick, you should know that better than anyone"

"I do. But why are you even considering it then?".

Neil stared into the field. He remained silent for a few moments before replying; "I consider myself a businessman, you know this. Now, what kind of businessman, or man with half a brain in his head, lets bad feelings come between himself and a profit, especially a four-hundred percent profit? One thing I learned from my father's mistakes was, run a business with the head, not the heart"

"Neil, I get what you're saying. It makes sense, but I asked to buy that field first. I'm your friend, for fuck sake. You hate those bastards, and it's my families land after all"

"Ach", Neil gestured wildly; "Don't give me that shite. If your father thought that much of the ground, he wouldn't have sold it to me in the first place. Let me tell you my reasons for considering his offer"

Pete laughed bitterly and went to walk away, before stopping himself and turning back; "Ok, tell me then. I want to know."

"Right", continued Neil; "First, he's offering quadruple what I paid for it. Secondly, I want to see if the little prick actually does get it up and running. I severely doubt he will, but if he does, I can't see there being enough rock in that ground to last for as long as he thinks. Finally, I want to do something good with the money."

Pete let out a theatrical laugh.

"Oh, do tell me what this good deed is? End world hunger, cure cancer, please tell"

His response angered Neil. He rattled the gate in rage, the cattle grazing nearby running away in surprise and fear. "I was goin' to help you and your father out, you whingeing, ungrateful prick. That's what I was goin' to fuckin' do", he shouted.

They both fell silent.

Pete broke the silence after a few moments. "How were you plannin' to do that?"

"Máire and I spoke about this the last night. We both agreed that, as good a businessman I am, or think I am, I'm not a greedy bastard. I want to help my friends out. Listen, I'm gettin' four times for that field of rocks up there beside your fathers. Let me tell you, it's not worth a tenth of what I'm getting' for it. You know that and I know that. So, what I was planning to do was to take the little pricks money and give half of it to you and your father. Call it my way of thanking you for the years of help you have given me, never once taking a penny for it."

Again, both men stood in silence for a few moments before Pete broke it; "You owe me fuck all. I'm your friend. I was glad to help and never expected anything from you", his voice sounding croaky.

"I know, Pete. You've been a good friend to me, my only friend. Please, forget about that quarry, it's good for nothin'. You're a butcher, a fine butcher, not a quarryman. I'm goin' to screw these pair of weeds and help out my friends, what better outcome could I ask for. So...please let me do this. I'm not taking no for an answer by the way"

Pete smiled at him; "There's nothin' I can do to change your mind, ya thick cunt?"

Neil smiled back at him; "You know me. My minds made up. What'd ye say?", he said, extending his hand towards him.

Pete shook his hand. "All right. Thanks Neil. Only do this if you're sure. I don't want you to do this because I've been whingeing at you."

Neil shook his head. "You know me. I don't operate with my heart; my head always rules. But, to buy land from my friends and sell it for four times what I paid for it, wouldn't sit well with me. I have doubled my money on the investment, so you can rule out any charity. Why not share my good fortune with friends?"

Pete laughed. "Well, when you put it that way. God bless you Neil Dillon"

The two men shook hands and walked back down the road, towards home.

The next night, Neil and Pete went to the pub. McNamee and Paddy Gray were sat at the bar. Neil walked up to them.

"Right, about that deal", he said...and the deal was done that night.

CHAPTER 22

And there I was. Back, and as happy as Larry, on the building sites. All the old crew were back too (apart from Blondie, I think he was eventually found out in the end). Even Mickel McKeown was back, much to my delight.

Life was treating me well. I was earning good money, a lot more than what I was earning in the school, which helped. To ease my conscience, I gave Dan a percentage of my pay, every payday to give it to Kathleen, so she could give it to my mother. There was no way I was going around there again- we were well and truly finished this time. My life was good, happy for once and I didn't need my mother's poison seeping into it again.

I had a new girlfriend too. Andrea, the cleaner from the hospital. I rang her a week after leaving hospital. I told her all about what happened with Dixon and Herbert. I told her about getting my job back on the sites and found her very easy to talk to. I knew we would have a good time together.

Our first three dates, however, were catastrophes.

The first date was on the Friday night of my first full week back on the building site. I couldn't wait to get home, shower, change and get a few beers down my neck. I had arranged to meet Andrea in a little Italian restaurant on the Highgate Road. I arrived ten minutes early and ordered a pint and a whiskey chaser. I wasn't a whiskey drinker but thought it would be apt on that occasion to steady the nerves. It did the trick.

Andrea had to walk right up to me and call me by name before I recognised her. She looked completely different to the last time I had seen her. Sure, she was beautiful before, but now she took it to a wholly angelic level. Her hair was long and blonde, where it had been in a bun in work. She wore a beautiful, flowing yellow dress and a pair of high heels that made her almost the same height as I was, and I stood at six feet one. I felt very inadequate standing next to her, she was well out of my league, but didn't know it. She was the most beautiful woman I'd ever seen. As corny as it sounds, but after one glimpse of her that night, I knew I would never want for another woman. Fired up by the whiskey, however, I was all talk and conversation flowed easily between us.

We were shown to our table, where we sat and had a few drinks and our meals. It was a very pleasurable experience. Low lights, mellow background music, delicious Italian food and Andrea sitting across from me, giggling, and flirting through the evening. I felt like James Bond. I wasn't used to such sophisticated and enjoyable experiences.

There was a party of three sitting opposite us. I sat facing them. The three were in their sixties by the looks of them, perhaps kicking the ass off seventy. Two women and a man. Nothing unusual initially, but things began to get stranger as the evening progressed. The old guy looked like a retired head teacher, very well read looking, thick glasses, an air of authority about him. The old women looked like stereotypical church-goers. Both looked very pious, the type who would attend W.I functions. It appeared the old guy was married to the old girl sat beside him, the level of weariness in their manner towards each other a giveaway. Sat across from them was the other old lady. She seemed to be the focal point of the evening between the old guy and his missus. At first, I hadn't paid much attention to them, just noticing them in the background, but I couldn't help but notice as the evening progressed, that whenever the old guy's wife went to the toilet, he and the old lady sat opposite him would begin to peck each other on the cheek and hold hands, gazing lovingly into each other's eyes. When the wife came back, they would stop and continue as they were. It got worse through the evening as they began full on snogging and fondling, in the wife's absence. I told Andrea about what I was witnessing and she laughed and told me they were obviously swingers. Apparently, it was common in the area, there was a large community present and most seemed to be of a certain age. It all made sense to me at that point and I thought nothing more of it.

When the night ended, I paid the bill, got up to help Andrea with her coat and put on my own too. As we walked past the swingers on the way out, all three of them gave us pleasant smiles and Andrea engaged in some small talk with them. They were very well spoken, nice people, not the type one would expect to partake in the act of swinging.

"Do you do this often?", I asked, pointing at the three of them.

"Do what, sorry?", the wife asked.

"The whole swinging thing?"

The old man's face turned to stone. Andrea gasped.

"Excuse me?", the wife asked. I was far too drunk to see I was putting my foot completely in it.

"You know, your man here. He's riding both of you, isn't he?"

The old man's face suddenly turned ashen.

"He's doing *what* to us?", the wife asked.

"Well, I don't know about you, but he's definitely shagging this one", I said, pointing to the old lady sitting across from them.

The man squirmed in his seat, and replied; "How dare you. This is my sister in law, my wife's sister. How dare you". He was shouting now.

"Shit, sorry, didn't mean to drop you in it Mister. I just thought..."

"Shut it, shut the fuck up you little shit", he roared back at me. Everyone in the restaurant was quiet now.

The wife stood up. She pointed at the two sitting down; "I knew it. I bloody well knew you two bastards were up to something"

All hell broke loose between them. Andrea grabbed my hand and we slipped out. Once the cold evening air outside hit, I only realised what I had done.

"God, Andrea. What did I do that for? I was just making small talk- I was sure they were swingers. I'm sorry, Jesus…"

She walked up to me and kissed me full on the lips. She stopped and laughed heartily, at one stage having to bend over for air.

"Tommy, you're nuts. What the hell were you thinking?"

I didn't know what to say. I was genuinely trying to be nice to the old people.

"You're not cross, Andrea?"

"I like you. At least you're not boring…anything but"

We talked for a bit, kissed another few times, then she hailed a taxi home. We arranged another date in a weeks' time, much to my surprise and delight.

On the night of the second date I decided to calm down a little on the drinking. I felt more comfortable around Andrea and didn't feel I needed the Dutch courage. I also didn't want to do anything stupid again and mess things up with her. I stuck to beers and had a few glasses of wine with the dinner.

We went to a little seafood restaurant on the St. Paul's road Andrea had recommended. Once more, she was easily the most beautiful woman in the restaurant. I told her this and she laughed and said I was a smooth operator. I told her I meant it and wasn't saying it for the sake of it. She liked that and accepted the compliment very graciously.

The thing I liked about her, amongst many others, was she made me feel like a silver-tongued fox. I never had been, and knew I wasn't, but she had a way of understanding what I was trying to say. I had always been misunderstood with most other women, being greeted with; "And what does that supposed to mean?", when I delivered a compliment or was trying to strike up a rapport. Andrea was different. She got me. It was a beautiful quality in her.

We were shown to our table and took our seats. A very friendly middle-aged couple sat at the table next to us. The woman was a Scouser and the man a Cockney. They had a small baby, probably no more than twelve months old, sitting between them in a high chair. They seemed like a nice couple, the man was a little sleazy around Andrea, but I couldn't blame him for that. Their main courses sat in front of them, but they were barely touched. I couldn't work out if they were a little mad or just pissed. Surely, I thought, they couldn't be that pissed as they were looking after the little boy. A girl came to their table with two glasses of wine.

"Facking 'ell Samantha, what's this?", the man asked.

"Your wine you ordered, sir"

The man laughed. "We ordered two large glasses, those aren't large. Bring us large 'uns"

The girl laughed. "You're funny" she replied, nervously.

"Samantha, two large glasses...please", the man responded, very sternly.

The girl went to get the two glasses and came back with what looked to be two buckets.

"Good girl Samantha", the man said, his eyes following her ass all the way as she walked off.

The two polished off their glasses in double quick time, calling for Samantha constantly for refills over the next hour and a half.

They seemed like nice people, a little crazy, but nice. They doted on their little boy, feeding him ice cream, and cooing over him all evening.

"The little boy", asked Andrea, "Is he your son?"

The two cackled with laughter.

"Wowsers, no way, love. He's our grandson", the woman answered. "Our daughter is working tonight, so we thought we would treat him and take him out with us. Ha-ha, did you hear that, Gordon? Is he our kid, ha-ha-wowsers."

"Wowsers", seemed to be her word. "Wowsers" got a little annoying as the night progressed.

Andrea and I continued to enjoy our night. I was watching my alcohol intake, and the food was delicious. Thankfully, the mad couple befriended an elderly couple on the other side of them, which deflected the attention from us.

An hour or so later, I called for the bill. The man next to us sat on his own, putting a coat on the little boy.

"Aah, you're very sweet around him", Andrea said to him, "I see you both completely dote on him".

The man smiled. "We do. You know, both him and his mum live with us. Don't get me facking started on his father, though. Scum of the earth. You know, he told social services that we shouldn't have little Jay living with us. He told them we're alcoholics. I mean...for fuck sake."

Andrea and I sat shaking our heads. "Oh, that's terrible", we said, however I was thinking the guy had a point.

We sat talking to the man for about fifteen minutes. I whispered into Andrea's ear; "Where's the wife?"

"Probably torturing some poor soul in the toilet", she whispered back. We both laughed.

Just then, we noticed a lot of the staff running up and down the stairs. One of the waitresses came over to the man, and took him to one side for a quiet word. Without saying a word, the man left the restaurant with one of the waiters. The poor little boy was taken to a corner of the restaurant, where he was given a bottle by one of the other waitresses.

"I'm going up to see where she is", said Andrea, "Look at that poor little boy. This isn't right".

I agreed, and off she went.

I sat nursing my drink and wished I could have done something. I felt bad for the little boy. I began to fear the worst, maybe the woman had a heart attack in the toilet?

Two minutes later, Andrea came back down the stairs, looking haunted.

"Oh God, Andrea. What happened?"

"Oh, Tommy, it's horrible. Oh, my God."

A cold shiver ran down the length of my spine. We had just been talking to the woman twenty minutes or so before, and now she was...

"Tommy, I didn't know whether to laugh or cry"

My ears pricked up-maybe it wasn't as bad as I feared. "Why, what happened, Andrea?"

"Oh Jesus, the smell. I almost fainted with the fumes. She has *shat* all over the toilets."

"She did what?", I tried my best not to laugh.

Andrea still wore a haunted expression. "It's as if her ass exploded all over the toilets. She is up there now with a few of the girls. She's sitting crying in the cubicles in a pool of shit, saying she couldn't help it. She's saying that as soon as she got into the toilets and pulled her jeans down, the shit just started flying out everywhere. I mean, Tommy, you should see it. There's specks of shit on the mirror and even on the ceiling"

I couldn't help it, I burst out laughing.

"Oh, you git. It's not funny", she replied, beginning to laugh too.

"Where is the husband away to then?", I asked.

"Oh, him. He's away home to get her a change of clothing-her clothes are drenched."

I couldn't help it, I was pissing myself laughing, but when I looked over at the little boy, I stopped. Poor little guy. People like me were laughing our asses off at his crazy, drunken grandparents, and in a perverse sort of way, that meant we were laughing at him too.

It made me think about my own crazy, drunken mother and about how her actions affected me as a child. I felt my laughter was suddenly going to turn to tears. The poor child was surrounded by strangers in a strange place, it was upsetting him. It wasn't right. I almost suggested to Andrea that we should kidnap him, steal him away to live with us, so we could try to give him a decent upbringing. Then I felt nauseous, as I knew there wasn't anything we could possibly do to help him. We were just strangers and it was none of our business. We just had to stand by and watch the car crash unfold before our eyes.

I couldn't enjoy myself after that. I didn't want to bring Andrea down after a good night, so outside I kissed her and got her a taxi home. I walked home and drank until I fell unconscious.

For our third date, Andrea thought it would be a good idea that I meet her brother. I was chuffed she wanted me to. She must have liked me after all, even after our first two disastrous dates, not to mention how she first saw me in hospital, after my bar room brawl. I must have been doing something right.

She rang me the night before and gave me her brothers address, as we were to meet there for around seven. I told her I was nervous to meet him so soon, but she assured me we would both get on well.

She wasn't wrong.

I arrived at the flat the next night where Andrea answered the door. She wore a pair of jeans, red high heels, and a stripy red top, and looked like she had just stepped out of a movie set. She beamed from ear to ear, and so did I. When we walked into the living room, hand in hand, Fleetwood Mac boomed from the stereo. I liked her brother already.

His name was Dean, and he stood up to greet me with a hearty handshake, introducing me to his girlfriend, Nicole. Dean didn't look much like Andrea. She was tall, blonde, and pale, where Dean was short, tanned and had a head of thick, black hair. He was very well built, and from noticing the weights bench and various weights in the corner of the room, I could see why.

Dean and Nicole were my type of people. Right from the off, there was no bullshit, no pretence, they just wanted to get drunk and have a good time. Dean was a mechanic and Nicole was a receptionist. They couldn't have cared less if I was a brain surgeon or a road sweeper. They asked, just to be polite, but in no way to judge.

These people could certainly drink. I had brought a half bottle of vodka around for Andrea and me to share, and a bottle of wine for the hosts. Dean and Nicole had drunk a full bottle of vodka between them already, before they opened the wine, drinking it directly from the bottle between them. I slipped out to buy another bottle of vodka, after about an hour or so. The bottle was polished off by the time we left at around nine.

We went to a nice little steak house on the Holloway Road. I knew I wasn't sober, but I was aware how much soberer I was than Dean and Nicole. Andrea was at about the same level I was, which pleased me as I didn't want to play catch up and make a fool of myself in front of those people.

It was a pity it didn't pan out that way.

We arrived and were shown to our seats. Wine, beer, spirits, and shots were all ordered. The conversation and laughter flowed as much as the booze. What great people, I had never felt more comfortable around relative strangers before in my life. I looked at Andrea and realised at once she was the one for me. We played footsie with each other and we laughed and joked. Life had never been more pleasant.

We began to run low on drinks, such was the consumption rate, so I tried to get the attention of a passing waiter to order more. Just then, I noticed the couple sitting at the table next to us. They sat staring at us, mouths agape. I made eye contact with the man and nodded at him.

"Nice evening for it. Hard to get a bit of service around here though?", I said, smiling at them. Neither replied. That pissed me off a little. On closer inspection, both were very smug looking. Mid-thirties, middle class, both reminded me of asshole teachers I had in school. He had a little beard and she looked like a beard would improve her features. I didn't want to let the fuckers annoy me and ruin our evening, so I averted my gaze from them, tracked down a waiter and ordered more drinks. We had barely received the drinks at our table, when Dean ordered more. I knew it was going to be one of those nights. My only saving grace was that I had drank a skinful the night before with the hoodlums from the building site. I knew I could keep up with them and not get too drunk, as I found it almost impossible to get roaring drunk two nights in a row. That predicament mostly annoyed me, but on this occasion, comforted me.

Dean got up from his seat to go to the toilet. "Oi, Tommy. I'm going to the pisser", he announced, "I'll give ya a shout if I need you to put a shoulder under this thing. It can be a bit heavy sometimes, can be a two-man job getting it back into my trousers", he said, referring to his penis.

"Yea, Tommy", said Nicole, "Don't forget to bring a magnifying glass to help him find it first"

We all laughed and Dean stumbled off to the toilet, almost falling into the smug looking couples table.

Again, they looked outraged. His hand cupped his mouth and he muttered something to his wife. I smiled to charm them a little. "Look folks, my friends have had a little to drink. If we are annoying you or disrupting your evening in any way, just say so and I will have a word with them to tone it down. Is that OK?"

I thought that would put them at ease, so they could keep their noses out of our business for the rest of the evening. I expected a response too, either a; "No, they're fine, it's OK", or a; "Yes, could you have a word, they're a little rowdy", either would have been good. However, I was met with silence, an expression of both curiosity and revulsion on both their faces. I swore under my breath at them and decided to ignore them from then on.

Dean came back from the toilets. "Who wants another fuckin' drink?"

The two girls giggled, and shouted; "Yay", in response.

Our mains arrived and we all tucked in. I couldn't really relax and enjoy myself because of the two smug looking fuckers sitting at the table next to us. It felt like we were like animals in the zoo, the way they were looking at us. Dean and Nicole *were* quite loud, but inoffensive. They weren't in any way making a scene, merely having a good time. Almost everything said at our table was met with an audible gasp from the table next to us, followed by the hand cupping around the mouth, raised eyebrows, secretive speech followed by more gawking. It was really beginning to piss me off. I didn't want to alert our group to them. I didn't want these fuckers to ruin our night. I turned around to them when Dean went to the toilet again and the girls were in conversation and said; "Listen, you people are starting to annoy me now. I feel you are judging our group very harshly. If you would, I would prefer if you'd turn your attentions elsewhere, as I feel very self-conscious in your company."

Again, no response. I was met with two blank expressions, the hand cupping around the mouth and the whispering followed.

"Look, pal. Have you something to say? I find your manner very rude and disrespectful."

Still, no response.

I was beginning to get very angry. Dean came back and nearly fell off his seat when he went to sit down. Nicole howled with laughter, "You daft prick, Dean."

The smug couple were now sat, arms folded, almost leaning forwards to get as close to the spectacle as they possibly could, without actually sitting with us. It annoyed me that I was the only one noticing them, as the rest were so drunk.

"Right mister", I finally snapped, "If you don't turn around, I'm gonna ram your head right through that fuckin' wall."

That didn't work. I was about to get up and execute my promise when Andrea reached over for me and said; "Give me a snog, you handsome devil". This cheered me up, momentarily letting me forget about them.

We asked for the bill and paid. Just as we were about to get up and leave, Dean noticed Andrea had a half-eaten steak on her plate.

"You not eating that sis?", he asked.

"No, I'm full", she answered.

He reached over the table, sticking his fork in the steak and dangled it in the air, eating straight from the raised fork. We all laughed. The couple next to us went into shock and awe overdrive. He almost fell off his seat in eagerness to share his comments with his wife.

I saw red. I got up and walked over to him.

"I've had enough of you, cunt", I hissed at him. He sat still, staring at me as if I was a primitive animal in the zoo. I grabbed him by the scruff of the neck. His wife shrieked and I was suddenly conscious of what I was doing.

Everyone was now looking, including my own party. I grabbed his neck tight, very tight, as tight as I could, knowing I was really hurting the fucker. I considered punching him. He was saved from that fate, though, when I noticed the cream cake he was having for dessert. I grabbed his head and plunged his face into it, dunking it a few times, before reaching over to lift his bottle of wine, pouring it all over his head. At that point, his wife was on her feet and attacking me with her nails. I considered punching her too, but thought better of it as I wasn't the woman hitting type (although it was hard not to when she was using my face as a scratching post). Suddenly, she stopped clawing me.

She had disappeared.

I looked over to see Andrea had her in a headlock. She was walking around the restaurant with her, probably wondering what to do with her, until Nicole ran over and poured a jug of water over the woman's head. Andrea let her go and the woman sat defeated, sobbing on the floor.

We got out of the restaurant at once.

"What the fuck just happened?", Dean asked, laughing hysterically. "My sisters going out with a fucking crazy man."

Even though Dean was laughing, I decided to tell my full side of the story to prove I wasn't a complete lunatic. I apologised profusely to Andrea, telling her I would understand if she didn't want to go on any more disastrous dates with me. Much to my relief, she laughed and told me she knew her life would never be boring with me in it.

That night, as they say in the movies, we made love for the first time. We *were* in love. Life had never been better.

She moved in with me a few weeks after that. We lived in non-marital bliss and all was good in the world. Work was going well and I began taking classes at night college, in joinery. I was drinking less and life had structure, meaning and routine.

But, as usual, the good times wouldn't last long.

About two years later, one Friday evening after finishing work, I went to see Dan to receive my pay packet. As always, I handed some of it back for him to give to Kathleen, for my mother.

"Give it to Kathleen yourself Tommy, she's coming up in a minute", he told me.

A few minutes later, Kathleen arrived.

"Here's that few quid for my mother, Kathleen"

I knew she wasn't going to give me good news, such was the look she gave me.

"Tommy, sweetheart, it's your mum…she's not well. She's…well, she's very sick. I think you should go and see her, son."

I felt like I was sinking into the ground.
The day I always dreaded had finally arrived.

CHAPTER 23

McNamee paid for the land in cash. Neil had never seen such an enormous amount of money. He took the money home that night and split it into two. He put Pete's half to one side and split the other half too. He kept half of that for himself, it was after all what he had paid Pete's father. He would reinvest the money in machinery, or more land. The other half of it, he was going to put in the bank for Seamie, a trust fund. Neil had sworn to himself when Seamie was born that he would not repeat the mistakes of his own father. He had stood on his own two feet and found his niche in farming, not running a failing mill as was his father's wish. He would encourage Seamie to do the same with his life, find a passion and pursue it. He wouldn't burden Seamie with running the farm if he didn't want to, instead he would encourage him to follow his own path.

Oddly, McNamee's return to the country didn't upset Neil as much as he thought it would. Whenever he met him on the road, McNamee was always civil, waving his hand and smiling. Neil would return the gestures, merely to keep the peace, but always muttering under his breath; "Ugly wee fucker". He was sure McNamee was doing the same. The only issue that annoyed him was the re-kindling of Maggie and McNamee's friendship. Pete told him that he had seen McNamee visiting Maggie a few times in Dunbay. Maggie confirmed this, when Pete brought her around for dinner one Sunday afternoon.

"Dessie McNamee's back in the country", she gleefully announced. Neil grunted an inaudible response.

"He tells me he is going to make a quarry out of that land you sold him." she continued.

"And...?", Neil asked, feeling himself beginning to get angry.

"Why couldn't you have done something like that?"

"Maggie, I'm a farmer. I'll stick to what I'm good at. What do I know about quarries?". Neil could feel his blood beginning to boil.

"Ach, farming. Sure, it's a fool's game. Everybody's at it and who's making any money from it? Now, a quarry, that's a business, a viable one at that. Your father was a businessman, obviously that didn't filter down into you. It's in young McNamee though.", she almost hissed.

Neil had recently begun to smoke a pipe, especially in the evenings after his dinner when the day's work had been done. He found the whole ritual of packing the pipe with tobacco, smoking it and then dismantling and cleaning it out, very relaxing and therapeutic. He found it a more enjoyable experience than smoking cigarettes, however, at that moment he found himself desperate for one, and quickly.

"Give us one of your fags, Máire", he said.

"They're in my bag, over in the corner"

He almost ran over to get them. He clumsily fondled the packet, his hands shaking with rage. He got one out, lit it and inhaled deeply. The surge of nicotine did the trick for him. He tried to remain calm, trying not to play into Maggie's hands.

"Businessman, Maggie, is that what he is?", he asked, now smiling.

She sat, reverently, almost smirking, looking into her half empty cup of tea, but didn't reply.

"Did he tell you how much he paid for the land, Rockefeller himself?"

"I don't think young McNamee is so crass as to talk about such things. And, why would I want to know?"

"Well, *I'll* tell you how much he paid then. He paid four times what I paid for it. Four times. So, who is the smart fella now?".

Maggie remained as she was, no reaction in her body language either. It slightly infuriated Neil, he was itching for an argument. She was too crafty, she wouldn't get angry and show her true colours. She would always remain calm, Neil would lose his temper and come out of the confrontation looking like the fool.

"Now, don't talk to me about money. It holds no interest to me…unlike you", she eventually replied.

Neil took a drag on his cigarette, trying hard to calm himself. It worked. The years had certainly mellowed and matured him.

"Maggie, do what you want. You seem to like the man, fair enough, but don't compare us. He'll do his thing, I'll do my thing. Our battles are over. I have moved on, so has he."

She nodded her head in agreement, and got up, putting her coat on.

"Righto. Thanks for the dinner Máire, it was delicious. Peter, are we ready to head back up the road?", she said.

Pete nodded and got up to ready himself. Neil followed Maggie outside.

"Maggie, hold on a second."

"I'm in no mood for an argument, mister. I'm tired", she protested.

Neil waved her protestations away. "I've not come out to argue, woman. Here, take this…put it in your purse."

He produced a brown envelope from his pocket and handed it to her.

"What is it?", she asked.

"It's a few quid. Its money I got for that land I sold to McNamee. It'll come in handy for ye."

Without saying a word, she put it in her handbag and got into Pete's car.

"Aul cunt", Neil muttered under his breath. "She says she doesn't care much for money, but she's fond of taking it", he thought. He had given her an eighth of McNamee's money. He thought it should do her the rest of her days. It was one less burden for him, as he always saw she was well looked after- it was what his father would have wanted.

After they left, Neil went back into the house, played a little with Seamie, loaded his pipe and went outside to smoke it. The smoke, the sound of the birds and the dimming evening sun finally relaxed him. A little later, as he was finishing the pipe, Máire came out, carrying Seamie in her arms.

"Bed time daddy. Say goodnight to wee Seamie"

Neil kissed Seamie and wished him goodnight. He stayed out for another while. Máire came out, after getting Seamie to bed, putting her arms around him from behind.

"What are you pondering, big man. What's on your mind?"

Neil sighed. "Ah, Máire. I don't like it that McNamee's back sniffin' round Maggie."

"But what can he achieve from it, Neil? He can't get anything from Maggie, can he?"

Neil thought for a moment, before replying; "If you're locked up safe and sound inside your house, but you look outside the window and see a snake slithering about, hissing at your front door, you can't help but feel anxious and insecure, even though you know the fucker can't get in. That's sort of how I feel."

Máire hugged him tighter. "Ach, poor Neil. Don't worry about him, he can't hurt us."

Neil smiled and looked up towards Seamie's bedroom window, "I suppose you're right. And a lot of that is down to that wee man's presence in the world. God bless him."

Neil, true to form, bought more land with the money from the sale. His farm went from strength to strength, family life was good and life in general was great. He heard various stories about McNamee's fledgling quarry but stayed well clear, never being tempted to visit it. It wasn't in his nature, he despised nosiness in people, and it was rife around the country. He didn't begrudge McNamee any success, but wouldn't be devastated if he heard the quarry failed spectacularly.

His life was good and he was determined not to let anyone else destroy his happiness. He treasured his life, every day was a privilege to see Seamie grow and develop. He and Máire were trying for a second child too.

It was a bitterly cold evening when Pete called out for him. The thermometer hanging on the wall of the out-house had read five degrees Celsius for most of the day, not a particularly cold temperature, but there had been a biting Eastern wind, a wind that seemed to blow straight from Siberia itself. Neil had been glad to down tools for the day, eat dinner and wash, in preparation for his night in the pub.

The two men walked into the pub, the fire blazing in the corner, much to their delight. Neil ordered and paid for their drinks and sat at the bar.

McNamee and his hangers on, as usual sat in their corner. Neil had grown used to McNamee's presence in the pub by now. McNamee usually stayed in one corner and Neil the other. Neil didn't even notice him most of the time as the craic between him, Pete and whoever else was in the pub was so good. The atmosphere in the bar was usually good natured, but on that night, it seemed different. He could sense a mischievous, prickly atmosphere from the corner where McNamee sat, a heavy tension seemed to float amongst the cigarette smoke.

The night grew later and more men sat slouched over the bar, a mixture of drunkenness and tiredness. Friday night seemed to take its toll on a man, especially a farmer. Neil and Pete sat talking, drinking, and smoking. Plunkett Walsh, the barman and proprietor shouted for last orders. A few men shouted their orders, most had either gone home or were being woken up by Plunkett's shouting.

Neil ordered a drink for Pete and himself, and reluctantly, to boost public relations shouted over to McNamee's corner; "What'll it be, men?"

There were four of them sitting. McNamee, his right-hand man, Paddy Gray and two young men who Neil didn't know, but guessed they must have worked for them.

"Are you buyin' drinks with all that money you made off me, Dillon?", McNamee asked.

His tone had no usual sarcasm or even joviality, it had a definite edge of bitterness.

"I'm only ordering. You're payin'?", Neil joked.

"You can stick your fuckin' drink", Paddy Gray interrupted.

Neil almost laughed, but composed himself before saying; "Now, now, Paddy. That's not very nice. Is there a problem here?"

McNamee and Gray both laughed. The two younger men looked nervous, awkward.

"Jesus, Dillon. I knew you were many things, but I didn't think you were a tattle tale", McNamee replied, finishing off what was left of his whiskey.

Trying to compose himself and work out what the problem was, Neil turned to the barman to order.

"Plunkett, give them four half 'uns and four bottles. It might settle them a bit."

Plunkett brought the drinks down to them on a tray. Neil sat talking to Pete, however his mind wasn't focused on the conversation. Cutting Pete off halfway through one of his anecdotes, he turned to McNamee's corner.

"McNamee, what's this tattle tale shite all about?"

McNamee laughed without a trace of humour, more a mocking cackle. "Why don't you run home and ask Auntie?"

The penny finally dropped for Neil. He realised at that moment Maggie had went to McNamee and relayed the information he had given her about the sale price. He suddenly felt a flush of embarrassment, his cheeks beginning to redden.

"I didn't know it was supposed to be a secret.", he replied.

McNamee sniffed. "It's bad craic. A sale is a private transaction. It was no-one else's business apart from ours and yours."

"Hold on a second, now. It's not like I broadcast it all over the country, for God's sake. She's my family after all, she has every right to know."

"Oh, she's your family *now*, is she? Your family when it suits you more like.", Gray replied.

Neil tried to remain calm, although he knew he was on the verge of losing his temper.

"What are you talkin' about, Gray?"

McNamee, interrupted; "Now, Dillon. We all know you're a great man for family when you think you can get something off them. All over Maggie when she holds the purse strings. When your father was alive, you treated Maggie like a dog, however all that changed when everything was left in her control, funny enough."

Neil suddenly felt like he had all those years ago, a mixture of shock, embarrassment, and untamed range.

Gray added more insult to injury, before Neil could reply; "Your poor father wasn't cold in the ground before you were sellin' up everything he worked his whole life for."

"And what about poor Kathy?", McNamee interrupted.

"Aye, poor Kathy too. Left with fuck all, poor lassie. Last I heard she was livin' on the streets of America.", Gray continued.

Neil's temper finally flared. Pete grabbed his forearm so hard and tight it almost took him by surprise. "Neil, don't rise to it. It's not worth it, you'll get yourself locked up for fuck sake."

Neil smiled at him, a smile failing spectacularly to mask his madness. He shook his head and wagged a raised finger.

He strolled over to where they sat. Gray stood up, yelling; "Ye big fucker, what do ye think you're doin', do ye want some of this?", raising his fists, fear perspiring from his every pore. McNamee grabbed him by the belt, pulling him back down to his seat. "Cool it, for fuck sake, Paddy", he scolded.

Neil stood over them. Almost whispering, he said; "You two come back here, after all these years, spouting shite about me and my family, and expect me to sit here and take it. Well, you have another fuckin' thing coming.". Stopping to point to the two young men who sat with them, he said; "You two, I don't know who you boys are, but I have no issue with ye, unless you have with me?"

The two shook their heads, nervously. "No", both replied almost in unison.

"Now, you two", he continued, pointing at McNamee and Gray; "I have a serious fuckin' problem with".

It almost frightened him how calm he remained. His rage felt electric, savage.

Gray stood up again. "What are you gonna fuckin' do about it then?", he roared.

Neil nearly laughed. He remembered at that point a film he had once seen, a Western, where a character tells another if a group of Indians ever encountered him alone, he should act like a mad man, to scare them off. He felt like asking Gray if he had seen the film.

"You were at this craic years ago, Gray. Belittling me in front of the whole country, bringin' up my sister and family to use against me. Well, I'm puttin' an end to it now. Outside, both of ye. We'll soon see who the big men are."

Neil turned and walked out towards the door.

"Wait", McNamee said.

Gray looked nervously at McNamee. "Right Dessie, come on. Let's give this fucker a hidin' he'll never forget."

"No", McNamee replied. "I don't need anyone's help here. I'll sort him out myself. Let's go."

It was music to Neil's ears.

A crowd of men gathered outside. The night air was so cold, a cloud of steam rose from where the men stood, from their breath in the dim light.

Once both men were outside, they squared up.

Neil threw the first punch, a long jab directed at McNamee's jaw. He seen it coming late and moved his head, Neil's fist scuffing his right ear. McNamee moved in quickly and landed two punches into each of Neil's sides. Almost winded, Neil tried not to panic and pushed McNamee away with one arm. He came at Neil once more, trying to duck in and go for his ribs again. Neil seen him coming, reading his intentions, and cracked a hard right to his mouth. McNamee stumbled backwards, his low centre of gravity preventing him from falling. He threw himself forward again, this time Neil threw a right hook, his fist connecting sweetly to McNamee's jaw. A gasp of astonishment was audible from those watching. The punch almost lifted McNamee off the ground. He lay on the concrete, making inaudible grunts and moans. Neil looked down upon him and against his better judgement almost felt sorry for him. Just as Neil was about to turn and walk away, McNamee somehow managed to get himself to his feet.

"Come on, come on you bastard", he shouted at Neil.

"Go home, McNamee. You're beat. Give it up.", Neil replied. Just then, McNamee rushed at him again, pushing him against the wall. It took Neil by surprise and he could feel the air being rushed from his lungs. He felt light headed, McNamee pummelling his stomach with punches. Again, composing himself and trying to block the punches as best he could, he found the strength to sidestep and throw a punch into McNamee's guts. When he bent over in pain, Neil followed up with a powerful crack to the side of McNamee's head. He toppled at once to the ground.

It was over. Neil knew he wouldn't get up for a while, and if he did, he certainly wouldn't be for fighting.

"Right", Neil shouted. "Where's Gray-he's next"

Paddy Gray stood on the edge of the crowd of men, his face noticeably pale in the pale moonlight. He stood silent and motionless.

"Well, Gray, what are you waiting for, let's go."

Gray stood shaking his head. "No, Dillon. I'm not fightin'. You've made your point."

Neil put on his coat and laughed, looking straight at Gray.

"Coward".

Gray looked anywhere but back at him.

The crowd of men began to disperse. It was too cold to be standing around with no fighting to watch.

McNamee began to stir on the ground, much to Neil's relief. He wanted to teach him a lesson, he didn't want to inflict any long-lasting damage on him.

He got on to his knees and vomited. He looked up at Neil, his face a mess, his mouth a grotesque mixture of blood, spittle, and vomit.

"You bastard, Dillon. I'll fuckin' get you for this."

Neil bent down towards him.

"We're even now. Do you remember the hidin' you gave me when I was only a gasun? You beat the shite out of me, in front of my father and the whole country, and you, a fuckin' grown man. How could I ever forget that? Let's call this payback. As far as I'm concerned, our quarrel is over."

He offered a hand to help him to his feet.

McNamee spat at his hand, the horrible mixture of blood, spittle, and vomit.

"Our quarrel has only fuckin' begun.", he started, his eyes alight with rage, "I'll kill ye. Just you wait and see. I'm gonna fuckin' kill ye".

Neil could see he fully meant it.

"Any day you're fit...you fuckin' weed", he hissed back at him.

He made his way towards his car, where Pete stood, looking shaken.

"Watch your back, Dillon. Watch your fuckin' back.", McNamee shouted after him.

"Don't you worry, McNamee. I'm used to watchin' my back when you're around, you snake", Neil shouted over his shoulder as he walked to his car.

CHAPTER 24

I knew it was only a matter of time before she got sick. I had always known it, but strangely my anticipation didn't dull the shock any when the sickness became a reality.

She had been a force of nature. A small waif of a thing who could drink any hairy arsed builder under the table, any day of the week. Her body withstood unbelievable self-abuse for many years. I had always thought it was because of her strong Irish genes, a sort of evolutionary response to her ancestors being heavy drinkers. I thought those genetics would render her immune to the ravages of alcohol abuse. I half hoped I had the same immunity by default.

Kathleen had told me it wasn't good. I didn't realise how bad it was until I eventually went to see her. Kathleen had been keeping an eye on her throughout the week, regularly visiting and bringing her meals. She was trying to get her to eat, but mostly in vain.

Kathleen surely was a saint. I had never met such a good person. She wasn't the usual do-gooder, hungry for credit and praise at every opportunity, the woman was Biblical good. Humble, caring, good hearted and a sensitive soul- the kind of person who gave one faith that God existed and lived in some people.

I went to see her the next day. I made sure Kathleen would be there, if only to break the tension. Again, I was heavily hungover. I had encouraged Andrea to have a night out with her friends, and stay in her brother's place as I needed an early night. The truth was, I drank myself into a stupor on my own, barely sleeping at all.

I knocked on the door, thankfully Kathleen answered. I noticed the smell first. There was no pleasant way to describe it, the room reeked of stale urine. That broke my heart. For all my mother was, she had always been hygienic. No matter what state she would get herself into, she would always wash regularly, using deodorants and perfumes. The smell of urine felt like a metaphor for her deterioration.

When I walked in, I couldn't see her. The television was on, horse racing.

"Where is she?", I asked Kathleen.

"Over there, sitting in her chair."

The chair sat in front of the television, it's back facing me. Usually I could see her head sitting above the top of the chair, not then. I walked over and sat on the sofa.

When I first caught sight of her, I had to bite hard on my lower lip to stop the tears and sobbing taking effect on my body. I had to breathe deeply and slowly to keep a lid on my emotions. This wasn't my mother. My mother who had always been proud of her seemingly eternal youthful complexion. True, she had aged recently, aged badly, but what I saw before me was not a direct result of ageing, this was a body preparing for death. My mother was slowly dying, rotting from the inside out.

She was tiny, that was the first observation I made. No wonder I couldn't see her sitting in the chair, her body had wilted like an autumnal leaf, the winter of her life imminent. Her eyes were yellow, the whites long gone. I couldn't distinguish where her eyes ended and her skin began, both sets of tissue merging into one sickly, yellow hue. Her eyes sat caved into her skull and her skin was pock marked, sores adorned her arms. Her hands were those of a skeleton. She sat smoking a cigarette, the cigarette looking like a baton in her hand. It was heart-breaking. If I saw a stranger looking the way she did, it would upset me, but this was my mother, the woman who carried me for nine months in her womb. She was a part of me, my only family in the world and she was going to die soon, painfully, and there was nothing I could do about it.

"Ach, ma.", were the only words that came to me.

Kathleen came over, smiling sweetly, compassion, pain, and empathy writ large across her face. She plumped up a pillow and placed it behind my mother's back.

"I told you Tommy would come, didn't I Mrs Smyth", she cheerfully said.

My mother stared at me. It made me uncomfortable. I wanted to reach out, take her in my arms and hold her, be with her, be there for her.

"It's about time you came to see me", she finally spoke, her voice laced with bitterness. But, her manner was different. The bitterness seemed forced, as if to try and drown out the sadness.

"Fuck it ma, let's let bygones be bygones. Let's just concentrate on getting you better."

She laughed and shook her head. "I'll be getting no better. I'm done. It's the wooden over coat for me"

I turned to Kathleen. "Kathleen, this can be fixed. I mean, doctors, hospitals, they can work miracles these days. Can we get her into one?"

Kathleen sadly shook her head. "I've been trying my best, but you won't go, will you Mrs Smyth?"

My mother shook her head. "If it's the Lord's will, then so be it. If it's my time, who am I to argue? I don't want any doctor's hoking about inside me- no way."

"Ma, don't be stupid, come on. We can get you help, we can get you fixed."

I was pleading now, I was almost ready to get on my knees.

She looked at me and almost smiled, like her old self, on a good day. "No. I'm happy here. It's my home now. I'm not going to any hospital."

I knew there was no point in arguing.

"I'll go and make some tea.", Kathleen said, breaking the silence. "You two have a little time on your own."

I nodded my head and smiled.

I sat and updated my mother about my life. I told her about working on the sites and training to become a joiner. I told her about Andrea and even about our first three crazy dates. I told her she would like Andrea. It was nice being with her and talking, no arguments, no bad blood. She didn't say much, just sitting watching the horse racing, but she didn't need to talk. I knew she was listening and seemed content to do so.

Kathleen came in with the tea. She told me health visitors were calling out regularly to check on my mother. She had arranged it, making sure my mother was always supported.

I stayed for a few hours. When I got up to leave, I once again pleaded with her to reconsider the hospital. I knew deep down I was wasting my breath. She looked up at me, shook her head and said; "Next time, bring your girl. I'd like to meet her. And bring a bottle, I'm dying for a wee drink."

That was the saddest part of the day. I knew my mother was going to die, sooner rather than later...and she didn't seem to care.

Andrea, through the next few months was always there for me. She knew when to talk to me, and more importantly when to leave me alone. Life had to go on, and I continued with my training. Dan even promised he would try and get me a start with a few of his joiner mates, when I got my papers. It gave me something to aim for, taking my mind off my mother's tragic demise.

For the first time in my life, I could save some money. Andrea and I even had a plan to save for a down payment on a place of our own and move out of the shit hole we were renting.

Ironically, even though my world was falling apart, life in general was being good to me. Beautiful, loving girlfriend, work going well and money in the bank.

But, yet again, the curse that seemed to hang over my life struck again.

I knew something wasn't right the morning I arrived on site and Dan wasn't there. Dan was always first on site. Always there, organising, planning, directing, but mostly slagging and having a laugh. The atmosphere was strange that morning though. Even Mickel McKeown wasn't his usual self. He seemed subdued, he wasn't actively looking for a victim, it unnerved me. Dan, in all the time I knew him had never pulled a sickie. When I asked him about it once, his response was; "Don't have time for sickness. Don't believe in it.". He never even had a sniffle or a cold.

Sean Carragher was there, filling in for Dan. Most of the time Sean floated about, leaving the hands-on stuff to Dan, so it was strange to see him there at that time.

I called him aside when we were alone. "Sean, what's wrong? Where's Dan? It's not like him not to be here."

His shoulders slumped and his face registered surprise and shock, like rainclouds slowly passing by, darkening a summers day.

"Ach Tommy, you don't know?"

I nearly laughed. I suppose it was anticipated shock.

"What, Sean. What's happened?"

He walked over to me, and placed a hand on my shoulder; "It's Brian, he's in hospital. He's in a bad way, a very bad way."

The news stunned me into silence. I had felt like I couldn't forgive him after what happened to me. I hadn't spoken to him in over two years, but the last thing I wanted was something like this to happen to him.

Sean told me I could take the day off if I wanted to go to the hospital. I told him I'd rather work. Work distracted me, it meant I concentrated on the job in hand rather than all the other shit going on in my life. I worked hard that day, concentrating intensely on everything I did, but the day went by too quickly- it seemed to be over before it even began. Then I had to go home and think about things. None of the crew went to the pub that night, purely out of respect for Dan and his family.

Brian was in hospital from an overdose. Heroin. He had been dumped unceremoniously outside a hospitals admission unit late the night before. When the medical staff had found him, he was unconscious, needle still in his arm. He was in a coma and his chances of pulling through were deemed slim.

I went to the hospital that evening. Outside in the waiting room I was greeted by his sister, Maura. She had moved up north a few years before with her boyfriend and now had a little girl. She was still as beautiful as I remembered, only now friendlier. The surliness of her teenage years had surely been cast aside. When I first met her, she sat wiping tears from her eyes. She looked exhausted and it was obvious she hadn't slept. Beside her sat young Francis, Brian's younger brother. It appeared he had inherited Maura's old teenage surliness.

She stood up and hugged me tightly.

"Oh Tommy. Long-time no see. Mum and Dad will be so pleased you're here"

I shrugged my shoulders, not really knowing what to say.

"I'm so sorry, Maura."

She burst into tears and I held her tightly.

"Tommy, what the hell was he playing at? We all knew he was fond of a drink, maybe the odd spliff, but this shit?"

She looked at me like I had all the answers. I wished I had. I wished I knew how to fix things. I knew he had been taking a lot of coke with those assholes that night, but I didn't think he would ever go to those extremes.

"It'll be OK, Maura. Everything will be all right", I said, trying to reassure both of us.

She calmed down a little and we talked, trying to pause reality for a while. She told me about her little girl and life with her boyfriend in Leeds. She worked as a HR manager in a meat processing factory. I told her about Andrea and life in general. I neglected to tell her about my mother though, as she had enough on her plate. When the conversation eventually dried up, I knew it was time to go into the room.

I took a deep breath. When I entered the room, Kathleen rushed to me, hugging me tightly, bursting into tears. Dan sat at the bedside, tenderly holding Brian's hand. I had never seen that side to him and it hit me hard, to see the affection and love he had for his son. I could see from his eyes he had been crying too, but he would never let me see that.

Brian lay in the bed, hooked up to all sorts of wires and instruments.

"How is he?", I stammered, instantly feeling very stupid and embarrassed for asking such a question.

Before Kathleen could respond, Dan jumped in with; "He's fine. Aren't you kid. Us McManus' are made of tougher stuff than to let a wee thing like this beat us, aren't we son?"

It was strange to hear Dan refer to Brian so tenderly. Usually Brian would be referred to as "kid", "gasun" or mostly "gobshite". It unnerved me a little, I knew things weren't good, and I knew Dan knew it too.

"Sit beside him, Tommy. Talk to him, he can hear you.", said Kathleen.

I didn't know what to do. I sat at his bedside. When I looked at him, I had to restrain myself as much as I could, to not let the tears fall. True, we had fallen out, in a big way, but when I saw him the way he was, brotherly love rushed to the surface and the bitterness and anger I felt towards him instantly dissipated. I just wanted him to get better and resume living his life.

When I began to speak, I felt awkward and self-conscious. I didn't know how to address him, and felt stupid.

"The doctors reckon he can hear everything around him, he just can't respond yet", said Dan.

Knowing he could hear me, I just went for it then, putting all shyness and awkwardness to one side. I told him about what I had been up to. I told him about Andrea and about what happened in the school with Dixon and Herbert. I told him about all the craic we were going to have when he got better. I told him we would all go on holiday to Ireland, and go drinking with Mickel McKeown and the rest of the boys in their home towns. I meant everything I said to him. Life was short, this proved it. There was no point in holding grudges, especially against those who meant the most to us.

As I left, the atmosphere had become a lot more positive. An outside perspective was probably just what Dan and Kathleen needed to refresh and reenergise their weary bodies and minds. To be fair the atmosphere couldn't have been any worse than when I entered the room, but I was glad to help those people in any way I could.

I hugged Kathleen and reassured Dan that we would look after everything in work. Then I went home and demolished a six pack of beer and a bottle of vodka. I slept for an hour or so on the sofa, before getting up for work again.

Between the time I spent visiting my mother, Brian and drinking to fill in the gaps, it was no wonder my relationship with Andrea began to get rocky.

CHAPTER 25

The evening was growing late, the shadows becoming braver, creeping along the room, as the light dimmed.

Neil had been unsuccessful in his attempts to gather firewood that day, although he had tried, his heart just hadn't been in it. He sat at the table, his breath now visible due to the plummeting temperature. He knew he would suffer that night, but he didn't care. The pain and suffering of the freezing house would make him feel alive. He considered it a very mild form of pain compared to what he had already experienced.

No matter how hard he tried, he couldn't help his mind from racing back to that night. He tried everything...routine, self-discipline, endurance exercises, anything that would occupy his mind for a short period. They only delayed the inevitable though, and his will would eventually waiver. Once caught in those memories, a tangled mass of torment and suffering ensued, until the only escape came from sleep. If he was lucky, the nightmares wouldn't take over during his slumber, but mostly they did. He would awaken in the morning, sometimes reaching over for Máire, for her warmth and loving touch, half expecting Seamie to come racing in. That blissful bout of temporary amnesia would last all but a few seconds, until the horror of reality would unfold, making him want to scream in despair. The dull, throbbing sensation in his heart he hoped would turn out to be a heart attack, never so kind to strike.

He sat further, listening...listening for nature outside. He longed to hear the birds singing, the cows mooing, sounds he used to hear. He wanted to hear life, but he knew his wishes were all in vain. Life seemed to have deserted the place after what happened that night. He realised long ago that the place was cursed.

His mind, eventually was transported back to the night it all happened. The day had been uneventful, a Sunday- the day of rest. Pete had been for Sunday dinner and had taken Maggie out with him. Maggie's health had deteriorated badly in the weeks leading up to that day. She had caught a bad flu which had really shaken her. Neil noticed she had barely touched her dinner and hadn't smoked either, which was very unlike her. The biggest giveaway that she wasn't feeling herself came when Pete and Neil engaged in conversation about business, and she hadn't scoffed, offered her opinion, or rolled her eyes in disdain. His guard was always up around her, but he knew he could take it down that day. The fire in her eyes had turned to fear, defeat perhaps. He had seen the same signs in the eyes of his father, her own brother and he knew then, she hadn't long left. It stoked up very mixed feelings in him. He had many battles through the years with her, losing most of them, but she *was* family, his own flesh and blood. Even though she had treated him badly, he still wanted to protect her.

When the time came for them to go, Neil helped with her coat. He noticed a shakiness about her, from the ice queen herself. Never had he even noticed a tremor, when she sneezed she didn't even move. It had worried him when he felt her shoulders. She had always been a thin woman, but she was now skin and bone, certain people couldn't afford to lose weight, Maggie was one. When she got into Pete's car, Neil kissed her on the cheek and she didn't attempt to shrug him off. Neil then knew for certain her days were numbered.

A few hours passed by after Maggie left and Neil and Máire spent it playing with Seamie. Máire sang sweetly as she cleared up the dinner plates. The windows were open, as Máire complained about the smell of the pipe smoke, and the breeze floated gently through the house carrying the sounds of outside's nature with it.

Pete arrived back at the house around seven thirty that evening. He looked shaken, angry.

"What's wrong, Pete?", Neil asked.

"I took Maggie into the pub. She said she needed a hot whiskey, to warm herself a bit."

Fearing the worst, Neil anxiously asked; "And what? Is she all right?"

"Yes, yes...Maggie's fine. She's home and all, we just went in for one. But, when we were in the pub, McNamee was sitting in the corner with his usual cronies. As usual he came over, smarmy as anything around Maggie- you know what he's like."

"Aye, aye- I do. But what happened?"

"Just when we had finished our drink and were about to leave, McNamee came up to me and said; "Your friend, Dillon. Tell him he's a fuckin' dead man. He's got another thing comin' if he thinks he's goin' to get away with batin' me that night. I was too drunk and he done me. I'm gonna fuckin' kill that bastard."

Neil thumped his fist on the table, the ashtray jumping about three inches, spraying its ashes everywhere. He got up and put on his coat.

"We'll fuckin' see about that", he said, trying not to shout, but the ferocity in his tone was immense.

"Máire, I'm goin' to the pub for one. Shouldn't be too long", he shouted up the stairs.

Before Máire could reply, he and Pete were in the car driving to the pub.

When they arrived at the pub it was typical Sunday night fayre, packed full of people, mostly very drunk from drinking all day, after they had been to mass that morning. They ordered a double whiskey each. Neil gulped his down and ordered another. He knew the whiskey would dampen his temper, for a while at least. He didn't want to act on impulse, he was afraid of what he might do. After all, he had a family to look after and support, he wouldn't be much use to them in jail. He waited for the band to take a break, before walking over to McNamee's corner. As usual McNamee sat, holding court with his hanger's on. Paddy Gray sat to his right, taking his role as right hand man much too literally, and another group of men sat around the table, mostly employees and acquaintances.

Neil stood in front of them, swilling his drink in one hand.

"McNamee. You've been shooting that big mouth off again.", he said, the whiskey giving a sureness to his voice.

"Ach, if it's not the bold Dillon. Watch out boys, Tarzan here might get angry and start beating us all now.", McNamee replied. All the men laughed.

"No, no, Dessie. The only man I'll be batin'...again, will be you, if you keep that smart-ass mouth of yours goin'", Neil replied.

McNamee squinted at him, a look of malevolence in his eyes.

"Can I help you with something, or are you just gonna stand there like an overgrown gobshite?", he asked.

Neil leaned down towards him.

"If you're goin' to make threats to my life behind my back, at least be fuckin' man enough to do it to my face.", Neil replied, almost snarling, barely able to contain his rage.

It was now McNamee's turn to look shaken.

"What? Are you away in the fuckin' head? What are ye talkin' about boy?"

"You know what I'm fuckin' talkin' about, and don't call me boy. Sittin' up there, shootin' that big mouth off. If you want to go outside again, be my guest."

McNamee sat and took a sip of his drink, before replying; "This is the second time you've humiliated me in front of my friends. I'm gonna let it go this time. Do it again...we have a problem- a serious fuckin' problem. Now, go home you fool...and take your boyfriend with ye."

Neil felt like a child again. He was enraged and felt at a loss for words. It was him who felt humiliated then. The pub stood deathly silent. He knew he had to reply, to say something and retaliate, but he couldn't find the words until Pete suddenly spoke up; "Ladies and Gentlemen. The great Dessie McNamee. Makes a threat to a man's life and then shite's himself when the man confronts him face to face about it. A complete fuckin' coward."

Neil turned around to stop Pete. He could see Pete was getting very irate, very unlike him. Never had anyone fought his corner before, and although grateful, he didn't want to get Pete embroiled in his troubles.

"Go home now boys. You won't get a rise out of me tonight", McNamee replied, dismissing both men.

The band's break was now over and they started to play once more. Neil and Pete sat at the bar and had another few before leaving early. Outside, before parting ways, Neil thanked Pete for standing up for him.

"Don't worry about those pricks", Pete told him.

"You know me, Pete- I don't worry about anything.", Neil replied, lying through his teeth.

That was the last time he would see Pete. He wished it had been the last time he had seen McNamee.

He walked home that night, letting the cool night air wash over him to cool off. The last thing he wanted was to go home and snap at Máire over something. He had never done that. She was the one, alongside Seamie who brought happiness to his life. He never let anything that happened in the outside world affect his home life.

Máire, surprisingly, was still up when he arrived home. She sat watching television when he came in. She smiled at him, although Neil could tell she was tired, and worried about something.

"You didn't come up to see Seamie tonight."

"Ach Máire, I know. I'm sorry. I just had to rush out about something."

She considered his eyes, a look that cried out for reassurance and asked; "Is everything all right?"

He walked over to her, took her in his arms and kissed her.

"Of course, sure why wouldn't it be?"

She sat silent for a few moments. "I worry sometimes, Neil"

Neil laughed.

"Máire, sweetheart, you have nothing to worry about, absolutely nothing."

He went to hug her again, but she got up and walked to the worktops, busying herself with the laundry.

Neil stoked up his pipe, fired it up and let the smoke relax him.

"Sometimes I wish it could just be the three of us more often"

Máire's statement surprised Neil.

"What...what do ye mean? Sure, it is the three of us, is it not?"

Máire sighed. "Ach, maybe I'm just overthinking things. But...it seems Pete's here an awful lot. Look at today for instance. He was here most of the day, then when I get you for a bit myself, he arrives back and steals you away to the pub."

Neil took another puff on his pipe, if nothing else to give himself a moment to think about his reply.

"Ach Máire, Pete's a good fella. He helps us out here an awful lot, does he not?"

Máire sighed once more, a slightly disgruntled sigh, very unlike her.

"That's not the point Neil. We are a family now. I don't think it's very appropriate a grown man is here most of the time. He takes a lot of your time, time you could be spending with Seamie and me. I mean, we hardly ever see you with the amount of time you spend on the farm alone."

"Máire, for God sake. Where is all this comin' from? Pete's always been around from the day and hour we got together. And, let's not forget, was he not the man who introduced us?", Neil replied, trying to stay calm, not wanting to snap at her.

"I know, I know", she responded, sensing that Neil was getting angry, not wanting to upset him. Biting down on her lip, as if to try and hold the words back, she continued; "I just think he's...well, just a bit of a bad influence."

Once the words came out, she reddened and continued to busy herself with the laundry.

Neil sat, almost in shock at Máire's harsh assessment of his friend, before adding; "For the love of God woman, how the hell do you think that? Pete Kelly's my best friend...the only real friend I have. How could you think that?"

Máire straightened up at that point. As gentle a soul she was, she could be feisty when she had a corner to fight. "How is he not, Neil? You're a married man with a child, he's a single man with a colourful history. He's dragging you to the pub most nights and he's drinking, gambling and probably whoring too. I just worry he's putting you to the bad, that's all. I worry you're being badly influenced. Seamie and I should be enough for you."

It was too much for Neil to take. Against his better judgement, he slammed his fist into the kitchen table. Máire didn't flinch. She had a steeliness to her when she was up against it.

"For God sake Máire, I don't need this. Of course, you and Seamie are enough for me, don't be so silly. If you feel...jealous about Pete, well, that is your problem- not mine."

Máire stood, looking aghast. "Jealous, ha. If that's what you bloody well think, then you don't know me. I'm going to bed. You cool off before coming up, Mister, or you can sleep on the bloody sofa."

At that she left and retired to bed. Neil sat at the table in silence, regretting what he had said. He felt bad. Very rarely did he and Máire row about anything. He made up his pipe and took another few puffs.

Once cooled off, he climbed the stairs and got into the warm bed beside Máire. He took her in his arms, she was still awake.

"Máire, I'm sorry. You and Seamie are *everything* to me. If you want me to see less of Pete, no problem. I love you and Seamie with all my heart, no one even comes close. Good night, sweetheart."

"Oh, you silly big oaf. I know that. I'm sorry for what I said too. I just worry sometimes. I love you more than anything too. Good night and God bless, darling."

At that, they kissed and made up. Both went to sleep happy.

Neil remembered that night for having a very vivid and terrifying dream. It was about the Gentle bush. He dreamt of it standing alone in the middle of the field. Over time, it began to wither and die. When it had finally withered away to nothing, he dug up the roots to re-seed the area with grass. As he dug down to where the roots sat, deep in the ground, he fought back the urge to vomit suddenly. He frantically tried to claw his way back out. He roared out in horror for someone to come to his aid. In the hole, just inches from his feet, lay two grossly decomposing bodies, side by side. Worms protruded from the faces of both. It was hard to see who the bodies belonged to, so badly decomposed they were, but he couldn't help but to look, out of grave curiosity. Suddenly, the shock of the realisation of who the bodies belonged to caused him to lose his footing and fall on top of them. No matter how hard he tried, he couldn't get out of the hole, or even onto his feet. The horror so overwhelmed him it woke him from his sleep, sweating and gasping for breath.

Before he had time to dwell on what just happened in his dreams, he realised the gasping for breath reflex was indeed a real one. He reached across and found the warm, sleeping figure of Máire. Looking back on that night, the decision not to wake her there and then would haunt him forever. He couldn't understand why he didn't. Over the years that followed, he believed he must have thought he was still in the nightmare and didn't want to contaminate her with it.

As he got on to the landing, his gasping for air grew more intense. His eyes began to sting and the fight for air turned into a more sinister choking sensation. In a lucid, half-awake state, he found himself rushing down the stairs. To his horror, he found the downstairs room filling up with a thick, murky smoke. It was then he roared at the top of his lungs for Máire to awaken, to go and get Seamie. He was about to go back up to make sure Máire and Seamie got down safely, when he heard the commotion in the hayshed, attached to the house. His reflex actions kicked in and he found himself bolting for the outside door to see what was happening in the shed. Still screaming for Máire to wake up, he opened the door and rushed into the adjoining hayshed. He stood deathly still for a second, his senses conveying sight, sound and smells he couldn't comprehend.

The shed was on fire. It had been no accident either, the harsh smell of petrol in the air confirmed that. Then he heard rapid footsteps coming from behind him. Just as he was turning to see who they belonged to, he received a sickening blow to the side of the head. At that, the flaming scene before him seemed to swirl and encapsulate him. As he descended into unconsciousness he tried in vain to roar out the names of Máire and Seamie. He wondered if the words ever came out.

He hoped he was still within his nightmare. Just as easily as he had woken from it, he slotted seamlessly back into it. He was back in the hole, with the two rotting bodies, screaming out for help. He was tearing at clumps of soil to try and get a grip, but the soil turned to sand in his hands. He looked up and saw the Gentle bush beginning to grow again above him, from seedling to plant, to fully grown bush. As it grew, the hole he lay in became smaller, the roots embedding themselves in the two rotting corpses. It was feeding from them. He tried desperately again to get to his feet only to realise the roots were beginning to enter *his* body, needling the life out of him. At that, in his nightmare, he fell unconscious, only to wake to reality.

When awakened, he would have gladly returned to the horror of his nightmare. As he looked up, amid the searing heat stabbing and licking over his body with its brutal energy, he saw none other than McNamee stooped over him, roaring and screaming into his face with a demented expression, animating his already hideous features.

Neil tried, with every ounce of his being to fight back against him, to claw at his face, to kick, to try and defend himself...all sadly in vain.

His strength had gone. McNamee had finally got the better of him. Neil knew then, in those desperate few seconds that the bastard had finally gained his terrible revenge.

CHAPTER 26

The few weeks after I visited Brian in the hospital had been hard. As if things weren't bad enough with my mother and her health, what happened to Brian almost drove me over the edge. But, one only realises how hardy the human spirit is when they are up against it and amazingly, I held it together…for a while. It was important I went to work, remained positive and visited Brian constantly. Enough people were on the verge of complete breakdown, without me adding to it. I knew I had to remain strong, and I did…until it all caught up with me.

Good news finally began to filter through about Brian. I was at work one day when Dan arrived on site. He looked different, not exactly happy, but more at ease. He didn't look as beaten as he had.

"We've a bit of news on Brian, Tommy."

My heart began to pound, my mouth dried up. The saying, "No news is good news", ran around my head. I gripped hard on my shovel.

"Yeah?", is all I could say.

"He's out of the coma."

In life, very few moments occur when the system is overloaded with relief, adrenalin, euphoria, and anxiety all at once-a strange and unique feeling.

I let out a massive sigh of relief, wondering where all the air had come from, and where it had been stored.

"Oh, thank God. Jesus, it's good to get some good news at last, eh?"

Dan nodded his head sombrely.

"It is. He's not quite out of the woods just yet. He's awake and responding to people around him, but the doctors don't know if he'll ever be the same again."

Choosing not to listen entirely to all he said, especially the last part, I replied; "Ach, he'll be fine Dan. We both know that. He's as strong as a bull, he *will* recover-I have no doubt about that."

I was glad I said that. I believed it too, but the effect it had on Dan was remarkable. His shoulders raised and pulled back, he even seemed to grow in height before my eyes. He smiled then, an unforced one at that.

"Bejaysus you're right, Tommy. You're fuckin' right.", he replied and walked off, almost with a spring in his step, which visibly lifted the mood of all the men on the site too.

It's remarkable how a person in despair can cling on to the words of others. To obtain a crumb of comfort and hope, because, as I would find out later, Brian had quite a fight on his hands…even by his standards.

The overdose he took caused him to have multiple mini-strokes. These strokes culminated in loss of many of his normal brain functions, particularly the ability to walk and talk. His face seemed to be frozen, drooping at the mouth and at one of his eyes. He couldn't lift his arms or control his mouth or tongue muscles, making him drool constantly. When I went to visit him that evening, again, I had to bite hard on my bottom lip to stop myself from breaking down. The guy, along with his father, had been a lifelong friend, a brother and sometimes a hero of mine. To me, he was invincible, and there he lay, a young man looking like a ninety-year-old. It was heart-breaking. To be honest, I couldn't see at that time, how he would ever recover.

That all changed whenever he looked at me, though. I could see that glint in his eye. That certain rascality that lived within him. I could see he was glad I came, that our feud had ended.

Looking into those eyes, seeing that steely resolve, gave me a lot more hope. I believed then. I knew he would recover.

Kathleen sat at the bedside. She tenderly wiped the drool from his mouth. The poor woman had aged ten years, she looked exhausted and beaten.

I sat and continued my story about what we were going to do when he got better, trying to project positivity through my words. I just spoke, most of it bullshit, but I knew Brian and Kathleen were listening. I knew they were enjoying it. I couldn't help but feel it was like talking to someone's soul, like prayer. His body resembled a corpse, but his eyes had all the fire and life of his youthful years.

I left after a while and went home. Andrea had cooked dinner and left it covered in tinfoil on the kitchen work top. She was in bed. I didn't visit her. I sat and drank a bottle of vodka, wallowing in self-pity, Brian's piercing eyes never leaving my thoughts.

As usual the next morning, I woke on the sofa. Head pounding and my stomach losing its battle against the booze, I quickly changed and got out. Andrea was away already. She must have been thinking things were getting bad between us. The scene that had played out was becoming more of a regular occurrence. I knew I had to make amends...and quickly.

The day passed, the work and fresh air taking my mind off Brian, my mother and mostly my hangover. I came home that night and told Andrea I was finally going to introduce her to my mother. She knew how big of a deal that was and immediately busied herself getting ready.

I had never introduced a girl to my mother before. Never felt the need to. No-one had ever come as close to me, as Andrea. I knew she was the one for me. I resolved not to let her slip away, although deep down I knew I would fuck it up too.

On the way to my mother's I told Andrea we would need to go for a drink first.

"Another drink is the last thing you need, Tommy.", she said.

"You're probably right, but the drink is mostly for *your* benefit.", I told her.

We had a few at the bar at the bottom of the road where my mother lived.

When we got there, against my best nature, I couldn't help but to feel embarrassed.

The curtains were pulled, as usual, but the place smelt *bad*. It smelt like decay, death. It was a kip too. Empty bottles of gin and cigarette packets lying everywhere. Her record collection was strewn across the floor too. It was obviously like that because Kathleen hadn't been around as much, being with Brian most of the time.

Again, she sat, watching television, barely registering our presence. Her condition hadn't improved any. She still looked like a corpse in waiting.

"Ma, this is Andrea. My...girlfriend."

My mother looked up, surveying Andrea up and down, and said; "Oh, you're a doll.", and continued to watch the television in silence.

She was drinking. *Still* drinking. It looked like cider, I had never known her to drink that before.

"What's that ma, cider?"

She laughed- a genuine laugh.

"It is. I'm not fit for the hard stuff anymore, so I'm drinkin' this stuff. It's not too bad. Gives me a serious dose of heartburn from time to time though.", she sat smiling, taking another sip.

"You shouldn't be drinkin' anything, ma. Hard stuff or not."

Again, she smiled. I could tell she was in one of her better moods, or on some strong medication.

"What's this girls name again?"

"Andrea"

"Angela. Look at this one telling me to go easy on the drink- he's one to talk, eh?"

Andrea laughed, nervously and politely.

"So, Angela" (neither of us corrected her), "What do you do with yourself?"

Andrea told her about her job, even told her about how she met me. My mother sat smiling and listening, her eyes still fixed on the television. Andrea spoke further, telling stories, and filling the awkward silence.

It was soon time to go. As we got up, like a nagging wife, I pleaded again; "Ma, please go easy on that stuff. How about seeing the doctor again? I think you maybe need a bit of help?"

At that, she drained the remaining liquid in her glass. Still smiling, she replied; "I'm done. No point in seeing doctors and having them rooting about inside me. It's time to stand in front of our Lord."

"Fuck sake ma, catch yourself on- see a doctor...please?", I replied, exasperated and a little irritated.

Still smiling, she shook her head.

"A wee drink and a smoke are the only comforts I have in this life. Now, you young people mightn't be able to believe this, but there comes a point in your life when you get tired. Tired of living, tired of life. Eat, drink, sleep.

Wake up, do it all over again. It's fuckin' monotonous, that's what it is. You are young, enjoy yourselves. Plan and build a life together, there's lots left for you, all in front of you. I'm not feelin' sorry for myself, I am genuinely looking forward to the future, whatever that holds... most likely death, but whatever is around the corner, let it come. I'm ready for anything."

She poured herself another drink, drank deeply from the glass and nodded towards Andrea.

"This girl- I like. She's a good 'un. You've chose well. Bring her around again.", she said.

What more could I say? What more could I do? I bent down and hugged her, her bones jutting into me.

That was that. Andrea and I left to go home. I knew my mother's fight was over. I tried to get on with my life as best I could. If drinking myself unconscious every night and not having any recollection of how much I drank, or what I did, was getting on with my life, then that was what I did.

A few months passed. Brian was still in hospital. I tried to stay positive, for him and his family. I was in danger, I thought, of turning into an insincere fucking cheerleader. There was only so much encouragement and positivity I could bring. I didn't want to overdo it and sound false. It wasn't in my nature, I wasn't a bullshitter, so didn't want to bullshit them too much. There was a fine line between inspiration and desperation, I was balancing on the edge.

The truth was, I really despaired for Brian's predicament. Yes, he was making progress, but at the rate he was progressing, he would be back to his normal self when he was about one hundred years old.

It was that bad.

Small things, like moving his fingers when asked to in a sequence, were huge accomplishments. Everyone got excited when he blurted out a noise that vaguely sounded like a word. But, what could I do? Throw my head up and say; "It's all fucked- he's fucked. Forget about it."?

Of course not. I had to play along- trying to find a fleck of gold dust in a lagoon of shite. Not the easiest task when my mother was also in the process of dying a horrible death, and the love of my life was slipping away by the day.

Poor Mrs McManus was starting to build a shrine to what looked like a saint.

"Who's the saint?", I asked.

She stopped what she was doing and looking mournfully at Brian, and replied; "Poor St. Jude, the patron saint of lost causes."

A saint I could relate to.

I tried not to let things get me down too much. After all, I had a beautiful girlfriend at home. I should have been looking at the positives in life. I actually did feel positive most days, after the hangovers wore off, around mid-day. Once feeling more normal I resolved to visit Brian after work, spread some cheer, then go home and sweep Andrea off her feet and take her out for a no expenses spared meal, make a fuss of her. However, as the day ebbed on, the positivity ebbed away. By the time work was finished and I visited the sick, the desire for a drink, for complete obliteration, took hold in ways I couldn't resist, no matter how hard I tried.

It would always begin as a sociable meeting in the pub, fooling myself it was like the old days when alcohol was merely fuel for the wit and craic that ensued. I knew deep down, though, the alcohol was now the main event, fuelling my despair and sadness. Most of the time I found myself sitting at the bar on my own, away from the others, as the craic I used to enjoy so much, now distracted me of the main job in hand…drinking. Then, on the way home, the off licence. I always left the pub just before the off licence closed. It would have been unthinkable to go home without a carry out.

Once home, I would attempt to eat the dinner Andrea had lovingly prepared. Cold and soggy, or lukewarm and cardboard-like, the texture of most foods after they had sat for four or five hours after cooking.

I drank, listened to music, looked at photographs of years gone by, drank some more, and fell unconscious on the sofa, only to wake again the next morning. Andrea would have already left for work an hour beforehand- like every other day.

God only knows how long that toxic routine lasted for…five, six months, maybe longer? My joinery course had been abandoned, I didn't have the self-discipline to keep that going. The only reason I got up to go to work was because I had to. I didn't want to let Dan down, and I couldn't afford not to work.

I began to have recurring dreams, horrible nightmares that I was being abusive to Andrea. Nightmares where I was roaring at her, threatening her with violence. I could see her crying, lying in bed, looking at me with fear in her eyes, her face red and flushed from her tears. I saw her in the living room, wearing her red dressing gown, the cute woolly one with white spots on it, a look of terror on her face as I roared and screamed at her. She was crying. I could almost smell her tears, like fresh seawater, such was the ocean of tears she wept.

I could hear her in my dreams; "Tommy, please stop. Come to bed. I only want to help you. You're going to end up like your mother at this rate. Please…please, stop this baby."

Then I could hear myself roaring at her; "Fuck you. Fuck you and my mother. Fuck Brian, the druggy cunt, he had it comin' to him. Fuck the lot of you- now get out of my sight before I do something I regret..."

Then she ran off to the bedroom, crying and terrified.

What horrible nightmares.

What was wrong with me? I knew I would never lay a finger on *any* woman, but in these dreams, I had felt perilously close to it, like I was out of my mind.

I would wake, again on the sofa, sometimes retching from the stench of vomit, pooled either on the floor or on the cushion beside me. I would clean it up, trying not to be sick again, toxic sweat emanating from my every pore. Then I would shower and go to work. Again, the positivity would come to me, like shards of light seeping into a darkened room through the blinds, only once again to be drowned by the evening darkness that inevitably came.

One day, my positivity lasted longer than usual. I decided to embrace it, to shower another person I love in the rays of sunshine. So, that night I gave Brian and my mother a miss. I decided to get home as quick as I could before the darkness took over, like a child running for home before the sun went down.

I got home, still in good spirits.

"Andrea, baby. I'm home. Get your glad rags on, I'm taking you out tonight."

Full of satisfaction I finally got around to doing this, I walked into the kitchen to embrace her. She wasn't there. I noticed a forlorn piece of paper sitting on the kitchen table. I sat at the table and read it;

"Dear Tommy.

You know I'm no quitter. I never wanted to give up on you. I know you're going through a lot these days, but I can't deal with this anymore. I vowed I would never give up on you, but it is hopeless now, since you have obviously given up on yourself.

You have frightened me recently. I can't live like this anymore. You probably don't remember what you have been doing as you get so drunk, but the name calling and the roaring and shouting is unbearable. You say you would never hit a woman and you haven't hit me, but I feel like it is only a matter of time. I can't hang around and wait to see if you finally do.

You complain about your mother all the time, about what drink has done to her, but you obviously can't see you are on the same road to destruction.

I can't sit back and watch this happen. I can't live like this anymore.

I love you with all my heart, but love can only put up with so much.

I wish you all the best and I hope you get some help- I really do, but I need to leave before something bad happens.

Please don't call or try to find me. I think its best we go our separate ways.

Love, Andrea xx"

I read the letter about five times over. I felt nauseous. Those nightmares I'd been having had obviously been real. How could I have thought I was dreaming, how drunk had I fucking been? I had never felt so disgusted with myself. I couldn't even look at myself in the mirror, I felt uneasy living in my own skin.

So, what did I do?

Man up and get back on the straight and narrow, sober up to win Andrea back and be strong for Brian and my mother?

Did I fuck.

I went to the off-licence, stocked up for a few days and drank myself to oblivion.

Sometime later the phone rang. Dan.

"Where are you? Are you sick? You haven't been in work the past few days."

Then the nightmarish scenario descended upon me once again, where I felt like I was having an outer body experience, unable to stop what I was saying or doing. I saw myself roaring down the phone; "FUCK OFF! LEAVE ME THE FUCK ALONE!"

Then the stunned silence on the other end. Then I hung up.

Then the black outs, veering in and out of consciousness. I lost all track of time. Time didn't matter anymore.

There were times when I'd run out of drink and had to get up off the floor to go out. I would sometimes think- "Just stop this. Get your shit together, go after Andrea. Visit your mother, visit Brian. Be strong. Go to work and get back to normal.". Sometimes I attempted to shower and wash the badness away. Shower, shave, fresh clothes, fresh resolve. But, then the negativity would seep back into me. It's too late, I would reason. Too many people have been driven away. People have seen my true colours. It's too hard out there. It's easier to stay in, drink and forget about everything.

That reasoning would win every time.

Kathleen rang a few times.

"Tommy, please don't hang up...", I already had, at that point.

I knew bad shit was coming. I wasn't working, so I had no money. I couldn't help my mother out and my landlord would be on my case looking his overdue rent. The worst-case scenario would be that I couldn't afford any more drink...unthinkable. To counteract that problem, one day I visited the off licence four consecutive times, carrying as much drink as I possibly could home. Each time I arrived home, I guzzled enough booze to down a small army. Obviously, I didn't remember the third and fourth visits to the off licence.

A week or so must have passed. I woke up lying on the floor, completely naked.

Why naked?

Probably because I had been lying in my own shit, piss and vomit for so long, that clothes became more of an inconvenience.

The phone was ringing. I hoped it was the phone and not the alarm bells my body was sounding out. My head pounded like it had never pounded before, the pain was insanity in a physical form. I reached out for the nearest bottle that lay beside me, like a discarded lover. Vodka. Took a huge hit and fought with all my being to keep it down. Then I took another one, it being a little easier.

The phone rang off, then rang again.

"FUCKIN' PHONE!!", I roared, and picked it up by mistake. I had meant to pull the plug from the wall, but deep down had been hoping it would be Andrea, so my subconscious had probably instructed me to answer it in false hope.

"Yes", I slurred aggressively down the line. There was a slight pause at the other end.

"Tommy. It's mum. Don't hang up on me. I'm...worried about you, son."

That word at the end got me. She very rarely referred to me as "son". To hear that *she* was worried about *me,* God, that drove the message home. I didn't let it show though.

"What'd ye want?", I grunted in reply.

There was another slight pause.

"Son, I want to see you...soon. The thing is, Mrs McManus came around the other night with a doctor. They took me to hospital. Son...I'm dying. They reckon I don't have long left, a few weeks...if I'm lucky. So, I'd like to see you. There are...things, I need to tell you before I go."

She was telling me this very calmly. It was as if she was going on holidays and needed me to water her plants or feed the cat, not that she was going to die.

My eyes were filling with tears. The expression one had a lump in the throat never seemed so apt, it actually stopped me from replying. My face burned with emotion.

The line was quiet. She awaited my reply.

"Where are you? I'll come soon."

She told me the name of the hospital and ward she was in. I put the phone down. The vodka fumes wafted out of the bottle and into my nostrils, enticing me to drink further. In my darkest moment, I nearly laughed, as it reminded me of a cartoon were the characters are attracted to the visible lines coming from the cooked food.

I lay on my back, a million thoughts rampaging through my twisted, tortured mind. I had to be strong.

I had to.

I had to stop drinking, shower, change and visit my mother. I had to make amends, somehow. Andrea was gone, but she wasn't dying. She didn't need me...my mother did. Thoughts such as; "Where am I going to bury her?" swam through my head.

Horrible.

I pulled myself off the floor, and took a freezing shower that bolted me back to sobriety. I thought about eating something, but dry retched at the thought, the retching saving my disappointment, as there was no food in the flat anyway.

I looked at my reflexion on the way out the door. The man in the mirror looked like me, only if it was Halloween, and I was made up to look like a ghost.

The scariest thing was, I looked like her.

Then, I went out through the door, sober and sick, to find my mother.

CHAPTER 27

Neil sat at the lone chair, puffing at his unlit pipe, and breathing in the sub-zero Irish morning air.

"When is this fuckin' winter goin' to end?", he muttered to himself.

There seemed to be no sign of spring, never mind summer. He took a few pulls on the unlit pipe, the stale tobacco smell stirring his senses and memories to better times. He sat for a moment and basked briefly in them. They were still vivid in his mind, the way he wanted them to be. He remained thrifty with his memories. Yes, they were still vivid, but to use and dwell upon them may render them over used and colourless, he reasoned. He thought of his memories as works of art, beautiful, poignant...although they would always leave the connoisseur feeling unfulfilled, frustrated. The yearning to view the original sight, instead of the replica, no matter how life-like and awe-inspiring it was, would never be the same as it had been on original view.

He sat further, trying to stop himself from delving into his memories too much, when suddenly, a rustling outside startled him, a crunching of frozen gravel under a human foot. It felt almost supernatural to him, the sensation of sound from another human being.

He froze for a second, then decided to run. He leapt from his chair and bolted up the stairs, trying to find a place to hide. He stood at the top of the stairs, listening, barely breathing in case he would be heard. Then the front door swung open. He heard heavy wellington boots squelching on the floors, smelling the cow manure from them.

"Neil...Neil. Are you here?", the man called out, his voice tinged with anxiety and fear. Neil recognised the man's voice instantly. It had been so long since he heard another human voice.

It was Fintan Smith, his brother-in-law.

"Oh God", thought Neil. He thought how much the poor man's life had also been ripped apart. Neil had lost a wife and child, Fintan had lost a sister and nephew.

He wanted to answer, to call back to him. He wanted to descend the stairs, and reach out to him. Go for a drink and talk. Relish human company, company from a *good* human, but he couldn't. He knew if he even tried to respond, he would open his mouth and no sound would come out. He had become too stuck in his ways. It seemed strange to him that he now relished solitude, he couldn't bear to interact with other humans. How could he trust humanity after what they had done to him, he thought?

So, he didn't respond. He stood there, in silence and watched as Fintan moved furtively around the rooms. Finally, he watched as Fintan moved back to the front door, took a last glance around the place before taking one scanning glance. Neil remained frozen, almost in horror as he was sure

Fintan had spotted him. He had locked his eyes on Neil's. He didn't say anything. He just stood for a split second until it appeared something jolted him into life. He reached his hand behind him to find the door knob, quickly turned and almost ran out through the door. Like a flash, he was gone.

"Surely, he didn't see me...he would have said something?", Neil thought.

He felt relieved he had escaped the encounter. To speak to Fintan would be like speaking to the man in the mirror. His pain and suffering being reflected in the eyes of another man.

Trying, mostly in vain, not to let the episode rattle him too much, Neil's mind, against his strongest will, raced back to the night and following morning of the tragedy that destroyed so many lives.

Unlike the good memories, where he felt he should dwell on them sparingly for fear he should dull them with over-use, the opposite seemed to be true for those most horrid memories. Over time they appeared to intensify and grow more vivid in their wretchedness. Once he was transported back, it seemed he was locked in, held prisoner until the images blurred and faded out.

He had regained consciousness. McNamee was nowhere to be seen. He didn't know how long he had been out for. His body ached and he fought hard against the reflex to retch from the smell of stale smoke in his nostrils. Why stale, he wondered. Why was there no fire, or even smoke? Luckily, the shed hadn't been damaged too badly. Most of the hay had been destroyed, but that didn't concern him.

He got to his feet, "Máire...Seamie", he shouted, no answer. He walked towards the door, still shouting; "Máire...Seamie", but, as he walked out through the open door, he stood, frozen to the ground.

He vomited immediately on the ground, for what he saw in front of him was the image no father, or person, should ever have to witness.

A black line ran from the charred hay, out of the shed and around, into the house. He knew it was where the bastard had poured the petrol, letting the fire from the burning hay lead to. Inside the house, the walls were blackened from the smoke. He walked closer to the door. A hive of activity ensued. There were people everywhere. He walked through the house. Policemen and other uniformed people were present. He ignored them all.

"Máire...Seamie", his voice now more desperate.

He walked outside, almost in a daze. The air was cold, but his blood boiled from anxiety and rage.

"Máire...Seamie, where are you?"

No answer, no sign of either. Then...the hustle and bustle of the people in and around the house dulled down, slowly at first, then totally. Like the calm before the storm. Neil stood on the periphery, watching. Then the people in the house and those standing in the doorway began to make way.

"Let them through, give them some room", a man shouted.

Neil's heart soared. Relief washed over him. At that moment, he knew a shaken and scared Máire and Seamie were being interviewed and treated upstairs. He knew then the reason for all the people around the house- investigating the cause of the fire. He began jogging to the door to meet them, expecting to see them any second, blackened, and covered in blankets, but alive and well.

Just as the men came out through the door, he lost his balance and fell to the ground. He looked up, the world swirling before his eyes. Time appeared to slow down for a few moments. He didn't feel anything at that moment. A feeling of nothingness. No anger, hurt or sadness, just a feeling of emptiness. The anger, hurt and sadness all crashing in like waves later, but at that point all his emotions abandoned him.

The image he viewed at that moment would be forever ingrained in his memory.

Men carried two stretchers out of the house.

A figure on each one.

White sheets were placed over both, including the faces.

One larger figure, one smaller.

Máire and Seamus had both been killed in the fire, he knew that then.

The bodies were put into a van and taken away.

With that, Neil's life was taken away too.

CHAPTER 28

It was the same hospital Brian was holed up in. I supposed it would kill two birds with one stone when visiting them all.

When I got there, I met Kathleen in the waiting room. I felt embarrassed, really embarrassed. She put me at ease immediately with a kind, understanding smile.

"Good to see you, Tommy"

"Yea, Kathleen. You too. Listen…I'm really sorry for my behaviour recently. I'm embarrassed to show my face, to be honest with you. Behaving like a petulant brat, and you people…"

She stopped me there, putting her hand up; "Tommy, don't worry about it. You've been going through a rough time, these things happen. The most important thing is you are here now and you're going to be strong for your mum."

I felt such a rush of love and affection for her right then, I had to use all my restraint to not break down and lose myself in her arms. As I had always thought, the woman was a saint. I didn't respond. I just nodded my head sombrely and let her lead me up to my mother's room.

I knew things were bad when she led me to a private room. People like us weren't in such privileged positions for a private room, unless there was something majorly fucking wrong!

Kathleen stood at the door, before we entered. Again, smiling sweetly, she took my hands in hers.

"Tommy, love. Your mother, she's…well, she's not doing too good at the minute. But, she's one of us, she's got that Irish fight in her. She'll not give up easily. Be in her corner. Encourage and be there for her, just like you've done for Brian. You've been great with him and we all respect that. It goes without saying that we are here for you both. If you need anything, all you have to do is ask. You understand?"

I nodded.

"And another thing, Dan said call him if you are still interested in resuming work after what he calls your "little episode". He will give you details of where to be tomorrow morning."

I had fully expected the sack after my behaviour, no questions asked.

"OK", I replied, and we both walked into the room.

The woman lying in the bed, I didn't recognise. I almost told Kathleen we had entered the wrong room until I locked eyes with the woman, only then recognising her as my mother. The eyes hadn't changed. Steely, mischievous, all the things my mother had been…a fucking mystery wrapped in an enigma. Most heartbreakingly of all though, fear overshadowed all the other old traits. For all my mother's bravado and talk of relishing the imminent arrival of death, I knew deep down she was scared, very scared.

Awkwardly, I sat at her bedside. Bones jutted out from everywhere on her body. Having lived in London all my life, I had met a lot of damaged people. People with all sorts of afflictions and diseases, but never had I met anyone with a green hue to their skin like my mother had, like an afterglow. The woman almost looked like a ghost.

She gazed upon me for a moment, then took my hand in hers- her skin fragile and brittle to the touch. At that point, speaking was even a strain on her wracked body.

"Tommy, enough is enough. I've heard things you've been up to."

I glanced at Kathleen, wondering what my mother had heard.

"Don't be cross at Mrs McManus. This woman, I realise now, is the mother I should have been to be to you all along. I've heard you've been drinking, really drinking...my type of drinking. I didn't realise you were so bad. Son, I need you to stop it. There are things I need you to do, things I couldn't do because I was too scared. For you to carry out my wishes I need you to stay strong, not like me."

I thought she must be losing it, talking about crazy stuff like that.

I looked at Mrs McManus. She was busying herself tidying things away.

"Ok ma. Whatever you wish. I'll knock the drinking on the head for a bit, things just got on top of me a bit recently."

She still had my hand in hers. Her grip tightened. "Tommy, I don't know how long I have left, but I need to tell you some things. Things about your past, our family's past. I had been too scared to tell you these things when you were growing up. There are things, people, I cannot ever face again. You, on the other hand are young, strong, and able bodied. I'm relying on you, son."

For a woman who was in such declining health, her grip was vice like. I was beginning to get anxious. What were these things I had to do?

"What, ma. Tell me what you want me to do. I won't let you down, just tell me what it is."

She let go of my hand and the fire of her previous convictions seemed to fade. She lay, as if wilted on the bed now, where before her body had been taught and tense.

"Son, there's a lot to tell you. It's going to take a lot out of me telling you these things. Come back tomorrow night and I'll start my tales. It will take a while. These things require a lot of energy for me to relive, but I want you to be patient. Give me time and you will know everything, you have a right to know everything. But it will take a while, so be patient."

Excitement and anxiety pulsed through my veins. "Alright ma, I'll give you time. Take as long as you need, anything you want me to do, I'll do it."

She smiled. Her eyes conveyed sweetness and warmth.

"Good. First, and I want you to heed this, I want you to keep off spirits. Vodka, gin, whiskey- those spirits are deadly, they have done this to me". She pointed at herself, a look of sadness polluting her features.

"These past few months I have stuck to beer and cider. I know…I know. I shouldn't have been drinking anything, but those two, I could drink all day and not a button of harm they would do to me. Strangely, I've felt better the last few months than I have done in twenty years. If you're going to drink, stick to those two and you'll be all right. You'll get full up, you'll get tired and sleep, drinking them. Spirits, for God's sake, you know as well as I do…you could stay up for a week drinking them."

I nearly laughed. Pearls of motherly wisdom, drink beer and cider, not spirits. I took her advice over time though, and sure enough, she was right.

"OK, ma. Whatever you say.", I replied.

She smiled, and the ruins and blackness of her teeth made me deeply sad. My once pretty and proud mother now a doppelganger for Shane MacGowan at his lowest ebb. It pained me to see MacGowan looking like he did, a man I idolised, so like me in many ways in his outlook and heritage. So, you could gather how it pained me to view my once beautiful mother as she was then.

"Come back tomorrow night and I will begin my tales."

She closed her eyes and immediately fell asleep. I tucked her in before leaving, kissing her on the forehead.

Kathleen and I left her sleeping and went to see Brian for a while. Then I went home.

Once home, I sat for a while, deciding not to drink as I wanted to be fresh for work the next morning. I debated with myself whether to ring Andrea or not.

I wanted her back, needed her back, but those nightmare memories of abusing her, tortured me enough into thinking that maybe she was better off without me. On the other hand, I knew if I took my mother's advice, got strong, laid off the hard stuff and focused on helping the people in my life rather than wallowing in self-pity and despair, I could be a good addition to Andrea's life.

Lost in my thoughts I was bolted back to reality by a knock at the door. It was about ten thirty. "Who the fuck could this be?", I thought.

"Who the fuck is it?", I shouted.

"Me", came a voice from behind the door.

"Who the fuck is "me"?", I shouted back.

"Me. Now let me in you dumb fuck."

Blood beginning to boil, I bolted for the door, opened it, and glared at the man standing before me.

"Who the fuck are you? What do you want?", I growled at him.

He looked at me as if I were mad.

"Tommy. What the fack, you crazy cunt?", he asked, obviously very startled.

I leaned in closer to him, "How do you know my name? Who are you and what do you want?", I asked, trying to remain calm, for fear I would rip the little pricks head off.

Baffled looking and scanning my features for some sort of give-away sign, he asked, "You for real?"

"Listen dickhead, and yes, you do look like a dick too with your little purple head, I'm gonna count to three and if you don't tell me who you are before then, I'm gonna throw you down those fuckin' stairs. OK, one...two..."

"OK...OK", he replied, obviously panicked, "I didn't realise you had some mental issues when we were partying together."

"What?", I asked, thinking there obviously had to be some sort of wind-up now.

"Tommy, it's me...Lee. Do you not remember?"

"Lee? Sorry, but I haven't a clue who you are.", I responded, wracking my brains to see if I could place his face somewhere from my past.

"Where do I know you from? We go to school together or something?"

He laughed, not a normal laugh, more an annoying guffaw.

"Tommy, I've been around your flat about five times these past few weeks. We drank some booze and shit, but fack, I didn't think you were so out of it you wouldn't remember anything that happened."

Shit, how out of it had I been? I didn't believe him, didn't want to believe him.

"Prove it. What do you know about me then?"

In one movement of his little shoulders, his body language changed from being frightened to condescending. "Andrea left you, your best mate and your mum are both facked, your quitting your job, your..."

"OK, OK, stop", I instructed him.

I couldn't believe it. Here was a total stranger who I hadn't recognised, yet he had been in my flat and I had spilled my guts to him. I was worried, my drinking and black-outs must have been worse than I thought. I thought my mother had exaggerated about how bad I was, but God, she must have been right.

I looked at him. Small, bald, and pot-bellied with shifty little eyes. I would have crossed the street to avoid him normally, but I had let the little creep into my flat, drank with him and poured my heart out to him.

"Is it all right to come in?", he asked.

I almost laughed in his face. There was no way I was letting this creep into my flat.

"I bought a crate of beer earlier. I'll go and get it from my gaffe and bring it over, will I?", he asked.

"OK", I replied.

He *was* bringing beer after all. My mother told me to drink beer, so I'd drink beer.

He went to get the beers and was back within a minute. We drank a few and talked. He did all the talking, but I enjoyed the company. I had never met anyone like him. He certainly didn't seem to have much going for him physically, but he had an unshakeable self-confidence, or perhaps arrogance, that I had never encountered before. He amused me greatly.

He was a university graduate and had let me know this on many occasions throughout the night. He had a very high-powered job in computers, that, according to him paid "fuck loads of money". When I asked him why, if he was earning so much money, was he living in such a shit hole and not a pent house flat in the middle of London, he side-stepped my questions expertly.

The guy was a piece of work all right, I couldn't work him out.

He had grown up in Hertfordshire in a huge house. His mother was a teacher and his dad was an architect. He went to all the best schools, received the best education money could buy, but the guy had zero people skills. The way he interacted with me (as he deemed me beneath him) was to speak in trash talk, toilet humour to the maximum. When we went out (rarely) to bars at night and he bumped into workmates or people he knew, his personality would completely change to that of a dullard, a posh well-spoken bore. If he was to interact with a regular person, say a shopkeeper, barman or God forbid, a female, he seemed completely confused as to what persona to take on. An example of how he would get on came one evening after work when we went out for a few drinks. We went to a bar on the outskirts of the city, popular with yuppies and upwardly mobile desperados- a place where he could relate to his own kind. A girl was at the bar waiting to order a drink. He winked at me and turned to her.

"Hard day in the city dear?"

She smiled and nodded politely, trying to win the barman's attention.

"I know all too well about the pressures of the city. You know those computers you sit at all day? Well, there's a good chance that a key processing device, essential to the efficient running of the machine, had been researched and developed by a team of highly trained experts, headed up by a guy like yours truly", he continued, pointing to himself.

The girl looked at me, as if to ask; "Is he for real?", before quickly moving to the other end of the bar. Later, that evening, a woman with a leopard print coat arrived at the bar and sat beside him. To be honest, I too thought she was a hooker from the look of her. Blonde, big breasted and trashy looking. It was well known working girls frequented such establishments to offer a recreational pursuit for the middle-aged millionaires who had been toiling in the city all day. Once more, he winked at me.

"All right, dahling?", he asked in his mock cockney accent. So fake and ridiculous it was, the woman actually smiled at him, put down her wine glass and replied; "All right geezer?", playing the game too.

Encouraged, he asked; "So, sweetheart, you looking for trade?"

Her smile vanished, the hardness of her features now visibly prominent.

"Looking for what?", she scowled.

Lee was out of his depth. We both knew this woman was going to eat him for breakfast, but he persisted, "You know, trade?".

With one hand, he made a circle and the pointed finger of his other hand came across, to mimic penetration.

"I know a lot of blokes. I could put a lot of facking trade your way...if you know what I mean?"

The woman snapped immediately, grabbed his pint, and poured it over his little bald head.

"You filthy little toad", she screamed, "Thinking you can pimp me out, are you?"

Just then, a very important looking man in a business suit rushed over, looking aghast.

"What's wrong darling?", he asked.

"This little rat, Oscar. He accused me of being a prostitute and even attempted to pimp me out."

The man turned to Lee, anger, and outrage writ large across his face. He called another important looking man over.

"Adam, this man has insulted my wife in the most disgraceful fashion, can you do something about it?"

The other man walked towards us, grabbed Lee by the arm, told him he was the owner and instructed him to leave immediately or he would set the bouncers on him. We got out sharpish at that.

That was Lee. An asshole of the highest degree!

I don't know why I put up with him. He amused me, he was my muse in a sort of way, if a person from a low-class demographic like myself was entitled to have one. However, we did strike up an uneasy friendship over those next few months, and deep down, I was glad to have him around. He took my mind off deeper and darker matters, and for that I appreciated his presence.

That first night he called around, we sat and drank all the beers in the crate. That was one thing I liked about him, when he opened the crate he wasn't going to leave until it was finished- we had at least one thing in common. He didn't leave until about four thirty in the morning, and I had to get up at six thirty.

The next day, I could already see my mother's logic was applying. Even though I had only about two hours sleep, and still half drunk, the hangover slowly drifting over me like a large raincloud, I still got up and prepared for work. If I had been drinking spirits, I knew I would still be drinking them.

I was glad of the half-cut haze I was seeing the world through, it eased my nerves of having to face Dan after all that time.

I arrived at the site half an hour early. Dan was already there. He seen me, but there was no usual friendly greeting. He was busying himself setting up for the day. He walked past me to the van, to get tools and machinery out.

"What do you need me to do, Dan?", I asked, feeling awkward, like a spare part.

He ignored me, continuing to set the machinery out in his customary neat and organised manner. He walked back towards the van, stopping just in front of me, gazing into the distance like he had forgotten something. Then, quick as a flash, I never saw it coming, he drew back and punched me right on the side of the head. I lay on my back inside the boot of the van. He grabbed me and threw me on the ground, standing over me.

"That's for fuckin' me off all those times I rang ye. Fuckin' drunken monkey."

Then, he drew back and kicked me in the ribs. I knew he held back though, because I was only partially winded, "And that's for being a wee fuckin' cry baby."

I coughed and spluttered before getting to my feet again. After all the beers I had drunk the night before, and the punch and kick I received, all before breakfast, you could say I wasn't feeling too great.

Dan was now sitting where I had been sprawled in the van, smoking a cigarette.

I went and sat beside him. We both sat for a few minutes before he said, "I expected better from you Tommy."

I nodded sombrely. "I'm sorry, Dan. I barely even remember speaking to you on the phone, you know I would never speak to you like that."

He mockingly began to rub his eyes. "Oh, boo-hoo. Poor wee Tommy. His bit of fluff leaves him and he completely falls to pieces. Fuck sake kid, catch a grip. After all the shit you went through as a child, you let something like a girl leaving you drive you over the edge? Look at the rest of us. Look at our son, could be a fuckin'...vegetable for the rest of his life. How do you think we feel?"

His voice began to break a little with those last words and he stopped himself there.

"Dan, it's not all about my bit of fluff, as you like to call her. It's just everything got on top of me. Your son, my best mate, remember. Then there's my mother. She's...*dying*, for fuck sake, and there's nothing I can do about it."

It was my turn to stop myself, before I busted into tears making a complete fool out of myself.

Dan took the last draw on his cigarette, threw it to the ground and stubbed it out with his boot.

He put his hand on my shoulder and patted it.

"I know...I know. I'm sorry, too. But Tommy, you need to hang in. You can't let everything go to fuck now. If you really want that girl back, you'll get her back. But your mother and Brian need you, need all of us right now. Try to bear that in mind the next time you want to disappear up your own arse."

He patted my shoulder again, and I had to fight back against the urge to hug him. I think he read my intentions, as he looked at me in mock horror.

"What, have you fuckin' turned queer on us too?"

We both laughed and got up to go about our day's work.

"Fuck me", said Dan, "It's a bit early in the day for these so-called heart to hearts. The only time I ever talk like that is after about twelve pints and a bottle of Jameson"

We laughed.

Feeling rejuvenated and inspired from my father figures pep talk, I went that night to visit Brian and my mother.

It was then I would be told the tale of our lives.

CHAPTER 29

I was just about to enter the room Brian was in, when I heard much amusement from outside the door. Laughter, a sound I hadn't heard in so long. Desperate to hear the reason for the sweet sound, I almost ran into the room like a man running into a chip shop after a long bout of starvation.

I saw Kathleen first. Her hands were grasped together in pure joy and happiness. The look of sheer glee on her face made my stomach flutter with butterflies. I burst out laughing, for no particular reason.

"What's goin' on in here?", I asked, still laughing as the laughter and joy in the room was so contagious.

They were all there, all the McManus'. Even surly little Francis was there, all standing in a circle, beaming smiles all round. Amazingly, I saw Brian standing in the middle of the circle, resting on a pair of crutches.

"Brian, who is this?", Dan asked, pointing towards me.

Again, I could see the spirit in Brian's eyes. He looked at me like he always had, the look that made you think he knew something that you didn't. A look laced with pure rascality.

He said my name, it came out stuttered, but it *was* audible.

The elation was immense. I could imagine then how it must feel for a parent to hear their child's first word. We danced around the room singing and laughing.

"Kathleen, what the hell. When did this happen?", I asked when we had tired ourselves out.

She still had to wipe his drool from time to time, whereas before she had to continually mop it up.

"Just this evening, Tommy. The doctors have been in with us. They said he started speaking the odd word this morning and walking near enough unaided. They reckon they've never seen a recovery happen so fast-isn't that right Brian?"

Again, he stammered his words out, "It is, yes."

I couldn't believe it. I grabbed him in a tight embrace, and when I let go, he looked at me with a mixture of surprise and embarrassment, then I really knew he was going to make a full recovery.

"They reckon there is no reason he can't be fully recovered within six months to a year. Obviously, he has a full rehabilitation program to go through, but they think all the signs are very positive."

I looked at him. "Bullshit. This beast will be recovered in a couple of months. He's like a bull.", I said, grabbing him by the shoulders, feeling the strength that remained in them.

He smiled at me, then pointed towards the bed. "Rest...bit", he said. Then the clucking began, Kathleen and Maura plumping the pillows and folding the sheets.

Dan walked me out of the room. It did me the world of good to see those people so happy. Dan was a smiler, a naturally happy person, but the smile he wore then was different- the smile of happiness a father could only express for a child of his own.

God, I wished at that moment someone could have smiled that way about me!

"What do you think of that?", he asked, nodding his head in the direction of the room.

"Don't mean to be a "told you so" type of prick, but didn't I always say this would happen? I know him. I know the backbone and guts the guy has."

Dan shook his head, almost in disbelief, smiling from ear to ear.

"You know, I've never been overly religious, Tommy. But...Kathleen and I have been on our knees every night since this happened, praying to our Lord up there, and he listened to us. Thank God, our prayers seemed to have been answered."

He smiled and looked at the floor, his body saturated with relief.

"You know, Kathleen always threw in an extra prayer for your mother too. Every night she would get a prayer, and we will keep praying for her."

That choked me up. To think people would perform such a selfless and personal act as praying for another person, especially my mother who needed every prayer she could get, almost drove me to tears.

"Speaking about your mother", Dan continued, "Go see her now. Brian has plenty of people molly-codling him. He'll be fine, now go see your ma.".

I walked off quickly, my face burning with emotion and happiness.

Outside my mother's room, I tried to compose myself with a few deep breaths. The phrase of the unarticulated; "Rollercoaster of emotions", seemed apt at that point. From the noise, joy, and hope of the McManus room to the despair of my mothers.

She lay on the bed, agony evident on her face. A young, pretty nurse was taking blood samples from her hand. I winced, as her hands were skeleton like and covered in dark bruises. The phrase; "blood from a stone", never felt so apt.

A middle aged Asian doctor entered the room. He took one look at me and asked; "The son?".

I nodded, and he asked me to come outside for a quiet word.

There was no small talk with him and his English was a little broken. I supposed his job was to keep people alive, niceties probably weren't high on his agenda.

"We've tried our best for your mother. We have used various treatments to give her more time, but she is not responding. I'm sorry to say she will be gone in the next few days- absolute tops. You may want to say your goodbyes."

With that he walked up the corridor to see his next patient.

A mass murderer getting a death sentence would have received more compassion from the judge, than my poor mother did from that doctor for hers!

The nurse walked out past me with her samples and I entered the room again. I sat next to the bed.

"Jesus, Tommy. This is desperate. How did I let myself get to be such a case?", she said.

I didn't know what to say. Trying to break the tension, I said; "I've just been to see Brian. He's made a miraculous recovery. The whole family are over the moon. You know...the same might happen to you."

She let out a small chuckle.

"Ach, that's great. It's a shame to see the poor gasun like that. He has youth on his side, Tommy, I don't. I have no chance, son. Don't be getting your hopes up for me."

We sat in a heavy silence for a few moments.

"As they have probably told you, I am almost out of time, so I need to get started. I am going to start from the beginning, so listen carefully and don't interrupt. I need to get it out before I go."

She tried to sit up in her bed and took a long deep breath that rattled her entire body.

"It all started when I was a young woman in Ireland..."

She spoke for about half an hour. She spoke quickly trying to get as many words out as she could, before a frenzied attack of coughing took her breath away for a few minutes at a time. I drank in every word and digested them when I got back to my flat that night. There was a lot to take in, I had never been as fascinated by anything in my entire life. This story she was telling was piecing together the jigsaw of our lives.

She told me that one of her family members would contact me soon after she had gone. During her entire story telling, I had only interrupted her once, to ask how this person would know when that happened. She told me she had given Mrs McManus the man's contact details. Kathleen had already contacted him, under my mother's strict instructions not to let him know where she was, for fear he would come over to get her. It was arranged the man would phone and arrange for me to go to Ireland, to carry out her wishes. I understood then that I would have a big role to play, so I shut up and let her continue the story.

The Asian doctor had been wrong, thankfully. If he had been right I wouldn't have heard the full story, always being in the dark about what happened. The entire story took two weeks to tell. The reliving of her tales seemed to stoke up fires of passion within her soul, seemingly keeping her alive until it was completely told. I went home every night in a daze. The story got deeper and darker every night and my rage mirrored that darkness.

When the entire story was told, she breathlessly told me to come again the following night to hear what her plans were. Finally, I felt I had a real mission in life. Unfulfilled lives and lifetimes rested on my shoulders to be validated and avenged.

The next evening, I walked into the hospital like a man possessed. I had a purpose now. I called to see Brian quickly. Again, the entire family were there. He was walking slowly around the room, aided by his crutches.

"Tommy", he called to me, smiling broadly. His speech was still a little slurred, but the improvement was no less than miraculous.

"Guess what?", he asked.

"What"

"They reckon I can go home in a couple of weeks or so."

"Shit", I looked at Dan and Kathleen. "This St. Jude is some boy. You must have him on speed dial."

Brian didn't get the reference, but Dan and Kathleen appreciated the joke.

I laughed and joked around for a while, everyone's high spirits contagious, until I bid my farewells and went to see my mother.

When I entered, she lay sleeping. I sat for a few moments and watched her. I sat and thought about all the heartbreak and torment the poor woman had endured. I was sure she would have been a different person, had life not dealt her such a tragic hand. She would have been every bit as good a mother as Kathleen, I was sure of that.

I felt ashamed of the way I had treated her at times. Had I known her history I would have understood her better, been more tolerant and helpful. I had judged her harshly…and who of all people was I to judge, the mess I had made of my own life. She had reared me single handed. I had spells in the home from time to time, but I couldn't imagine the demons this woman had niggling at her. A lesser person would have given up on me completely, taking the easy way out. Not my mother though. She never gave up on me. *I* had given up on *her* many times, but I wouldn't now.

She began to stir. Her lips were like sandpaper, cracked and adorned with sores. There was a sponge lying next to a glass of water. I dipped it into the water and put it to her mouth for a few moments, letting the moisture relieve her parched lips. She opened her eyes and looked at me. The sleep had brought a rosy tinge to her cheeks. For a split second, just a fleeting moment, I could visualise the youthful, beautiful mother I once had, before the ravages of alcohol and despair had taken their toll.

"Ah, Tommy. You're here", she whispered, a little smile brightening her features. She sat up a little, with great effort; "Now, this is what I want you to do next."

She spoke for about twenty minutes. I underwent more emotions in those twenty minutes than what I had in the previous twenty years. Anger, fear, excitement, anxiety, shock, and adrenaline all pulsed through my body in waves. It was exhausting. I felt it difficult to merely sit and listen, but I had to as she didn't have the energy for conversation.

When she finished, she wilted back into her original position, the healthy hue the sleep brought now replaced with the deathly pallor her inevitable permanent sleep would bring.

I took a huge breath. "OK ma. Thank you for telling me all this. Your wishes will be fulfilled, I promise you this. Now, lie back and let *me* tell *you* a few things- no interruptions."

It was then my time to talk. I spoke for about twenty minutes too. I told her everything that was in my heart. I apologised for judging her unfairly. I told her I appreciated how she never went from man to man, like many of my friend's single parents in school. Men who brought disruption, violence, and annoyance to those children, because their mothers couldn't bear to be on their own. I told her I realised now, it was out of loyalty and respect to my father that she never had one affair with a man, and I loved her for that. I told her I understood why she drank so much and assured her the same wouldn't happen to me. I realised she had felt lost and alone without a purpose, I knew because that is the way I had felt. I told her she had now given me my purpose in life, a meaning, and thanked her for it. I assured her not to worry about what was going to happen. I promised, swore to her, from the depths of my heart that I was going to make amends for everything that had happened.

Eventually, when I emptied my heart to her, I sat exhausted, almost wilted like her. She lay in bed, a little river of tears streaming down her face. She didn't attempt to wipe them away, I didn't want her to. It felt like a much-needed rain storm after a long deadly drought. When the tears ceased to flow, she spoke.

"Son, whatever happens, I know you'll do the right thing. I may not be here, but let me tell you, wherever I am, I'll be with you. I want you to always have that comfort."

I nodded and held her hand.

We embraced. I didn't want to let her go. I could feel her heartbeat, it seemed to fall into rhythm with my own. I kissed her and put the sponge to her lips again. I realised then how thirsty I was too, after all the talking.

"Ma, I'm gonna pop out and get a coffee from these machines."

Out of courtesy and trying to maintain a level of normality alone, I added; "You fancy one?".

Sensing what I was doing and playing along, she smiled and answered, "Only if you put a good skite of brandy into it."

We both laughed. I realised then how good that felt, and how much of a rarity it had been in our lives together.

I stepped outside the door and typically, the closest available machine was out of order. I walked a little further, finding the café at the other end of the hospital. I bought my coffee and walked back towards the room. At that moment, I remembered a funny story from my childhood. It involved a Frank Spencer type painter and decorator we had known, Mr Goode, our flat, a bucket of paint, a stepladder and slapstick accidental comedy. Even though our flat had been in complete disarray for the next few days, despite all our attempts to clean up, I had never known my mother to laugh so heartily. Even when we brought it up in the years that followed, she had to sit down from the force of her laughter. I wanted to share this with her again, so I half jogged back to the room.

When I entered the room, I started; "Ma, what about Mr Goode…".

The Asian doctor, and a nurse were in the room. The room felt colder than it had. The Asian doctor pulled a pair of rubber gloves from his hands, and threw them in the nearest bin.

"Ah, Mr Smyth. Your mother took a turn just now. I'm afraid she's gone."

He was writing on a document on a clipboard, my mother's life and death recorded simply by a few dates and times.

As the doctor exited the room, I called after him.

"Doctor"

He stopped and turned to face me.

"She proved you wrong. You said a few days. She lasted a few weeks."

He didn't say anything, just turned, and walked towards his next patient.

The nurse left the room as I entered, and I was left alone with my mother once more. I doubted the medical staff did it, as I was sure it was more of an undertaker's role, but her eyes were closed and her mouth was shut. The expression she wore was one of peace, she seemed to be half-smiling. She looked like she was sleeping peacefully. The silence in the room was deafening, however.

I held the hot coffee cup in my hands, relishing the comfort it gave me from the coldness of the room. I pulled the blanket up to her chin, I wanted to tuck her in.

It was only when I put my hand on her forehead and felt the coldness of her, did it begin to sink in. It wasn't a deathly coldness, more lukewarm, like a bath that was cooling down, soon to become uncomfortable.

Then it hit me.

My mother's little body, warm no more, lifeless. She would be freezing cold soon. She would become stiff. She was my mother no more, she was a…corpse. I hated that word. I thought I would have been stronger than I was, I knew her death was inevitable for the previous few months. But at that moment, knowing what was done could never be undone, the sobs of despair came, totally overwhelming my body until I could only curl up in a ball and lie beside her, my hands wrapped around her little face, the horrible coldness becoming more intense.

Kathleen entered the room after a few minutes had passed.

"Oh, Tommy", she cried, rushing towards me. I stood and hugged her, the warmth of her body a comforting contrast to the coldness of my mothers. Her sobs rocked my body in powerful waves.

We went to the café about an hour later. Dan assured us he would sit in the room with my mother, as I didn't want her to be alone.

We sat on the steps of the hospital, sipping from our cups. We didn't speak. Suddenly, Kathleen let out a large gasp that took me by surprise.

"What's wrong Kathleen?", I asked.

She smiled and pointed to the step below us.

"Tommy, I was looking up towards the sky just then and I noticed something floating towards us. Look...",

"What is it? A feather?", I asked, confused.

"Yes. Do you know what that means?", she asked, now beaming from ear to ear.

"No."

"It's a white feather. According to folklore, if a white feather falls into your path, it means an angel is close by, watching over you. God has given your mother her wings, Tommy."

The smile Kathleen wore *was* that of an angel. They surrounded me. What comfort in my hour of need.

I picked it up. A beautiful white feather, as pure as the driven snow. I put it in my pocket.

"Do you think she's here with us now?", I asked, desperately trying to stop my sobs taking hold once more.

"Yes, absolutely. I truly believe she is."

I looked up at the sky. At that point, I swear I could see a beam of sunlight break through the most miserable darkest sky.

I realised then, my mother's promise about looking out for me was being fulfilled.

"God bless her.", I whispered.

Then, Kathleen and I prayed for her, together, on those cold hospital steps.

CHAPTER 30

Neil jolted awake. To waken in the dead of night was nothing new to him, but this time it seemed different. His body was drenched in sweat, even though the room was freezing cold. His face felt cold, though, and when he touched it, he found cold tear tracks running along his cheeks. He had been crying in his sleep. He didn't think he had ever done that before. Again, a new low in his tormented existence.

He sat on the edge of his bed and tried to piece together what had happened, trying to work out why he had jolted awake so violently, and the reason for the tears during his sleep.

The weather was brutal outside, in the countryside night. He knew a storm had been brewing all day, but he didn't get to see it materialise before he retired to bed. The room, in complete darkness was momentarily lit up by shards of light cracking through the night sky. It had been a while since he had seen lighting, and he couldn't remember seeing it as intense. The lightning cast an eerie pallor in the room when it struck, making objects look a lot more different and sinister than they looked in the light of day. He felt scared, feeling like a child again. His top coat lying on the bedroom floor looked like the little sleeping figure of Seamie. The bedclothes on the bed, looked in a certain light like the peaceful, resting pose of Máire. The bush outside the window, swaying in the storm seemed to cast images of terrifying demons into the room under the seemingly supernatural light. He wanted to scream, but he didn't. Aware of his faltering sanity, he knew those were the moments when it would be tested. He knew he had to ride it out, another few minutes and the lightning would stop. He knew if he snapped, lost control of his senses, then that would be it...he would descend into madness forever.

It was the bush cracking against the window that stirred Neil's memory of the dream. It had been the continuation of the terrible dream he had all those terrible years before, where living nightmares had crept from sleep into conscious days. In the original dream, he remembered the withering gentle bush had eventually died away to a mere stump. He had wanted to dig up the roots and re-seed the area, only to find two grossly decayed bodies when he dug down. On closer inspection, after the horror of seeing the worms crawl in and out of eye sockets in the skulls, he noticed the roots of the fallen Gentle bush had been embedded into one of the bodies. He stood in silent horror. Like the culmination of all his nightmares blended into one, he viewed the full horror of the picture that unfolded before him.

The two bodies in the hole belonged to Pete, and himself.

The body of Pete had thick roots embedded into it. The roots that grew upwards out of the hole were slightly transparent, and seemed to be feeding from his blood. It seemed his body, although decayed and rotting, still had a blood supply, but the blood wasn't feeding *his* body, nourishing the bush instead. Its roots, much like veins and arteries carried the blood to its core. The bush was growing before his eyes. The roots were extending into twigs and branches. It grew bigger and bigger, leaves finally forming to bring it back to its former glory, the rotting stench wafting from the decaying bodies nauseating.

He vomited once more on the ground. The body that lay beside Pete's, his own, while just as decayed and horrible had escaped the root network. Feeling a little braver, he moved closer to the edge of the hole to take a closer look. Then, in a split second, losing his footing, he found himself in the hole with the bodies. Scrambling around, trying to get to his feet and get a grip on the soil, he felt a piercing sensation in his left side. Frozen to the spot, he realised, to his great horror, that the root network had eventually penetrated *his* body. He looked up, panic flowing through his body like electricity. To his great terror, the hole began to fill with soil, the dreaded roots taking control of his body. Blood flowed through them until the bush above the ground grew bigger and bigger, eventually masking the sun until total darkness replaced the light. His body became cold, like stone, and his screams were muted by the soil that began to fill up his mouth.

Only then, to his sheer relief, he awakened.

He sat further in the darkness of his bedroom, the shadows growing shorter as the morning light began to fill up the room. The storm had subsided a little.

He almost jumped off his bed when the thought struck him. The dream- it must have been a warning. He only thought of him then, Pete, his dearest friend. He hadn't thought, over the years, about how the events of that dreadful night would have affected poor Pete. Because his own self-inflicted reclusiveness would not allow him to venture out into the world to visit him, he found it strange that Pete had not come to visit *him*. A wave of nausea suddenly hit him. Had McNamee got to Pete too? What had happened? Something, at that point didn't feel right, and he felt a sudden urge to go to Pete, to at least warn him about what he felt was happening, or about to happen. McNamee had destroyed *his* life, he couldn't let the same fate befall his dearest friend.

He dressed and pulled the curtains open. It was strange for him to do so, as he had left them closed for as long as he could remember. To his amazement, the early morning was bathed in light, instead of the usual darkness that greeted him every morning. The sun was beginning to break through the clouds.

He hadn't seen that traitor in such a long time, he thought.

The grass seemed greener. The dead, yellow-brown mess that once lay in the fields, now replaced by a dark, lush green. The sunlight rained down upon the dew on the grass, giving the illusion of a field of dazzling diamonds, shimmering, and shining beautifully.

How long since he had witnessed such a scene? It wasn't months, it had to have been years, many years. Impossible, he knew but since the night his life had ended, his days had been colourless and without warmth, the sun turning its back on him, along with everything else.

Amid the tragedy and sorrow that had taken permanent residence in his heart, he felt a new day was dawning. The winter was finally showing signs of decline, the green shoots of recovery seemed to be on their way. He knew there was nothing he could do to save his own life, there would be no point anyway. But...he couldn't give up on the life of his only friend.

CHAPTER 31

The McManus' took charge of organising and arranging my mother's funeral-to my great relief and appreciation. Who knows how to plan a funeral?

I didn't, wouldn't have had a clue where to start...but *they* did.

They even paid for it.

I hadn't the money and was ready to go to a loan shark, when Dan told me to catch myself on. Dan, being Dan, tried to rationalise his kindness by telling me he would take a few quid out of my pay packet each week until the debt was paid. I told him to take fifty pounds a week until it was paid. He laughed and said he would take a fiver instead.

"Fuckin' hell, Dan. At that rate, it will be time for my *own* funeral before I get you paid back.", I told him.

He laughed it off, but rcfused to take more than a fiver a week.

What would I have done without those people?

The funeral went by in a blur. I had never been one for pomp and ceremony, neither had my mother. It was just as well we weren't, because there was a depressingly, disappointing attendance.

There were a few old biddies making up the numbers. Auld biddies who lived in the chapel, probably seeing standing at a graveside as a refreshing change of scenery. The McManus', of course, were all there, Brian too, even though he was confined to a wheelchair. A few of the building site crew turned up. Mickel McKeown, Larry Dolan, Sean Carragher, Fergus Fox and even Blondie.

Blondie hadn't done too much work on the sites, but his bluffing must have burned *some* calories as his weight had ballooned since he stopped working. He had been big before, but now he was almost American fat. It felt a little ironic too, calling a man Blondie, who's hair had almost completely turned to silver. It had been good to see him, though. A bluffer extraordinaire, but a harmless big lump at the same time. Not an ounce of badness in him, to borrow one of my mother's expressions.

During the service, it seemed the priest had better things to be doing with his day, than presiding over my mother's funeral ceremony, as he rattled through it, barely taking a breath.

The one thing that annoyed me the most, was he kept mispronouncing her name, referring to her as Mary.

He could have had at least got her name right, a little respect for the dead.

I was going to have a word with the fucker, but decided against it. The poor woman had had enough turmoil in her life, she would at least have a peaceful funeral.

When the ceremony was finished, the coffin lowered into the ground and the congregation dispersed, I stood there, alone, for a few minutes.

A wave of panic suddenly hit me.

The coffin lay in the wet, cold ground. It was now to be smothered in six feet of soil, letting the worms begin their dark magic. I remembered my mother in her more youthful years. The baby-faced freshness, the perfect little white teeth, the dark brunette hair that hung to her shoulders, and slightly moved and bounced when she moved her little head.

"Oh, God", I cried aloud. I almost physically threw-up at that moment, the horrible realisation of what was going to happen to my mother's little body finally hitting me.

That little body, the little body that carried me as an unborn, and then after as a child, was going to rot and decay. She was going to fall to pieces, bloat first, then disintegrate.

I didn't know what to do at that moment. I wished I had taken more of an active role in the funeral arrangements, been more forceful and had her cremated. There would have been no decay, no rotting debris for the worms to thrive upon. It wasn't too late, I was going to get that horrible coffin out of the ground and get her to the crematorium. In a flash, she would be a neat little pile of ashes. I could deal with that, I knew I wouldn't have nightmares about that.

Just as I was about to turn, and run for someone to help lift the coffin out of the ground, a gentle touch brushed my shoulder. I knew who it was without even turning. When I turned, she stood there, like a beacon of hope amid the drizzly grey surroundings of the bleak graveyard.

"Andrea...you came!"

She stood in front of me, looking awkward, wearing an uneasy smile.

"Sorry I came late. But...I thought maybe better late than never."

She fumbled in her bag for a moment and handed me a mass card.

"I was told it's what you do- you Irish."

I smiled and thanked her. I always knew absence made the heart grow fonder, but the feeling I had in my heart made a mockery of mere fondness. The million little butterflies in my stomach seemed to be lifting the despair in my soul.

I looked into the grave once more, noticing the gravediggers hovering in the distance, like hungry vultures.

"Jesus, Andrea. My poor mother, lying in that cold ground. Its...fuckin' barbaric to let this happen."

The tears again stood in my eyes. Andrea hugged me and guided us over to a bench on the edge of the graveyard. She told me it was how she felt when her dad passed away when she was only twelve. She told me how she got over it, as she viewed the body simply as a prison to the soul, someone could only be truly free when they escaped from it. She assured me my mother was in a better place. I had to agree with that.

She couldn't possibly have been in a worse place than where she was.

The McManus' had even organised a meal, and booked an upstairs room in our local, O'Reilly's.

Real Irish shit.

A burial then a piss-up…I knew my mother would heartily approve. I told Andrea about the plans and she agreed to come for a drink, only one though as she had to baby-sit that evening for a friend. I understood. I certainly wasn't going to push things.

"Give me a minute please Andrea.", I asked her, and I made my way back to the grave. The gravediggers were still hovering. They had just stubbed out their cigarettes and were about to move in when they noticed me heading back. They looked pissed off, but stood where they were and lit another. I glared at them for a second, luckily for them they didn't react.

I knelt over the grave and whispered; "Don't worry ma. I'm goin' to sort everything out for us. You can rely on me, everything's goin' to be fine. I love you. I love you more than you'll ever know. I'm gonna go now. We're goin' to have a party in your honour. Don't worry, I'll stick to beer."

I had a little chuckle to myself at that.

"Look out for us up there, ma. Put a good word in for us with the big man."

Andrea's hand once again touched my shoulder and things suddenly appeared a little brighter. I wondered at that moment whether my mother had put Andrea there. I looked to the heavens and smiled.

I stood, and signalled to the two men to begin their ghastly work.

Andrea walked with me to the pub. We talked a lot. I told her I was heading over to Ireland for a while, although I didn't tell her what for. I detected a hint of disappointment from her and my heart soared because of it. There were obviously feelings in her heart for me. I knew mine would never leave my heart for her.

She was true to her word and stayed for one drink. When she was leaving, I tried to play it cool and not spill my heart out to her. I didn't want a sympathy vote from her and I wouldn't guilt trip her into staying with me on that horrible day. She kissed me on the cheek and suggested we go on one date a week to see how things played out between us. Even though I felt giddy with joy, I told her not to suggest something like that if it was out of sympathy. I told her to walk out the door and not look back if it was- no hard feelings, trying to make it easier for her to get out of something she didn't really want to do. She smiled sweetly and hugged me tightly for about twenty seconds. She pecked me on the lips, wrote her number down (in case

I had thrown it out- I hadn't), gave it to me and made me promise to call her. It was an easy promise to keep. She smiled at me once more and walked out to her taxi.

I walked back to the pub, my body exhausted by the bombardment of the many mixed emotions it had been subjected to that day. The saying; "Every cloud has a silver lining", came to mind.

On that cloudiest of days, Andrea's presence was the silver lining I had been crying out for.

I walked into the smoky bar and found all my friends well on the road to drunkenness, having a good time. It made me happy. It was the way things were supposed to be. There had been enough sadness during the day, now, the magic of alcohol was beginning to wash it all away.

Dan came up to me and put a pint in my hand, and, most importantly, a comforting hand on my shoulder. We walked over to where the rest were gathered in the bar. I put my arm around Mickel McKeown, and said to everyone; "Listen, I haven't fuckin' turned gay all of a sudden, but does this cunt not look damn good in a suit?"

He looked up at me with that cheeky grin, the eyebrows raised, the tongue protruding slightly.

"Like a young Robert De Niro.", I continued.

He shrugged his shoulders to get away from me, and stood directly opposite where I stood. His expression changed to one of pure menace. I had seen that look before and things had gotten fairly violent on both those occasions. I stood momentarily in shock, just like everyone else. Shit, I thought, had I insulted him? I hoped I hadn't, as he was not a man to insult, or get on the wrong side of.

Then he spoke;

"You talkin' to me?"

I burst out laughing. We all did, half out of relief, half out of appreciation for his comic timing.

"You're a funny guy.", I replied.

"I'm gonna go get the papers, get the papers", quipped Brian.

A few others chipped in with quotes from De Niro movies, until Blondie (after about a minute, or so, after we had stopped doing it) said;

"Life is like a box of chocolates."

"No, Blondie, no. You've missed the boat by about ten miles, ye eejit.", said Dan.

But, Blondies quote had us all in hysterics.

With all my friend's there in the bar that night, it ended up being a good time.

Thank God for small mercies.

CHAPTER 32

My mother was gone, so I was officially without a family. To be the sole member of a family left surviving in the world was a daunting one, to say the least.

Awkwardly, I had asked Kathleen about the contact she had been given. I knew my mother had a plan she wanted me to implement, but impatience and intrigue got the better of me. I shouldn't have asked her. Kathleen was a people pleaser and seeing me anxious and impatient pained her visibly. I regretted asking her and tried to laugh it off by changing the subject, but she asked me to sit with her at the kitchen table.

"Tommy, you and I both know your poor mother had her troubles in life. Well, these instructions she has set me seem to be her way of gaining redemption. She wanted to put things right, to make things right for you. She wanted you to get closure on everything, and to get what is rightfully yours."

I stopped her; "Kathleen, it's OK. You don't need to explain."

She waved my protestation away.

"I promised your mother I would do as instructed. She gave me the man's number and told me what to tell him. I rang him twice, once when your mother was in hospital and then when she…went. He has been given your details and he will ring in a few weeks' time. Your mother wanted a little cooling off period to let you grieve, so the man has been given instructions not to contact you, until your mother thought you would be up to it. God love her, Tommy, the poor woman didn't have many earthly possessions to leave you, so this is her will and we should respect her wishes."

I sat for a moment, reflecting on Kathleen's words, before she continued; "Have patience, son. The man has verified everything your mother told you in the brief time I spoke to him. But, my job is done now. It is left with him now. This is your family business and I'm going to leave it between you people from here."

I nodded and clasped her hands in mine. "Thanks Kathleen."

We sat and spoke for another while, mostly about Brian and his progress. As much as she loved him, he seemed to be getting on her nerves a little. That *was* something, as to say Kathleen had the patience of a saint would have been an understatement.

Brian, being himself, was not content with making small daily improvements, he wanted to be back out working and drinking with his mates like he used to. They kept telling him he was lucky to be alive and to count his blessings, but he wanted to go from zero to one hundred in an unrealistic period. Like she was always there for me, I tried to be there for her, and told her to call me any time it was getting too much for her. I would gladly call to see Brian, or take him out for a while to give her a break, offer him a different perspective on things and encourage him further. I told her that even though I wasn't family by blood, I certainly felt it in spirit. Brian and I were kindred spirits and I knew what made him tick, I felt I could offer something in his recovery. She smiled and looked a little more relieved and I was glad I could do something to help *her*.

We sat further, drinking tea, smoking cigarettes, laughing, and joking. It was nice. When Dan arrived home, he came in and accused us of having an affair with each other, much to Kathleen's amusement. Brian came down from his nap and the slagging and blackguarding really began in earnest. The same old mischievous wit was still there, it never left him. Brian and Dan joined us at the table, even surly young Francis came down at one stage. He showed signs of the family wit at times too, casting aside his usual surliness. It was about time too, him being in his early twenties, probably the result of Kathleen's over eager parenting, him being the "baby" of the family.

When it was time to go, I reluctantly said my goodbyes, conveniently just before I knew the off-licence was about to close. Then, I went back to my flat and drank a dozen beers.

I sat then for half the night, thinking. Thinking of my mother, about the stories she told me about her life and thinking about what I was going to do. I thought about Andrea too, about how I wasn't going to mess it up with her again. We stuck to our arrangement of one date per week and the magic was still there. I knew it would, and always would be. I thought about Brian and the McManus'.

I knew I had so much to look forward to in life. Despair and futility clouded my past...hope, and happiness, I hoped would brighten my future, alien concepts as they were.

When I drank the last of the beers at around two thirty a.m., I went to bed, woke at six thirty, worked all day and repeated that cycle for the next few weeks.

Until the man finally called.

CHAPTER 33

The man stood in the office, looking down upon the dimming daylight drawing over the quarry. It was his favourite time of the day. To see the lorries park up in the yard and the breakers and JCB's halting their work did him good.

The men would enter the office, tired, hungry, and thirsty. Clock out and the fun would begin. The girls in the office, Irene and Petra would tally up the orders for the day and from there he could calculate the profit. Always in profit, even in the winter months. He had the knack, an excellent businessman, he had even thought of branching out into other avenues. Pimping, now there was a business he knew he would be good at. He looked at the two girls, both innocently working away. He laughed aloud.

No-one asked why.

"I could definitely pimp those little hoors", he thought.

His mind raced back to the nights he had spent with both. Perhaps he could fuck them both some night, he wondered, and again he laughed. He paid them well, probably not as much as he should for personal services rendered, but his ego wouldn't allow him to believe both girls slept with him because he paid and looked after them well.

It was because he was irresistible, a real lady-killer.

A few of the men entered the office. Paddy Gray and Carl Donnelly, his favourites. Carl was his longest serving lorry driver, there were five in total and Carl was the boss amongst them. He took charge of the maintenance of the lorries and organised all the insurance and road taxes that came with them. Paddy was the utility man of the company, a handy man. He broke the stones, organised the blasting, fixed machinery and generally kept the quarry ticking over. They enjoyed a few pints after work and enjoyed the man's company.

On many occasions, Carl had drunk too much. When Carl would drink, whiskey especially, on a Friday night, he usually lost control and sometimes fell unconscious at the bar. The man, on many of those occasions had bundled him into the back of his car and drove him home. His wife, Rosie would answer the door, disappointment etched on her face at her foolish husband's antics. The man would carry Carl into the house and plonk him on the sofa. Then, he would turn to Rosie and grope her tits. Rosie had the best set of tits he had ever seen. Two children had suckled upon them, but they had still defied all forms of gravity. Pert, huge, and voluptuous. She would look upon him in disgust as he fondled her breasts.

"Now, now Rosie. Sure, you wouldn't go and tell Carl about this, would you? It'd be terrible if he ever found out. He'd probably try and kill me. And then what? The poor fella would lose his job and he couldn't afford this house...or these.", he said, nodding towards her breasts, smiling.

He would grope her breasts for a few minutes before kissing her on the cheek and leaving. A sly wink before he left on his way.

Carl was well paid, no doubt about it, probably grossly overpaid. He knew he wouldn't get close to those wages anywhere else and maintain the lifestyle he, and his family had become accustomed to. Rosie was well aware of that fact too.

That evening, the man, along with Paddy and Carl went to the pub, as was their habit. The same routine, each man drinking about five pints before heading home.

He arrived home at around ten that evening. His wife sat watching television.

"Is that you dear?", she called from the living room.

"It is dear. Any dinner for me?"

"Yes. I made it earlier, but sure you didn't come home. Anyway, I put it in the oven for you."

"Thanks honey."

The man walked into the kitchen. A huge kitchen, his wife's pride, and joy. They had built the house ten years before. The quarry had made him a lot of money, so he had built himself a mansion.

He walked to the fridge and lifted a can of beer. He cracked it open and took a drink. He opened the oven door, the food smelt delicious. He took the plate out and sat at the table. Two pork chops, peas, and a few potatoes. The nights drinking had given him a voracious appetite. He cut into the chop, it was a bit too tough for his liking, but he supposed it had been in the oven for a good while. He put it in his mouth and chewed. The flavours were still there but the texture was slightly leathery. He put down his knife and fork, put the can to his lips, sank it in one go, burped loudly, and smiled to himself. He walked into the living room. His wife lay on the sofa watching the television. Something in her stirred as she noticed his body language was different, as he entered the room. She was a larger lady, having over indulged in the finer things in life over the years, the fruits of her husband's success. She had always been a slightly larger woman, even in her youth, but the years had piled it on and it had annoyed her, the weight being her Achilles heel.

"Enjoy your dinner, dear?", she asked, trying to mask the nervousness in her voice.

"Hmm, not really", replied the man, standing picking his teeth with a toothpick.

She sat up, anxiously. "Why, what was wrong with it, darling?"

Smiling, the man remained standing over her, engrossed in picking his teeth.

"The pork chops were like leather".

He looked at what he had produced on the toothpick, before throwing it furiously to the ground.

"LIKE FUCKING LEATHER.", he roared.

The woman sat frozen to the spot. The man bolted towards her, taking her by the throat and slapping her face three to four times.

"How many fucking times, eh? Turn the fucking oven down a bit, then this won't happen. You stupid, fat bitch."

He stormed out of the room, slamming the door behind him.

The woman lay on the floor, sobbing for almost twenty minutes before getting up, finding the courage to go up to bed with him.

Once undressed, she got into bed.

He turned to her, holding her tenderly.

"Oh, my darling. When will you ever learn? I don't know why you do these silly things that make me so angry. I hope you can stop though, honey, I really do. I love you.", he said, gazing into her tear sodden eyes.

"I'll try to do better, honey. I'm just so stupid sometimes.", she replied.

Even in the darkness, she could see he was smiling. He turned his back to her and she could feel the ripples of laughter rocking his body back and forth.

She didn't ask why.

CHAPTER 34

After waiting for what seemed an eternity, he finally called.

I sat on the bed and gazed out the window. It began to steam up with my breath as the room was so cold, although I didn't notice at the time. For about an hour that night I didn't feel anything. I just sat there, from time to time wiping the window clear, so I could look out on north London and its piss coloured streetlights.

I drank whatever beers I had in the fridge, then went out and bought some more. I sat in silence in the darkness for several hours after that, drinking and thinking.

It had been arranged for me to fly to Ireland on the Thursday of the following week. I had plans to make, I had people to see. I had to get my shit together.

The next day I went to see the McManus'. I sat down and told them the full story. We sat in silence for a short time afterwards until I asked Dan if the Wednesday before I flew out could be my last day on the site. He waved me away and told me not to be so stupid. I was to take the whole week off as I needed to organise a lot of things. I felt disappointed but didn't want to appear ungrateful for his generosity. I wanted to go to work until the day arrived. It would keep my mind off things, offer me a distraction to my thoughts and anxieties.

More silence fell between us, until Brian was the first to break it. He jolted out of his chair.

"I'm fuckin' comin' with you", he said.

"No, Brian. You can't. You're not fit enough son.", Kathleen protested, desperation etched in her voice.

"I am. I swear to God, I am. I can't let my man here face all this shit on his own. He needs back-up, it's too dangerous for you to go on your own Tommy."

Brian's words were aflame with the passions of friendship and true concern.

"No, Brian. You can't, I won't let you.", Kathleen again protested, her emotions beginning to get the better of her.

"I am", Brian shouted in reply.

"Shut it.", said Dan, speaking gently but sternly.

"Shut it for a second. Please, son. You're not goin' anywhere.", he continued.

"But...da, why not? You can't stop me.", Brian replied, sounding more like a stroppy young Francis, rather than himself.

"I agree with you, Brian. I don't want Tommy goin' over there on his own either.", Dan interrupted.

"So, what's your problem then?"

Dan looked at me. "You're not goin' on your own Tommy. *I'm* comin' with ye."

Before I could say anything, Brian butted in.

"Well, I'm comin' too then."

"No, Brian. Listen to your mother. You're not fit enough yet. Ye still need more time to recover."

Brian went to butt in again, but I got there before him.

"Listen to your parents, Brian. You owe me nothing. I don't expect you to come over. You are flying with your recovery at the minute, add this stress to your system and it could set you back years. You have nothing to prove to me."

I looked at Kathleen.

"Kathleen, I don't expect this one to come over either", I said, pointing at Dan. "Please talk some sense into him. I want to do this on my own."

To my surprise, she shook her head.

"No, Tommy. I want Dan to go with you. It's too dangerous on your own. You need back-up. You have never even been to Ireland before, so to expect you to go over all on your own to tackle your demons is madness. Dan will go with you...and that's that."

What more could I say? They had decided and there was nothing I could do to change their minds. I was happy, but at the same time I didn't want to drag Dan away from his happy family for my sake.

Afterwards, when I got up to bid my farewells, I thanked them all for their concern and help.

"Sure, what are ye thanking us for?", asked Dan. "I'm only using this as an excuse to get away from *her* for a while, and to get over for a piss up."

We all laughed.

"Bastard", said Brian, "Those were my fuckin' reasons for volunteering."

They always knew how to diffuse a tense situation.

Next, I went to see Andrea. I phoned her first and she insisted in meeting me for Sunday lunch and a drink. I was delighted, to say the least.

I told her the full story too, from beginning to end. After I told her everything, she began to cry. I held her, her sobs rocking both our bodies.

Just like the McManus', she said; "I'm coming with you."

Inside, I wished I could bring her with me, but I couldn't put her at any risk.

I told her she couldn't come and explained why. I told her Dan was coming with me. She seemed relieved that I wasn't going on my own...so was I.

We sat in the pub for most of the day and it was one of the best evenings I ever spent- certainly the best evening I had spent in a pub.

We talked about a lot of things. She told me what I had been like during my drunken black-out episodes. She cried telling me those stories. She didn't hold anything back. She told me I had acted exactly like how I described my mother in her worst drunken frenzies. I was horrified, but I had to hear the truth. I promised her it would never happen again, and told her about my mother's advice about only sticking to beer. She laughed and fully agreed.

That night, after the pub, we went back to my flat, and again, as the Americans put it, "made love" all night, and for the two days afterwards. Working in the NHS, she certainly didn't have a problem pulling a sickie for a few days, certainly administering some Florence Nightingale comfort to me in that time.

She left on the Wednesday morning. She held onto me with all the desperation of a person clinging onto the edge of a cliff, before getting into the taxi.

I laughed. "Andrea, for God's sake, let go- I can't breathe."

She didn't laugh, but stared deeply into my eyes.

"Be careful, baby. Call me every day. I love you."

"I will. I love you too, baby.", I replied, trying to choke back the tears.

After she got into the taxi, she looked back at me, her eyes heavy with tears. I waved and ran quickly back into my flat, the lump in my throat making me feel awkward.

That day, I got organised, tying up any loose ends that needed tying. Sitting alone in my flat that night, I fought the urge to go to the off-licence. I waited and waited until it was too late. Then I went to bed, alcohol free and slept until the next morning.

I was awakened by the phone ringing, Dan. He came by and picked me up, the two of us travelling in near silence the whole way to the airport.

When we got there, Dan had to direct me everywhere. I felt like an idiot, having never been in an airport before and not knowing any of the procedures.

Once on the airplane we sat side by side, again in silence. The flight was enjoyable, nevertheless. I felt like a child, looking down upon the towns and cities getting ever smaller, then the cloud's appearing right in front of my eyes. A short while after, I viewed what the exiled Paddy's always spoke so fondly and sometimes poetically of. The lush emerald greens, the mist covered lakes and rivers. So much countryside. From first viewing, Ireland looked as if no-one even inhabited it, fields, and rivers as far as the eyes could see. Then, a few little houses, speckled here and there, like little ornaments. As the airplane began to descend, I could begin to make out the roads and the tiny cars driving on them

The closer we got to landing, the more I began to realise that the man would be waiting for us at the airport. It all began to get very real then, as the pilot came over the Tannoy to announce we were about to land soon, giving his instructions to the cabin-crew. A cold sweat broke over my forehead...and I couldn't even blame the alcohol. My heart began to pound, not because of the ensuing touchdown, but because of what lay beyond it.

I was every bit as useless, descending the plane as I was boarding it. Dan guided me through it all nicely, laughing heartily at my incompetence. As soon as we touched down, he was in his element, like a giddy teenager, seemingly forgetting the nature of the business we were on. I didn't want to put a dampener on his mood. It had been a long time since he was home, so I wanted him to enjoy it as much as he could.

"Smell that good air, Tommy. That's God's own stuff. Not that smog shite we're breathin' over in London.", he exclaimed once out of the plane, taking a huge suck of air into his lungs.

"Fuck, Tommy, it's too healthy for me. Let's get our bags and get a few fags smoked before I conk out from all this lovely pure oxygen. I'm not used to it anymore."

We laughed and quickly went to get our bags. Dan's good humour and all his messing around distracted me for a while. Then, just as we were walking towards the exit, I spotted him.

It was strange, I had never even seen a picture of him before, and I'm sure he hadn't of me either, certainly not as an adult, but we both instantly recognised each other.

He had all the features my mother had. He was a few years older than she was, but he looked twenty years younger than she did, at the time of her death. He was obviously a man who lived a healthy lifestyle and looked after himself. It hit me at that point that my mother could have been like that, living easily another twenty years, healthily and happily, maybe with a few grandchildren to cherish.

A fresh surge of anger and with it, purpose, came over me. Someone had to pay for my mother's lost youth alone.

The man put his hand out.

"Tommy? It's you, isn't it?", he asked, to be completely sure.

I shook him by the hand.

"It is. Boy, it's good to see you. I can't believe how much you look like her."

He laughed, the good natured, pleasant laugh my mother had when she hadn't been tortured by her demons.

"Sorry, this is my friend, Dan. You spoke to his wife, Kathleen, on the phone a few times."

The two men shook hands and exchanged pleasantries. I couldn't take my eyes off him, it felt comforting to look at him. It seemed my mother lived on, like she wasn't gone. This man seemed to share all her best traits, minus the bitterness and hurt.

We walked to the car, making small talk. Unlike meeting a stranger for the first time there was no awkwardness or silence between us. The conversation flowed, Dan waxing lyrical with him like he did with the Irishmen on the sites. It seemed to be a trait the pure Irish had, those born and reared in Ireland. I resented it a little, as I didn't have access to the true Irish lexicon.

I sat in the back, knowing Dan liked to take the alpha male role, sitting in the front. A man like Dan wouldn't look right taking a back seat, literally, or metaphorically.

My uncle turned to me, his expression now more serious, the steeliness my mother had in her eyes evident in his.

"We are goin' to head to my house, the house where your mother was raised. I have a few documents and things for you to sign, then I will take you to your parent's home. It's what your mother wanted. I can imagine this will be upsetting for you, but I will try and make it as easy for you as I can. We all will.", he said, looking to Dan.

"After that, we'll go to the police. Your mother has confirmed the sequence of events, and I believe she gave a written statement too?"

"Yes, I have it with me.", I confirmed.

"Good. Justice needs served and there is no better time than the present to do it. Are you happy to go ahead with all this, Tommy?"

I nodded.

"It was my mother's dying wish. Of course, I'm more than happy to do it."

"Good lad.", he replied, putting the car into gear.

With that, the journey to my parents' home began.

CHAPTER 35

Neil remained at the kitchen table all that day. For once he boycotted his daily routine, the routine that had saved him from the baying insanity and gave him a daily purpose. He boycotted it that day without fear of consequence because he knew his purpose lay ahead that night, after darkness. The thought that he was becoming some form of ghoul, a bogeyman, that shouldn't be seen in the daylight hours, having to tend to his business after dark, amused him so much he almost let out a howl of laughter.

He asked himself why he couldn't walk out the gate, walk those country roads he had walked years before. He hadn't done anything wrong, he hadn't killed or hurt anyone. He wasn't the beast that should be cowering in the shadows. No, the beast who should be hiding away under the cover of shame of what he had inflicted, was at large, he thought.

At large and thriving. He had probably bought up more of the country too, the country that had once been Neil's.

He had thought at length in the past about what he should do with him. Oust him for the vermin he was? Kill him? Seek some form of judicial justice?

No.

The reason he wouldn't…shame. Shame he hadn't seen it coming. Shame his quarrels with him had brought tragedy upon his family.

He sat, at that moment, shaking with anger, then suddenly shivering with remorse.

His family were long gone. Of course, he blamed McNamee, but he knew he could never control other men's desires, or read their minds. No man could. In the past he had anticipated trouble, snuffing it out before it escalated on many occasions, but he had grossly underestimated McNamee. He certainly hadn't seen it coming. How could anyone think another man, even one's sworn enemy, would have enough evil in their soul to kill another man's family. It was way beyond his comprehension.

He remained sat for another while.

There had been a change. The seasons were slowly turning. The perpetual winter was beginning to thaw. He had noticed a bud or two appearing on the starved tree outside his bedroom window. How long had it been, he wondered? It had felt like years, many years. Again, he tried to steer his mind away from his train of thought. Thoughts of a winter lasting many years surely had to be tell-tale signs of madness.

The air had appeared different though. Crisper, cleaner…there was more life in it. He had always been able to judge a change in the seasons by the feel of the air, by the smell of it. The air he had become accustomed to had been heavy and stale, but the new air was light and fresh.

Finally, the dusk began to settle. Not yet he thought, he wanted to wait for the complete cover of darkness. He wondered how people would react to him if they saw him. How would he react to them? To even speak to another person after all that time would be excruciating. The pity, people would undoubtedly have pity for what had happened, it was only human nature. But he couldn't deal with the pity of others. Their pity could only act as a weapon for his shame. His shame was a living, thriving parasite, omnipresent and hungry for encouragement, to encompass his whole being. Once it would take hold, it would overpower him, and all rational thought and reason would be lost.

People and their pity were poison to him, he *had* to avoid them at all costs.

Finally, the darkness surrounded him. He could view everything perfectly, so accustomed to it he had become. He knew the average person's vision in the dark wouldn't be as good as his, so already he would have a huge advantage. He could blend in with the shadows on his one and only mission.

He stood, his body stiff from sitting so long, and shook himself off. It hadn't been cold throughout the day, again to the average person it may have been unbearably cold, but he was used to it. He began to feel the cold then, however, opening the door to see the beginnings of a light frost settling upon the landscape. The winter hadn't cleared completely, he knew that then. He put on his long, black top coat and shivered with the cold.

He walked to the top of the lane. He heard a car in the distance, driving slowly down the road. He could just about make out the headlights amid the bushes and trees that lay between it and him. It made him nervous, but he knew at the end of the lane, life went on regardless. There *would* be cars, tractors, people. He *had* to expect them, he had to be smart about taking cover.

Mid-way up the lane, there stood a gate. The same rusty old iron gate that had been there since he had been a child. Máire used to complain about it all the time. It made him smile, the thought of her. Every time they left the house it was the same routine. Neil would stop the car halfway up the lane, jump out, open the gate, drive forward a little, jump back out to close the gate, then back into the car.

"Ach, you and that aul gate", she would complain; "Why do you have to have it. I mean, if you insist in keeping a gate, then why can't we buy a new one. It's awful looking, and the flipping weight of it, it kills me trying to open it."

Neil would always laugh and promise to fix it. He had been true to his word. He had put hinges on it, a new handle, even new gate posts to hold it in place. He painted it red, but the rust would always prevail. It hadn't stopped her from complaining though. He had always liked to have a gate, he felt he was keeping the outside world out.

That night though, the gate blended in with everything else in his world, old and ruined. It had done its job in keeping the evil of the world out, he thought, with pure sarcasm. He held back the urge to kick it, out of anger and contempt.

He leaned over it, contemplating what he was going to do next. His thoughts turned to Pete. Poor Pete, his only friend. The only person apart from Máire who ever understood him. A good man. But where had he gone, he wondered. Why had he not visited? He needed to find out what happened him, to make sure he was safe. The thought that McNamee had gotten to him, possibly on the same night made him physically shudder.

Maggie. She was another of the people Neil had dwelled upon since everything had happened. He had never cared much for her. She was family, yes, and he looked out for her, but that was as far as it went. He hadn't worried about her, she could certainly look after herself. But...the will. That God-forsaken will. He always knew it would haunt him. He hadn't worried about it in years, not since poor Seamie had been born. Neil himself wasn't going to live forever, so what was to happen to the place when he was gone. He knew that Maggie, without a second thought would gleefully sign it over to her beloved McNamee. There was no doubt about that. How could he ever rest in peace knowing the Dillon legacy, the legacy both he and his father had worked so hard to create, would be inherited by a devious murdering bastard? He would climb out of the fires of hell if he had to, to stop it. Anger rose in him like mercury in a thermometer. He felt like roaring, never had the urge to rattle the gate off its hinges and roar at the top of his lungs been so great. He resisted, though. Mad men did such things. Besides, his anger was best stored within, it would act like fuel to propel him in his mission. He had to do it. He had to do it then, immediately. He had to visit Pete, to make sure he was safe and still alive.

He didn't plan to speak with Pete, it would be too much for him. He didn't want to speak to anyone, but he *had* to speak with Maggie. He had to travel the five miles to Dunbay, first to check on Pete and then to speak with Maggie. He would tell her exactly what happened, she had to know. The legacy of her brother's home and property remained solely in her hands. He couldn't let her sign it over to a monster like McNamee. He would explain all, and instruct her to sign over one half to Pete and the other to Fintan, Máire's brother. He didn't expect she would object too much if she knew the truth. She would then go to the police, get justice for what happened and McNamee would be arrested the next morning.

On the way back home, he would call into Fintan's farm, a keen huntsman. He knew exactly where Fintan kept his shotgun, it wouldn't be too difficult to break into his garage and steal it. Then he would return to the house, sit at his table one last time, and suck on his pipe to let the good memories flood back.

Then he'd put the shotgun into his mouth and blow himself to kingdom come.

He smiled to himself. A great plan. Why had he not thought of it earlier, he wondered. Finally, he was going to get some form of justice. He could rest as close as possible to some form of peace the next day.

He stood for another moment at the gate, desperately trying to pluck up the courage to finally scale it and embark on his journey.

Just then, to his utter horror, he felt a human touch upon his shoulder...then the darkness descended upon him.

He woke once more in his bed, the next morning. The sunlight streaming in amongst a million dust particles. He had experienced the worst ever recurring nightmare about the Gentle bush and the bodies. It had lasted the whole night, never had he experienced it's like before. He had awoken exhausted, the sound of the chirping birds outside doing little to lift his spirits. Then he remembered what happened, his mission hadn't been accomplished. Another day of waiting, the torture, he thought never to end.

He didn't bother to get out of bed that day, his routine could go to hell.

There was no point, he thought.

His hellish prison had trapped him, and he knew then, there was nothing he could do to escape.

CHAPTER 36

We drove for just over an hour. Through various small towns, villages, and hamlets.

I couldn't believe how quiet everything was. To my surprise, it unnerved me a little. I always thought I would embrace the silence. I had always liked to sit in my flat, alone with my thoughts, but the hubbub of the city always lay beneath. The small towns and country areas we drove through didn't have the intensity of background noise I was used to. They were deathly quiet.

Perhaps I was a true London boy at heart, after all?

We arrived at my uncle's home. We drove up a small incline to reach his house on the top of a small hill. The first thing that struck me was the view. Spring had sprung and the nature was breath-taking in its beauty. Rolling green fields lay beneath our line of vision, trees of all varieties, mostly oak, lining the small country roads, small buds slowly turning to leaves.

It struck me then, the house being my uncle's family home, that this was the house my poor mother grew up in. The view before me what she would have witnessed every morning, noon and night, the seasons making the landscape look differently beautiful as the years progressed. A dull ache pounded at my heart just then, as I thought about how she was ripped from such a place of beauty, to a soulless, sprawling city where she knew no-one.

My uncle led us into the house where we were met by his wife. She stood at a very impressive looking stove, cooking what looked to be a very hearty and delicious looking stew. When she seen me, she took a step back and stood, shaking her head.

"Jeepers, are you not the spit of your father?", she said, almost as if she meant to say it to herself.

"Sorry, you must be Tommy? And you, Dan?", she asked.

We both nodded and she hugged us warmly.

"I'm Veronica", she said, introducing herself.

"I hope you boys are hungry. I have a drop of stew made for you both.", she continued.

"Ach, God bless you Veronica. We'll take a drop surely.", Dan replied, beaming from ear to ear at the prospect.

Veronica looked at me. "You're like your father in nature too, Tommy...quiet?"

"Ach leave the poor lad alone, Veronica", my uncle interrupted. "The poor fella has a lot on his mind. He's hardly goin' to be singin' and dancin' now, is he?"

I felt a little awkward. I hadn't really said anything. I felt a little in shock. This was my mother's home, I could almost sense her spirit in the place. It unnerved and comforted me in equal measures.

"Veronica, enjoy him when he's quiet, because you'll be fed up listening to him when he gets started, believe you me.", Dan quipped.

We all laughed, and I felt further indebted to him that he came. There certainly weren't any awkward silences when Dan was around.

My aunt and uncle had two children, a boy and a girl who were both grown up and moved away. Patrick lived and worked in Dublin, and his sister Deborah, lived in Australia with her husband and baby girl. Veronica told us Deborah would be coming home for a family wedding in the summer, so we could all get together for that. Cousins. Two months before I had no-one, apart from my mother and the McManus'. Now I had a whole family network.

It would take a while to get used to it all.

We sat eating the stew, and talked. It was nice, it felt like it had done in the McManus household. Of course, they loved Dan, it was nigh impossible not to. We skirted around the heavier issue, the elephant in the room. It would rear its ugly head soon enough, so it was nice to enjoy some light-hearted conversation in the meantime.

They showed us photos of my cousins. The similarity of the daughter, to my mother was almost uncanny. Of course, there was a resemblance to Veronica, but the main features, she shared with my mother. The eyes…the steeliness, the fullness of her face. It was nearly impossible to tell her age because of the youthful pallor in her cheeks. The dimples, the features were all the same.

Veronica seemed to read my mind, perhaps from how long I stared at the photo.

"Uncanny, isn't it?", she asked.

I knew what she meant without asking.

"It is, yes.", I replied.

"And she has every move of her too. The feistiness, it's all in her. She's a Smith through and through. You'll like her, she's a good girl."

It had comforted me seeing the similarity between my mother and uncle, but seeing a younger, happier version of her, cheered me up no end.

We sat around for another while, drinking tea and smoking until Veronica got up and began tidying away the dishes. She turned to my uncle.

"I'm sure Tommy wants to go and see where he was reared. Why don't you take them?", she said.

My heart began to pound, Goosebumps suddenly appearing all over my body. My uncle sat back in the chair, stretched, and got up.

"OK. Are you both ready?", he asked.

I nodded. I hoped I was.

We drove a short distance, through small country roads ensconced by more trees and fields than I had seen in a lifetime. The sheer beauty was breath-taking, I felt humbled to even breathe the purity of the air. But, something lay beneath. There was a presence, an underlying energy that my sixth sense just couldn't tune into. I knew amid the beauty and tranquillity of the countryside, lay a malice and evil, that felt as much as out of place as the stench of an occasional dead animal lying in the hedgerows.

Sensing the melancholy washing over me, once more Dan stepped up and cracked a few jokes, lifting the mood momentarily.

My uncle slowed up, and turned to me.

"Tommy, we're here. It's just down this lane."

He drove down a long, tree lined lane that led to the house. A shiver ran down my spine, but no memories of the place came back to me.

Then, I spotted the house. Still, no stirring of memories, just a stirring in my guts. Nausea almost overwhelmed me. Dan patted me on the shoulder.

"Home, Tommy. Your rightful home.", he said, smiling.

I looked blankly back at him. I was stuck for words.

We got out of the car and walked towards the house. No-one spoke for a while. It seemed like the stillness of the place would suck up any sound, like a vacuum. We walked slowly around the perimeter of the house, before my uncle spoke.

"Tommy, this is your home. Your mother wanted you to reclaim what is yours, what belongs to your family. It mightn't look like much, but by God this place has history. History and potential- what a combination. Take it in, it's yours. Once we get this job done and dusted, we'll get the wheels put in motion to get it into your name."

His words weren't sinking in. The place meant nothing to me, in fact I quite despised it. I didn't want anything to do with it. It wasn't home, it was a place of torment to my mother, a place she ran away from her entire life. How could I be expected to live there after what happened?

"Listen fellas", I said, addressing both. "Would you mind letting me spend a bit of time here on my own? I have a lot of thinking to do."

My uncle nodded his head. "No problem. We will call back for you in a few hours. Is that all right?"

I told him I would ring him when I was ready to go. He agreed to call for me when I phoned.

"Take this man to the pub for a few hours.", I said to my uncle; "I can tell by the head on him he's gasping for a few pints."

Both men laughed, and drove off in the car, leaving me alone at the house.

I sat on a pile of blocks, piled up at the door of an out-house, looking directly at the house itself. I must have sat there for a few hours, the hours slipping away like minutes until dusk fell on the early spring evening. The air began to feel chilly, so I got up and walked a little to warm myself up.

I walked around the perimeter of the property, peering into various windows of the buildings, never entering any of them. I wanted to, but just couldn't bring myself to do so.

The place was deathly quiet, but strangely comforting. I never had as many contrasting feelings about anywhere before. I felt it was where I belonged, but also had an urge to get on the next available flight back to London. I fought the urge though. I had promised my mother. I couldn't let her down.

Then I decided.

It was time.

I had to do what I had come to do.

I set off, hurriedly down the lane. I jogged down the long lane towards the road. I almost admitted to myself that I was scared, very scared. The dimming daylight, along with the hunched over, intertwining bare trees made the lane very eerie and dark. I almost laughed to myself. The big city boy who had survived his whole life on the tough streets of North London, afraid of the darkening countryside landscape. I could only imagine how Dan would laugh. I wished at that point I had let Dan and my uncle stay with me, company would have neutralised the devastating loneliness of the place.

My jog turned into a three-quarter paced run, then into a full sprint. My heart was pounding and my breathing accelerated, the cool evening air gushing into my lungs, making them feel like they were on fire.

At last, I could see the gate that led onto the road. I quickened my pace even further, my legs feeling like jelly.

Then I saw it.

I stopped immediately. I bent over, gasping for breath, praying I wouldn't collapse from my exertions. I looked up, still it was there. I rubbed my eyes and tried to regulate my breathing, to make sure I wasn't hallucinating from the lack of oxygen.

But, it was still there.

I walked towards the gate, the object didn't move, its darkness clearly marking it out against the background of the murky evening light.

There was no doubt about it, it was the figure of a huge man.

The closer I got, the image grew in definition. The huge figure was dressed in black. A long black coat hung down to his knees. He was leaning over the gate, still as a statue. His size was immense. He was taller than I was, even as he leaned over the gate, so I imagined his height at full length to be around six-four or six-five. But, it was his presence, the sheer width of the man, the breadth of his shoulders coming close to the width of two men.

I got closer. Still, he didn't move.

He must have heard me, I thought, as my breathing hadn't yet returned to normal, and I was still panting heavily.

It had to be him. His sheer size and presence alone uniquely identifying him as to what I was told about him. Even without seeing his face, I knew it was him.

The mythical Neil Dillon. The man mountain. The legend.

I walked slowly up behind him. I didn't want to completely surprise him, so I shuffled my feet a little, hoping he would hear me and turn around.

He didn't move. I got closer. I coughed.

Still, no movement. Then, my voice sounding small, pathetic, and scared;
"Neil".

No movement, no response. I moved closer still, now smelling the pipe smoke from him.

"Neil. Can you hear me...Neil?".

Still nothing.

Then, my heart pounding, my breathing again becoming out of control, a sudden nausea swimming in my stomach, I spoke again;

"Neil...its me."

A lump immediately came to my throat, but I managed to spit the words out before the lump made it nigh impossible to speak.

"Neil. Turn around. It's me. It's OK. Everything's going to be OK"

I put my hand on my father's shoulder.

Then the world turned black.

CHAPTER 37

The pub had been unusually busy that night, for a week night. There had been a funeral in the nearby chapel, so there had been a throng of mourners making a day of it after the ceremony.

The man sat in the corner he always sat in, with his sidekicks, Paddy, and Carl. They sat and talked about the deceased old woman for a while, occasionally going to the bar and mingling with some of the family members, before Paddy and Carl eventually got caught up in the heavy drinking themselves.

The man had been nursing a brandy all evening, before deciding to get himself another. It was a little celebratory drink as he knew he would be driving a drunken Carl home, getting a grope of Rosie's nice big tits in the process.

He took a sip of his brandy, the initial sweetness followed by the searing heat a moment later. He loved that little kick, almost always taking his breath away. The exhalation of breath after the sip always felt like he was breathing fire. He had a little smile to himself at the thought of actually doing so.

Fire...his old friend. He had a vision of himself walking around, bottle of brandy in tow, breathing fire, bringing devastation and fear to the people of the country. He had a little laugh to himself, no one asking why, as the mood was good in the pub...the Irish making a party from a tragedy.

He sat watching Carl. He could see the signs already, the heavy hooding of the eyes and the slowing down of his senses, his drinking becoming heavier. He would soon black out. Then, he would dump him in the back of the car and take him home. He had a delicious thought just then;

"Maybe I'll even get my fingers wet tonight?"

He laughed aloud once more and took another swig of his brandy.

At that moment, Fintan Smith entered the pub with a tall, black-haired man he had never seen before. He thought it unusual to see Fintan in the pub as he had never been much of a drinker, preferring the quiet life at home instead.

Fintan was someone he had always kept close tabs on. He had found himself at times driving up and around Fintan's home to see if anything was happening, monitoring any comings and goings that could be deemed suspicious.

Keeping a close eye on Fintan was essential in maintaining his empire. Fintan was a key figure in the man's elaborate game.

Fintan found a seat at the bar amongst the crowd, a few feet from where the man and his workmates sat. The man hunched himself forward a little, trying to listen to Fintan's conversation with the black-haired man. They hadn't noticed the man amongst the busy crowd in the bar, so he knew he could eavesdrop nicely from behind where they sat.

The black-haired man did most of the talking. Most of the conversation was about someone called Tommy. The man's mind was busily trying to figure out who Tommy was. He tried to reason with himself, to calm himself down, paranoia getting the better of him. It was likely that Tommy was the black-haired man's son, an irrelevance. The tall black-haired man was obviously a contractor, a builder perhaps who was doing work on Fintan's property.

He had almost convinced himself that this "Tommy" was irrelevant, until Fintan began to speak about him with warmth and affection.

The man's hairs stood on end all over his body.

"Fuck", he thought; "What has turned up now?"

Then, he almost felt sick to his stomach, when the black-haired man took a sip of his pint, wiped his lips, and said;

"Well, Fintan. I hope this sorry story ends well when Tommy goes to the police tomorrow, and tells them just what that fucker did."

The man sat in the corner, momentarily frozen to the spot. A cold sweat swept across his body, shocking his system into a shiver. He felt like someone had walked across his grave.

His drunken friends hadn't noticed his state of shock, both sitting staring at him, as if awaiting a response.

"Sorry", the man said, "What did you say, Paddy?"

"Another drink, boss?", Paddy asked, his words becoming badly slurred.

"Ah, no. No thanks Paddy. I'm gonna hit the road here, men. I don't feel too well. I'll head home and sleep it off. I'll see you both in the morning."

He stood up, noticing Fintan had gone to the toilet and slipped out unnoticed, the tall black-haired man now engaged in conversation with the locals around him.

"Fuck it. Rosie's big tits can wait for another night", he thought.

He had to get himself home. He had to think, to plan.

Could he kill again, he wondered? He smiled to himself.

"Of course.", he thought; "It worked so well the last time."

He started up the engine of his car, and drove home.

Home, to plan his defence.

CHAPTER 38

For the rest of that day, Neil stayed in bed.

He no longer cared if madness finally took hold. He welcomed it. Perhaps, he thought, being truly mad, wholly insane would numb his tormented mind.

For so long he had yearned for spring to arrive. Now that it had, the birds and nature outside beginning to awaken, he longed for the dark, cold winter once more. He longed to lie in his bed with the elements at their worst outside. The protection his creaking house provided, a reminder that even the most broken-down vessel could still function and stand up to the most devastating forces.

For then, the sun hung in the sky. He could smell spring. He knew outside, the daffodils were winning their battle against the heavy soil of winter. He felt it should be giving him a sense of hope. A sense that something so beautiful, being prisoner to a dense mat of heavy dirt for such a long time, could, year after year, eventually prevail and show the world its true beauty.

The daffodils and spring plants...true survivors, never defeated.

They didn't inspire him, not anymore.

He slept for most of that day, even with the promising spring sunshine pouring into his room. He dreamt of the Gentle bush and Pete's decaying body, his blood feeding the branches. He woke up screaming mostly, always the same urge to break out and go to Pete, to warn him and make sure he was all right.

He didn't though, he couldn't. He lay and waited for sleep to take him again, the unconscious hell merely a respite for the conscious one he inhabited.

Next, he dreamt of a shabby old office. Papers and files were strewn carelessly across an expensive looking table. A vaguely familiar looking man sat at the desk rifling through the papers. Just then there was a knock at the door and two people entered the room. An elderly woman and a younger man. The haze in his mind slowly dispersed until he could finally make out who the two people were.

Maggie and McNamee.

Even in his dreams, his blood ran cold. He knew exactly what was happening. Both signed some papers, then embraced each other warmly. McNamee slyly winked at the man at the desk, a look of satisfaction enveloping every fibre of his being.

McNamee and to a certain extent, Maggie, had gotten what they wanted. The heir to the Dillon estate was dead, the loophole Thomas Dillon had implemented in his will, executed, and McNamee had won in the end.

Again, Neil awoke, his body shaking and drenched in a cold sweat.

Just then, whilst staring up at the ceiling, he finally realised he didn't care anymore. His fight had been lost, the fight *in* him gone too. What difference did it make if McNamee had robbed him of his family's inheritance, he thought? The fires of revenge and justice that had burned in him for so long, now extinguished.

He knew he was done. His rage, all that was left, now gone.

To hell with it all, he thought, as sleep took him once again.

CHAPTER 39

Not for the first time in my life, I awoke in a strange bed.

My head pounded and my clothes were drenched in a cold sweat that made them cling to my clammy body. It took me a moment or so to work out where I was, the absolute silence confirming I was in my uncle's home.

Why did my head pound so much? Why the cold sweat?

My headache was obviously because of complete dehydration, due to the excessive sweating. But, I hadn't drunk the previous night, I was sure of that. Maybe I had come down with a fever, or some type of flu?

Then, it hit me. The memories of the evening before coming flooding back.

I had seen him.

Neil...my father.

He stood at the gate and I had approached him, calling his name. Then, when I touched his shoulder I must have blacked out.

That is when the horror began. The dreams, those horrific visions had come to my subconscious. Again, and again they bombarded my mind all night long. They were so real, so lifelike. I could smell the rancid decay of the body. I could hear the cries of Neil in the hole, crying out for my help. I saw the roots of the bush embedding themselves in the decaying man's body. I saw blood pumping through roots, the leaves of the bush illuminated by the man's blood. The bush had a red hue to it, a ghastly sight like I had never witnessed.

The idea of a plant feeding from a decaying human body, made me physically retch.

I couldn't work out what it all meant. It had been more than a dream, that was certain. I had experienced every second of it. I had physically been there, there was no doubt about that. It had felt like a nightmare replaying on a loop. Every time it replayed, it got progressively worse. I noticed horrid little extra details each time, like how the roots progressively got more tangled around Neil's legs, the look of horror on his face becoming more intense.

The man beside him, the dead, decaying one, I didn't know, had never seen before. His body had been horribly destroyed by the hideous plantation that gorged on his blood, but his face had been relatively untouched. It was the expression the man wore that haunted me the most. The look of absolute horror was grotesque in its intensity. I had never seen a human expression like it, like the expression of a man who was already suffering the eternal damnation of hell.

That poor man.

I couldn't work out who it was. It was obviously someone Neil had a lot of fondness for, as his own look of horror seemed to be mostly out of concern for his friend.

In those dreams, Neil had begged me to save them both. The futility of his screams to save the other man, heart-breaking. Even in his deepest hell, I sensed Neil's great spirit, generosity and concern for his friend, his courage evident.

It gave me hope I could summon his spirit and courage, to complete what I needed to do.

I drew upon that very courage there and then, to force myself out of bed. I heard footsteps on the landing, outside the room. I sat on the edge of the bed and tried to regain my composure.

There was a knock at the door, and in walked Dan. He sat beside me in silence for a few moments.

He put his hand on my shoulder.

"Are you all right, kid?"

I shuddered at the touch of a human hand. It seemed to bring back the memories of those horrible nightmares again.

I tried not to dry retch.

"I'm OK, Dan. Tell me, what happened last night."

He straightened his back and took a deep breath.

"Well", he started; "Fintan and myself went for a few drinks after we left you, in the local pub. Then we came back here, had a few tins, and waited for you to call. As it got later, we both began to worry about where you were, why you hadn't called. Then we drove to the house, and there...we found you."

He stopped at that point to take a breath. Then, visibly shaken, he continued;

"Jesus, Tommy, we thought you were...dead."

He laughed, not a normal good-natured laugh, but one that tried, in vain, to disguise his nervousness and emotions.

"I mean, you were just lying there, at the foot of that aul gate."

He stopped again, looking at the floor, attempting to regain his composure, and continued;

"You scared the shit out of us. When we got out of the car and went over to you, we could hardly hear a breath out of ye. We tried to find a pulse, but because the two of us were half-cut, we could hardly find one. And you looked like a fuckin'...corpse. I've never seen anyone like that before, Tommy. By fuck, ye scared the shite clean out of us."

Again, he took a deep breath and looked at the floor. I cut-in before he continued.

"So, what happened then? I can't remember any of this shit, Dan."

"Well, the two of us eventually calmed down. We could feel warmth from your body, so we knew you weren't a gonner. We managed to bundle you into the back of the car and got you back here. We were glad to get the fuck away from that place, to be honest. It gave me what the yanks call, "the creeps.""

"So, did I act weird. Did I talk in my sleep or anything?", I asked, thinking the nightmares I suffered, had to have somehow manifested themselves physically on my unconscious body.

He sat and thought for a moment. When he spoke, his voice was laced with emotion;

"No...nothing. You know, you reminded me a bit of Brian...when he was in that coma. It brought it all back...really scared the shit out of me."

He smiled, leaning across to punch me on the arm, "Ye prick.", now laughing.

We both laughed, it was the only thing we could do to lighten the mood a little.

"We got you to bed, and as soon as you were in you began to warm up...and snore like a pig."

He looked at me, his eyes searching for answers.

"What happened up there, kid?"

I lied and told him I was fine, told him I lay down for a rest and fell asleep by mistake. He knew I was lying, but seemed satisfied enough. I didn't feel guilt for lying, sometimes it being better to protect people from horrific truths.

He punched me on the arm once more and told me to get ready and come down for breakfast.

When I got myself up and ready, I went downstairs where a mountain of food awaited us. Veronica clucked around us, never sitting to eat anything herself.

I looked over at Dan.

"She reminds me of someone, this one.", I said and we both laughed and got the reference.

Fintan wore the same worried expression Dan had earlier, until I told him the same lie. He didn't buy it.

He put his knife and fork down by his side.

"Bullshit."

His reaction shocked me, shocked us all.

"You're lying, Tommy. I've been up there on my own before. Something happened. Tell us what it was."

At that, the room fell silent.

I laughed nervously, trying to diffuse the tension.

"Honestly, Fintan, I fell asleep. Yesterday was the first time I was on a flight. Maybe I was jet-lagged."

Dan and Veronica chuckled at my ridiculous excuse. Fintan didn't though, sipping at his tea, never taking his eyes off me.

"I think something happened up there last night. There's something…strange about the place, I've felt it. I think you seen…something. Maybe you feel scared, or embarrassed, but I think something happened and you don't want to tell us."

"For God's sake, Fintan. Leave the poor lad alone.", Veronica interrupted, much to my relief.

"I'm not getting at the lad, Veronica. I just don't think what happened last night is as straight forward as he's makin' out…and I'm worried."

He looked at me. "If there's anything you want to tell us, Tommy, speak up. We're here to help, son. We're on your side. Tell us what happened, we can help."

I took a sip of my tea, trying to buy myself some thinking time.

What could I do? Tell the truth and project those horrific images into the minds of those lovely people and their lovely lives. Tell them it was no nightmare, but a night-long hellish episode that felt as close to reality as an icy tingle down one's spine?

How could I?

"It was nothing of the sort, Fintan. I had a long day. Tiredness and excitement just got the better of me."

He still didn't look convinced, no-one did. Then I added, for a hint of authenticity; "And it didn't help that I was nursing the mother and father of all hangovers from the night before."

To my great relief, Dan laughed, a nervous one, but still it was something to break the tension.

"I can vouch for that. This boy doesn't do normal hangovers. I've seen him some days where he's been green in the face."

Veronica chuckled, but Fintan remained stony-faced, still staring at me.

"Are you sure everything's all right, Tommy?", he asked.

"Couldn't be better, Fintan.", I replied, giving him my best poker face.

We sat for a while afterwards. Dan and Veronica chatted about the weather, the price of petrol and other awkward silence fillers. The food looked delicious and everyone ate with gusto, but I couldn't bear to eat any of it. The images from my nightmares left a toxic void in my stomach that vomiting or any other physical process could never eradicate.

I drank tea and played with my food, blaming a dodgy stomach for my lack of appetite. Fintan drained his tea and went to the sink to rinse his cup.

"So, Tommy.", he said, standing at the sink, "What time do ye want to head to the police station?"

"Whatever time suits you, I don't mind.", I replied.

My stomach performed summersaults.

"I know you have a few bits and pieces to do around the farm, first.", I continued; "Sure, why don't you get them out of the way and then we'll head down?"

To my great relief, he contemplated my suggestion, and answered; "Aye, all right. Give me an hour or so and then we'll go. Only if that's OK with you, as I know you probably want to get this done quickly?"

"Don't worry about me. Get your work done first"

Fintan nodded in agreement.

Veronica made a fresh pot of tea and we sat around making small talk for a while more.

"So, Fintan. My mother spoke a lot about Pete Kelly. Is he still around?", I asked.

Fintan let out a small chuckle. "Aye, Pete's still around all right."

"He was a good friend of my fathers?"

Fintan took a sip of his tea and looked melancholily out the window.

"Ach, he was...he was. He was good to your father too, helped him out a lot. But..."

"But what?", I asked.

"Well, the problem with Pete was, well...he was a fuckin' eejit."

He stopped himself to apologise to Veronica for his profanity. She chuckled and agreed with him; "You're right Fintan- he was though."

"You see.", Fintan continued; "Pete had spent a lot of time living in England...not that there's anything wrong with that.", he quickly interjected obviously for my benefit. I waved him away to let him know I took no offence.

"When he came back to rural Ireland, it must have been a culture shock to him. You see, according to a few sources, he...well..."

Veronica laughed and interjected on his behalf, to spare his blushes; "He hoored around a lot in England."

We all laughed.

"I was going to say he had a colourful past, Veronica", he continued, laughing too.

"Well.", he continued, "He was a buck eejit and he loved the wine, women and song. A good fella, don't get me wrong, but he *did* seem to be a bit of a third wheel in your mother and father's marriage. He and Neil were inseparable. Your mother would have preferred if he hadn't been around as much, complaining that he "put your father to the bad". Your father would work himself to the bone all day, sometimes fifteen or sixteen-hour days. Then, after that, he and Pete would be off to the pub, mad for craic and beer. I suppose, over time it put a bit of a strain on your parents' marriage."

I nodded in agreement and understood, realising how alcohol and socialising with my mates put a strain on my own relationships. I felt a little tingle in my stomach at the thought of Andrea and the second chance she was giving me. The sensation was so strong, I promised myself, there and then, that I was going to head back to London afterwards and ask her to marry me.

No more fucking around.

"You two fellas would get on well with Pete.", Fintan continued, referring to Dan and myself, "There was always plenty of craic when Pete was around."

"So, does Pete still live locally or did he move back to England?", I asked.

"No, Pete's still around. He used to live a few doors up from your great-aunt Maggie in Dunbay, God bless her soul. Even Maggie liked him, which showed just how much of an affable fella he was."

Veronica laughed, "That's terrible, Fintan. Speaking of the dead like that."

"I know, sorry.", he continued; "But, Maggie couldn't ever be described as a "people person". Don't get me wrong, a good woman, but she didn't suffer fools gladly. I'm sure your mother told you about her?"

"She did", I answered, "My mother actually kept remotely in touch with her by all accounts, up until her sad passing a few years back."

Fintan looked surprised by my last statement.

"Really?" he asked.

I nodded and said nothing more on the matter.

"Well, Pete lived up beside Maggie anyway, until his father passed away. Then he built a big house on his father's land. He only lives about two miles away from here, you know. If you ever wanted to visit him, I'm sure he'd love to see you."

"Does he?", I asked. "God, I'd love to meet him. I've heard that many stories, it would be great to talk to him. A friend of my father's is a friend of mine after all."

Fintan drained his tea, getting up to put on his coat.

"Well, I'm goin' to head out and get this work, done."

He looked up at Dan; "Fancy givin' me a hand, Dan?", he continued, a little smile colouring his features.

Dan was in his element being on the farm. With all the eagerness of a child, he almost jumped up and put on his coat too.

"Fintan.", I said, "Just when I have a spare hour or so, would it be OK to call up to see Pete? I was just thinking, he might have some extra information for us to give to the cops."

Fintan stood buttoning his coat, thinking.

"Aye, I suppose. Sure, it wouldn't do any harm. After all, Pete always did ask after you and your mother over the years. It'll be a nice surprise for him."

He reached into his coat pocket and pulled out a set of keys, throwing them to me.

"Here, take my yoke. I'm sure he'll be about the house as I don't think he works on a Saturday."

He gave me the directions to Pete's house and I got up to put my coat on too.

"Don't be too long, Tommy. Pete's a talker, so don't let him ramble on too much."

I nodded in agreement. He put his hand on my shoulder.

"You can tell Pete that at the end of today, McNamee will be exposed for the Judas bastard that he was. What he did to you and your family will be brought to light for the whole country to see. Pete will be pleased, mark my words."

I nodded in agreement once more.

"Oh, he'll be exposed today all right, Fintan. I'll see to that."

The steeliness my mother had was evident in Fintan's features once more, as he squeezed my shoulder and nodded sombrely.

"Good man, Tommy. Today is the day you get redemption for your poor parents."

With his words ringing in my ears, I went to see Pete.

CHAPTER 40

I drove the few miles up to Pete's house. The countryside was breath-taking in its beauty. There was a freshness in the air, freshness that only spring could bring. New life, new beginnings.

The presence of the sun and the extended evenings made people more optimistic, the darkness of the winter months slowly fading away to be replaced by light.

Even through the beauty of the burgeoning spring day my soul felt as heavy as my mother's coffin, the weight I could almost physically still feel upon my shoulders. Those dreams, I couldn't work out what they were about. Even the thought of them almost made me pull over and vomit on the side of the road. I felt like I had been on a mammoth bender, the queasiness and nausea that engulfed me. I felt weak too. The past few weeks had weakened me considerably and probably aged me ten years too.

More than anything, I felt scared. This was now the point in my life where I had to stand up. My mother and father would judge me as a success or failure, depending on what I was, or was not to do.

If I had been at my strongest, I knew I would have a good chance. But, here I was, a shivering, nervous wreck…I didn't know if I had the stomach or the balls for it.

I drove on regardless. I had to see Pete.

When I arrived, I parked in his driveway, took a deep breath, hoping in vain to alleviate the nausea flooding my body, and got out of the car.

I rang his door bell. A few seconds passed until I heard the footsteps in the hall and eventually keys opening the grand-looking door from the inside. My heart raced and I felt weak at the knees. I was to finally meet my father's dearest friend, a direct link to the past and a window into the soul of my father, and indeed my mother. This man had known both at their best, had shared in some of their greatest and most treasured moments.

The door opened, and there stood a tall, grey-haired man. I could see the looks were still there, a little jaded with age but there was no doubt this man had been a looker in his time. The first thing that struck me about him was how he reminded me of Dan. He had that certain glint in his eye and his features were similar too. The height, the handsomeness, and the look of playful menace, that blackguard look.

He looked at me and I could see he was registering me as a perfect stranger, though something was stirring in him, telling his subconscious that he recognised something about me.

"Well, young fellah. What can I help ye with?", he asked, his manner as amiable as Dan and Fintan. It was perfectly obvious to me then, that my father and I shared the same set of standards to judge our friends on.

"Hello.", I said; "My name is Tommy Smyth. I'm a nephew of Fintan's."

He stood for a moment, his mind trying to piece together who I was exactly, and why I was standing on his doorstep.

"Right...right.", he responded, obviously in the hope that I would fill in the rest of the blanks.

"Sorry, let me explain.", I began, "My name is Tommy Smyth, but you would have known me years ago by a different name...Seamie Dillon. Neil's son."

A wave of surprise washed over his face. He held onto the doorframe for fear he was going to collapse.

The term "he looked like he had seen a ghost", had never been so apt.

He looked deeply into my eyes, as if he were scanning me to see if there were any features he recognised, or remembered.

"Forgive me, Tommy...Seamie, but I'm in quite a state of shock. I didn't think I'd see the day."

He looked embarrassed as he spoke. I laughed, to ease his embarrassment.

He stared at me further, his face ashen with shock.

"Sorry...sorry, come on in.", he continued.

I entered his house and was shown into a large living room. It was very impressive. A large room adorned with tasteful paintings, three large sofas in the middle of it and a roaring open fire, enclosed in a grand looking fire-place. It surprised me he lived in such opulent surroundings. I expected a much more rustic, more rough and ready type home for a man of his character.

He told me to take a seat and offered me a cup of tea. I told him I was fine, and we sat down. We sat in silence for a few moments. I could see he was in a state of shock by the way he stared at me. I finally broke the silence;

"So, you and my father...you had some good times together?"

He looked into the fire and smiled.

"We did, Tommy. Sorry, do I call you Tommy or Seamie, by the way?"

"Call me Tommy.", I replied.

"Yes, we had some good times Tommy. He was some boy, your father. The best friend I ever had...a good, good man."

He continued to stare at me, seemingly still in a state of shock.

He shook his head and seemed to suddenly snap out of his shocked state.

"Well...I tell you, I never thought I'd see the day.", he said, getting up to walk over to the fire where he began to stoke it with a very heavy and impressive looking poker.

"Well, fair play to you son, it's good to see your doin' well. I truly feared the worst for you and your mother, after what happened on that dreadful night."

He finished poking the fire and placed the poker back in its container.

"You and your mother were the talk of the country, Tommy. You disappeared in a flash after what happened. The whole country was worried about you."

He stood, now gazing out the window of his living room.

"But, thanks be to God here you are, safe and sound.", he continued, flashing me a charming smile. A look of concern suddenly clouded his features.

"What about your mother, Tommy. Where is she? Is she all right?"

"She died recently, I'm afraid."

He visibly wilted.

"Ah no. Ach, poor Máire, the poor woman."

He looked at the floor very solemnly.

"Can I ask what took her, Tommy?"

"The drink got her in the end, Pete."

A confused look coloured his features.

"The drink? Sure, your mother was never a real drinker. When did that start?"

I half laughed and answered; "She might not have been a drinker when you knew her, but the shit that befell her after that night would have driven the most righteous of assholes to drink."

He walked over to the window again and looked longingly out of it.

"You've had hard times Tommy, God love you son. Things could have been different for you two, if that bastard hadn't done what he did."

He turned and looked at me, almost apologetically

"You *do* know the full story, don't you?", he asked.

I smiled. "Oh yes, I've been filled in about what happened all right."

He nodded. "Good, good. Do you need help with anything when you are here, son? I'm your God-father at the end of the day, Tommy, so it's my duty to help you in any way I can. I promised your parents on your Christening day."

His voice was beginning to quiver a little.

"I know, Pete. Don't worry, if I need help I'll ask."

He straightened himself up, regaining his composure and walked over to the fireplace, where he poked the embers once more. He laughed to himself, then spoke;

"The stories I could tell ye, Tommy. Your father and I had some good times together...what a man."

He stopped poking the fire to look directly at me.

"You are very like him, too. The same features, the same mannerisms, not quite the height or size, though, not many have."

He laughed once more, then his features changed to one of a more solemn nature.

"He loved you, boy. God, he loved you and your mother. Thank God he didn't see what happened to your mother, as that surely would have been the death of him, or more accurately the death of the bastard who caused all of this."

I nodded my head and agreed with him.

He sat down on one of the very grand looking and comfortable sofas, directly across from me. He sat staring at me for a few moments, obviously mentally comparing me to my father. He shook his head and let out a good-natured laugh.

"I honestly didn't think I'd see the day, Tommy. It's great to see you son."

He stood up.

"Tommy, I don't know about you, but I could do with a drink. This has been quite a shock, to say the least. I've got a nice expensive bottle of brandy I bought on holidays last year. I've been dying to open it, and this surely merits a special occasion. Will you join me?"

I nodded, trying to reign my enthusiasm in a little.

"Go on then, I suppose it would be rude not to."

We both laughed and he disappeared into the kitchen to open the bottle.

I roamed around his living room for a little while, admiring his taste in vintage antiques and furniture. A few photos of him, and what looked to be his wife adorned the walls and mantelpiece of the room, no photos of children, so I guessed he didn't have any.

He walked back into the room a few minutes later with two chunky, expensive looking glasses, both containing a generous portion of brandy. He gave me a glass. I took a large gulp. It was good. The guy certainly had good taste. He took a large swig himself, breathing out theatrically upon doing so.

"Wo... it's like breathing out fire. It's good stuff this, eh?"

I nodded enthusiastically. He laughed.

"Well, don't be afraid to get it down ye, there's plenty more of where that came from. The missus won't be home for another few hours so we can enjoy ourselves, nag free."

He rolled his eyes and we both laughed. He walked to the other side of the room and delved into a stack of papers, rummaging around for a moment or so, before lifting a stack of aged looking documents.

"A-ha", he said as he held the papers above his head.

"What are they?", I asked.

"This, Tommy, is the key to your inheritance, young man.", he said, walking towards the table in the adjoining room before sitting down to put on his glasses.

"Come over here to I show you this.", he said, beckoning me towards him.

I took another swig of the brandy and went over to sit beside him.

"You see, Tommy, I don't know how much you know about this, but your fathers will was not so straight forward."

My mother had told me about this, but I wanted to hear the details from another party, so I shook my head; "I don't know much about it, no. Go ahead, tell me."

"Well, you see, your father and grandfather didn't exactly see eye to eye a lot of the time, so your grandfather put a clause in the will. He didn't quite trust your father, so he willed his land and property to your father's children. I think he wanted to keep it in the family or something, and he must have thought your father would sell it and piss it up against the wall."

He stopped and let out a howl of laughter.

"Fuck, he got your father completely wrong."

He took a swig of his brandy and continued; "Your great aunt Maggie was put in charge of the estate. It basically meant that if your father didn't have children, it was left to her, to will it to whoever she wanted."

He stopped, and removed his glasses and looked at me directly in the eye; "Now, here is the interesting part. Your father knew Maggie had a soft-spot for that cunt McNamee and dreaded the idea that everything would be left to *him*, if anything ever happened to him...or you. Now, here is where his smartness comes into play. To safeguard that from happening, your father pleaded with Maggie to will everything to another man she had a soft spot for...yours truly. This way, he knew the family property would be in good hands in case of any disasters. He knew I would do the right thing for his family."

His eyes began to well a little and his voice began to crack with emotion.

"Your father trusted me, and by God I am glad to repay that trust today." He lifted a few of the documents and placed them in front of me.

"These, Tommy, are yours. They are the deeds to your family's property. It's all yours and it makes me a happy man to give these to you today. Your father placed his trust in me and I would never have broken that trust, never in a million years."

He stood and drained the last of his drink. "We have a few forms and bits of pieces to get signed off first, then we can go and see the solicitor and you are good to go- all yours. But first, let's enjoy ourselves a little...another drink?"

I emptied my glass and replied enthusiastically; "Sure why not, Pete."

We both laughed and he disappeared into the kitchen to refill our glasses.

I had never really been a brandy drinker in the past and had to admit it was hitting me hard. Sure, I had promised my mother never to drink spirits again, but this merited a special occasion, and it was vintage stuff. It's not like I was going to drink the whole bottle. But, I was surprised at how strong it was.

Pete re-entered the room with two full glasses in hand and handed me one.

"To your mother and father."

I echoed the sentiments, and we both took a good swig. He sat across from me at the table, observing me, much like a doctor would look at his patient.

I laughed. "You look like you've seen a ghost."

He remained as he was, never taking his eyes off me. "I feel that way, Tommy. I just can't believe the resemblance between the two of ye. It's like someone rewound the clock thirty years, and I'm back sitting drinking with him again."

With that he suddenly became more animated, snapping out of his trance like state and waving his arms at me.

"Come on, Tommy, get that down ye. Your father would put ye to shame. If he were here now we'd have to go for another bottle."

I took another large swig. Wiping my mouth, I replied; "No, Pete, I don't want to drink all your good stuff on ye."

He laughed; "Nonsense, sure this is a special occasion. Get it down ye, for God's sake."

"Fair enough.", I replied and drained the rest of what was in the glass.

It was beginning to really hit me hard. I noticed, to my embarrassment, that I was beginning to slur my words a little. I knew I was beginning to get the taste for it, starting to get into my stride. Also, it was taking the edge off me from those horrible nightmares I had, from the night before.

He came back into the room with another two full glasses.

"Right, let's get this shit signed and finished before we get completely blocked.", he said, slurring a little too.

"Fair enough.", I said, "Just tell me what I need to sign and I'll get down to it then."

He put his glasses back on and rustled through a few papers.

"Right, these lands are in my name currently, as we all thought you were, well...gone. Now, this document here is basically a waiver. It means that I give up my right to the lands, and you, once you sign under where my name is, become the owner. As simple and straight forward as that."

I glanced at the document, a few pages long, legal jargon with the usual dotted line at the bottom for signatures and dates. I noticed Pete had already signed and dated his part.

"Feel free to read through it if you want, Tommy, but it's all the usual bullshit, legal mumbo-jumbo. The gist is, it goes straight from me, to you when it's signed."

"Fuck it, Pete. I'm not wasting valuable drinking time reading all that crap. Pass me that pen."

He laughed and handed me a silver plated, grand-looking pen.

"A man after my own heart.", he said, taking a large swig from his glass.

I clicked the nib of the pen into place and set about signing the document.

"I feel great about this, Tommy. If only your father could be here to see this. He would be proud of us both, boy. The land stays in the Dillon name, we are making sure of that."

I nodded in agreement.

Just as I was putting pen to paper, I asked him;

"Pete, you reckon all the land is in your name? Is that right?"

He looked a little confused at my question.

"Yes. It is. Why do you ask?"

I glanced at the document. God, the brandy was taking effect all right. I could barely read the words on the page, they all seemed to conglomerate into one indecipherable blur, no matter how hard I tried to focus on them.

"It's just, I don't understand how everything *is* in your name."

Again, he looked even more confused.

"Well, there's nothing *to* understand. It's there in black and white. *I* own it and now I'm signing it back to you. What part don't you understand?"

"Well.", I answered; "Sorry, by the way...do you mind if I smoke?", I asked.

"No.", he replied, "Only if you give me one too."

We both lit our cigarettes, and sat smoking for a moment or two.

"Sorry, the thing is, Pete...you said earlier that the land would have been willed to you, had any harm came to me or my father."

Pete drew hard on his cigarette, simultaneously letting a long, continuous stream of smoke jet out of his nose.

"Yes, that's right. But, do you not see, we thought you weren't coming back. You and your mother were never seen, nor heard of again. The powers that be simply wrote you both off."

He drew hard on his cigarette and took a sip of his drink. He pointed at my glass. "Another?"

I resisted the temptation. I would end up legless at this rate. I sat back in the chair, stretching out a little, putting my hands behind my head.

"Here's the part I don't understand.", I said.

He sat forward, putting his head between his hands, staring straight at me and smiling.

"Shoot. Tell me what you don't understand, Tommy."

I composed myself as best I could. I didn't want my words to be delivered in a slur. Failing miserably, slurring very heavily, I continued; "My mother sent various letters and photos of us when I was growing up, to Fintan and Maggie. Fintan passed these to our solicitor, proving we were still alive, negating any will Maggie put into place thereafter. So, you see, that's how I can't understand why the lands are in *your* name."

It was now my turn to smile.

To my surprise, *his* smile brightened and he laughed.

A full, hearty laugh.

It was the first time his façade of sanity began to slip.

"You're not as dumb as you look then...Seamie?"

He laughed again and stood up, beginning to pace the room. I fixed my eyes upon his every move.

"You killed my father...you cunt.", I said, although the line hadn't been delivered as forcibly as I intended. The brandy was getting the better of me. I had to snap out of the drunken haze, and quickly!

He stood by the window and smiled at me. But, for the first time I noticed the true malice hidden in his eyes, the anger and insanity that lurked behind the cold, dead stare.

"I suppose you're not goin' to sign these papers then?", he asked.

I looked at them, my eyes trying to focus on what was written, but I got the gist of what it said from the wording at the bottom of the page. My signature would have been enough to sign everything over to *him*...the sneaky bastard.

"Do you think I'm fuckin' stupid?", I shouted, my voice sounding pathetic, my words heavily slurred.

"Just a bit, yeah. I've been waiting for you coming to get me, you know. Fuckin' took you long enough, thirty odd years, eh?"

I thought to myself then that he must have had a death wish, he must have wanted some punishment for what he did all those years ago, until he continued; "What, are you the big tough guy now? Gonna come over from England to seek revenge on me for what happened to your parents, eh, Seamie?"

He let out a mocking laugh.

"Well, what the fuck are you gonna do about it?", he roared.

I knew exactly what I was going to do with the devious, murdering bastard.

I was going to beat him halfway to death, and then haul his pathetic ass down to the cop shop, telling them what he did. Then the scumbag would spend the rest of his miserable life behind bars. Then, hopefully he would get buttfucked out of his mind every night, until death finally caught up with him...then he would burn in hell for eternity.

Very simple plan.

I began to tell him exactly what I was going to do, before noticing my words were being delivered like those in a dream. They weren't words, more slow, incoherent noises that came from my mouth.

He laughed at my sorry state.

That fucking brandy.

"Slurring your words a little, Seamie? What's wrong? Can't handle that good brandy you've been drinking, or maybe it's all those sleeping pills I've been slipping into it?"

He reached into his pocket, and produced an empty packet of sleeping pills.

"Usually two to three of these puts that fat pig of a wife of mine down, but it's taken a bit more for you. You must have had, oh, maybe ten or even twenty. But sure, who's counting? You're my guest and I'm a very hospitable man."

He laughed again. It was a laugh that to the naked ear appeared very amiable and good natured, but sounded every bit as twisted and insane when one learned of the vileness of the man. I panicked at seeing the empty packet of sleeping pills. Deep down I knew the brandy hadn't caused my grogginess. I now feared for my life, but mostly feared I was about to let down my father and mother. I felt sick to the stomach, not knowing if it were through fear, or a by-product of the sleeping pills. I rammed my fingers deep down my throat and immediately threw up on his floor, producing only a small volume of brandy flavoured vomit.

I needed to get those sleeping pills up and out of my system.

"Nice try, Seamie. But, I've been dosing you since you came in. Let's face it...you're fucked."

A surge of anger erupted inside of me.

I had to act, fast.

I charged at him, attempting to take him down so I could call someone quickly before falling unconscious. I summoned up all my power to charge him, but as I did, I had that dream-like sensation once more of running through quick-sand. Seeing me coming, he moved out of the way, just as I was about to make contact, putting his foot out to trip me.

I tripped and fell to the ground.

No matter how I tried, I couldn't get to my feet. I watched him from where I lay, walk slowly to the fireplace, where he picked up the heavy-looking poker.

Then he walked back towards me, paused for a moment and grinned, before he swung the poker forcefully down towards my head.

I felt no pain.

Then, just as the night before, the world turned to darkness.

CHAPTER 41

I dreamt of my mother. I dreamt of the harrowing story she told in her last days, when she recalled what happened the night my father died. Her stories were so horrendous they embedded themselves into my mind, making my dreams as vivid, and as real as a moving picture, like a film.

I dreamt I had been there that night, like a helpless spectator. I followed my father and Pete to the pub, after Pete had come to our family home, telling tales of what McNamee had been up to in the pub.

All lies.

McNamee had been minding his own business, never even mentioning my father's name. Pete knew if he spun my father a tale that McNamee was making threats in the pub, my father's hot-headedness and pride would overtake any semblance of reasoning he had in him. He knew that my father would be straight over to sort McNamee out.

I stood there in the bar, alone, as my father and Pete walked in, my father eyeing up McNamee before confronting him about making threats to his life. There was an exchange of words, then Pete stepped in, shouting at McNamee, calling him a coward about making threats to my father behind his back. McNamee looks enraged and a little baffled, but surprisingly lets it pass. Then my father and Pete drink at the bar before they go their separate ways.

Pete goes home, drinks further, then jumps into his car and drives to our home. He parks the car at the bottom of a lane, a few fields away from our house, carrying two five-gallon drums of petrol with him.

I watch from the front door as he staggers down the lane. He heads for the out-house, adjoining the dwelling house, packed full of hay-bales. He opens the door, walks in, and douses the place with petrol. He uses up one five-gallon drum in the hayshed and intends to use the other in the dwelling house. He lights a match and flicks it high into the air, the match extinguishes halfway down towards the ground. He repeats the process, this time with success, and the trail of petrol alights from the middle of the floor, all the way up to the bales packed high in the shed. The place immediately bursts into flames. He then heads towards the front door of the house. Just as he is about to pour petrol through the letter box, he suddenly hears my father running down the stairs. He panics, momentarily frozen by fear, knowing that if my father sees what is happening, there will be only one winner if it comes to blows...and it's not going to be him. At the last second, just as my father opens the door, bolting straight for the hayshed, Pete quickly side steps his way to the other side of the house, knowing my father is only headed in one direction. He waits for a moment then follows my father into the hayshed. As he enters, he notices an old rusty horse shoe hanging by a nail on the door. He lifts it, tip-toes up behind my father and smashes it into the back of his head. My father collapses and Pete runs out of the smoke-filled hayshed, the flames beginning to grow more intense. He closes the door on the way out, fully intending the fire to burn my father to death.

He quickly moves on to the second part of his plan, to burn down the house, killing my mother and I in the process. Just as he is about to douse petrol all over the interior of the house, he hears men's voices coming down the lane. He realises then, that the flames coming from the hayshed and the smell of smoke, must have alerted someone as to what was happening. Anger rises in him as he finds himself frozen in shock once more. Suddenly he realises who the voices belong to, seeing Dessie McNamee and Paddy Gray running towards the shed. He smiles to himself. His original plan of putting both men in the frame for the murder seemed a solid one, although he knew solid alibis could possibly free them of suspicion. But, here they were, at the exact scene of the crime...perfect.

He laughed a nervous, almost hysterical laugh, before quickly pouring petrol all over the kitchen floor. Running out of the house he strikes a match and throws it towards the petrol trail, watching the flames arise from the darkness like a beautiful demon, its fury soon to decimate everything lying before it. Remembering to discard of any evidence, he lifts the two five-gallon drums and hurls them towards the flames, the small volume of petrol left in each, further fuelling the great growing flame.

He sprints from the scene, a few fields south and he'd be on the lane where he had parked his car, knowing the car would not have been spotted in that quiet little area.

I dreamt that I could feel the heat from the flames. I saw my mother rushing into my room, her features awash with panic and fear. I saw her bundling me up, carrying me down the landing, only to be met by a wall of flames at the bottom of the stairs. I could feel the choking fumes at the back of my throat, my mother's body shaking manically in fear and pure desperation. I could hear her crying for help, the futility of what she was doing, heart-breaking and petrifying in equal measure.

Then I heard the man's voice.

My mother began screaming louder, calling my father's name, "Neil, Neil, help us, *help us*."

I knew though, that the voice did not belong to my father. I could hear him trying to reassure us, telling us to stay calm as he was going to go get some water to try and extinguish the fire, although his voice was far from reassuring, riddled with panic. I watched as my mother ran back up the stairs, I could feel the tremors of fear running through her body. Then, I heard the man downstairs throwing buckets of water upon the blazing inferno, his yells of frustration telling us all we needed to know about his progress.

My mother suddenly had an idea, and shouted down the stairs, "Fuck it, I'm going to jump."

"No, Máire, no. You'll break your neck, hold on, hold on, I'll get this fire out.", he shouted back, his voice conveying no confidence at all.

She put me down on the floor, ran into her room and lifted the little wooden chair she sat at each night, at her dressing table, then ran into my room, the room with the biggest window, and threw the chair through it, the glass shattering into a million little pieces. She went back into her room, hauling the mattress from her bed, and squeezed it through my window. Then, she took my duvet and placed it onto the window frame. She looked down to see Paddy Gray standing beneath her.

"No, Máire, no.", he shouted in desperation.

Ignoring him, she took me into her arms once more. In one movement, she sat upon the window ledge and fell out through the window. Her body completely cushioned mine as we hit the ground.

I heard the sickening crack of her leg bone. She roared in agony, but the adrenalin kicked in and she quickly got up and hobbled towards the shed, pulling me with her, where Paddy Gray was now standing at the door, trying in vain to enter, the roaring flames barring him from doing so. He was crying, actually crying, the sobs of a small child coming from a grown man. My mother, wincing in utter agony, but trying to compose herself, shouted; "Paddy. What's wrong?"

He looked into her eyes, the look of a man completely lost, not knowing what to do, utterly helpless.

"Máire, they're in there."

My mother looked lost.

"Who? Who's in there?"

I knew from her reaction she hadn't even let herself fathom that my father might be.

"Dessie. He's trapped. I can't get him out."

"And who? Who else?", my mother snapped at him.

Paddy Gray looked at her, confusion writ large across his face. It was as if he didn't need to respond, the answer so obvious.

"Dessie...and Neil, of course. Máire, what are we goin' to do?"

At that moment, he fell to his knees and continued to sob uncontrollably.

It took my mother a moment or so to digest what he told her, then she began screaming; "Neil, Neil, get out...come out...Neil"

She tried to enter the hayshed, realising only then, the intensity and heat coming from the fire. She stood back for a moment, trying to work out how to get in. When it dawned on her what Paddy Gray had realised moments before, there being only one entry and it was completely blocked, she too lost all fight and crumpled to her knees, her wails, and sobs of anguish enough to melt even the hardest of hearts.

I could see what had happened inside the hayshed. Dessie McNamee, upon running to the scene of the fire had seen my father lying unconscious in the middle of the floor. The fire was gaining in size when McNamee entered the building, stooping over my father trying to wake him up. He tried dragging him out, but my father's bulk was too much for him, so he straddled him, trying desperately to waken him. When my father eventually came to, the shock of seeing McNamee at the scene panicked him. He tried to fight frantically against him, McNamee trying in vain to tell him what was happening. Then, the fumes eventually got to the two of them, both falling unconscious simultaneously.

My mother and Paddy Gray remained as they were for a few minutes after, until the heat of the fire became too much and they had to retreat. My mother hopped on one leg towards me and bundled me into her arms. Paddy Gray took off his coat and placed it around both of us. He asked us to come with him in his car, so he could go call the fire brigade. He carried me in his arms, and my mother held onto him for support on the long walk to the car. Not a word was spoken. When we got to the car we drove to the local telephone box and he called the emergency services. He came back and sat in the car with us for a few moments.

"I made an anonymous phone call. I didn't give my name.", he said.

My mother turned to look at him, anger brimming under the surface. He immediately reacted, seeing what was coming next.

"Máire, we had nothing to do with this. *Nothing*. I promise you. You know we didn't see eye to eye with Neil, but we would never have taken things this far."

My mother's eyes bored into his.

"Well, answer me this, Paddy Gray. What the fuck were you and Dessie McNamee doing on our property at that fucking time of the night, eh? And if *you* didn't do this, who the fuck did?"

Her voice remained flat and very calm, the proverbial calm before the storm. Paddy Gray composed himself as best he could, knowing if she didn't believe one little part of his story, she would literally scratch his eyes out. He took a deep breath, then spoke; "Máire, you need to believe this, this is the truth. This is what happened."

He took another deep breath, once more trying to compose himself, my mother's glare intensifying upon him.

"Speak", she hissed.

"Dessie and I left the pub shortly after our argument with Neil. We headed into town and ended up at a dance. We drank too much, me more than him, so we left and went to the chip shop to get a feed into us. Dessie then drove us home. I began to feel sick, the bumpy roads and the drink a bad combination. We were driving past the top of your lane on our way home when I shouted for Dessie to stop. I couldn't hold it in any longer, I had to throw up. I fell out of the car and vomited at the side of the road, all I could hear in my ear was Dessie laughing..."

He smiled a sad little smile at that, and continued; "The fucker. Anyway, after I threw everything up I thought I could smell smoke. I shouted in through the window to see if Dessie could smell it too. Once he stopped laughing, he said he could and we quickly realised the smell was coming from your house. Dessie jumped out of the car and I slowly followed him down the lane, my stomach doing summersaults. Halfway down the lane, we saw a man moving around. I thought it was Neil, but my vision was still a little blurry. Then Dessie slowed down, eventually stopping completely. When I got level with him, he was staring in disbelief at the scene unfolding in front of us. He looked like he had seen a ghost. I asked him what was wrong and he pointed towards your house.

"Look, Paddy", he said, "It's Pete Kelly. Holy mother of God, he's tryin' to burn Dillon's house down."

I stared, dumbfounded, by what he had just told me. I mean, Máire, Neil's best fuckin' friend...doin' something like *that?"*

My mother's face drained of any colour that was left in it. She began to shiver, uncontrollably, her teeth actually chattering. She began to rub her torso, embracing herself, trying to warm her body and stop the shivering.

"Máire, at that moment, just as Dessie said it, I seen Pete Kelly throw two drums into the house...then he ran off down the field. We stood for a few moments, completely shocked, before Dessie began to run once more towards your house. "We have to stop this.", he kept shouting. When we got to your house, we split up. He went to the hayshed and I went to the house. That's when I saw you and spoke to you. I tried my best to get a few buckets of water to stop the fire, but it was like pissing into the wind. I didn't realise what Dessie was up to until after you jumped out of the window. When I knew you were out of danger, I bolted quickly towards the hayshed, only to realise what had happened."

He stopped and searched my mother's eyes. "Oh, Máire, what the fuck? Why would he *do* such a thing. Dessie and Neil, God love them, they're gone. What a thing to happen..."

At that, he broke down, sobbing like a small child, his body shaking with shock and heart-breaking sadness.

My mother turned to me in the back seat and said; "Son, we are leaving here tonight. We can't live here anymore, no way, never again."

Her inner steel began to shine through, even after such devastation.

Paddy Gray wiped his face clean, trying to compose himself a little.

"But Máire… where are you goin' to go? *You* haven't done anything wrong. You don't need to go anywhere. We'll help you get through this, your family and the community."

My mother solemnly smiled at him and replied; "Paddy, I can't live in a country that breeds people like that. He was Neil's best friend. Neil thought the world of him…and he went and done *this*? What in God's name?"

"But…but, Máire, we'll go to the police and get him locked up. We'll tell them what happened. He'll not get away with this."

My mother smiled once more, this time the smile of the utterly defeated.

"Don't you see, Paddy? He has everything wrapped up. You're going to get the blame for what happened…you and Dessie. You understand that?"

Paddy Gray broke down once more, large sobs overwhelming his exhausted body.

"But, Máire, I didn't do anything. *We*, didn't do anything. You believe me, Máire, don't you?"

My mother put a reassuring hand on his shoulder.

"Of course, Paddy. *I* believe you…but the court wont. You, Neil, and Dessie had a blazing row in front of everyone in the pub tonight. Dessie threatens his life, then his house gets burned down with you and Dessie at the scene of the crime. Dessie accidently gets killed in the act, then you blame Neil's best friend for doing it- a man who will make sure he has a cast iron alibi. Come on now, Paddy, what do you think is going to happen?"

Paddy entered another fit of sobbing.

"Oh Jesus, Máire. But…you still have no reason to leave. You're an innocent victim in all of this."

My mother paused for a moment, obviously thinking hard about whether she was doing the right thing or not.

"I have young Seamie to think about. How can I bring him up safely, knowing a psychopath lives down the road, fearing he will come again some night, any night, to finish what he started? How can I, Paddy? How can I live in a house, a home…a home I loved, a family I loved…adored, only to view it as a haunted, horrible thing? I can't Paddy, I won't. This place will never be the same again, my life here is over. I can't live here without Neil. That man was my life, my one true love. A part of me has died tonight, Paddy. If it wasn't for wee Seamie here, I'd throw myself into the fire with him. I would. To be with him, to hold his hand on the other side. But…I can't. Seamie needs me. I'm his mother. He's young enough not to remember this horrible night. If he grows up around here he will be reminded of it for the rest of his life. He will grow up bitter and twisted by it, just like I will. I don't want that, Neil wouldn't want that. I'll do what I can to protect that boy…anything."

Paddy sat at the wheel of the car, and nodded his head in understanding.

"Fair enough Máire, I see your point. But where are you going to go?"

My mother sat and thought for a moment before replying; "I will leave shortly after the funeral. I am going to go to England, London perhaps. I want us to slip into anonymity, go to a place where no one knows about this. Hopefully I can rear Seamie on my own, hopefully to God I can rear him well and give him a life worth living. Now, Paddy, please drop me over to Fintan's house."

Her eyes darted over to Paddy's anxiety ridden face, before she added; "I will leave this part of the story out. I won't mention you, don't worry. You must find yourself a solid alibi, just like that bastard Kelly is doing as we speak. It doesn't take a genius to work out Dessie is going to get the blame for this, but so what, he is dead, they can't lock him up now. Do as I say, go home and live the rest of your life, keep your mouth shut and nothing will come of this."

Paddy Gray's lower lip started to quiver, and again he broke into a fit of sobbing that rocked his body violently. My mother reached her arm over and rubbed his back gently; "Come on now Paddy, just do as I say and let's get this over with."

He complied with her request, straightening himself up to drive us to Fintan's house. When we got close to his house, my mother instructed Paddy to drop us off about a quarter of a mile from it, so the car wouldn't be seen by anyone. Without saying a word, my mother opened the car door, reached into the back seat, and carried me in her arms.

"All the best, Máire", Paddy said, through a river of tears.

My mother gave him a sad smile and walked away.

I dreamt further. I dreamt about the next morning. Dawn had just broken, the air was damp and heavy, the sickening smell of smoke hung upon it. I stood outside our home and watched, a hive of activity around me-police, ambulance, local press, and nosy neighbours. The mood was sombre, as one would expect under such circumstances. Then...a deathly hush as the men carried the bodies out, covered in white sheets.

The bodies. One large, one small.

The two dead men. Dessie McNamee and my father, Neil Dillon. The people all hung their heads. Even in my dreams, I shook uncontrollably, sobbing like a child. I was the only one shedding any tears.

The bodies were put in the back of a private ambulance and driven away. The crowd dispersed and the house grew quiet once more. Not a sound could be heard, but anyone with an inkling of a sixth sense could feel the spirit of the man inside. The man who wouldn't get to rest in peace.

Well, I hoped he soon would.

I dreamt of the funeral. I saw my mother walking behind the hearse, holding my little hand in hers. Although her face was etched in complete torment, she wouldn't let a tear drop. She knew if one fell, they would all follow, and she wouldn't be able to continue. She remained strong, but the tears caught up with her afterwards, staying with her constantly for another thirty years.

Pete Kelly didn't show up for the funeral. The story went that he couldn't bear to see his best friend's young body put into the ground. He maintained that if he didn't see the body, didn't see the coffin then he could convince himself nothing had happened.

All the signs of a guilty conscience? The people of the country never once thought of such a thing. Poor Pete, they thought. God love him.

I watched on at Dessie McNamee's funeral. His sister opted to have his already badly charred body cremated, and a tiny funeral ensued. No-one wanted to attend the funeral of a murderer. His soul would be burning in hell before too long, and people just didn't like the thought of any of it.

A day after the funeral, my mother was driven to the docks by Fintan. Against much pleading, my mother had made up her mind. She couldn't bear to live in the country any longer, deciding to make a new life for both of us in England.

With that we both boarded the ferry.

For her, that was the last she would ever see of her homeland.

CHAPTER 42

It took a while to realise I was conscious once again. The sickening bolts of searing pain in my head confirming I was. The first thought that came to me was; "Thank fuck I'm not dead."

On many occasions, I had woken up feeling the opposite, but not this time. I was alive, there was still a chance of redemption, of revenge. Then, when I realised I was bleeding heavily from my head, with both my feet and hands tied up, I realised I had been a little optimistic about my chances.

I appeared to be lying in the back of a moving vehicle, a transit van I guessed. The vehicle was moving very quickly, objects dangerously flying all over the place. There was a pick, a shovel, and a spade in the back where I lay. It didn't take a genius to work out what he was planning for me. I tried not to panic too much and keep a clear head, the pounding pain making it nigh impossible not to. I knew he planned to kill me and bury me somewhere. Again, the thought of imminent death had never been that daunting in the past, but the idea that I was going to die at the hands of this monster who killed my father, and ruined my mother was unbearable.

What could I do, though? How long did I have? If we were only minutes away from where he was taking me, I was fucked, I didn't have time. An avalanche of panic suddenly fell upon me at that moment, debilitating me completely.

"Come on, Seamie!", I said, under my breath. It was now or never, I couldn't let panic take over and fuck everything up. I snapped out of it. Mind over matter, I pledged. I was bleeding profusely from my head, but I tried not to worry too much about it. To die after I thwarted him didn't bother me, to die before I got at least one crack at him would be unthinkable.

A sudden moment of clarity dawned on me. Panic was momentarily kept at bay and time seemed to slow down, letting me think logically and clearly. I knew my mother was around me, pouring strength into me at that moment as I focused entirely on the spade.

Like everything else, it bounced around the back of the vehicle every time we went over a bump. The first few bumps made it bounce further away from me. I almost roared out in frustration. Then, after a minute or so, the vehicle went over several bumps, more-so pot holes. Again, panic almost got the better of me. This was no road we travelled on anymore, this was an off-road lane...we had to be close to where he was taking me. I swallowed hard, trying to physically swallow the panic that was beginning to rise from my stomach. I had to concentrate, I had to find that inner strength, that inner faith that my mother was with me, that she wouldn't forsake me at this desperate time.

Just then, we hit a huge pot-hole. The contents of the van all flew high in the air, I knew this was my chance. The spade bounced against the roof of the vehicle and landed upright between my knees. I clenched my knees hard on the shaft and very carefully aimed the head towards me. I had never concentrated as hard on anything before in my life. Luckily, the spade appeared almost new- nice and sharp, the way I needed it to be. Blood still pouring from my head and feeling increasingly faint, I furiously began rubbing the rope around my wrists on the spade head. A few times, whenever we went over a large bump, I missed the rope and grazed myself badly, my flesh breaking, blood oozing from the wound. The blood began to soak onto the rope, making everything slippery. The pain in my wrists was sickening and I prayed to God I wouldn't pass out again. I finally began to make progress, the ropes beginning to feel a little loose, the blood that didn't ooze from my wrists beginning to filter back into my hands once more. But, still I was nowhere near being able to wriggle my hands free. I had to continue rubbing the rope against the spade. Between blood pouring from my wrists and the effort spent rubbing the rope against the spade, I began to experience extreme fatigue. I sat back against the side of the van to take a breather. Only then did I notice the bumps becoming less frequent and the speed dropping. Shit, I thought, we must be near the destination, the vehicle now travelling at around running pace. I immediately went back to work, rubbing the rope as hard as I possibly could until I became breathless and exhausted. The van finally came to a stop. I made one last attempt, and to my huge relief the ropes were beginning to come apart, not enough to free my hands, but weakened enough, so that if I continued to apply pressure it would soon break.

The engine was switched off and I heard the front door of the vehicle open. Then the sound of squelching footsteps. He opened the back door, and as if anticipating that I may have broken free, quickly sidestepped to his left in case I rushed him. Visibly relieved his bondage had worked on me, he laughed, one of relief.

He grabbed the rope that had been tied around my feet and jerked me out of the van, in one quick movement. I fell to the ground, the wet and cold grass jolting my system into life. To my great discouragement, he grabbed the spade from the back of the van, any hopes I had of utilising it to further free myself, slowly dissipating.

He lit a cigarette and took a deep pull. As he exhaled, he turned to me and asked; "Do you know where you are?"

On my knees and still applying pressure to the rope around my wrists, trying to buy myself some time, I answered; "No, where are we?"

He laughed, shaking his head.

"Well, big time land owner, you are sitting on your own land. This is your field, well...was supposed to be your field."

He took another pull on his cigarette before pointing to a small looking bush standing directly in front of us.

"Know what that is?"

I shook my head.

I tried to readjust my eyes to the outside darkness. Dusk had fallen and a murky light that masked almost all visibility, fell over the landscape. Before my eyes adjusted to the limited light available, I could see he was quickly getting to work, digging up the sod around the little bush.

Suddenly, to my horror, I realised just what the bush was. It was the same one I had seen in my nightmares the night before, the same plantation that dominated my subconscious from the moment I laid hands on my father.

Forgetting the predicament I was in, I blurted out; "What is this? What is it about this bush?"

He paused for a moment resting his arms on the spade, smiling once more.

"This, sonny, is what is known as a Gentle bush. Your father was very fond of it. Bit of a superstitious man, your father."

He laughed and got back to digging once again.

A cold shiver ran down my spine. Those dreams, nightmares I had, were the most horrific, yet realistic I had ever encountered. Now here I was, right back in the nightmare, gazing straight at the wretched thing, its roots now exposed and ready to perform their terrible work.

I continued to apply pressure to the rope and to my sheer relief it had loosened enough so that I could almost free my hands. I knew I had to be careful. Blood still seeped from my head and wrists, and I felt beyond weak. If he got wind of what I was up to, I knew he wouldn't hesitate for a moment in whacking me over the head with the spade.

He continued to dig. For a man of his years he was making incredible progress. I was perhaps half his age and I couldn't have dug it as quickly. His power was evident, so I had to be clever. I worked away, quietly trying to free my hands. He dug further until he had dug about two feet below the ground. I knew he was almost done, the psychopath wouldn't be too concerned about a shallow grave. If my feet hadn't been tied up I could have charged at him.

I had to bide my time and wait for my moment.

Still relentlessly digging, he continued speaking; "You see, your fate as you may have guessed, is being buried below this bush. Why, you may ask? Because I fuckin' hate you, and because no-one will ever dig up this precious Gentle bush...fuckin' stupid superstitious pricks that they are."

He began laughing again, then broke into a little song. To the casual observer, a man content at his work.

Finally, my hands became free. Relief rushed through my system, but I had to wait a few seconds, the blood rushing back into them leading to a moment of debilitating pins and needles. I slowly reached my left hand into my jacket pocket and expertly found, first time, the little plastic device I was looking for. I coughed so he wouldn't hear the click on the little Dictaphone. I knew if I died and was buried with it, it may be found one day, many years in the future and the truth would eventually out. So, I knew the exercise was not completely futile.

"So, why did you do it?", I asked.

"Do what?", he answered, still not stopping from his work.

"You know, why did you kill my father?"

He stopped digging and looked deep into my eyes.

Had he worked out what I was up to?

Then he began, much to my relief to answer the question.

"As a child, I wasn't well- a weakling I was known as. The boys in the area used to bully me, your father was one of them. The names they used to call me, the fuckin' names. They never laid a finger on me, probably for fear they would kill me if they did, but by fuck they tormented me. To be fair, your father wasn't the worst out of them, but let's just say he never stood up for me, happy to stick the boot in instead. Anyway, I got better, grew stronger, grew up and fucked off to England. I went to escape those bastards, I couldn't live side by side with people who treated me like they did, I would have ended up killing the lot of them. So, I lived over in Bristol for a good few years. The women seemed to like me and I certainly liked them. I was ridin' every night of the week, fuckin' life of Riley it was. I trained as a butcher and worked in a shop for a few years, but I wanted to have my *own* business. I contacted my father and asked if he could help, and he said he would. He asked me how much I needed. I told him what the figure was and two weeks later the cheque arrived. I bought myself a butcher's shop, and was up and running in no time. I was flying, money was pouring in and the going was good. It didn't occur to me at the time where my father got the money from, until I rang him one day. I told him how well I was doing, how I would soon have enough money to return home and finally do what I always dreamt of doing."

He stopped and almost forgetting what he was doing sprang into action once more, digging the hole.

"What did you always want to do?", I asked.

He stopped digging once more and answered; "We owned a few acres of land up beside our home place. My father always said there was great rock in it, and if it could be mined, a great quarry could be made of it. From a young age, I had been fascinated by machinery...diggers, lorries, dump trucks and the likes. My father one day, when I was a child, brought me to visit an old friend of his who owned a quarry in County Monaghan. I fell in love with it, became fuckin' fascinated by it. It became my life goal. I wanted to return home, having made my fortune in England and run my own quarry. To my horror, my father told me he had sold that little piece of land to fund my butcher shop business. To add insult to injury, he told me who he sold it to. None other than little bully boy, mill owner son, privileged prick, Neil Dillon. I couldn't bear it. What the fuck did he want with our land? Did the greedy cunt not have enough of his own?"

He spat viciously into the hole in the ground.

"So, what did you do then?", I asked.

"Well, I came home. My father told me to forget about the quarry, pursue the butchery trade instead. He told me the long-standing butcher in Dunbay was selling up, and he had a readymade customer base who would keep me in business for years to come. I done as he asked, as I could see his pride was hurt because of selling the land I had wanted to keep. I wanted to make amends and show him he made a good decision in buying me the business."

He stopped talking and began digging once more like a man possessed, seemingly forgetting about the telling of his story.

"What happened after that?", I asked, trying to conceal my impatience and frustration with him.

"Your father came into the shop one day. We got talking- I liked him, genuinely liked him. He was a likeable fella, I have to say, to be fair to him."

He stopped, looked scornfully upon me and added; "Unlike you, ye hateful lookin' Brit cunt."

He laughed manically once more and my blood boiled, although I kept my cool...on the surface.

"We went out and had a few drinks and you know what...he actually apologised for what he had done to me when I was a child. He fuckin' meant it, too. I forgave him and from then on, we became best friends. We did, that's the truth. There was no malice, no bad blood. Over time, however, I did become...resentful, jealous maybe. I had half expected him to sell my father's land back to me, but he never did, never even mentioned it. He must have known my pride was hurt, him more than anyone. Everything he touched seemed to turn to gold. He met your mother, married, and continued to thrive in his business. He bought land like it was goin' out of fashion, but never did he mention selling me back my little family inheritance."

He gazed off into the distance, then set his sights on the bush and continued to laugh.

"You see this fuckin' bush here?", he asked, "The Gentle Bush.", he mockingly gesticulated towards it; "Load of aul shite, but people believe in it. People actually believe fairies live around it. I mean, for fuck sake, no wonder the English call us dumb Paddies. Your father believed in it, and I knew he did. So, one night when we were working in this exact field, I took the fuckin' saw to it, tried to cut it down as I knew it would piss him off. I did it out of pure badness."

He laughed loudly once more; "You should have seen the reaction I got from him. Fuck, I knew I'd get one, but I didn't think he would get on like he did. Jumpin' up and down like a spoilt child, crying and whingeing...I never seen the like of it. Inside I was laughing my balls off, but played dumb and pretended I knew nothing about it. He believed me, but I knew the superstitious prick would think bad things would happen to him and his mindset would gradually become more negative. Someone had to bring him down a peg or two, and I fuckin' did it."

He turned to resume digging again and I got to work once more on trying to free my feet.

"So, when did you decide you were going to burn our house down?", I probed further, controlling the fear and anger in my voice surprisingly well. He glanced back at me, this time he didn't smile or laugh. He looked angry and I hoped I hadn't hit a raw nerve. I had to keep him talking, to metaphorically let him dig his own grave.

"The thing about your father was, he had a big mouth sometimes, especially when he had a few drinks. He told me all about his upbringing and let it slip about the way his fathers will had been left. That really bugged him, that complete lack of trust his father had in him. It seemed to drive him, though. He wasn't content to sit on his father's property and make a living out of it, he was hell bent on proving him wrong. To be fair to him, he did. It didn't impress me, as the saying goes, money goes to money. It wasn't hard to make a lot of money and buy property when it was already there to begin with. So, he told me about the way he was treated and how much it annoyed him."

Anger rising in me, in response to his calm and reasoned approach, I asked; "So, you burned our house down so you would get in on the will?"

His face changed once again to one of sheer menace. He walked slowly towards me, and hit me hard on the side of the head, with the butt of the spade. A wave of nausea hit me, flashing lights appearing in front of my eyes. I feared I was going to fall unconscious at that moment, but thankfully I didn't. My head, that had only stopped bleeding moments before, began to gush blood once more. I began to feel weaker by the second.

He looked down at me and sneered.

"Shut the fuck up. Don't go thinkin' you know everything that happened...Brit"

He glared at me for a few moments before walking back to the hole, to continue his work.

"Now, I knew about the will thing for a long time. Never once did it occur to me to sweeten Maggie up, so she would add me as an executor. I looked after her out of genuine friendship-nothing else. Now, the turning point of my friendship with your father came after he sold my field to McNamee...*fuckin'* McNamee."

I had guessed as much. My mother had told me the whole story so it was no surprise, but I played along to keep him talking.

"He sold a field to *McNamee*? But...he hated him?"

He stopped digging once again and looked at me in a different way, as if I had suddenly become an ally, like I understood him.

"Yes. Did you not know that?"

"No.", I lied.

"Yes. McNamee comes home from England, all suited and booted, throwing his weight around like he's Billy fuckin' Big Bollocks. He asks your father if he can buy my father's field from him and your father fuckin' agrees to it. He thinks he's being the smart fella by sellin' it for four times the price he paid my father for it..."

He stopped talking, looking at me knowingly, before continuing; "Oh, he did give me a few bob from the sale, but it was guilt money. He knew deep down he was in the wrong."

I knew he was lying. My mother told me my father gave him half the money from the sale, not a "few bob". He gave Pete double what he had paid his father for the land. I still played along though. Looking shocked, I continued; "I can't believe that. That's not on. I didn't think he would do something like that."

Encouraged by my apparent disapproval of my father's action's he continued; "Oh, he did it all right. Now, I had told him it was my ambition to quarry that land, but he laughed. He also laughed when McNamee told him the same thing, then McNamee went and proved him wrong by getting it up and running. He thought he knew everything...he knew fuck all."

He went back to his digging.

I struggled with the rope once more. My head pounded and I tried not to panic too much. Too much nervous energy would zap me completely, I could end up falling unconscious once more, waking up in a fucking shallow grave. I had to probe further to buy myself more time.

"So...what about the fire? Why did you do it?"

Again, he stopped, lit up another cigarette, sat down and smiled a satisfied smile. It was clear from his body language that he had taken pride in the murder, there was absolutely no remorse in him at all.

"Refusing to sell back my father's field to me, selling it instead to his sworn enemy, was the ultimate act of betrayal."

He puffed on his cigarette, looked straight into my eyes, and for once looking solemn, continued; "I make a great friend, but an even greater enemy if I'm crossed. Your father, he crossed me, and you...you will see how much of a horrible enemy I make, just like your father did."

I simply nodded in submission, as he continued; "He had told me about the situation with the will. I had never even thought about it. You see, it was never in my nature to be a treacherous bastard."

Then, stopping to look at me again, he shouted; "Unless I'm fuckin' crossed."

He took a pull on his cigarette, obviously attempting to calm himself down. A snake like him operated best in cold blood.

"Well, after your father refused to sell me back my father's land, I put a plan in place. Firstly, I planted a few seeds in his head, reminding him that if anything happened to him, or you, then Maggie would most likely sign everything to McNamee.", he stopped to laugh loudly; "Fuck, did that not put the shit up him. The next evening, he took me aside and told me with that big sombre head of his that he had spoken to Maggie. He told me that he begged her to make me the executor of the will. He knew she liked me so he thought it was a certainty she would agree. He was right. A few days before I burnt the bastard out, Maggie came into my shop and asked me to go with her to see Mr. Blayney, the solicitor. I agreed and that day she put the clause in the will that if anything happened to you or your father, then I would take control. I could keep it for myself or give it to another living family member…so easy. So, when that was signed and done, I put the next part of my plan into place…to do away with you fuckers entirely."

He finished his cigarette and threw the butt in my direction; "Little did I know it would take thirty odd years to finally finish the job off."

He got up and began digging once more. From the looks of it, the hole was now long enough to put a body into. About two and a half feet deep, arguably deep enough to bury a body in too. I had to keep him talking, I needed desperately to buy more time. I reached down once more and struggled in vain with the rope at my feet.

"Tell me what happened the day of the fire."

He swung around quickly, almost quick enough to see me fondling with the rope.

"Oh, you really are a glutton for punishment.", he replied, his words drenched in sarcasm; "Well, on that day we had dinner in your home. Maggie was there and I drove her home afterwards. On the way, I noticed McNamee's car outside the pub, I knew he had probably been there since mass that morning and would be there until closing time that night. I had a delicious plan. After I left Maggie home, I went to bed for a few hours and drove back to your father's house. I told him McNamee was shouting his mouth off in the pub, saying he was goin' to do this and that the next time he saw him. Knowin' how much of a hot-head he was, and his hatred for McNamee, I knew it'd be enough to lure him to the pub with me."

He began to laugh again, continuing; "Well, the mad big bastard busted into that pub and started on McNamee right away. McNamee didn't know what the fuck was goin' on. Angry words and threats were exchanged. Fuck, they couldn't have played into my hands any better if they'd been attached by strings to my fingers.", he laughed, before continuing; "The whole thing settled down and we parted ways. I stalled about for a few hours, then I loaded the boot of the car with a few five-gallon drums and headed for your house. When I got there, all the lights were out, so I got to my work. I had the shed outside nicely burning when the big bastard came bolting out, the fucker had obviously smelt the smoke. He met me at the door of the shed, realised what I was doin' and went for me. I sidestepped him, big clumsy prick that he was, and socked him one in the belly. He bent over and I uppercut him right under the jaw, knocking him spark out."

My blood boiled. To have done what he had done, but to lie and say he beat my father in a one-on-one situation was too much for me.

Against my better judgement, I stupidly reacted; "Bullshit. That didn't happen. You sneaked in behind him and hit him from behind, like the yellow bastard you are."

That statement hit a nerve. I knew it would, was glad it did, but now I would have to face the repercussions.

His slimy smile dissolved into his bitter features. He rushed at me immediately, jutting the butt of the spade into my jaw.

Oh, fuck.

I panicked, as I heard the crack, then the nausea in my stomach arrived, followed quickly by the searing pain. I spluttered and coughed, my mind spinning, my will to remain conscious tested to breaking point. To breath, I had to spit out the contents of my mouth. Thick dollops of blood flowed from my mouth, mixed amongst it were three or four broken teeth. My face felt like a hollowed-out sausage, the urge to throw up, overwhelming. He stood over me for a second, visibly taking great pleasure in my pain, then walked back to resume digging the hole.

"You see, shithead- you weren't there. You don't know everything...smartass."

He was really pissed off. I concentrated on staying awake and he continued; "I knocked the fucker out."

He stopped and stared at me, this time I gave him no reaction, "Then I went to finish the job off. To do it properly I had to get rid of you and your mother too, so I went to work on the house. Just as I put a match to the petrol, I looked up and saw McNamee and Paddy Gray running down the lane. I couldn't believe my luck, stupid fuckers or what, talk about walking into it. So, I fucked off and left them to it, hoping they would try and save you and get badly burned, proving they were at the scene of the crime. How could they explain their way out of that? Dumb fucks."

He stopped digging and let out a large guffaw, before continuing; "So, the next day, I got word my plan had worked...well, to a certain extent."

He paused, looking at me with contempt before adding; "I didn't get you and your fuckin' mother...but I got *him*."

I was confused. If he had planned to get his hands on my father's land, but couldn't, because I was still alive, then why was he so happy? His plan, after all, had failed. I asked him that question, horrified at how my voice sounded with so many teeth missing.

"I didn't give a shit about your father's land. You see, I'm not greedy, not like him. All I cared about was gettin' my own back. If I'd gotten rid of you, that would have been a bonus, but I was soon to get my father's field back regardless."

Feeling more confused I asked how he got it back, if it had been sold to McNamee. He looked at me, the same mad glint in his eye beginning to glow.

"Again, you don't know anything. Fuckin' gobshite. You see, I'm a smart man. Your father underestimated me. I saw Gray at the scene, he seen me too. Because of the events in the pub and McNamee gettin' killed in the fire, Gray was runnin' scared. He knew the cops would be on his doorstep the next morning. What was he goin' to do? Blame Dillon's best friend, when it was so obvious to everyone that McNamee did it?"

"So, what happened?", I asked.

"First thing next morning, he arrived at my house. He was cryin' and whimpering like a stray dog. I calmed him down and gave him a drink. I told him what we were goin' to do. I told him, I would tell the police he was drinking with me in the house all night. He would have his alibi. Talk about a relieved man. The tears dried up, the colour came back to his cheeks…he was reborn. I told him his alibi came at a price. Because he was McNamee's business partner, I ordered him to sign my father's land back to me the next day- the quarry. He agreed and asked what I was goin' to pay for it. I laughed at him, told him it was the price of his freedom. He didn't bat an eyelid and signed it over the next day, true to his word. He had his alibi, I had my legacy back. He showed his true colours, though, the snake bastard. Instead of tryin' to clear his best friends name, he sold out and let the country believe McNamee was a murderer.", he laughed; "Nice friend, eh? I took pity on the prick eventually though. As bad as he was, he knew how to run a quarry. I put him on the payroll and he has worked for me ever since. We eventually became good friends too…although, let's just say, I wouldn't trust him as far as I could throw him."

He laughed at his last statement and went back to his digging with renewed vigour.

"By the way,", he continued; "How did you know *I* did it? How did your mother find out, when the whole country was fooled into thinking McNamee did it?"

Through an avalanche of pain, I smiled knowingly this time at him, and replied; "Your mate…Gray. He didn't tell you that…did he?"

He leaned on the shovel, shaking his head, and talking to himself; "Snake bastard! After all these fuckin' years, eh? Well, I'll be comin' for *him* after I'm finished with you."

He laughed, shook himself off and continued his digging.

I was relieved the blood flow inside my mouth began to stem. I worried about the amount of blood that was left in my body. Summoning up all my strength, I lifted myself into a sitting position, sat forward and once more began to fiddle with the rope around my feet. To my sheer elation, I thought I could find the rope loosening. I hoped I wasn't hallucinating, my fears easing as I could feel pins and needles tingle my feet. The blood was slowly entering my feet once more, the rope had loosened considerably. I fiddled some more, the rope becoming less tight until eventually I could take my feet out of the noose altogether.

I knew I had to play it carefully. My life depended on the next move. Even though I was free of the bondage I had been in, I knew I didn't have the strength for a fight. I knew if I stood up, I was likely to fall back down again owing to the blood loss and abuse my body had been subjected to. I knew I would have one crack at him, get it right and I would avenge both my parent's deaths, get it wrong and I would spend an eternity in hell, dead and rotting under those terrible roots. I had seen a vision of my afterlife in those dreams, and it was beyond horrific.

It hit me then, that even though I had endured some extreme loneliness at certain times, this was by far the worst. Literally at death's door, alone and beyond terrified, I very nearly cried out for Andrea, the McManus' and my poor, dead mother and father.

This was it. It all came down to the next few moments.

I braced myself.

"No matter how much you talk, no matter how much you try and validate what you did, you *know*...you know in that black heart of yours what you did was beyond wrong."

I surprised myself how calm I was, delivering those words.

I wasn't surprised at his reaction.

He stopped digging, threw the spade hard to the ground, smiled and began to roll his sleeves up. Unfazed by his attempts at intimidation, I continued; "You think you were hard done by? Boo fucking hoo. You couldn't buy your daddy's land back- so what? Does that warrant killing a man, not only a man, but your best friend...in cold blood?"

It was my turn to laugh at him now, instantly regretting it, my ribs and jaw immediately taking their revenge, shooting disabling pain to all my senses.

I immediately grimaced, before continuing; "You kill a man over a piece of land, and in the process, ruin the lives of his wife and child. You completely ruined our lives, you cunt. I hope you're proud of yourself. No matter how you dress up what you did, you know you're a psycho bastard at the back of it all."

He walked towards me, a manic grin on his face.

"Oh, I'm goin' to enjoy this.", he replied, barely able to contain his excitement.

I knew this was it.

I waited.

Two more steps.

One more step.

My heart pounded, the pain searing, but the adrenaline putting it on the back burner, momentarily.

Just as he stood over me, about to lunge, I drove my boot up, as hard as I could. I caught him straight between the legs, right in the bollocks. A mixture of pain and utter surprise animated his features, before he dropped to his knees.

He lay at my feet for a second, paralysed by pain. I tried, as best I could to get myself off the ground, but the state my body was in made it incredibly difficult. I eventually got to my knees, but he had quickly realised what I was doing. He was slithering towards the hole like a snake. I crawled towards him and caught him. I punched him a few times, his hands shielding his face. I had to weaken him before he got up. I threw another few punches, but, because my strength and reactions had been diminished so much, he kept blocking my blows.

I began to doubt myself, did I have the strength for this?

He began to recover, starting to hit back, as well as block. We rolled around on the wet grass, both trying to get a stranglehold. Once he got on top, I could see him trying to reach out for the spade. Desperation kicked in. If he got hold of the spade, he would bash my head in, and it would certainly be lights out.

I summoned up one last ounce of strength. Rotating my hips, I yanked his torso to the left, throwing his body off mine. It took us both by surprise when we rolled into the damp, rocky hole.

It took my breath away. He landed on top of me, his entire body weight the cause of the sickening crack of my ribs on landing. The hole was so tight there was no room for manoeuvre. I tried hitting him a few times, but my arms were trapped beneath his body. Realising I was trapped, his hideous features formed into a smile once more. He pulled himself onto his knees, and against all my attempts to hold him off, he wrapped his hands around my throat.

I don't know how many times in a man's life, he is convinced he is going to die. Probably only the once, when death is imminent.

This situation I was in, I knew it was coming.

This creature who had risen from hell, this wolf in sheep's clothing, who had masqueraded himself as my father's only friend, who in cold blood, murdered my father, and ruined my mother's life, was about to kill me too.

There I lay, in a ready-made grave, the hole in the sod where I had the most horrendous, grotesque, and realistic nightmares about. There was nothing but silence, the only sound coming from him, the effort and power he was inputting to strangle the life from my body, making him grunt like an animal struggling with its prey. The darkness behind him grew brighter. I was beginning to see all the colours of the rainbow, because of the lack of oxygen going to my brain. Then, they began to die off in their vivaciousness, becoming darker until I knew when the darkness fell completely that would be it... all over.

I thought of my mother and father, realising then I had finally let them down. To let one's parents down as I had, with the way my life turned out was bad enough, sad even. But this, to let the man who had ruined our whole existence get the better of me, kill me...and get away with it, whilst stealing our inheritance, was unforgiveable. I could only imagine my parents disgust.

Just then, as darkness was about to finally dominate, just as I was about to slip into death, the nightmare returned. I could see the roots of the bush that stood over the hole growing quickly, seeking out a body to embed themselves into, seeking blood to gorge themselves on. Then the visions grew stronger, and it was now clear who the body belonged to, the grossly decayed one that fed and cultivated the thriving plant.

It was *his*.

I felt an irresistible urge to let him know this, to give him a taster of how he would end up. Like an alcoholic has a moment of clarity, my imminent death gave me a moment of complete understanding. This feared and sacred bush, as my father had always believed, as folklore taught generations of children and adults alike, would take its revenge on anyone who lifted a hand, or a weapon to it. It was going to take its revenge on him, finally. He, and him alone had taken the chainsaw to it years before. He had done that on purpose, out of pure malice to try and bring bad luck on his supposed friend. The gentle bush did not forget, nor forgive. It was, as always to have its revenge – I *had* to let him know this.

The nightmarish visions vivid in my mind, my brain almost out of fuel, I summoned one last ounce of strength from my body.

I freed my right hand, somehow, and grasped it around his wrists that were being used to squeeze the very last drop of life from me. Then...an amazingly unexpected thing, his grip began to loosen. I took an almighty gulp of air into my lungs, and, as before, my vision portrayed the world around me in various greens, blues and purples before my normal vision was restored, viewing only the darkness around me.

I looked up at him, my hand still gripped around his wrists, now completely limp. I felt the visions leaving my mind, like they were being drained out of me, into him, by the touch of my hand on his wrists, just like how the visions were transferred to me in the first place, when I had touched my father's shoulder. I seemed to be infecting him with this ghastly virus like entity, and his strength was draining now, just like mine had.

The expression on his face, which had been hideous in its malevolence before, now just as hideous, portraying agony and horror instead. One of his hands had broken free from my clutch, now grasping his chest instead.

I realised he was having a heart attack.

Those visions, so real and horrific were dominating his consciousness, his body couldn't handle it.

His face became more gruesome, he was entering hell...finally. He was going to die in utter horror and agony. His face, even in the pale moonlight could be seen turning a deathly shade of white.

His body fell on top of mine. The sheer weight, I thought was going to kill me on its own, so weakened and fragile I had become. I managed, somehow from pure desperation to shove him slightly to the side of me, where at least he wasn't lying directly on top of my major organs. He lay there, in that cold and soggy ground, his eyes open and staring into mine. I realised then that he wasn't dead yet.

I was glad.

I looked into his eyes, now *my* time to smile.

"You know you're goin' to die now, don't you? Those terrible visions you're having...guess where they came from? They only came straight from my father, you're supposed best friend. I saw him last night, as clear as day, just as I'm looking at you now. I touched his shoulder and I caught these visions off him. Now, I'm giving them to you, let's call them a parting gift from my father."

His face, although I didn't think possible, filled further with terror. He let out a small, pathetic groan. I laughed in his face.

"And you thought you had gotten the better of Neil Dillon?"

His eyes became glazed and I knew then, he was dead.

I lay back in that cold, shallow grave and gazed up at the clear night sky, completely convinced I was now going to die. I didn't care, but on the other hand I desperately wanted to live. I reached down and felt in my pocket, pulling the Dictaphone out, rewound and hit play. There it was, the full confession of the dead man.

I finally had it.

When the police would find us, he would get recriminated, posthumously, and justice would finally be served.

I took a deep breath and agony ensued. I knew it could possibly be one of my last, but felt relaxed. I had gained justice for my family. My once pathetic existence now felt validated, the feeling more euphoric than all the drinks I had ever had, all served up at the same time.

Blood still oozed from my wounds and my heart rattled restlessly in my chest. I didn't have the strength to climb out of that hole. I would soon lie dead beside that evil creature, but I didn't feel afraid.

I thought of Andrea.

I had a vision of her lying in bed at night, crying inconsolably over me. It broke my already battered heart. I longed to lie on that bed with her, my arms cradling her, reassuring her, and letting her know our lives were only beginning. I longed to tell her of our wedding day, paint a portrait of our beautiful children we would have together. I wished to give her a glimpse of the happy life we both pined for together. Building a home and family with one another. Holidays, picnics...day's out. I wanted to show her how proud we would be of our children, and then our grandchildren.

I wanted to live more than I ever wanted to at that moment.

I wanted to die, as an old man, in a warm bed, my family around me, happy I was leaving the earth in peace. Satisfied with a full, happy, and meaningful life.

But, here I was...lying in a cold, ready-made grave next to the scourge of our family.

Our families dead scourge. Dead at my hands.

My body began to shiver uncontrollably, as if only then registering how cold it had been. I struggled for breath, my heartbeat now more of a dull throb.

I realised now it was over.

No happy ending for me.

I almost smiled at the thought I could have been so deluded there might have been.

Before I fell into permanent unconsciousness, I put the Dictaphone to my mouth.

"To whoever finds this tape, I, Seamus Dillon, leave my inheritance to the following people. I wish to leave half of my lands to Fintan Smith. The other half, and the dwelling house of our family, to Dan McManus and family. I wish to leave any money willed to me, to my fiancée, Andrea Hart. I love you all. Be happy and enjoy life. I will look down from heaven, if I make it, upon you all."

At that moment, the battery on the little device ran out of power.

Just as I did with Kathleen, after my mother died, I looked to the heavens and prayed to our Lord Jesus, asking Him to forgive my sins and comfort me in my final moments.

The night grew darker before I closed my eyes, but I felt a presence around me that made me no longer afraid.

I'm sure whoever found me would wonder why I wore a surprising half-smile.

CHAPTER 43

Neil woke once more. He lay for a moment or two, before pulling himself up into a sitting position on the edge of the bed. He rubbed the sleep from his eyes and looked around the room. Rays of inspiring and beautiful sunlight illuminated it, seeping in through the moulding, decayed curtains. An alien feeling of optimism arose in him. He wouldn't allow it though, how could he. He tried to swallow it down, assimilate it and drown it into his misery.

He dressed, for once not feeling the need to don his top-coat. It had to be years since he had neglected that item of clothing. Had it been when they were…still alive, he wondered? The thought of them stirred a queasiness in him, the misery and loss he felt at that moment almost a welcome tonic to the optimism he had felt a moment before.

He descended the stairs and once more sat at the kitchen table. He couldn't figure out why, but the house seemed completely different. The sunlight seeping through the windows seemed to heal the charring the house had suffered years before. He almost had to rub his eyes again, so convinced he was they were deceiving him. Finally, it seemed, the winter was beginning to subside.

He wondered how he would cope.

The winter brought a form of peace and solitude. Once the sun fell and darkness arrived, one could sleep. All sense of time is forgotten, becoming almost irrelevant. An eternal night, he felt would be a beautiful concept- he could sleep and forget.

What then of the spring and summer? It would never be dark, he would have to wait longer to be able to sleep, the longer he remained awake, the more torment he would have to endure. The smell and hope those seasons brought would prove a false dawn, only tending to stir up memories of days gone by, days that would never be regained.

Insanity would certainly ensue.

But, as he sat there, alone at the table, he couldn't help but feel differently. He didn't know why. Maybe, he wondered, it was because he had spent a night where he hadn't suffered any nightmares.

That strange feeling bubbled and fizzed once again in him.

What was it?

Hope, change, optimism? But, how, he wondered…why?

As he sat contemplating his feelings, there was a sudden knock at the door. He almost leapt out of his chair in shock. How had he not seen that coming? He froze, not moving a muscle for fear he would be heard. Again, a light knocking at the door, more a tap.

He recognised it at once.

He sat and put his head in his hands once more, rubbing furiously at his hair, trying to wake himself, to snap out of the daydream.

Then a voice.

The voice sounded to him, like a musical note played straight from the angels of heaven. Then again, that beautiful note oscillated through the door and into his home.

"Neil...Neil...Neil."

He got up from the chair and walked slowly to the door, much like a child about to unwrap a Christmas present, relishing the build-up.

"Neil...Neil", the voice spoke again.

He put his hands on the door handle and opened the door. He almost fell backwards into the house, on viewing the beautiful sight that stood in front of him. The sun hung high in the sky, its golden rays encouraging new life to bristle and burst into existence. The vision in front of him, like the most beautiful dream, spoke;

"Neil...there you are."

It was Máire.

She was young. She was just as he had remembered her. Young and more beautiful than ever. She looked rested, fresh. He couldn't speak. She noticed that and threw her head back and laughed. That sound of laughter, to him, was like the most melodic, uplifting piece of music he had ever heard. Almost alien to him, his face muscles involuntarily began to form a smile. How long since he had smiled, he wondered? Many, many years. At least since the last time he had seen her.

When she finished laughing, she considered his eyes, smiling a smile that seemed brighter than the sun hanging in the sky behind her.

"Neil Dillon, don't play the bashful soul with me, now."

There was a pause, he waited for a second to wake up. He would have woken happily at that point, the one solitary, happy dream enough to sustain and satisfy him for another few years of torment.

He didn't wake up. Euphoria blazing through his system, he spoke, again the physical mechanism feeling completely unnatural; "Máire, I thought you were...where have you been?"

She smiled again, only this time it was tinged with an intense sadness. Neil's heart, if not broken years before, would certainly have broken at the sight.

"Oh, Neil, my poor sweet love. You...you don't know, do you?", she asked, her eyes welling up with thirty years of tears.

Neil, confused and dismayed at his wife's obvious show of emotion, asked; "Know what, Máire? I thought you were...dead."

At that, he did something he had never done before in his life, he openly cried in front of another human being. Máire walked towards him and threw the most loving of arms around him. His sobs rocked both their bodies as one, like an earthquake that had suddenly erupted after hundreds of years lying dormant.

"Don't cry, my love.", Máire whispered, "Everything is wonderful now. Your...our suffering is finally over, it's all over."

When his sobs finally subsided, he held her tightly in his own arms.

"Máire, where's Seamie?"

Again, she looked deeply into his eyes, her own eyes conveying a pain and suffering that had not been there before-it dismayed him more than anything. He wished he could absorb her pain and pile it up with the rest of his own.

"Seamie is all right", she smiled.

Again, Neil completely broke down. He fell to his knees and noticed a small pool of tears forming on the ground beneath him. Máire knelt with him.

"But...", Neil began, through a deluge of tears, "I thought Seamie was..."

He couldn't bring himself to finish the sentence. Even though he thought it, he couldn't speak it aloud.

"No, Neil, not at all. It kills me you thought that for all these years. He didn't die, Neil...*we* didn't die. I'm so, so sorry you were led to believe that, my poor love."

"But...what happened? Why have I been on my own for all these years? Where were you Máire? Where was Seamie?"

Máire wiped his tears away, kissing him tenderly on the lips.

"It's a long story, my love. But, don't worry, I have an eternity to explain it to you. You're suffering is over, our lives together are only beginning."

Neil smiled at that prospect. His poor, stone-cold soul beginning to crack and thaw with the warmth of happiness.

"Máire, I know one thing for sure."

"What's that, sweetheart?"

"The winter is finally over."

Máire once again threw her arms around him; "Yes, my love, it is. Never to return."

She took him by the hand and led him up the lane.

"Where are we going, Máire?"

"I want to show you something, my love. Something very important, something you need to know."

The two of them strode out of the gate, onto the road, hand in hand. They walked up the country roads for miles, the roads Neil didn't think he would ever walk again. They didn't speak, only glancing at each other from time to time to smile and giggle, like a pair of love struck teenagers. The sun shone like it had never shone before. The little country roads remained calm and still, only the sounds of the sweetest birdsongs breaking the peaceful blanket of silence enshrouding them.

It all felt like a dream for Neil. He knew if he awoke then, to continue the tortuous existence he had grown accustomed to, it would be too much for him. But, somehow, he knew it was real.

Purgatory had been paid, Heaven to be reaped.

Máire beckoned him towards the churchyard. He hadn't expected to be taken there. He followed in silence, following his wife's lead. Once more, to his surprise, they walked past the doors of the building and out towards the graveyard. They walked halfway down the length of the graveyard, towards where the Dillon family grave lay.

The graveyard hadn't looked at all like the way he remembered it. Instead of the grey, rain-sodden, and almost God-forsaken place he had in his mind, it now seemed almost…serene. Bathed in sunlight, the grassy areas bustling with daisies, the smell of spring rife in the air, it seemed to him a place of regenerated life, certainly not one of death and defeated dreams. His soul was full of hope, the emptiness of yesterday becoming a welcome distant memory.

As they approached the family grave, Máire gave his hand a little reassuring squeeze. She knelt at the gravestone and rubbed her dress lovingly over the grand marble marker of the dead.

Totally confused, Neil asked; "Máire, why do you bring me here? You say Seamie is all right. You're all right too, so what significance does my mother and father's grave have for us? I don't understand."

Máire stopped polishing the headstone, and looked up at her husband.

"Oh, my poor darling. As I have said, Seamie is fine, don't worry. I bring you here to explain the…final, *and* the beginning of our story together."

Neil stood for a moment, trying in vain to work out what his wife meant. He laughed, and asked; "Máire, what do you mean? Am I just being stupid? I don't understand any of this."

Máire's features suddenly changed. It was like a cloud of great sadness had just passed over, drowning out the happiness that had been there.

"Neil, my love…read the headstone."

Neil grew even further confused. He had visited that gravestone hundreds of times since his father's death. He had even erected the new headstone and knew every word written on it like the back of his hand. But, to honour his wife's request, he did as he was asked, reading the names and dates aloud, for Máire's benefit. He finished reading out his father's birth and death dates and was about to look down upon Máire to question her further, when, he noticed another name on the headstone. He almost recoiled in horror and disbelief as he read the name;

"NEIL THOMAS DILLON. BORN 22-APR-1930-DIED 29-OCT-1973. AGED 43 YEARS. REST IN PEACE"

He couldn't speak. His mind raced in a million different directions. He fully expected to wake up again to the nightmare existence he had endured for so many years...but he didn't. He looked down at Máire, once more, to find she had tears streaming down her face.

"Máire...what is this? How is this so?", he asked, like a child asking its parents for reassurance.

Máire wiped her eyes, but the tears still ran down her cheeks in great rivulets.

She took his hand, and stood. Looking directly into his eyes, she nodded her head.

"It's true, my love. Seamie and I survived the fire. *You* didn't. Your poor soul has been in turmoil all these years."

She gazed down at the headstone, letting out a mocking laugh.

"Bah...Rest in Peace. How *could* you? You have suffered my poor love. But it's over. I am here, you will never suffer like that again...I promise you."

They both embraced tenderly, comforting each other like never before. Suddenly, Neil drew away and asked; "But Máire, if I'm...dead, then how come you are here with me, if I'm a...ghost, a spirit?"

At that, Máire bowed her head. Neil realised everything then, from his wife's subtle little expression of sorrow. He embraced her again and this time the tears that flowed were his. In that moment, he mourned the life of his poor, beautiful wife as he would have if she were not with him at that time.

Máire drew away from him. Wiping the tears from his face, she said; "Neil, my love, don't cry. You have been waiting for me. You were in hell without me. I was in hell without you, a hell on earth. I didn't want to be there, but I *had* to, for Seamie. But we are here now together, and we will be for eternity. We have so much happiness in front of us, the past will become a minor speck of dust on the horizon."

Neil smiled at the thought, then his features became darkened with an anger that lay dormant within his soul.

"What about the bastard who did all this to us? I want to see him burning in hell."

Máire once again looked into his eyes, trying to pacify and bring reassurance to him. She took his hands and squeezed them tight.

"McNamee is at peace, Neil."

She could feel the tension instantly rising in her husband's body. Before the eruption, she immediately flung ice on his rage; "Shush now my love. Dessie McNamee didn't do this."

Neil's anger deflated like a used balloon. Drawing away from her, confusion writ large across his features, he asked; "What...of course he did, Máire. Who else would do such a thing?"

Máire walked to him and took his hands once more in hers.

"Neil, I want you to close your eyes. I'm going to show you what happened that night. Also, I'm going to show you what happened just last night too. You are going to be completely shocked, but...I know you'll be satisfied at the retribution gained. Now, close your eyes."

At that, Máire closed her eyes too. The two of them stood above the grave and were transported back to the fateful nights, both watching at first hand the events unfolding. When finished, both fell to the ground.

Neil was the first to speak; "Oh, Máire. How could I have been so foolish?"

Máire smiled sweetly at him and drew him close to her, embracing him tightly.

"Oh, my dear. You weren't to know, nobody can comprehend such evil in someone's heart."

She paused, before adding; "Our Seamie got him in the end, though. We can be so proud of that boy...he came through for us."

Again, tears formed in her eyes, this time tears of pride instead of sorrow.

Neil nodded in agreement.

"A fine man he grew up to be. He's a credit to you Máire. I just wish I had been there to watch him grow up."

"Don't worry, dear. I've told him all about you and he was very proud to have you as his father."

Neil sat gazing at the ground, his mind a blur. Máire stood and reached her hand out to him.

He took it, and was led along by his wife.

"Where are you taking me?"

Máire smiled; "Let's go get our son."

Neil leapt to his feet at once.

"Yes, my love. Let's go get Seamie."

At that, the two-walked hand in hand out of the church grounds. Spring had finally arrived, summer certainly on its way. Blooming, golden daffodils appeared, as if by magic in front of them as they walked along the country roads. Neil looked upon the scenes in front of him and it filled his heart with so much joy and hope that he afforded himself a rare smile. He looked down upon his wife who gazed lovingly back into his eyes.

"The winter is at last over, Máire. Isn't this wonderful?"

She nodded in agreement.

"But Neil, this is only the beginning. Wait to you see what awaits us. You cannot imagine."

They stood in the middle of that quiet little country road, the sun's gentle beams dousing them in a comforting warmth, holding each other in a loving embrace. Then, hand in hand, they set-off together, happily.

Towards paradise...and their only so

To my great relief, I heard voices around me. I had been found, saved from that horrid hole in the ground.

I thanked God.

To lie there, beginning to rot simultaneously with *his* body, to merge into one rotting mass and share a grave with that hideous creature, the devil who robbed me of my family, my childhood and innocence, would be a fate worse than eternal hell. I smiled to the heavens and praised God under my breath once more.

I was sure I was in hospital. I could hear equipment, medical devices. I didn't feel any pain, absolutely none. I couldn't remember the last time I had awoken pain-free.

I wasn't well, that was obvious. I could hear the doctor in ear-shot taking a sharp intake of breath, much like that of the best builders I had worked with, when pricing a big job. I knew from the doctors exaggerated response I was in a very bad way.

I remembered thinking when Brian was at death's door, I would have gladly sacrificed my own life for his. Without a second thought, I would have, to save my friend from death and to save Dan and Kathleen the agony of losing a child. At times, I had prayed to God to take me instead of him. Back then I hadn't cared about my own life. I had nothing to live for, no purpose.

Now I felt I had.

I wanted to marry Andrea and start a family. I wanted to offer the children we would have, a life I had never known. A life full of love, happiness, and opportunity. I wanted to get to know my family in Ireland. I wanted to help the McManus'. I knew how dearly they wanted to move back home and I wanted to make that happen for them. I wanted to share in their happiness, to somehow repay them for all they had done for me in my life.

Typical.

Now that I wanted to live, I couldn't. If I was fit enough to laugh, I would have.

I had experienced vivid dreams after falling unconscious in that horrible hole in the ground, beneath that little fairy tree. Not the horrid dreams I had endured the night before, but beautiful, poignant dreams-full of hope, full of happiness.

I dreamt of my mother and father. My mother had looked like she did when I was a child.

Ageless. Beautiful.

But, she looked happy. I had never seen her happy in her life...never. My father, he looked a lot like me, only taller, stronger, and healthier. He looked happy too.

It made me happy seeing them that way.

The beeps and noises of various medical equipment sounded around me, but still I was numb. The room grew quiet, no priests yet to read me the last rites.

Did they still do that?

I remembered making my will into that Dictaphone before I fell unconscious. I smiled inside and wondered if my features conveyed the emotion. I had done the right thing. To enable the McManus' a move back to Ireland, giving them a place to live, helping them realise their dreams of moving out of London, did me good.

Even if I lived, I wouldn't move back to Ireland. How could I live in that house, where those atrocities occurred? To live in a land that produced people who could perform such acts, would be too much. A big scary city like London, full of all sorts and indeed evil, had, to its credit never harmed my mother or me. If anything, people had helped us. Mrs Kingston, the McManus', various neighbours over the years, even the social services, to a certain extent. But, here, in this whimsical, little corner of Ireland, evil, bitterness, jealousy, greed, and ridicule had loomed large. Of course, I didn't tar everyone with the same brush, everywhere had its share of good and bad people, but this to me would always be where the bogey man lived. As much as I loved this country, I couldn't live in it. It remained in my heart, but London was in my blood.

If I survived, I would live in London, but always I would come back and visit my family, which of course included the McManus'.

Although, I was pushing at deaths door, I felt joy.

I hadn't achieved anything in life, nothing at all. I had merely survived, a life spent, not lived. But, when I thought about what I finally achieved, outed the snake who had destroyed my loved ones, defeating, and condemning him to what I knew for certain would be an eternal hell, I couldn't help but to feel proud.

I could look my parents straight in the eye, and I knew they would be proud of me.

What more could a son ever wish for?

As I lay on my deathbed, the faces of two little children I had encountered in my life suddenly came to me. The little black boy who had been bullied in the children's home...I wondered what had happened him. I hoped he was happy, I hoped he had made it through the system unscathed, making something of himself. I prayed he hadn't let the traumatic beginning of his life taint and ruin the rest of it.

I thought of the little boy who had been in the restaurant with the drunken grand-parents, on one of my first dates with Andrea.

He had broken my heart.

I had thought of him many times since that night, fearing the worst for the poor child. The grand-parents, although well-meaning, could barely look after themselves, what care could the poor boy hope to have for himself. I had always regretted not sticking my nose in that night, making it my business to find out their names and where they lived. I would have left a big fucking chunk of inheritance for that boy, I swear to God I would have, if I had known what I was to inherit myself.

I could have been the convict to the little boy's Pip...real Great Expectations shit.

I wished I had done something like that.

Again, another good intention, this time dreamed up much too late.

Typical.

Thinking about those children made me angry.

Angry with myself.

When I had been a child, I had always relied on the kindness of strangers. It was all I had. It was all those children had, their only chance, and I hadn't helped.

What good had I been?

The anger began to drain my energy. Like a man who had endured an exhausting day and was fighting sleep, I now felt the complete restlessness of an all-encompassing weariness. I felt my right leg kick out reflexively. Was it restless legs...or my dying kick?

God, I didn't want to die.

I wanted to live. Become re-born. To help people, help those helpless children. To live a full, proper life and become a father figure to my children and others who needed me.

I didn't want to die here...not on my own.

Suddenly, I heard a commotion around me. Something was happening. I was taking a turn for the worse, or hopefully the better...I had absolutely no idea. My world remained in darkness, until finally...my eyes opened.

I saw no-one around me. Suddenly, though, to my sheer joy, I looked down a long, narrow hospital corridor. The room I lay in, and the corridor, was doused in a beautiful sunlight, a sight I thought I would never see again. Halfway down that long corridor, a couple of lovers strode towards me, hand in hand, their features brightened by wide, beaming smiles as they realised I had opened my eyes and looked upon them.

The man was tall, lean, and handsome. The woman, smaller, athletic, and beautiful, little tear droplets sitting on her cheeks, reflecting the light like tiny diamonds. Tears not of sadness, but of joy, of hope. They quickened their pace as they got closer to my room. My eyes tried to focus on who the couple were.

Was it Dan and Kathleen? Perhaps my mother and father?

I couldn't tell for sure, they weren't close enough yet to fully see.

Then, as they got closer, I finally realised who they were.

I laughed. They laughed.

And at that, I knew how true happiness felt.

23006686R00173

Printed in Great Britain
by Amazon